THEY MET ON THE SANDS OF DESTINY . . .

EMILIE SLOANE—fair-haired, cream-skinned, she would be a perfect young English lady . . . were she not driven by an uncontrollable yearning to know the ultimate heights and depths of a woman's passion

HENRI CARTIER—the dashing French nobleman, wise in the ways of love yet thunderstruck by Emilie's beguiling charms

PIERRE LOUVEL—the young doctor, loved by Emilie's sister, seemingly devoted only to his healing work . . . yet Emilie could not forget his eyes' frank appraisal of her body

TALEB AL-MU'MIN—the dark conqueror of the desert, whose ferocity in war filled Emilie with horror even as his skilled caresses brought her to undreamed-of pinnacles of ecstasy.

HADRA—the dusky beauty whose jealousy of Emilie's happiness was tempered by the knowledge that no man of Taleb's might could be content with only one woman

Their lives intertwine in a sweeping, tumultuous tale of love as glamorous as the bejewelled palaces of the Sultans . . . as stark as the vast Sahara . . . and as romantic as the teeming streets of the Casbah!

WINDS OF DESIRE

by

Marilyn Granbeck

A JOVE/HBJ BOOK

First Jove/HBJ edition published March 1978

Library of Congress Catalog Card Number: 77-91233

Printed in the United States of America

Jove/HBJ books are published by Jove Publications, Inc. (Har-
court Brace Jovanovich) 757 Third Avenue, New York, N.Y.
10017

for Leslie . . . . and far away places.

There lies not any troublous thing before,
Nor sight nor sound to war against thee more,
For whom all winds are quiet as the sun
All waters as the shore.

    *   *   *   *   *   *   *

This is the end of every man's desire.

                       .....Swinburne

PROLOGUE

She felt him watching as she looked about the flat, occupying herself intently with admiring its masculine simplicity and hiding her dismay at the shabbiness of the two comfortable chairs, a bookcase filled with cloth-bound volumes, and a walnut writing desk with a green blotter covering some of its scars. She moved to a small laquered table to examine a gilt-framed picture of James standing in a garden, a cap shading his face somewhat but not hiding the captivating smile. She lifted a leather tobacco box and ran her fingers over the tooled lid.

"Emilie."

She replaced the box exactly where it had been, as if somehow she could put life back into a comfortable niche as easily. When she did not turn, he spoke her name again and she heard the soft footfall of his steps on the carpet behind her. She closed her eyes and held her breath. She was insane to come here to his flat—

"Look at me," James said, taking her shoulders and forcing her about gently. Then she was in his arms and his lips were burning on hers.

The throbbing in her temples became a drum and she was lost in its echoes. Her senses reeled as the kiss stirred fire inside her. She was aware of his caresses, aware of the heat of his breath mingling with her own and the insistent probing of his tongue at her lips. She was weak with rioting emotion, knowing she should stop him but powerless to do more than whimper softly.

He buried his face at her throat and murmured. The words scarcely penetrated the velvet fog of her mind and she swayed against him.

"I've waited for this moment," he whispered. His breath sent shivers coursing the length of her spine. "Come, the bedroom is this way—"

He took her hand and started toward the hall. Emilie let herself be drawn in his wake as her conscience tried to scream denial of her need. She was a woman, and James was offering release for the turbulent passions that had been trapped inside her so long. She had flirted and played a tantalizing game of womanly wiles, and now she wanted the reward of winning. Still, fear numbed her as the thought of her father sprang unbidden to mind.

He'd raged at discovering she had allowed James to take her riding and drive her home. And he'd forbidden her to ever see that "presumptuous young pup" again. James was a junior clerk at Cote's bank which her father managed and had come into her life by chance when delegated to deliver some important letters to Roderick Sloane at his home. The messenger had been left to wait in the parlor while the banker drafted a reply, and it was there that Emilie had spied him and stopped to speak with him. He was a good looking young man, blond and fair, with eyes that seemed full of laughter. She was attracted to him instantly, knowing somehow that he was quite different from the stuffy, very proper young men who attended the various social functions to which the Sloanes were invited. Emilie had never had a gentleman caller, nor had Sara, her sister, older by one year than her own eighteen. Roderick Sloane would not permit it. He recognized the fact that his daughters were of an age to marry, but he

10

would not settle for any common suitor who had thus far put in an appearance. Until someone came along who met his high—and unreasonable standards, Emilie thought—his daughters would continue as they always had, attending engagements of his choosing, doing his bidding in all matters.

For the first time in her life, Emilie disobeyed her father in a major matter. There had been small daring incidents throughout her childhood, more often than not followed by a whipping that planted her rebellion more firmly, and tears from her mother begging her to "do try to be a good girl and not upset your father." But in the matter of James Pauling, Emilie dared to leave the house on the pretext of going to the dressmaker but instead walking in Hyde Park close to where James had mentioned his rooms were. When they met, he bowed politely and expressed surprise at his good fortune in chancing upon her, but there was a hint of laughter in his grey eyes. They took tea at a small cafe near the Marble Arch, talking of unimportant things—the weather, the opening of Parliament, rumors of the King's failing health—but studying each other with an intensity and curiosity Emilie had never known. For the first time in her life, she felt swept into a tide of emotion she did not understand. It excited her to be near James, to have his fingers brush hers as they rested on the table or when he handed her into a cab when she finally said she must leave for home.

"I want to see you again," he said simply.

And so she had come to the park again, and now she was in his flat. His intentions were as clear as her own thoughts were clouded. His kiss stirred her beyond sanity, and she was suddenly frightened. She was a virgin and had assumed that she would be until she lay on her marriage bed. It was expected . . . it was right . . .

James smiled as they entered the bedroom. Her heart was hammering and she clutched the door in a rush of panic. Gently, he uncurled her fingers and took her in his

11

arms again. His lips were warm and eager, claiming her so she shivered and went weak. His hands stroked the curve of her waist, a breast. She was trembling so violently she would have fallen had he not held her tightly. Her body was alive with the rampaging fire that was unlike anything she had ever imagined possible; it fogged her mind and left her helplessly caught in its stirring passion. His hand slid under her velvet jacket and she felt its heat through the thin linen shirtwaist. She knew she should pull away before it was too late, but her body ached with a wanting beyond control. He was murmuring her name, then lifting her and carrying her to the bed, undoing the blue jacket and the fastenings of the navy skirt. The air felt suddenly cool as he drew off her garments and laid them aside, smiling down with hungry eyes. Her breath caught as he slipped the straps of the chemise from her alabaster shoulders and drew the filmy silk from her breasts. Then he was in a rush, pulling off her slippers and stockings, divesting himself of his own clothing.

The sight of his nakedness shocked her and she squeezed her eyes shut. *Run,* her brain screamed. But it was too late. He was beside her, his flesh hot against hers, his lips exploring and his fingers lingering where none had ever touched before. She trembled as he moved over her and his maleness brushed where his hand had been. After a brief moment of pain, he was part of her, incredibly warm and forceful, demanding response from her body that was eagerly given. She clung to him blindly as an inferno erupted within her. All thoughts of right or wrong vanished and she was aware only of the incredible pleasure that built to terrifying proportions until it at last exploded in release and ecstacy.

She lay with eyes closed, savoring the delight that filled her completely. He stirred and moved from her, and she heard the whisper of his feet on the floor. When she opened her eyes, he had pulled on a dressing gown and was knotting the sash. His gaze swept the length of her nakedness and she quickly reached for the sheet to cover herself. He laughed gently and came to sit on the edge of the bed, brushing a pale tendril of hair from her cheek.

"Did I not know otherwise, I would swear that you are experienced in the ways of passion."

His curious smile disturbed her, and she held the sheet tightly at her chin. "I should not have come . . ."

"But you wanted to, and you wanted what happened to happen."

She looked away, ashamed that he found her so transparent. The enormity of what she had done engulfed her and her face was suddenly flushed. He took her chin in his hand and forced her to look at him.

"You cannot deny you found the experience pleasurable."

She bit her lip.

"The truth is clear in your eyes. There is no need to be ashamed of being a woman with a woman's feelings and needs," he said. "I don't hold with the notion that a woman is a chattel for a man's convenience. I've known many who carried smouldering desire within them waiting to be unleashed by the right man."

She stared. "There have been others?"

He looked startled for a moment, then laughed. "Did you imagine yourself the first in *my* life because you were a virgin? Hardly, but you are certainly the most beautiful." He rose and crossed to pick a slim cigarette from a box on the bureau. He held a match to it and inhaled deeply as he walked back to the bed. "I think it would be unwise for us to meet in the park again. There are several employees of the bank who live nearby. I would not like our meetings to come to your father's attention. He'd have me sacked for certain."

She was still staring, listening to his words with a numbness that erased all traces of the pleasure she had experienced.

"I will give you a key so that you can let yourself in

13

before the bank lets out. It won't be too difficult for you to slip out the back way afterwards."

He was assuming her agreement, taking for granted that she would willingly enter into a liaison with him! He blew smoke and sat beside her once more. She sprang away, scrambling past him and off the bed, reaching for her clothing as tears burned at her eyes.

"What the devil—" He gasped as though she had struck him.

"Don't touch me!"

"I didn't intend to. What has gotten into you? One minute you're all warm and cozy, the next in a tantrum—"

"I'm not in a tantrum!" She stepped into her chemise and drew it up over her nakedness. She was shaking with rage, and her fingers fumbled with the blouse as she tried to pull it on, only to be caught in a turned-about sleeve. Tears spilled as she shook the garment right side out.

"You *are* angry. Why?"

She did not answer but finished dressing as quickly as she could. He followed her into the sitting room, still waiting for her reply and staring as she gathered up her coat and hat and rushed out of the flat. In the lower hallway, she paused to put on the coat and pull the hat over her disheveled hair. She leaned against the door trying to calm the pounding of her heart and choke off her sobs.

When at last she felt steady enough, she walked out into the street and away from James forever.

CHAPTER ONE

A fresh breeze blew across the swells of green sea. The sky, bleached sapphire by the day's heat, began to deepen in colour, turquoise to cobalt, and small downy clouds settled on the horizon to cushion the lowering sun. Darkness descended quickly as the white puffs turned pink and mauve and the sea swallowed the day.

The S.S. *Ophir* was ten hours out of Lisbon, her only port of call since leaving Southhampton, and would arrive in Tangier shortly after dawn the following day. With the growing darkness, ladies in dinner gowns and men in frock coats and Kingston collars made their way to the dining room amidships. Strains of music drifted from the main salon where entertainment and dancing were scheduled as a farewell party for those passengers departing the ship at the African port.

At the railing, Emilie Sloane lifted her face to the spray flung back from the water rushing along the ship's grey hull. It hardly seemed possible that the journey was almost done, that tomorrow she would be in a foreign city that defied definition in her mind. Tangier was the other side of the earth! She had browsed through several books and magazine accounts of the African port these past months since her father's announcement that they were to travel there—no, not travel—*move,* actually change their domicile! The house in Belgravia had been let, their furniture and personal effects stored until her mother determined which could reasonably be brought to Tangier and which should be auctioned off or otherwise disposed of. And tomorrow, they would be in Tangier.

She stared at the rolling green water, trying to sort her thoughts. Would life take on new character and adventure? She shuddered and chewed at her lip when she thought about the interlude with James Pauling and its aftermath. She had rushed from the row of flats and along the street with only the thought of escaping James and her own conscience. A cab rounded the corner and she hailed it quickly, sinking against the cushions and sitting with eyes closed until she had the presence of mind to straighten her hair and resettle her hat. The incident was over, and she convinced herself that the turbulent emotions would dim with time.

But she had been seen. A toadying elderly clerk who lived several doors from James observed Emilie rush from the junior clerk's residence and took it upon himself to inform his employer—quite innocently, he declared, but knowing that he would be rewarded by the banker. Roderick Sloane confronted Emilie, demanding to know how she dared disobey his wishes and what she had been doing in the man's rooms. Had she no decency? No respect for the Sloane's position and prominence? The house thundered with his rage, and Sara and mother hovered at the head of the stairs, neither daring to come to Emilie's defense. Terrified but defiant, Emilie claimed she had met James Pauling by accident near the park several days before, and he had been kind enough to take her to tea. On leaving the tearoom, she'd inadvertently left a glove on the table and had gone to Pauling's apartment to reclaim her lost property. In spite of her father's anger, she stuck to her brazen lie and set her mind and heart against his

16

tirade. She thought he would strike her as he often had done when she was a child, but he effected a crueler punishment by locking her in her room until he could make arrangements to send her off to Rothingale's School in Kent, an institution far removed from busy city life and with a reputation for strictness that resembled a nunnery.

She might be there now except for the sudden announcement that he was to be transferred to Tangier to manage the newly-founded Anglo-French Bank of Lyon.

Once the shock waned, Emilie began to anticipate the journey and the prospect of an adventurous new life. From all she'd read, Morocco *was* adventurous. She'd been both disappointed by the paucity of information she'd been able to find and excited by the mystery the lack created. Tangier was a city where people from many parts of the world gathered in one small place. And father would be very busy with his new position, perhaps so busy that he would be forced to relent in the strict discipline he always effected at home. Hadn't he already been forced to withdraw the sentence of her imprisonment so that she could ready herself for the move? There'd been fittings at the dressmaker, shopping expeditions for clothes suitable to the warm climate of Africa, the countless hours of going through personal possessions to select those worthy of taking. During most of the time, her father had been absent; his new post required extensive study and preparation, conferences that lasted late into the evenings and continued day after day.

There had been one dreadful week when it seemed that the entire plan might be abandoned. The nation received the sobering news that His Majesty, King Edward VII, had died quite suddenly after an attack of bronchitis. The entire country mourned, and financial matters were left in limbo as the economy fluctuated sharply before restoring itself. The Sloanes joined the long queue that filed through Westminster Hall to view the monarch's body lying in state, and they watched the solemn funeral procession make its way through the streets of London before journeying to Windsor where the King was entombed. Emilie viewed the procession with sorrow and wonder, seeing the foreign sovereigns and special ambassadors who rode behind the black-draped funeral coach drawn by eight black horses. Even in her sorrow she was keenly aware of the international aspects of the occasion, and she could not help thinking that soon her own life would no longer be so purely and properly English. Surely in Tangier the family would have to adapt itself to many differences in life style.

She rarely thought of James Pauling anymore, though she had heard from Sara who heard it from father, that the young man had been sacked. The news brought a pang of guilt but also relief at the knowledge that she would never see him again. She had spoken to no one of the incident and the memory of it was beginning to dim, except for a very faint stirring of longing deep inside her body that she did her best to deny.

She drew the capelet of the beige taffeta afternoon dress about her shoulders as the breeze whipped it like a sail. She should dress for dinner, but she wanted to hold on to the beauty of the peaceful moment a bit longer. Each evening she and Sara were forced to stroll around the promenade deck with mother and father, to see and be seen, with father nodding to those fellow passengers worthy of his attention. Emilie hated the ritual, but she dared not ask to be excused from it. Father had decided notions about what was expected of the family of an English banker, including behavior aboard ship, and she and Sara—and mother—followed his wishes. Besides, Emilie did not want to call any attention to herself and remind father of her earlier disobedience that had ended so disastrously.

She felt her cheeks colour and pushed away the memory of James Pauling. He was part of her past, and the future lay ahead.

18

"Emilie?"

She turned to find Henri Cartier smiling at her. He was tall and slightly built, with a thin face dominated by dark eyes, and quite charming. Her father was impressed by the young man's aristocratic heritage, and her mother insisted on calling him "Count", though he protested that he preferred simply "Henri." He was a fencing instructor at St. Cyr, on leave from his post for an indeterminate period, necessitated—according to gossip among the younger passengers—by an affair of honor which had resulted in serious injury to the son of a prominent senator. Intrigued, Emilie had flirted covertly and been flattered by Henri's attention. He seemed to enjoy their conversation in the dining room, where they both sat at the Captain's table, and several times he had encountered her on deck and lingered to chat.

"I hoped to see you at the Captain's apertif party," he said.

She looked striken. "I forgot completely!" Father would be furious.

"It was rather dull, you missed very little." He leaned close to her at the rail. "Tonight's party will be crowded and noisy, and tomorrow we disembark."

"Yes. The time has gone quickly. Somehow the days seem shorter at sea." She smiled pleasantly but dropped her gaze when he regarded her solemnly.

"You have helped make my journey a very pleasant one," he said. "I hate to see it end, except that I am consoled by the fact that we will both be living in Tangier. I am looking forward to seeing you often."

Startled, she looked up and found him staring at her. He put his hand to her sleeve, and his touch jolted her. With a quick, elusive motion, she grabbed for the tulled and ribboned brown straw hat as a gust of wind tried to yank it from its pins. Several strands of wheat-coloured hair came undone and whipped across her face. She brushed them away but gave up the struggle when the hat

19

slipped sideways and she was forced to grasp it firmly After a moment, she pulled it off impatiently.

He was watching her with an amused smile. "When am I going to see you?"

She pretended to frown. "Why at dinner, and later at the party—"

"That's not what I mean, and you know it. We make port tomorrow, and I have no intention of letting you walk out of my life as though we'd never met."

She laughed, and the sound was carried off by the wind. "I'm sure we'll see each other from time to time Tangier cannot be so large that we will not meet."

"I want to see you alone, somewhere where we can be together without a thousand eyes to watch our every move."

She felt her pulse quicken and she turned to look out over the water. He was suggesting that their friendship develop into something deeper than a casual one. In spite of his charm, she found the prospect frightening. He was too sure, too powerfully in control of his feelings while she floundered helplessly. She had thought herself in command with James, only to be swept headlong into a situation from which she was unable to retreat.

He took her arm again and turned her about so she had to look at him. "When will you see me?"

"I—I don't know. My father has arranged—"

"Does your father control your life and spirit? I think not, Emilie Sloane. I see it in your eyes—a longing for freedom and for life."

She blushed and had difficulty meeting his direct gaze. "I do not even know where we'll be living." Confusion flooded her as she felt the pressure of his hand on her arm. She looked away as an elderly couple passed and glanced in their direction. "Please, I must dress for dinner. Father will be angry if I am late."

She tried to withdraw but he did not release her. In-

tead he slipped her arm through his and clasped her
and. "I'll walk you to your stateroom."

"That's not necessary."

"If I only did the necessary things in life, my existence
would be very dull indeed."

He was mocking her again, and she felt her cheeks
warm. They crossed the deck and entered the narrow passageway that led to the luxury suites at the stern beyond
the promenade deck. She was painfully aware of his
closeness in the dimly lighted companionway, and when a
portly gentleman with white hair and flowing mustache
emerged from a room and squeezed past, Henri pulled her
into his arms as soon as the man was out of sight.

"Say that you will see me in Tangier. I have a
house—a friend's. Promise you'll come."

She struggled, pushing at him and feeling her panic
rise. He was holding her so close she could feel the
pressure of his body against hers, his breath against her
cheek. "Don't—"

"There's no one to see us." He bent and crushed his
lips to hers, sending a heady whirl of excitement through
her and making her brain reel, but at the same time filling
her with emotion that left her trembling. When at last he
released her, she was shaken.

"You take liberties!" It was meant as an accusation,
but the words came out a breathless whisper.

He smiled. "Do I? Tell me that is not what you have
wanted ever since we met. Tell me that your flirtation was
a childish whim and not the longing of a beautiful
woman."

She could not answer. She wanted to pull away, run,
but she was rooted by the dizzying consciousness his kiss
caused. She felt the hard panelling of the wall at her back
and the pressure of his hands on her shoulders. His face
was only inches away, smiling, the eyes bold with passionate invitation. When she did not answer, he kissed her

21

again. Heat suffused her and her breath rasped in her throat. She whimpered as his tongue touched her lips.

Her fear took full shape and she pushed him away, twisting her face from his. "Stop it at once!" Her dark eyes flashed and when they met his amused look, all courage vanished. He released her but trapped her between his outspread arms when she would have fled along the corridor.

"Let me go," she whispered. Her throat was dry and she felt weak all over. The soft notes of the dinner chime sounded, and she looked about startled. "I'm late—I must change. Father will be furious."

"The role of innocent child does not become you, Emilie Sloane. You rouse a man then expect him to do nothing but smile and settle for the pleasure of holding your hand or perhaps dancing a time or two. You're eighteen, old enough to know a woman's passion and put aside childish games."

Her cheeks flooded with colour. No man had ever spoken to her that way except James, whose passion had also been aroused and who had claimed her in a heady surge of desire. She shook her head and refused to meet Henri's gaze.

"I must go—"

He stood aside abruptly, his head tilted as he studied her with a strange expression. He made no move to stop her as she turned and fled.

The suite was large and elegantly furnished, one of the luxury accommodations the *Ophir* provided for passengers who demanded the finest. The duke and duchess of York had sailed on the *Ophir* on the trip to inaugurate the new Commonwealth of Australia shortly after the death of Queen Victoria in 1901; and they occupied the suite which Roderick Sloane and his wife Charlotte now had, a fact which the elder Sloane was quick to bring to the attention of their fellow travelers on more than one occasion. Emilie and Sara's suite was only slightly less elegant, said to have been used by the duchess' lady in waiting. It was comprised of two rooms, with a large wardrobe and a water closet between. The sitting room floor was covered with a thick Persian carpet, delicately patterned in deep reds and blues with accents of gold. Gold velvet drapes covered a large window which looked directly out to the sea, with no deck to obscure the view or afford the distraction of passengers going by. There was a small Chippendale settee with blue upholstery, two chairs and a writing desk. Beyond, the bedroom was equally as large, with panelled walls and two beds covered with heavy damask spreads of crimson embroidered with gold. A night table stood between them to hold the Tiffany lamp and a telephone which communicated with other parts of the ship.

Emilie leaned against the door and buried her face in her hands. Her cheeks were hot and dry and her eyes stung with tears. She choked back a sob but it would not be contained, and she began to cry. From the bedroom, Sara rushed in with a frightened expression and looked at her sister questioningly.

"Em! Whatever has happened? Are you all right?" She came close and slipped an arm about her shoulders.

Emilie tried to stop crying, hiccuping and biting her lip, wiping at her eyes with the back of her hand. "I'm all right . . ."

Sara peered. "Are you sure?" She had never seen her sister upset like this and could not imagine what had caused it. Emilie was always so stable—so sure of herself. When Emilie nodded and managed to smile, relief flooded Sara. Gently she said, "Can you tell me what's wrong? It's not like you to weep—"

Emilie took a deep breath and let it out as a long, shuddering sigh. "I don't know . . . nothing, really. All of a sudden—" She broke off, unable to put in words what she did not fully understand herself. How could she ex-

23

plain the shame she felt that Henri Cartier, a man she scarcely knew, would make such a bold suggestion and claim that she had led him to believe he had the right? How could she explain the turmoil that raged inside her because she knew the words were true? She *was* a woman, and she wanted fulfillment of the longing and smouldering fire that lay within her, dormant at times but never extinguished, a fire that James Pauling had fanned to flames too quickly and easily and that she now had to guard against so desperately. She still sometimes woke at night to stare at patterns of moonlight across the bed and remember vividly the sensuous vitality that had been hers for a few brief moments before guilt masked them.

"Are you sure you're all right?" Sara still had a worried frown between her dark brows. She was not as fair as her sister, though they both had the creamy complexion of their mother's Viking ancestry. Sara's hair was a chestnut colour, with a hint of red that added soft highlights. Her eyes were hazel with flecks of green, while Emilie's were so deep a brown that they seemed black.

When Emilie nodded and sighed, Sara said, "The second dinner chimes have already rung and you haven't changed!" She crossed to the hall and flung open the door of the wardrobe. "I'll ring for Jenny. Do hurry, Em, father will be raging." Sara began to select gowns, slipping each hanger from the rod and holding out the dress for her sister's inspection.

Emilie crossed and took the gown from her sister's hand, setting it back in its place then taking Sara's arm and leading her toward the door.

"I don't want Jenny. Go on without me."

"I'll wait—"

"No, run along. Make some excuse, and I'll be there just as fast as I can. Hurry before father is upset with you too."

Sara hesitated, then grabbed up the brown gloves she

24

had dropped to a chair. She smoothed the skirt of the chocolate-coloured silk. "You're sure?"

"Yes, go on."

Emilie sighed as the door closed behind her sister, then quickly went into the bedroom, unbuttoning the bodice of the beige taffeta as she walked. She slipped out of the dress, tossing it to the bed, then sat before the mirror and uncapped a blue bottle of cucumber lotion and began to cleanse her face. The cool, moist cream seemed to soothe her fevered thoughts. Had she led Henri Cartier on? The thought made her cheeks flame, and she was flooded with a memory of the fiery kiss in the companionway. He had no right!

Recalling the time, she rose and went to the water closet to pour water from a pitcher into the basin and wash. She should have allowed time for a leisurely bath. She sighed and unpinned her hair as she walked back to the dressing table to pick up a silver-handled brush and begin to stroke with a firm hand. She had *not* led Henri on. He boldly assumed too much. She didn't doubt for a moment that the stories of his escapades were true!

When at last her hair gleamed to her satisfaction, she caught it back and pinned it to her crown with tortoise shell combs so it fell in a small cascade of curls. She studied herself in the glass trying to see the beautiful woman Henri had called her.

Sighing, she went to the wardrobe and drew out a green gown. She had saved it for this occasion because it was her prettiest and most festive. Lifting it from the hanger, she shook out the flared skirt that had fullness in the back but which did not hide the roundness of her hips or her narrow waist. The dress had a square neckline, with ruffled lace flowers at the shoulders and ribbons which fell over her breasts; the sleeves were tight to the elbows, then puffed into caps so large they gave the effect of a cape thrown round her shoulders. She drew on the gown and struggled with the hooks at the back. She should have let Sara call Jenny, and for a moment she considered ringing now, but Jenny would already be on her way to the second class dining room. Though she was personal maid to Sara and Emilie, father declared that second class passage would suit the girl's needs. No sense wasting extra prounds when she could scamper up and down the stairs between decks whenever she was needed.

Fastened properly at last, Emilie stood before the glass and straightened the skirt. Six rows of delicate seed pearls formed a band down the center front and around the hem which came just to her instep so that the black satin slippers showed. A scrollwork of pearls decorated the bodice, and their luster against the dark velvet was striking. With a last pat to her hair, she snatched up the black evening cape she'd had fashioned at a dressmaker's shop on Regent Street. She doubted she would need it this warm night, but the lining matched her gown so perfectly that it was more attractive than any of her lighter wraps. Not bothering to don it, she stuffed a lace handkerchief in her cuff and hurried out. A glimpse of herself in the glass as she pulled the stateroom door shut showed bright eyes and cheeks stained with colour.

The first class dining salon of the *Ophir* was a huge room on the second deck. The round tables seated eight or ten, except for a few smaller ones that had been arranged for passengers who wished privacy—a honeymoon couple who sat alone in one corner, an elderly couple with a nurse who wheeled the man's chair and was in constant attendance, a few others. The Captain's table was set apart slightly from the rest near the center of the room. Emilie made her way to it, smiling excuses when her skirt brushed an arm, or when a gentleman greeted her.

Her father and the other men at the table rose as the Captain got to his feet and drew out the vacant chair beside him. Emilie slid into it, nodding around the table so the men could resume their places. Her father scowled but said nothing. It would be improper to cause a scene; he would take her to task in privacy, not before guests at the table, but he would not let the incident pass unchallenged, she knew. His brooding gaze lingered on her as Captain Domeér gallantly took the cloak she slipped from her shoulders and laid it across the back of the chair before seating himself once more. A waiter in white coat readied a bowl of steaming soup from a tureen on a serving cart and placed it before Emilie.

Captain Domeér was middle-aged, with blond hair and pale eyes that were emphasized by his tanned complexion. He'd been educated in his native Holland and also at the Greenwich Naval Academy, and he'd served as an officer in the Dutch Imperial Navy before joining the steamship line and assuming command of the prized S.S. *Ophir*. His English was flawless with only a trace of accent, and he was tall and lean, with a firm manner that commanded respect. Emilie found him charming.

"I'm delighted that you have recovered from your indisposition," he said.

Emilie caught her sister's quick glance and realized the excuse Sara had given for her tardiness. "Yes, completely, thank you."

"A touch of sun, perhaps," the stout *Frau* Muller said. studying Emilie's flushed cheeks. "The vetter grows varm . . ." She let the thought drift off, conscious of her accent and the slight disapproving smile that came to her husband's lips. She was ill at ease much of the time, unable to enter in the lively conversation that usually filled the dinner hour. Graying, her blond hair was drab and she did little to style it according to fashion. She wore muted colours, a plum shade tonight, which gave her a dowdy appearance, though she was not yet forty. Her husband, tall and imposing, with a straight back and stern manner, seemed to watch her constantly with steely blue eyes. He was an engineer of some sort but he managed to avoid

27

talking about himself or his work whenever the subject was approached.

Emilie disliked both of them at first sight and this opinion had not altered during the six day voyage during which she'd sat at the same table with them and entered into desultory conversation when forced. They were headed for Rabat, with several weeks in Tangier first to allow *Herr* Muller to see to some business matters. Though her father and *Herr* Muller talked about business, she still did not have a clear idea of what the German did. Until today, she had concentrated her attention on Henri Cartier, the eighth person at the table, but now she avoided him except for a perfunctory greeting. She felt his eyes on her, and she fought the tide of colour that threatened. She was relieved when the conversation she'd interrupted resumed.

"Certainly the death of your King will make a difference in your country's policies in Morocco," *Herr* Muller said.

Roderick Sloane turned his gaze from his daughter to the speaker. "I think not. His Majesty's government recognized Moolay Hafeed's rule last year, and we've supported him despite his appeals to the French. Naturally we don't like to see the French take control, but there's little we can do about it, at least at present." He cast an apologetic look at Henri, who shrugged and smiled.

"Perhaps England would like to have a Moroccan commonwealth under her flag," Muller said, smiling so that the remark lost some of its sting.

"No more than the Germans would," Roderick Sloane said dryly. "The propaganda campaign your people waged back in '06 was insidious and the direct cause of more bloodshed than any of our diplomatic relations."

"You are misinformed, *Herr* Sloane. My people had no part in that trouble." Muller stared at Sloane as though to force a change of opinion.

Roderick Sloane knew there was no purpose to be

28

gained in antagonizing the German, and he turned to talk to Henri Cartier.

Roderick Sloane had taken the trouble to inquire into the background of the young French count, since the chap had been attentive to Emilie since the voyage's beginning. Good family, descendants of the House of Bourbon, with a handsome income from properties in Paris and the south of France. There were rumors that he'd been involved in several political affairs, though he spent most of his time at his own pleasures. There was another rumor, one as shifting and elusive as a vagrant breeze, about a duel in which he'd wounded an influential young Republican and which had necessitated his hasty departure from Paris until matters cooled down.

Roderick wondered again about Emilie's reason for being late to dinner. He suspected at first that she might be dallying somewhere with Cartier, but they'd arrived separately. If he caught her— He had not yet forgotten her disobedience in the matter of James Pauling, and his fury smouldered every time he thought of her daring to go to the man's flat. Though he suspected it was not as innocent as Emilie claimed, he did not let his mind dwell on other possibilities. She was a willful child who had caused him to deal harshly with her on many occasions, and he was beginning to realize that she was not a child any longer but a woman. Time to marry her off before she got herself into a scandal of some sort.

"Will you be spending your entire holiday in Tangier, M'sieur Cartier?"

Henri set aside his wine glass and waited until the white-coated waiter finished serving roast duckling onto his plate. "Yes. Perhaps we will run into each other from time to time. I'm told that the European sector of Tangier is similar to the *Champs-Élysées*, if one waits long enough he will see everyone he knows pass by." He smiled round the table and let his glance rest on Emilie a moment.

Flustered, she said, "I have never been to Paris but if it

is as lovely as people say, I'm sure you must be sad to leave when spring is so close at hand."

"Yes, but there will be other springs, all equally lovely. Perhaps one day you will see for yourself."

Sara looked up from the plate on which her attention had been focused. "It will seem strange to live in a place where the seasons do not change. I cannot imagine eternal summer."

"Tangier has change of seasons, and sometimes winter is raw," Captain Domeer said. "But you arrive at the best possible time. May is still cool. I do not think you will find it unpleasant."

Charlotte Sloane looked at him. "And the summers?"

Captain Domeer shrugged. "I have not had the fortune to touch at Africa for more than a day's call, winter or summer. Warmer, I'm told, but the levante blows steadily and helps cool the city. And unlike the interior, Tangiers experiences rain storms to relieve the heat and drought."

"We will be quite comfortable, Charlotte. I've been assured that our living quarters will be the finest. I'm sure the Arabs have found some way to build so that they do not swelter."

Herr Muller looked amused and his tone was a trifle caustic. "To be sure. Most houses are built with courtyards and thick walls to keep out the heat. Our own house in Rabat is comfortable the year round."

Frau Muller nodded and looked at Mrs. Sloane earnestly. "Ya." Her glance fell to her food immediately.

Captain Domeer looked at Emilie, then at Sara. "You two young ladies must do me the honor of dancing with me tonight. Our last evening aboard . . . I will be sorry to see such charming companions leave."

Sara smiled. "It has been a pleasant voyage. I'm sorry to see it end—but of course it doesn't for you, does it?"

"No, it is only beginning. Our final destination is Batavia, as you probably know."

Sara nodded, her hazel eyes wide. "How far that is! I don't think I would have the courage to go to such a remote place." She glanced quickly at her father, almost expecting him to tell her to be quiet. She knew she would go wherever he took them, and she thanked heaven it was no further than Tangier. Whatever was life going to be like there? It was frightening, and she did not share Emilie's excitement about the mystery and glamour. She would be far more comfortable in the familiar surroundings of London.

"It is a lovely city, it would surprise you," Domeer said. "And an important seaport. The Dutch have been there for three centuries." He launched into a description of the city and some of its history, and Sara listened, fascinated.

Roderick Sloane and *Herr* Muller revived their conversation about business conditions in Morocco, while their wives were silent. Henri spoke softly to Emilie beside him.

"You will not be so busy that you cannot take time to see something of Tangier. Let me escort you."

She fought the discomfort that thoughts of being alone with him brought. "You do not know the city, you've never been there."

He laughed. "I learn quickly, and you forget I have friends to advise me. Say you will."

"I—I must see what plans my parents have. I'm sure my father would be adverse to having me wander about." Deliberately she turned her attention back to the captain who was still talking about Batavia. Throughout the rest of the meal, she avoided giving Henri the opportunity to speak privately again.

At the farewell ball in the main salon, courtesy forced her to dance with him, but she refused to answer his persistent demands until at last he left her in peace. Several times she found him staring at her across another partner's shoulder or the length of the room. When she tumbled into bed at midnight, sleep eluded her for a long

31

time, and she stared at the dark sky beyond the cabin window.

The *Ophir* dropped anchor in the rounded bay of Tangier at 7 a.m. Emilie, awake since the first light of dawn crept across the sky, was up and standing at the cabin window, craning her neck to have a first glimpse of the city. From the water level, Tangier rose along the side of a steep hill, looking almost vertical in spots. Houses, square and whitewashed, were piled like so many boxes, some low, others several stories high, all flat-roofed except for an occasional dome or towering minaret. To the west, villas in the European style stood among gardens splashed with bright flowers and deep cool greenery. Near the center of the city, crenellated walls of ancient stone surrounded the old city, and she could make out the rounded dome of the Sultan's palace where a red flag snapped and fluttered in the wind that seemed to have come up with the sun. The sky was already an incredible blue, so clear that the outlines of the upper city were stark against it. On a hillside which fell away sharply to the water, the land was almost barren except for a few straggly, tenacious shrubs and weeds, but below, a crescent of beautiful white sand formed a large beach. At one end where the sand ended abruptly, a sea wall had been built; beyond it, a dismal looking shack appeared to be a center of activity. Boats were putting out from a jetty, some with men pulling at oars, others steam-powered launches of varying degrees of shabbiness or elegance.

Behind her Sara came awake with a start and seeing Emilie at the window, jumped from bed. "We're here?!" She was eager to look, and Emilie moved to let her close to the glass. For a moment, Sara was silent, turning her head this way and that to take in the sight. When she looked at Emilie, her expression was one of disappointment. "It's not very grand . . ."

Emilie laughed. "But it is different, you must admit.

nd we'll have to make the best of it since we've no hoice." At her sister's crestfallen look, Emilie made an ffort to cheer her. "It's not fair to judge by first appearances. We may find it quite exotic once we're ashore and an see things close up. I'm sure visitors to England are a it dismayed at their first glimpse of Southampton, don't ou think?"

She was rewarded by a determined smile from Sara. Yes, you're right, of course. And there are quite lovely illas, aren't there. Look—" She pointed to a particularly arge house whose gabled roof could be seen among the rees surrounding it. "Oh, Em, I do wish I could share our certainty that we'll be happy. Sometimes I think I vill wake and find this is a dream and I'm home in my omfortable room, with all of London outside my door."

"Poor Sara, you've no taste for adventure."

"I'm not good at meeting people—"

"Nonsense. You are intelligent and pretty. You are an ccomplished artist and can hold a decent conversation or lance or—"

"Oh, Em, stop it. You sound as though you're auctioning me off!" Her gloom vanished and Sara laughed.

"That would be one way to get back to London," Emilie said tossing her head and walking from the window.

"Whatever do you mean?"

"Not auction, but sell yourself in a manner of speaking."

"Sell—?"

"Find yourself a nice Englishman who wants to go ome and marry him."

"Emilie!" Sara was scandalized. "How awful—"

"Awful to marry? Isn't that what we've been preparing urselves for all these years? Our dear old nanny who onstantly reminded us to behave and do right so that we vould grow up to be proper ladies who could expect the ame behavior from our own little ones? The music

33

lessons, stitching, and dancing at Miss Dreyfus Academy—why even if we had been permitted to atten Royal Holloway College for Women, I dare say we woul have gotten only a smattering of knowledge and a heav dose of proper skills in homemaking and how to be goo wives."

"What's wrong with being a wife?" Sara looke puzzled.

"Nothing, but it can be crashingly dull. Look a mother, she doesn't dare to take a stand against anythin father does. She scarcely speaks when he's about."

Sara sank to the edge of the bed and looked at her sis ter. "Do you think mother is unhappy? I've always con sidered her most fortunate. She has a good life, far bette than many women."

"Not unhappy but most definitely bored."

Sara shook her head. "I don't believe that. She ha many interests and father never stints on anything sh wants."

Emilie sighed. She and Sara were worlds apart in thei thinking and there was no way to bridge the gap. "You'r right, of course." She grinned impishly. "But it's still good idea."

"What is?"

"For you to find a man and marry."

Sara blushed. "We don't know a soul in Morocco Besides, I'm not popular. At parties it's always you who i asked to dance while I sit and talk with mother and he friends."

"There was the young man from Oxford—Jeffrey Hen derson."

Sarah frowned. "He never asked to call a second time."

"But he did call on you once, and if you had give him some encouragement, he would have returned. That what I mean, you have to make a man believe yo are an exceptional woman who would make a marvelou wife. If there are as many Europeans in Tangier as father says, they will be standing in line to call on you."

Sarah laughed off the idea. "You wash up first, and we'd better hurry. Father expects us to have breakfast done and the last of our bags ready to go ashore by nine." She rose and walked back to the window, staring out across the bay to the dazzling white city.

"I'm frightened, Emilie, aren't you?"

Emilie turned, her hand on the door leading to the water closet. "Frightened? Good heavens no! This is 1910 and the world is civilized."

"Is it? I mean, can we really live in a place like this?" She gestured at the view beyond the window.

"Certainly we can, and we will. In a few hours we will be at our new house, and in a month's time we'll be completely at home. You'll see. Now ring for Jenny and have her close my trunks. I've laid out what I need."

CHAPTER TWO

Many of the passengers had already disembarked when the Sloanes and their three servants gathered at the rail to watch a sleek launch draw up at the boarding ladder which had been put over the side of the *Ophir*. They were to be met and escorted ashore, the arrangements taken care of by letter by the president of Cote's Bank through the Minister of Finance in Morocco. The opening of the Anglo-French Bank of Lyon was of considerable importance to the Moroccans as well as the English and French, and the manager, Roderick Sloane, would be accorded every courtesy.

Three men hurried up the ladder. The first wore a flowing white robe with wide sleeves and a hood thrown back from his turbaned head. His skin was deeply tanned and his eyes were set under heavy brows. As he grasped the rail and came through the entry port, an intricate gold ring set with a large diamond caught the sunlight and winked it in a dozen directions at once. He went immediately to Roderick Sloane and bowed politely.

"Mister Sloane . . . I am Yusuf Bacali. I have been sent by Ali Ibn Toumart, Minister of Finance. It is my pleasure to welcome you to Tangier." Smiling, he bowed again, first to Roderick Sloane, then in turn to Charlotte, Sara and Emilie.

"How do you do," Roderick said, bobbing his head.

Bacali motioned quickly to the two blacks who had followed him up the ladder, and they began to collect the Sloane's luggage which was piled near the rail. The men hefted heavy trunks and valises as easily as feathers, swinging them to broad naked shoulders of gleaming ebony. Each wore only a voluminous white cloth that was wrapped about his waist and drawn between the legs to form a loose pantaloon, secured somehow by tucking the cloth back into itself.

Charlotte looked about nervously, afraid to trust their belongings to the two savage looking slaves, and embarrassed by the sight of their nakedness. When she saw Emilie staring, she nudged her and frowned disapprovingly.

Yusuf Bacali was explaining that the launch would take them to the jetty, where his men would see the luggage through the customs house, and that he himself would escort them to the house on the Mountain which the Minister had arranged for them. He bowed and begged the ladies to proceed to the waiting launch. Charlotte hesitated, one hand picking at the buttons at the front of the dove-grey morning dress.

Roderick Sloane said, "Charlotte." It was a command, and the woman paled visibly as she moved toward the rail. Sara took her arm and Emilie smiled encouragingly and started down the ladder. A robed Arab offered his hand to assist her into the bobbing launch, his eyes downcast. Moments later Sara and Charlotte stood on the deck and Bacali was following Roderick down the swaying ladder.

The launch was modern and well appointed, with a glassed cabin to shield passengers form the spray. The bay, which had been glassy at dawn, now rippled under the wind. There were leather benches along one wall, and as soon as everyone was seated, Bacali spoke to the boat man in a rush of harsh Arabic. The engine chugged to life and the boat was underway.

Emilie could scarely contain her excitement, but with her father only a few feet away, she forced herself to sit properly, hands clutching a small black kid purse in her lap. But she could not prevent her gaze from flitting this way and that as she tried to absorb everything. Other boats, some rowed by ebony slaves, passed closeby, some so heavily laden with baggage and boxes of all sizes and shapes they seemed in danger of overturning before reaching shore. On the jetty, people hurried about; slaves naked except for the wrap-around garments that covered them from waist to thighs, lifted heavy crates and trunks that had been brought ashore, straining and sweating under the sun, their bodies glistening as though oiled; others with complexions of olive, copper, wheat and occasionally white, hurried about, gesturing and shouting so that the din carried over the sound of the boat engines. As the launch neared the quay, half a dozen men rushed forward to grab lines and make it fast and to assist the passengers. Bacali shouted to a man in a brown robe and white turban, who in moments had organized half a dozen blacks to unload the luggage. Emilie's heart thudded against her ribs as Bacali helped her to the jetty and she stood among the trunks and valises, gaping at everything.

The long, low customs shed was an ugly dilapidated structure that seemed to tilt in the wind, which was quite strong now, and warm. Bacali was leading them toward it, though telling Roderick Sloane all the while they would not be subject to delay, since the Minister of Finance had arranged everything. When a man in a brown robe hailed them, Bacali immediately shouted and waved his arms in answer. It seemed to Emilie that one had to outshout the other in order to win his point, and she was relieved when at last the man stepped aside and Bacali bowed to the Sloanes and bid them follow.

They went in solemn procession, Roderick immediately behind the Arab emissary, his back stiff and his bowler incongruous among the sea of white turbaned heads. He'd gestured once to the women and did not look back again. They passed through the customs shed where other passengers from the *Ophir* had been herded into a group surrounded by their baggage and a dozen screaming interpreters. Emilie glimpsed Henri Cartier standing off to one side with a tall, slender, sandy-haired man. He'd spoken of a friend in Tangier. . . . She turned away when he glanced in her direction, unwilling to meet his gaze.

Charlotte Sloane felt faint with the commotion. She would have clutched her husband's arm, except she knew he would not approve. Instead, she clung to Sara, who patted her hand reassuringly.

"We'll be at the house shortly, mother. Landings are always like this, you've told me so yourself: Colleen, come help madam."

"Yes'm." A middle-aged woman who had been Charlotte Sloane's personal maid for eighteen years stepped to her mistress' side. She looked pale and frightened, but she set her lips in a tight line and took Charlotte's arm.

The third servant, Roderick Sloane's man Hawley, stood slightly apart watching and waiting for any command from his master. If he found the sudden and dramatic change in his life disturbing, he was paid handsomely enough to hide his feelings. It had been Roderick's decision to bring three of the household servants from London. The family would require their services aboard ship, and he would not trust his own comfort completely to the hands of foreigners, he declared.

Charlotte was unable to speak for the din. She had traveled with Roderick several times during their twenty years of marriage, twice to France where boat landings had been bothersome and hectic, but never had she seen anything to compare with this! The noise—and the smell—the shed was hot and the proximity of so many

39

slaves and Arabs was overpowering, and though she had known that Tangier would not be as civilized as London, she had not expected such *primitiveness!* It was unbelievable that Roderick expected them to live here!

Sara and Colleen guided her past knots of people, trying to shield her from the push of the crowd. It was frightening to be thrust into such turmoil, and Charlotte prayed that Bacali would soon have them out and on their way to the house.

"Come along," Roderick said sharply, his words lost in the cacophony of clatter and voices. Charlotte squeezed Sara's arm and looked to be sure Emilie was close, then quickened her steps.

Bacali led them through the shed, bypassing inspectors who were seated along one wall pointing and gesturing as baggage was opened and interpreters struggled to translate descriptions of items to puzzled customs men. Only eleven of the *Ophir's* passengers were leaving the ship at Tangier; those who had come ashore for only the day were spared the bother of inspection and were taken directly through the building.

Coming out into the sun after the closeness of the shed was almost blinding, and Emilie shaded her eyes with a hand. She'd chosen a small hat that perched atop her upswept hair, tilting forward on her forehead but without a brim to shield her eyes from the light. It was stylish blue velvet with a long brush-like feather sweeping back at one side. She'd also chosen a blue linen suit with a full skirt that would not hamper her climbing in and out of the launch, and a hip length jacket with white piping over a frilly white blouse with a high ruffled collar. She had dressed with consideration of the heat, but already she felt hot and sticky. Would any of her wardrobe be suitable here?

They were standing in a narrow street of hard-packed earth and irregular paving stones, some worn smooth, others badly cracked and broken so they afforded a

40

treacherous path. There were no pavements for walking, and the street was no wider than a twisting alley. In the shadow of the shed, a squatting man, face leathered and wrinkled under sparse wisps of white whiskers, bawled a harsh, unintelligible cry as he poured tinkling coins in a tenuous stream from one hand to the other. Seeing the English family, he cried so loudly that the women drew back in fright. Bacali gestured and shouted imperiously at the old man.

"A money-changer. There is no need for you to worry yourself." Waving again, his signal brought a man leading several mules, each with two large straw baskets suspended on straps over its back. The animals brayed and shook their heads in an effort to escape the coarse ropes tied about their muzzles as halters, but the little man in the striped robe swat at their flanks with a switch and yanked the rope to keep them moving. Instantly, the blacks began to load the baggage that had somehow miraculously come through the customs onto the animals.

Emilie watched the beasts burdened with loads that seemed to bend their backs to the breaking point, but the animals stood still except for the swish of tails or a soft snuffing. She looked along the narrow street, wondering where the cabs were that would take them to the European sector and already anxious to get away from the stench. Smells of the sea, animals and, she was sure, garbage, were flung at them by the wind, changing subtly from one moment to the next but never improving. She had not expected such dirt and inconvenience; mother was pale and shaking. Emilie moved to her side with a smile that was meant to be reassuring.

The baggage stowed, the slaves, muleteer and animals set out at a snail's pace. Bacali clapped another command, and another string of mules appeared as though by magic. Instead of the huge baskets, each was fitted with a soft blanket and saddle. Bacali bowed and indicated the ladies were to have their choice of animals. Charlotte

41

looked from her daughters to her husband. Surely she wa
not expected to *ride* one of these creatures?! Sara's gri
on her arm tightened. Even Roderick looked surprise
and turned to Bacali.

"Surely you can accommodate us with a carriage, m
good man."

Bacali's expression was veiled. "There are none, sir. Hi
Excellency, the Minister, has arranged for good ridin
horses for your convenience, but the road from here t
the European sector is very steep and best managed b
mules. I'm sure the ladies will be quite comfortable." H
pointed. "English saddles." Apparently he thought th
contribution worthy of praise.

"But I've never ridden," Charlotte wailed. "Roderick
please tell him it's impossible—"

Roderick frowned, annoyed with himself for not havin
determined details of this nature beforehand but unwillin
to lose face now.

"Then you will learn now, Charlotte. I'm sure th
transportation Mr. Bacali has provided is preferable t
walking." He strode along the string of mules gazing a
each as though judging their suitability. They all looke
exactly and impossibly the same, but he nodded and indi
cated to Bacali that he would ride the first one. A
Bacali's clap, the mule driver scurried and knelt to offe
his back as a step for the Englishman. Astride the un
gainly beast, Roderick motioned the others to mount.

Emilie was fearful her mother would faint before sh
was finally perched in the saddle, sitting sideways an
grasping the pommel so that her knuckles were white an
her face ashen under her wide-brimmed hat. Neither Col
leen nor Jenny was any help. If anything, they were mor
terrified than their mistress as they allowed Hawley to as
sist them into the saddles of two fly-plagued creatures
Colleen's lips moved in a steady, silent prayer and onc
on the mule, she started to cross herself but thought bet
ter of it instantly and grasped the pommel as thougl

clinging to life itself. She looked ridiculous, but it was impossible to laugh when she was so terrified.

Sara and Emilie were helped up. They had the advantage of having ridden enough to make the task plausible. Emilie hid a smile as she pictured Miss Dreyfus' face if she could see her former pupils. All the instruction of ladylike deportment, the lessons in entering and leaving a carriage gracefully, always allowing one's escort or the footman to take a hand to assist with the step . . . it seemed laughable now. A glance at Sara showed her thoughts were similar, and they smiled conspiratorily.

Emilie quickly became too engrossed with the sights that surrounded them to care about the discomfort of riding the mule. As they set out, led at a slow pace by the muleteer who held the rope of the lead animal on which father sat, they came almost immediately to a gate. Its huge wooden doors with heavy pegs and thick metal hinges and bolts were open. At one side was a small guardhouse with a native policeman dressed in ballooning scarlet trousers and turban standing at attention, his rifle slung over his shoulder by a leather strap. He did not blink as the mules clopped by on the cobblestones, but his dark eyes followed them. From the other side, a beggar with the hood of his robe slipped back to expose a red, sunken socket where an eye was missing, rushed forward to push forth a begging hand. The muleteer cracked at him viciously with a switch.

"Balaak! Balaak!" the driver cried, and the beggar scrambled from the path of the caravan.

Charlotte gasped audibly and closed her eyes.

Once through the gracefully arched gate, the driver led them along a narrow, dim street. The squat buildings which were close together and shared common walls, cut off the sun so the roadway was in shadows. All manner of people were abroad, walking at a slow pace or standing in doorways or small groups here and there. Several men huddled against buildings, seemingly asleep and unaware

43

of the activity around them. All wore long cloaks similar to Bacali's, with pointed hoods standing upright or with yards of white cloth wrapped as turbans about their heads. They were strangely incurious about the shipload of foreigners who had arrived, and except for an occasional beggar or the covert glances of some small boys spinning tops on a flat stone, no one evinced any interest in the passing caravan. They stared with fixed gaze or chanted verses from the Koran in nasal tones.

Emilie was aware of the smell that still hung in the air though they had left the waterfront. She had seen no whites since leaving the customs shed, and she wondered how far a distance they had to travel. She dared not look behind to mother and Sara, concentrating instead on trying to glimpse bits of the city as they passed crooked side streets or came to breaks in the buildings where she could see beyond. They seemed to be following the outskirts of the walled city, the high stone wall solid at her right as the mule continued its plodding pace. What had Bacali said about the location of the house where they were to live? On the mountain . . . Not the peak, surely, but probably among the proper European villas she had noticed to the east. They would have a view of the city and bay, and no doubt a parlor no different from that at home in Belgravia. She sighed.

The sun was caught in the pit of the city where buildings cut off the wind, and heat rose with a heavy stench. They turned a corner from the narrow street and emerged with startling abruptness on an open square. The street was wide and surrounded with tiny shops, some with Spanish, French or English signs in front. Among the multitude of burnooses, there was an occasional gentleman in cork hat or lady in fashionable dress carrying a parasol to shield her from the sun.

They crossed the square and entered a wide street where trees offered shade. In the distance, Emilie saw several buildings that were definitely European, almost

Georgian in character. Flags of various nations flew over them. The muleteer took them past a small park, with green grass and a border of geraniums, irises and daffodils, then up another street lined by European houses. Emilie glanced at each, hoping with all her heart that they would not stop. Occasionally, a Moorish style house with whitewashed walls screening it from the street was set among gardens and trees. She was praying fervently that such a house would be their final destination.

They had been riding less than a quarter of an hour, but Charlotte was slumped in the saddle, too exhausted to hold her head up any longer. When at last Bacali called a halt, she sighed and would have slid from the mule except that Sara clutched her arm.

The house was surrounded by a high, whitewashed wall. Emilie's excitement stirred when they passed through the gate and entered a green, lush garden dotted with patches of colour of flowers growing on slender stalks or thick bushes. Vines climbed along the trunks of dwarf palms and tall eucalyptus trees. The fragrance of blossoms was a heady perfume after the odours of the street.

Emilie almost laughed aloud with relief, and she heard her mother's quickly drawn breath. Emilie was restored instantly. She slid from the saddle without waiting for help as a dozen servants rushed from a region hidden from view beyond another wall that screened the edge of the garden. In the center of the garden, a white stone path glistened in the dappled light, and at its end, wrought iron gates stood open. Emilie went in.

The house was so unlike the ones in the village that Emilie gasped with delight. It was huge, two stories high with a flat roof and a band of orange and blue tiles bordering the parapets. There were many horseshoe shaped windows with emerald green shutters and doorways recessed under cool shadowy arches. Directly ahead a gracefully curved archway, ornately carved and decorated with mosaic tiles, led to an inner courtyard where she could see greenery and the reflection of water. Large earthenware pots containing glossy-leaved plants were everywhere.

"Oh my word . . ." Charlotte looked about with a startled expression. She had believed herself near death, and suddenly she had arrived in another world. Her first disappointment at the house not being one of the European villas gave way to the overwhelming beauty and serenity with which she was confronted. She glanced at her husband, who was already following Bacali through the garden. Sara took her arm and smiled as they skirted the servants unloading the baggage. Through the long archway, they found themselves in a second garden.

The house was built around a courtyard with thick stone columns supporting a covered gallery. Above, a similar gallery formed a verandah outside the second story rooms, with a slatted roof on which thick bougainvillea gave deep shade. At two corners, wooden stairways descended to the lower garden, where an elaborate fountain played softly in a tiled reflecting pool. A gnarled olive tree kept the court cool, and it was delightfully refreshing after the ride from the waterfront.

Emilie turned to smile at Sara. "Civilized after all."

Sara nodded, too surprised to find her voice immediately. A bowing, olive-skinned Moorish woman with coal black eyes, her face flawlessly smooth, bowed and gestured toward a doorway at their left. Mother, Colleen and Jenny went inside, with Jenny staring about with mouth open in wonder. With a last look at the garden court, Emilie followed her sister.

If the garden had been a surprise, the interior of the house brought amazement. It was as cool as an April morning on the Thames. They were in a large room, a sitting room or parlor of sorts. Rich, soft carpets covered the floor. There were three low divans and two Queen Anne sofas upholstered in crimson silk. Several chairs were modishly English, and a Queen Anne table stood against the wall under a gilt mirror. Four huge brass trays rested on low pedestals, the Moorish adaptation of tables, and the whitewashed walls were brightened by large brocaded tapestries of exquisite design and detail. On one wall, two gleaming, crescent-shaped scimitars were crossed like dueling swords. The ceiling was made of finely carved, multi-colored woods and plaster.

Charlotte collapsed into a gold silk chair; behind her, Colleen was holding the wide-brimmed hat her mistress had pulled off. Like Jenny, the older servant gaped as though still not believing what her eyes saw. The Moorish woman who had admitted them clapped her hands and a Negress appeared soundlessly from an arch at the other side of the room. She was barefooted, dressed in a long white toga-like garment that left one ebony shoulder bare. The dress was tied about the waist with a thick gold rope that hung in long tassels near the hem. She pressed pink palms together and bowed before the housekeeper, who spoke softly in Arabic. The girl backed from the room, still bowing.

Bacali and Roderick Sloane seated themselves at one side of the room, the Englishman stiff and uncomfortable on the red Queen Anne settee, Bacali sitting cross-legged, his feet tucked under the white robe, on one of the low divans that was in actuality numerous soft pillows in a low frame. He was explaining the operation of the household.

"Asheema is the housekeeper. All other servants are responsible to her, if that is satisfactory to Madam Sloane?" He inclined his head toward Charlotte and when she nodded, he went on. "The servants sleep in quarters beyond the hedge of the rear garden. A dozen others come by day, but this can be altered if you have need. The Minister has arranged a very fine cook to tend your meals, though his knowledge of English cuisine is limited. Perhaps one of your own servants can instruct?" He

47

looked at Colleen, whose mouth fell open at the thought of stepping down to the level of kitchen maid.

"That won't be necessary," Roderick said. "I am sure we will manage."

"It is common practice for the Europeans to interchange servants for special occasions. If you dine somewhere and relish the food, in all likelihood the host will permit his cook to teach yours the art of making the dish." That matter settled, he turned to business affairs. "The Minister requests the honor of making your acquaintance at your earliest convenience. M'sieur Augustin has already arrived and met with the Minister. He too waits your convenience."

"I will see him immediately after lunch," Sloane said.

Without a flicker of expression, Yusuf Bacali corrected politely. "It is our custom to remain in seclusion from noon until four. I will be happy to inform the Minister that you are available at five?"

Chagrined, Roderick nodded, looking relieved when the black servant returned carrying a heavy tray, which she set on one of the brass tables. The housekeeper, a very attractive woman, arranged china cups and poured from a silver pot with a long, slender curved spout. She brought his first, bowing before him as his eye caught her dark impenetrable gaze.

When the sweet mint tea had been poured and the servants departed, Bacali said, "I have also been asked to extend to you the welcome of the British Consul-General. Mr. Phelps has asked the honour of your presence at dinner tonight, with the ladies, of course." He inclined his head toward each of the woman with a smile.

So they were to be accepted and welcomed quickly, Emilie thought, and she found comfort in the idea. Despite her assurances to Sara, she had worried secretly that they might sit about staring at one another until father got around to planning their social life. She let her thoughts wander from the conversation between her father and the assistant Minister of Finance. She had no interest in banking matters, and she was far too excited to concentrate on the mundane. She was anxious to see the rest of the house but knew she had to wait until their guest departed and father released them from their responsibility as hostesses. She sipped the mint tea, finding it surprisingly delightful and refreshing. Its delicate flavour and aroma were unlike any she'd ever tasted. She found herself wondering about food—would the dishes prepared by the native cook be as good or would father demand familiar fare? She longed for the gathering to end so that she might satisfy her curiosity about the house. Her growing impatience made it difficult to sit still, and she put aside her cup and studied the tapestries on the wall. She'd never seen finer, even in the museums of London. Costly . . .

Bacali was on his feet, bowing and taking his leave. The housekeeper materialized in a doorway without a whisper of sound to escort the family to their quarters.

The entire house was magnificent. Asheema led them from room to room, passing through a second sitting room only slightly smaller than the one where they'd had tea, then past a long, formal dining room, with mahogany table and Chippendale chairs with seats covered in petit-point of brilliant designs. All walls of the house were whitewashed, but color had been added with wall hangings to highlight the overall scheme of the room. And every floor, with tile polished to a gleaming luster, was partially covered by patterned carpet.

The hall widened to a large foyer, which was another entrance to the house. Wrought iron gates stood open to a tiny court, lush with potted greenery and a small wall fountain splashing softly. Through tall, narrow, arched windows, the garden beyond could be seen. The foyer was tiled in intricate patterns that formed sunbursts which seemed to shift and shimmer as Emilie stared at them. The stairway was white marble, with a curved and fluted balustrade supporting a marble railing, and wide enough for three persons to climb side by side.

Emilie clapped her hands in delight. "Oh, Father, it's beautiful!"

Her father's face relaxed to a smile. "I was forced to leave the arrangements in the hands of Ibn Toumart and his people. They have done quite well, I think." He nodded to Asheema, who moved soundlessly up the stairs.

"Isn't it grand?" Emilie said again.

Sara smiled agreement, and they went up after their parents. They were shown to bedrooms, the master suite nearest the stairs, occupying a front corner of the house shaded by tall eucalyptus outside the windows. Emilie and Sara each had a suite of her own, at corners so they commanded a view in two directions. Emilie chose the one farthest from her parents; it overlooked a high hedge at the rear of the house and a small garden of olive and citrus trees to the east. The walls were thick so that the windows were recessed deeply to screen the heat. There was a small balcony outside the bedroom, entered through an archway that had curtains drawn over it. The room was lofty, with a decorative tiled band below the curve of the ceiling. The bed was adorned by a rich, dark red quilt over which a coverlet of hand-crafted lace lay like a spiderweb. Underfoot, a thick carpet cushioned all sound; hangings of red and yellow concealed the walls. It was a strange mixture of Moorish and English decor but surprisingly effective.

Emilie saw that her portmanteau and trunks had been set in a large dressing room adjoining the bedchamber. Asheema spoke softly. "One of the slaves will unpack . . . unless the *señorita* prefers her own servant?"

Emilie had completely forgotten Jenny. "Send Jenny to Miss Sara. You may select a slave—" the word was strange on her tongue—"to attend to my things."

Asheema waited to see if one of the young mistresses of the house had further orders. When Emilie turned to inspect the rest of the apartment, the woman left, drawing the door to the corridor closed behind her.

The third room of the apartment was a private sitting room. It contained a chaise lounge, upholstered in smooth amber-coloured velvet, a small settee in the same colour and fabric and, to her delight, a low divan like the one Yusuf Bacali had sat on downstairs. She went to it and poked at the downy pillows, then pulled her skirts up so she could sit cross-legged as he had done. It was almost impossible in her dress, and she understood why the loose robe was a more suitable garb for people who squatted. Laughing, she unfastened the buttons of her shoes and kicked them off, wiggling her toes into the soft pillows, then flinging herself back to lie flat, arms spread. The ceiling above her was slightly domed, or at least gave that illusion because of the coping and tiles that seemed to converge at a central point. The entire apartment was done in amber, golds and touches of orange and yellow, and it was the most elegant thing she had ever seen!

She heard the door and scrambled up from her unlady-like position, then laughed aloud when she saw Sara.

"Isn't it marvelous!" she cried, struggling to her feet and almost tripping as her skirt dropped around her ankles once more. "I am going to have Asheema find a dressmaker who can make me robes like the Arabs wear! Their furniture is far more comfortable than ours!" she said, pointing at the cushions she had just vacated. "Does your apartment have such a magnificent room?" She whirled, arms outstretched as though to clasp the new pleasure to her forever.

"It's very nice . . ."

"Oh, Sara, you sound like mother! Admit it, the house is absolutely marvelous. We certainly shan't lack for anything. Comfort, servants, why it's even cool and pleasant, though I don't know how they manage with so many open arches." She ran to the doorway and thrust aside the am-

51

ber and yellow striped satin curtain and stepped out to the verandah. "Come and see!"

Sara joined her, and they looked down into the cool, pleasant courtyard through which they'd entered. "Now, can you ask for anything more delightful—or romantic?"

Sara had to smile. Emilie's exhuberance was contagious. "Yes, it really is. I expected something dreadful after that horrible mule ride. Poor mother, I thought she would faint."

"Mother is made of stronger fiber than you imagine, pet. It will be an adjustment but she'll manage, especially when she's had a chance to meet people and get into some social activity. She thrives on teas and afternoon calls, and there'll be parties, balls."

Sara scowled. "If she's forced to ride a mule everywhere she wants to go, she'll never set foot out of the house."

Laughing, Emilie agreed. "I know, and it's a pity. Perhaps we can convince her to take riding lessons—on a horse, I mean."

Sara looked dubious. "She'd be terrified."

"Then a sedan chair! There must be such things about. If not, father can have one made for her. I dare say he'd manage a carriage somehow if the streets were wide enough to accommodate it after he'd performed his miracle."

"It's hard to believe a city—country—can be so primitive as to not have coaches!"

Emilie nodded. Primitive, yes . . . but provocative and entrancing.

A Negress, ebony-skinned like the maid who had served the tea, saw to Emilie's unpacking, arranging garments in the long narrow dressing room and in the drawers of the chiffonier that occupied a corner. Emilie discovered an elegant bath, which had tiled floor, walls and ceiling. A large round sunken tub had, instead of faucets, a single spigot high on the wall that trickled water like the fountains in the courtyard. Several huge tall-necked pitchers, startling blue porcelain to match the tiles, stood about the edges of the tub. A wash stand, with basin and pitcher, was built into a shelf, and a tall, slatted screen could be pulled across to afford privacy. At a corner of the room, where a large window covered with carved lattice work looked out into the thick branches of a cluster of palms, a chamber pot had been fitted into a bench with a hole cut in the appropriate spot. Emilie giggled, thinking of the recently achieved luxury of the water closet in the civilized world.

The Negress was a silent girl, padding about on bare feet and staring curiously at Emilie whenever she spoke. She seemed to understand basic commands, but spoke not a word of English that Emilie could discern. Her voice was as soft as a breeze in rushes, and Emilie was at a loss to know what language it was. But the girl seemed to anticipate Emilie's needs and desires, and moved about quickly, filling the tub and scenting the water with oil poured from a white decanter. The room became a garden of jasmine. She unhooked Emilie's dress with nimble fingers, although Emilie was sure she had never seen or touched a fastener before. And when Emilie indicated a dressing gown of sheer pale yellow linen, the girl brought it and laid it upon a stool near the tub, then knelt and waited.

Slightly embarrassed, Emilie stepped from her chemise and removed her stockings. Her figure was slim and perfect so that she never endured tight corsets for style's sake and which would never do so in the warm climate of Tangier.

Silently, the girl readied a soft cloth with creamy soap poured from a small jar and would have undertaken the task of washing had not Emilie indicated she preferred to attend to it herself. Without a flicker of expression, the girl sat back on her haunches and waited. Even so, Emilie enjoyed a leisurely bath and soon grew accustomed to the girl's expressionless stare. She'd been trained to serve, and she probably did not have a thought in her head save to do her new mistress's bidding. Emilie would have to ask Asheema the girl's name.

When she emerged from the tub, she was surprised to find a tray on one of the low tables in the sitting room. Asheema appeared momentarily to explain that Mister Sloane had decided that the family would not gather for lunch, since they were tired and would wish to rest. Emilie noted the use of *Mister* in place of the earlier Spanish titles. Apparently father had set the matter straight.

Emilie chose the comfortable cushions she'd tested earlier and drew the tray to her. A spicy aroma met her nostrils; she realized all at once that she was famished, and she lifted the covers from the dishes. Lamb and fresh vegetables skewered on sticks, rice flavored with saffron that tinted it a delicate yellow, a flat, round bread, and a bowl of fresh grapes and small wedges of melon. And not a single piece of silverware! But there were two small towels wrapped tightly to hold their steamy heat. Father would have something to say about such table arrangements, she knew, but without second thought, she dipped her fingers into the rice and began to eat.

CHAPTER THREE

The house quieted after lunch; the slave girl removed Emilie's tray, drew the curtains at the windows, and laid back the covers on the bed, then retreated, drawing shut the door. Emilie realized this was the seclusion Yusuf Bacali had spoken of. She found it difficult to believe that grown persons required so much rest, and she knew most certainly that she could not force herself to lie still a moment. Her excitement was too much to contain. Besides, it was barely past noon and she'd been up less than half the day! She was not a child to be put to bed for a nap.

She searched through the gowns in the dressing room, deciding on one of pale yellow dimity sprigged with tiny violet flowers. It would be cool, with its full skirt, low bodice and sleeves that came only midway to her elbows. She threw aside the yellow robe and dressed quickly, then seated herself before the mirror in the bedroom to contemplate her hair. It was too much bother to redo the bouffant crown she usually wore. She brought the long tresses forward over her shoulder and divided them into three thick ropes, which she braided deftly, then wound the braid around her head and secured it with a dozen tortoise shell pins. From the shelf above her gowns, she took down a large round box which held several hats; she decided on a yellow straw with a row of silk daisies around the wide brim. It would be an effective screen from the harsh sun.

She slipped along the hall, pausing a moment at Sara's door to tap lightly. When there was no answer, she eased the door open and peered inside. Sara's figure was outlined on the bed, motionless. Emilie drew the door and made her way back to her room and to the gallery outside the sitting room. After making sure the drape was pulled, she tiptoed toward the steps leading down to the garden court. There was no sound from the house. Did the servants observe the long rest period too? She wished she had learned where the stables were. It would be exhilarating to ride and feel the wind on her cheeks, but to rouse servants and inquire now might defeat her purpose by wakening father. She made her way through the court to the outer garden, then stood a moment on the road along which they'd come earlier. She was tempted to descend into the native quarter, into the walled city of the casbah but she wondered if doing so might cause a stir. She had not seen Europeans except in the square. Perhaps sections of the city were forbidden to foreigners. It would be better to be a bit less daring on her first excursion. She turned in the opposite direction, where the road still climbed slightly though it leveled at places and other roads intersected it randomly.

It was strangely quiet after the raucous noise of the lower city. She was alone on the streets; it seemed most of the populace adhered to the custom of wasting the afternoon abed. There were long stretches of trees and bushes between houses that declared themselves by gardens and at least one tall palm or evergreen. Red and pink oleanders and yellow flowering gentia gave a delicate fragrance. Some houses were behind walls and she could only glimpse bits here and there; occasionally a narrow lane twisted among thick shrubs to cottages hidden behind green hedges. Several times, robed native servants, shaking out cloths or emptying dustbins stared at her curiously as she passed, but she ignored them.

The sun glared and made shimmering patterns of heat in the distance. The sky was as clear and blue as the background of a Monet landscape. The odours that had assailed her nostrils in the narrow streets of the lower city were gone. It was another world.

She paused near a patch of green, looking about to decide which direction to take. She seemed to be at the edge of the residential sector, with the houses farther apart now and more barren ground and scrub instead of tended plants. Yet it was pleasant, and the path curved along the top of a ridge so that she had a magnificent view of the city and harbor below and of the old city. She was looking over the walls that they had ridden past earlier, seeing for the first time the narrow, twisting streets that seemed barely wide enough to walk. Many were covered with lattices of rough branches and sticks; in one place, the sticks were hung with something resembling moss, but of brilliant blues, reds and oranges. No plant grew to those proportions, she was certain, and she shook her head in perplexity. She longed to find a way to enter the walled ancient city and see the sights it had to offer.

She thought of Henri, who had offered to escort her on just such a jaunt. The sun felt suddenly warmer and she chewed at her lip. She had no interest in Henri or his proposals. She would not allow him to show her the city or anything else!

When she turned, the sun had moved toward the sea, and she knew she must make her way back if she wanted to slip into the house before father noted her absence. She quickened her steps, only to slow them again when she noticed a pleasant park a short distance down a side street. It was unfenced, its green grass clipped and bordered with flowers. It reminded her so of the square on which the Sloane house in London faced, she felt irresistibly drawn to it. How delightful if there was a park for riding or sitting about—once she and Sara met people, of course.

The park was too small for riding but there were several benches and crisscrossing paths. Across it was a large building of grey stone freshly whitewashed over and with tall windows of European design. The front entrance was flanked by tall columns supporting a portico, and the stone steps were scrubbed almost as clean as the whitewashed walls. She considered crossing to investigate but thought of the time again.

She turned from the peaceful square to retrace her steps to the roadway. All at once there was a burst of noise that shattered the quite afternoon. Several horsemen were thundering toward her, the animals' hooves beating against the hardpacked dirt and stones like a drum. Six riders in flowing robes, their turbaned heads gleaming white in the sunlight, plummeted toward her. She scrambled from the roadway in fear of being trampled and ran back toward the park.

A magnificent stallion snorted and tossed its mane as the first rider drew in at the sight of her. The dark Arab face was hidden behind a coarse beard and the fluttering white veil of a turban. His lips curled in evil smile, and his eyes were fiery coals as he stared at her. Her palms went damp, and she backed away from him only to find herself ensnared in a thicket of shrubs. The man laughed and called out to his companions as Emilie tried to free herself of the branches. The horsemen were in motion again, swooping at her and screeching like tortured animals bent on savagery. Her heart raced in terror and she ran again as she heard her own screams mingle with the deafening noise. Then the horsemen were upon her, and one of them leaned from the saddle to swoop her up with an iron arm.

She was so filled with terror that she scarcely knew what she was doing. She screamed and struggled, beating

58

at the rider and kicking wildly against the horse. Her head struck the tight muscles of the animal's pounding foreleg, and her hat was knocked off to fly in the wind. She choked as dust rose beneath the animal's hooves, and her screams were muffled. Quite abruptly, they were off the road and on the soft grass of the park. Emilie gasped and sucked air into her lungs, then shrieked again. The man holding her clouted her on one side of the head, and she was knocked almost senseless. Sights and sounds were a dizzy kaleidoscope, reeling and swirling as nausea engulfed her. Pain pulsed wickedly inside her skull, and she longed for oblivion to remove her from the horror of reality.

The horse slowed . . . changed direction . . . once again, pain and sickness overwhelmed her. The Arab's arm about her waist was a band of steel threatening to sever her in two, and the horse's mane whipped at her face like nettles. The noise had become part of her; she had fallen into a pit of hell and demons were bargaining for her immortal soul. She tried to pray but no words would form in her thoughts. There was only pain and the towering fear.

A sound exploded so close that it seemed inside her head. It came again and again—a volley of gunshots. All at once the arm released her and she felt herself fall, rolling and pitching as she bumped against the horse and crashed to the ground. The hoofbeats were so loud she shuddered as she waited for death to bear down upon her. Inhuman screams erupted on all sides, more gunshots and a hoarse cry. Miraculously, the hoofbeats moved past and away, grew dimmer and at last faded.

Dazed, she smelled the warm grass under her face. Her body ached, and when she tried to sit up, she fell back in a spasm of weakness and tears. A hand touched her and she cried out and pulled away, finding new energy as her fear was born again.

"It is all right, mademoiselle . . ."

Not a guttural, harsh Arabic voice but gentle, English words with a hint of accent. In spite of her panic, she did not struggle as strong arms lifted her. She opened her eyes but saw only the pale linen of a man's coat. Her face was pressed against it as he carried her, cradled in his arms like a child, across the park. The relief was so great, her mind gave way to the oblivion she'd sought earlier.

She was only dimly aware of her surroundings. She was no longer under the merciless sun but in some cool place with a gentle current of air moving over her. A whisper of sound that she could not identify . . . soft voices . . . unintelligible words.

She opened her eyes and tried to sit up. Gentle hands restrained her.

"You are not quite ready to be up and about."

The man seated beside the sofa smiled, but his hand did not move from her shoulder. She lay back and stared, first at him, then about the room. In addition to the sofa, there were two dark leather chairs, one with an ottoman that held a deep impression of feet that had rested on it; there was also a large desk at one side, its top untidy with papers, inkwell, pens and more than a dozen books in precarious piles. The man was young, about thirty, she judged, and quite good looking, though his sandy hair fell across his eyes carelessly and his white coat was rumpled and stained. She realized with a start that the stains were blood—and she remembered being carried against the linen jacket.

She raised a hand to her head where a dull throb surfaced through the haze. He reached to draw her hand away as her fingers brushed a very tender spot and she winced.

"You've had a shock and a fall. I don't think there are any internal injuries, but I would like you to lie still awhile longer so I can be sure there's no concussion." His voice was firm but gentle, and she recognized the accent as French.

"You're a doctor?"

"Yes. I was fortunate to be crossing the square when the raiders—" At the quick terror in her eyes, he broke off. "But it is over, and you are safe. Please, do not upset yourself."

For a moment, the horrible memory made her shiver; the man reached to draw a light afghan over her. She closed her eyes to blot out the thought of the savage cries, the thundering horses and the man who had swooped her up. Tears scalded her eyelids, and she shivered again. The man moved about, touched her arm.

"Take this—" He was lifting her head, holding a glass to her lips. "A mild sedative." She swallowed.

"Thank you." It sounded inadequate after he had saved her life. Her lips trembled as she smiled. "Thank you. I don't know what would have happened if you had not come along when you did."

His eyes clouded. "But I did, so we won't think about that. Now, if you will tell me your name and where you are staying, I will send someone to notify your family."

She sat up abruptly. "No—" An image of her father's face swam before her.

The doctor looked surprised. "You must realize you have had a bad fright, *mademoiselle*. I cannot accept the responsibility as physician or gentleman of allowing you to leave unattended." He peered at her with a frown. "I know that you have a family, since I saw you at the customs shed only this morning as you disembarked from the *Ophir*."

Another memory came then. This was the man who had been talking with Henri! "You are Henri Cartier's friend."

"Yes." He looked surprised.

"He spoke of you, but did not mention that you were a

61

physician. I'm sorry, I did not mean to be rude. I am Emilie Sloane. I met Henri aboard ship."

"Ah . . ." The expression in his eyes was unreadable. "I am Pierre Louvel. As you say, Henri's friend." He pushed back the chair and got to his feet. He seemed to tower above her as he stared down. "All the more reason I cannot permit you leave when you are in no condition to travel under your own power. Excuse me, *mademoiselle,* I shall return in a moment. Take advantage of the sedative and rest."

He vanished through a doorway and his footsteps faded. Emilie relaxed against the cushion. The blinds at the windows had been drawn so the room was shadowed and cool. Overhead, a large fan moved lazily, stirring the air. Glancing again at the desk, she wondered if this was his office. Certainly it was a man's room. Little effort had been made to brighten the stark walls, and the furniture was more serviceable than fashionable. Was the house near the square?

His thoughts drifted lazily like a fan. The terror of the incident with the Arab horsemen seemed to fade. The sedative . . .

When Pierre Louvel returned, he saw that the medication had taken hold; the girl lay with eyes closed, her breathing regular and relaxed. She was beautiful, and she was obviously headstrong. She was a fool to be walking about alone, and damned unlucky that several renegade tribesmen chose that moment to pull their daring raid. No doubt they'd been hoping for a chance to kidnap some of the young women who worked at the hospital nearby, else why would they venture into the European sector in midday? It was not uncommon for the nurses to cross the park to the residence at the other side of the square; to capture four, maybe even five, at one swoop would be a prize worth risking the possibility of retaliation by the Army. And Emilie Sloane had the misfortune to be available when the nurses were not.

He shuddered inwardly at the thought of her fate had he not happened along when he did. She'd be hidden in a tent somewhere on the other side of the mountain, or trussed and tossed over the back of a camel crossing the dessert, on her way to be sold to the highest bidder at a slave auction in the dingy native quarter of Casablanca or Fez. One as beautiful and fair-haired as she would command a high price.

He wondered about her family and surmised that they did not know she'd slipped away. From the brief remarks Henri had made about the girl he'd met on the *Ophir*, Emilie was undoubtedly too daring for her own good, though all women found Henri charming. Pierre settled at his desk, looking across at her. Was it possible that she had been on her way to see Henri?

He looked about as soft slippers clacked along the hall and the curtains parted. Ali Rabun's solemn face peered at him, and the servant's glance flicked toward the girl. Pierre rose at once and stepped through the doorway.

"What did you learn?"

Ali's head bobbed. "The arrangements for housing the Sloane family were made by the Minister of Finance through Yusuf Bacali. The villa at the crossroads of *el Kebir* and *Rue de Fes*."

Pierre nodded; he knew the house. It had formerly been let by an English merchant who transferred his business to Rabat to take advantage of the growing shipping trade there. The Sloanes were wealthy then, and important. The Minister of Finance did not generally bother with the comfort of foreigners. Pierre once had been at the house and knew it was one of the most richly appointed outside the wealthy Moorish community. He thanked Ali and returned to the sitting room that also served as his study. Perhaps he should have taken the girl to the hospital, but his quarters were closer at hand. Once he had determined that Emilie was not seriously injured, he realized it would be better to spare her the questions

63

that were bound to be asked. If he took her home, the incident would be over.

She began to stir, lifting a hand to her brow and wincing as her fingers touched the bruise. Her eyes opened and blinked and she lifted her head.

"Best you move slowly at first. You may still be a bit fuzzy."

Her gaze found him and she frowned, then swung her feet to the floor and sat up determinedly. She clutched the edge of the cushions to steady herself as her head reeled. She breathed deeply. It unsettled her to have him watch her so clinically, and she tried to rise but the dizziness overcame her. She sank against the cushions.

"You shouldn't be up," he said curtly.

She felt a growing annoyance at his manner. She might be some organism under his microscope.

"I'm quite all right, thank you," she said unsteadily. She would not have him laughing at her. She'd seen the quick look of surprise and rebuke in his eyes when she mentioned having met Henri aboard the *Ophir*. The young doctor knew his friend's reputation then, and jumped to the conclusion that she had fallen under Henri's charms! "I must return before—" She would not speak to him of her father. "It's time for me to be getting back. I thank you again, Dr. Louvel, for the gallant rescue and for your medical attention. I would appreciate the bill for your services. I will pay it directly, there is no need to forward it to my father's attention."

"There are no charges . . ." Pierre scowled and pulled off the blood stained jacket he still wore. He tossed it to a chair and went behind a silk painted screen to emerge with another jacket into which he thrust his arms. It was beige in colour and did not match the white linen trousers, but he seemed not to notice. "Come along then, if you're determined. I'll see you home."

"That isn't necessary—"

"You were fool enough to venture out alone and nar-

64

wly missed becoming the concubine of some rich emir.
you hope to survive in Tangier, it's best you learn a bit
out the ways of the people here. This is not Mayfair or
yde Park where you can stroll about at will, tempting
ery man with your pretty and independent air,
a'm'selle. Now, I shall escort you home, if for no other
ason than to be sure the sedan chair I have borrowed
ts back to its owner in one piece."

Furious, Emilie let him help her to her feet and lead
r outside. She was quite unsteady and glad of his arm,
it she did her best to hide the fact. As they emerged
om the house, she saw they were across the park from
e large building she'd seen earlier. At her glance, he
lunteered the information that it was the *L'Hôpital*
ançais where he worked. His house was close by for
nvenience, though he frequently was called to all parts
the city to tend the sick. There were many Europeans
attered in various sectors, even a few in the casbah it-
lf, he told her.

The sedan chair was black velvet, braided and tasseled
e a fine surrey. There were no windows, and the open-
g through which they entered was the only aperture,
ith a seat barely large enough for two set deep into the
cess of the coffin-like box. She sat stiffly, avoiding the
ew of the park where she'd had such a narrow escape.
he sedative Louvel had given her was still in effect, and
e felt little aftershock of the incident.

Four burly Negroes lifted the poles of the chair and set
f at a trot, past the park and along the narrow street
at led to the crest of the hill. She had not told the doc-
r where she lived, yet the servants seemed to require no
rections. Already, Emilie's thoughts were racing ahead
what she would tell her father. There was little chance
at her disappearance had not been noted by now and a
arch underway for her.

They were at the house in remarkably short time, and
milie realized her own route earlier afoot had been cir-

cuitous. The house was actually only several blocks fr[om]
the park and hospital. Pierre Louvel would not listen
her protest that he did not have to escort her inside, [he]
gripped her arm firmly and walked through the gard[en]
and archway to the inner court. The doors to the vari[ous]
rooms on the lower level had been thrown open to w[el-]
come the cooling evening air, and Sara rushed out, [her]
eyes wide and her face pale. Behind her, her mother sto[od]
in the archway, hand to breast, eyes fluttering.

"Emilie! What happened?" Sara hugged her sist[er,]
looking from her to the stranger who'd brought her hom[e.]
"You're hurt!" Her glance went to the ugly bruise [on]
Emilie's head and the bedraggled appearance of the y[el-]
low gown.

"She is all right," Pierre said, smiling to reassure t[he]
two frightened women. Charlotte had emerged from t[he]
doorway clinging to the arm of an English servant dress[ed]
in grey merino and white apron.

"Yes, of course I am," Emilie said, annoyed that t[he]
doctor had taken it upon himself to answer for her. [I]
had a bit of a spill and was fortunate to meet Dr. Louv[el]
who saw to my injury and kindly escorted me home."

"Oh . . ." Sara sighed with relief and curtailed t[he]
dozens of questions that filled her mind. Belatedly, she [re-]
called her manners. "Please, come in," she said to Louv[el.]

"I must be on my way."

"Do have a cup of tea and let me thank you prope[rly]
for coming to my daughter's assistance," Charlotte sai[d.]
She extracted her arm from Colleen's and told the wom[an]
to fetch the tea tray.

"Father. . . ?" Emilie asked.

"He'd already left for his appointment with the Mini[s-]
ter before we discovered you were gone. Oh, Em, wh[at-]
ever possessed you to go off alone like that!?"

Emilie caught the amused expression that fluttered [in]
Pierre Louvel's eyes and tossed her head. "I simply we[nt]
for a walk. I expected to be back before I was missed a[nd]

…no point in making an issue of it. Now let's drop the …tter, shall we?" She took Sara's hand and smiled dis-…ningly at her mother.

For a moment, Charlotte was flustered, not knowing if … should demand an accounting of Emilie's highly im-…oper behaviour or let the matter pass. Courtesy won out …er discipline, and she ushered the handsome young doc-… into the sitting room. Colleen was already filling the …ps on the tray Asheema had brought. Charlotte handed …e to the doctor as he seated himself beside her on the …een Anne sofa. Emilie took the farthest chair and did … look at him.

"Louvel . . . that's French, is it not?" Charlotte said.

"Yes, *Madame* Sloane."

"There was a young French count traveling with us—"

"Henri Cartier, an old friend who has come out to visit …th me for his holidays."

"How pleasant. Have you known him long?"

"We were at school together in Paris as youngsters."

Not a penniless young physician then. Charlotte smiled … her gaze went to Emilie. "My daughter's injury. . . ?"

"It is not serious, lay your fears to rest, madame. She …ll be as right as new in a day or two, I assure you."

"How in the world did it happen? Where—?"

Before Emilie could speak, Louvel said, "A careless …ler did not have the good sense to slow his animal as he …proached an intersection, and your daughter was …ocked to the ground. I was nearby, and took her to my …rgery a few doors away. I live not far from *L'Hôpital* …ançais. Are you familiar with it? No, of course you …uld not be. Your daughter tells me you have just ar-…ed."

Amazed at his gallant lie, Emilie relaxed and smiled …preciatively at Louvel. She had expected him to blurt …t the truth and bring stern warnings upon her from …ther and Sara.

67

"Have you been in Tangier long, Dr. Louvel?" S
asked.

"A year last January."

"Why ever would you leave Paris to practice in s
a—here?" Charlotte asked.

Louvel shrugged. "One enjoys the adventure of n
places, and it gives me the opportunity to pursue my
terest in diseases that abound in hot climates. I stud
under Dr. Goulven in Vienna—" He broke off. "I apo
gize. I do not mean to bore you—"

"Not at all," Charlotte said. "I find it fascinating.
you minister to the natives as well as the French and I
glish?"

"I am afraid that the science of medicine is quite prir
tive here, with a few so-called holy men dispensing he
or sarsaparilla for all complaints. The poor are too ig
rant and superstitious to seek medical help even if it is
fered without cost, and their religion forbids the study
anatomy, so they prefer death to submitting to the s
geon's knife. A few wealthy Moors regard their li
above superstition and send for European physicians, b
we are not widely accepted." He smiled, realizing that
was explaining far more than any of the women desired
hear. *Madame* Sloane smiled politely but was a bit p
around the mouth. Emilie was watching him curious
with an interest he suspected had nothing to do with
subject. He sipped the tea and refused one of the sm
cakes the maid offered. There was no way to explain
feelings. He sometimes wondered if he understood the
himself. He'd left a lucrative practice in Paris, the chan
to work with Doctor Goulven, and eventually a chair
the Sorbonne. Still, he found satisfaction in the challen
and the hope that someday his work might help enlight
an ignorant people.

He finished the tea and set aside the cup. "Thank y
for your hospitality," he said, rising. "I am expected
the hospital and must be on my way."

68

"You must come again," Charlotte declared. "Roder—Mr. Sloane will want to thank you—and of course y you for your medical services."

"No charge. It was my pleasure, madame . . . made-oiselles . . ." He bowed, then took his leave without aiting for a servant to show him out.

"Such a nice young man," Charlotte mused. Turning to milie, she frowned. "How foolish of you to go off by urself! Really, Emilie, at times you are the most vexing ild! Whatever possessed you?"

Emilie said, "I'm sorry mother, I meant only to go for stroll. I'm not accustomed to being put to bed like a ild for a nap, and I was restless."

"Your father will be angry—" Charlotte's face clouded.

"Then don't tell him," Emilie said calmly.

Her mother looked scandalized.

"Besides," Emilie said as she got to her feet, "it was ite a minor incident and my injury is negligible. A uch of powder will cover the bruise." She smiled win-ngly and bent to kiss her mother's cheek. "Poor mama, have always been a trial to your serene nature, haven't " She touched fingers to the older woman's cheek, then n from the room and upstairs.

When she glimpsed herself in the glass, she gasped. nall wonder that mother and Sara had been shocked. er dress was filthy and torn at one shoulder, and there as a smudge of dirt at her chin, though her face had en carefully washed to remove all traces of the blood om the cut on her forehead. She leaned close to the ass to examine the purple swelling and touch it gingerly. he realized she had lost her hat and wondered what had come of it. A soft tap sounded and Sara entered.

"Oh, Emilie! I was frightened when I found you gone. rushed about looking for you—then mother became armed—I'm sorry I—"

Emilie took her sister in her arms. "No harm done, pet. think mother will let the matter slide. She has no desire

69

to upset father any more than you or I. I only pray th
he doesn't hear of the matter elsewhere."

"Why would he? A chance misstep?" Sara studied h
sister's flushed face. "No, it was something more. I c
tell by the look in your eyes."

Unable to contain herself, Emilie nodded and flung he
self about the room, pirouetting until her head rang a
she collapsed onto the low divan. Sara came to kneel b
fore her, a worried look on her face. She said nothing.

Emilie looked up at last. "It was the most exciting a
frightening adventure of my life and now that it's over
wouldn't have missed it for the world! You can be su
I'll be more careful in the future, but I consider it
omen that our life here will be quite extraordinary!"

"What are you talking about? What adventure?" Sa
thought of the young doctor who had brought Emil
home. Had she become involved—no, that was impo
sible!

Emilie grasped her sister's hands and leaned clos
Struggling to control her excitement, she related t
events that had occurred in the park. Sara listened in a
tonishment, her own heart racing as Emilie told of bein
swept up by the galloping horseman. She was weak at t
thought of what might have happened had not th
Frenchman intervened.

She was almost afraid to ask, and the words came o
a whisper. "Where would they have taken you?"

Emilie pretended nonchalance. "According to Dr. Lo
vel, to be one of the women in a sultan's harem!"

Sara paled, and Emilie caught her hand. "Not
frightening as the thought of being killed. You can l
sure that's what I believed was going to happen when
was being held against that racing horse! I thought I w
as good as dead." She pulled Sara close and put an ar
about her shoulders. "But it is finished, and I am ali
and home."

"You might have been killed none-the-less," Sara sa

70

ftly. "Promise not to do anything so foolish again. ease, Em?"

"I only went for a walk. I couldn't help what happened." Emilie began to unbutton her dusty shoes. "I'm rtainly not going to promise never to go walking again."

"You know what I mean," Sara chided gently. "Alone, strange places . . ."

"Let me be! You're beginning to sound like mother." mpatiently, Emilie pulled off a shoe and tossed it aside. t Sara's hurt look, she relented. "I'm sorry, I didn't ean to be cruel. Forgive me?"

Sara nodded, accustomed to her sister's quick flares of mper and equally quick restoration of good humour.

"And I shall promise to be more careful, all right?"

Sara smiled and Emilie hugged her briefly. "Now," she id, "I'd best freshen up before father returns or he'll ave a hundred questions. Do you think if I do my hair ith a wave across here it will hide the bump?" She be- an to undo the braid and fluff her hair about her face.

CHAPTER FOUR

Roderick Sloane was too preoccupied with his business a
fairs to notice anything out of the ordinary on his retur
His meeting with the Moroccan Minister of Finance ha
gone well, and there would be no delay in the opening
the Anglo-French Bank of Lyon. A building had been s
cured, subject to Sloane's approval, the former residen
of a Portugese minister who had been transferred to R
bat. Operations could being immediately, though some r
modeling would be necessary on the interior of tl
structure to accommodate the banking enterprises mo
adequately.

Sloane also returned with the news that George Phelp
the British Consul-General was sending sedan chairs f
their transportation to the dinner party, news that Cha
lotte greeted with relief. Her husband also informed he
that he'd placed an order for chairs for the family's pe
sonal use; they had to be made to order, but he had bee
assured delivery in less than a week's time.

The dinner party at the Consul-General's house wa
dull and lengthy. Emilie found herself bored with the co
versation and scarcely listened. George Phelps was
sparse man with a shock of white hair and a large flowin

mustache which gave him an intensity of appearance and manner. Mrs. Phelps was plump and matronly but sat ramrod straight at all times. She had a hawk-like nose which was emphasized by the severely drawn-back greying hair. They had been in Tangier four years, but neither had made any concession to the exotic locale. The house might have been plucked directly from Essex or Surrey and transported intact to its present location. It stood at the end of a sandy, semi-cobbled country lane, bordered with oak trees and hedges; it was built to English specifications, with no Moorish influence except for the walled garden that surrounded it, and was staffed by English servants. The lace curtains, heavy, plum-coloured velour drapes, Queen Anne and Chippendale furniture, and a tasteless abundance of bric-a-brac and framed portraits on the piano and mantle almost made Emilie giggle, and it renewed her belief in the charm of their own house.

There were no other guests. Mrs. Phelps half-apologized but said she was sure the Sloanes were too exhausted from their journey to be up to full entertaining. In a week's time, there would be a formal welcoming party at the Consulate, at which they would have the opportunity to meet fellow European residents of the city.

Selina Phelps was the dull, proper type Charlotte found comfortable to be with, and the two got on famously. The Consul-General and Roderick talked economic affairs, centering mostly on the new bank and the influence English money would have on the expanding economy of Morocco. The Sultan was said to have obtained loans in amounts of several million pounds, mostly from French sources. The new Anglo-French Bank of Lyon would soon become an important link in English-Moroccan affairs. Emilie was surprised to hear her father mention Henri Cartier as one of the people he would deal with in financial matters. Apparently, father's newly made business connections were acquainted with the Count and looking forward to his backing and cooperation. These

73

facts were mentioned in passing, and Emilie did not pursue them.

Emilie could not hide her boredom after dinner when the group reassembled in the sitting room, and she was vastly relieved when her father announced that they must be getting on since he was due at the bank early to meet again with Ibn Toumart. Mrs. Phelps insisted Charlotte keep one of the sedan chairs so that she could get about insisting too that she come for tea the following day when Selina would have several other women in to meet her.

When Charlotte left for tea with Selena Phelps the following day, Sara refused the offer to accompany her mother. Ever since their arrival in Tangier, she had been anxious to try to capture some of its magnificence on paper. She put on a wide-brimmed hat that would shield her from the sun, gathered her sketch book and pastels, and went downstairs. Earlier, Emilie had declared her intention to pass the afternoon with a dressmaker Asheema had found to make her some loose, Moorish-style caftans that would be comfortable in the unusual heat. Father would insist, of course, that they could not be worn outside the privacy of her own home, but Emilie was determined. Sara considered the idea but was in no mood to choose fabrics and colours; she preferred to spend the afternoon alone. Not alone—for she was not as foolish as Emilie to wander about and risk incident. She conferred with Asheema about the best place for her drawing, and then accepted the company of one of the household guards to escort her to a place near the end of the road where the view was unimpeded.

Following the swarthy servant who wore a white robe tied at his waist and had a rifle slung over one shoulder, Sara felt quite safe. Despite Emilie's casual dismissal of the incident of the near-kidnapping, Sara recognized the danger that was ever-present in this extraordinary place. She was aware of the guards father had employed to

74

watch the house by day and to sleep indoors at night so that the household could not be taken unaware. How different from the life they'd known in London. She was not sure yet how she felt about it. They would meet people soon, and the European sector seemed largely independent of most of the Arab city and customs. Settling in would be no more difficult than it had been going away to school, or moving from St. James to Belgravia when father was made manager of Cote's Bank. They would soon know their way about.

The hill was steep and the guide slowed his pace so she had no difficulty keeping up. They were beyond the last of the houses now, on a path that crowned the hill and was covered with thick wild grass. Here and there, patches of daisies and asphodel bent under the warm wind, swaying in the sun like delicate ballet dancers.

The guide stopped at a knoll with a circular depression at one side that was almost a flat shelf. When Sara nodded and said it was perfect, the man spread a square of cloth for her to sit on, then settled himself several paces away, gun resting across his knees. Sara looked at the panorama below. The city crowded the foot of the hill, white geometric confusion set against the blue of the bay. The sky was crystal clear, the light magnificent. The horizon seemed an arm's reach away.

She opened her chalk box and set it down carefully as she turned back a blank page of the sketch book. She enjoyed drawing or painting and recognized her modest talent. To sit and sketch gave her an inner quiet that she found refreshing. She studied the scene leisurely and finally began to sketch.

She became totally absorbed in her work, seeing the city now with an artist's eye and putting aside any troublesome thoughts. The sound of the wind soughing in the grass and the distant melodious call of birds added to the peace that descended over her. She lost track of time, blending colours and defining lines on the sketch until the

75

picture began to take shape to her satisfaction. From time to time, she heard the guard shift but he did not disturb her. She barely heard the intruding sound until the guard got to his feet and his shadow fell across her paper.

Squinting, she turned to see a man on horseback halted on the path. The Rif guard had the rifle at ready but on seeing the foreigner, lowered it slightly as he looked to Sara.

"Why Dr. Louvel!" She set aside her sketch book and got up.

"Do not let me disturb you," he said, swinging from the saddle and coming toward her. Sara sat again as Dr. Louvel seated himself on the grass beside her.

He glanced at the sketch pad. "That's very good," he said, picking up the pad and studying the picture. "You are a skilled artist."

"Not really, but I do enjoy it. I've had very little training."

"There are several artists in Tangier. Perhaps you can find one worthy of continuing your studies under. If you like, I can secure their names for you."

She smiled. "You're very kind. I would like to know more, but I'm not sure about a class—"

"If not a class, perhaps private tutoring can be arranged," he said, laying down the sketch pad.

"It is my father's permission that I am uncertain of," she said. "I know I could learn a great deal from any accomplished instructor." Strangely, she felt no embarrassment in admitting this truth to him.

"Is your father such an ogre?" Emilie had seemed frightened of him too, he recalled.

"Not at all, though he is strict. He does what he believes best."

He was looking at her strangely, and she wondered what he was thinking. She gazed out over the scene she had been drawing. "It is quite lovely from here, isn't it?

Distance hides the dirt and squalor, the smells and noises."

"Do you find Tangier unpleasant?"

"No . . . I really have not seen enough of it to make a decision, I suppose. We travelled through some unfashionable streets as we came from the ship. I imagine that colours my opinion."

"It's quite charming in many ways. I think you will like it when you come to know it better." He indicated the sketch pad. "Your artistic eye has already captured beauty. You will find it in many other places."

"I dare say you're right," she said, smiling. His serious expression gave way to an answering smile. He was good-looking, yet Sara felt none of the tongue-tied discomfort that usually beset her in conversations with young gentlemen.

He was quiet a moment, then sighed. "It would be pleasant to sit awhile and clear one's mind of all thoughts, but conscience will not permit me. I am on my way to see an injured man at a travelling camp a few miles beyond the city. I'm afraid I must go."

"Of course." She got to her feet as he did, and walked with him to his horse. "What is a travelling camp? I have never heard the expression before."

"When caravans are readied to go to any distance, the bearers set up a camp to insure that they have everything necessary. To get a day's journey into the desert and discover insufficient tent poles or utensils for preparing meals can mean a serious hardship or considerably delay if they must be sent back for. The experimental camp assures this will not happen." He took the reins of his horse from the Rif. "Thank you for a pleasant pause in my day, Miss Sloane."

"Please, call me Sara."

"Sara . . . thank you again. Please remember me to your mother. I trust your sister is recovered from her accident?"

"Yes, fully, and she has confided the truth of the matter to me. You must know how grateful we all are to you Dr. Louvel."

"If I am to call you Sara, you must call me Pierre. And now I have to be on my way. Until we meet again . . ." He took her hand and kissed it, then quickly swung himself up into the saddle and with a wave, rode off down the path.

She watched until he was out of sight, then gathered her supplies and started for home. The light was fading and her mood for sketching had passed. Her thoughts were completely occupied with Pierre Louvel. She blushed at the realization that she found him quite charming and she hoped they would meet again.

True to his word, the Minister secured several excellent riding horses, and Roderick selected a magnificent Arabian stallion for his own. Emilie chose a black mare with a flowing, glossy mane and a spirited nature. Sara preferred a more docile creature the color of a young fawn, with creamy mane and tail. There were two others, both gentle, and a young Rif lad to serve as stableboy and riding instructor to Charlotte when she resigned herself to learning the new skill. She protested that with a sedan chair, she would have no need of a horse, but Roderick was adamant. She would learn to ride; his only concession was to allow her several weeks to adjust to the idea before the lessons began. The matter was closed.

The stableboy was a dark, solemn youth with melancholy eyes and a dazzling white smile. He wore a white jellaba that was caught about his waist with a length of rope, and over one shoulder was slung a gun which he carried at all times. Roderick Sloane had been advised that the Rifs were the most loyal and faithful servants, and most Europeans had several on the household staff. Without alarming the women, Roderick saw to it that six Rifs were added to the staff; Mohamet had instructions

78

that he accompany the women whenever they rode away from the house. Mohamet had been employed in several European households and spoke a smattering of French, English and Spanish so that he could obey instructions and managed to make himself understood.

Excited about the prospect of seeing something of the city and surrounding countryside, Emilie convinced Sara to ride with her. Emilie dressed in a forest green linen riding habit, the skirt loose about her ankles so her movements would not be hampered, the snug vest fastened with mother-of-pearl buttons at front and cuffs. She wore a white silk shirt beneath and tied a flaming orange scarf at her throat for an added tough of color. Grey kid riding boots and gloves, and a perky black velveteen hat with an orange band that trailed filmy streamers down her back completed the outfit, and she surveyed herself in the glass with approval. Hurrying along the upper hall, she tapped at Sara's door; Jenny opened it, smiling at the mistress who never called on her services these past days so that her work was light indeed.

Sara had chosen a habit of dovegrey poplin, accented at the collar by black velvet, and she was pinning a high-crowned black silk hat with white band atop her upswept hair.

"Do hurry," Emilie said, tapping her skirt with the short riding crop she had providently packed before leaving London.

Sara laughed. "This country has not changed in a thousand years. A few minutes more won't make any difference." She was beginning to catch some of her sister's excitement though, and she was looking forward to her first real glimpse of the city.

At the stables, Mohamet had the horses saddled. His own white stallion had an Arabian saddle with rounded pommel and a high, square cantle. The single cinch strap was of beautifully tooled leather, with shining brass fastenings that winked in the sunlight, but the blanket under the saddle was so tattered it hung in shreds along the animal's belly. Mohamet grinned toothily, as he brought the other horses to the block so the girls could mount. As soon as they were seated, he leaped nimbly to his own steed and pulled at the bit as the horse pawed and reared, restless to be off.

"*Señoritas* wish to see Mountain first, *merci?*" he asked, settling the strap of his rifle so the gun hung at his back.

Emilie would have preferred the casbah but did not argue when Sara said the Mountain would be fine. They rode out of the rear courtyard, tiny puffs of dust clouding under each hoofbeat. Mohamet led them up a road which seemed to go directly to the crest. Glancing back, Emilie occasionally saw the road she'd followed on her earlier journey, and as then, the view was breathtaking. The day was brilliantly clear, with the sun already bleaching the sky like bones cast on the desert. Ships at anchor and the jutting quay were etched against the blue bay, and tiny figures scurried about like insects. They passed several houses hidden behind high walls and once or twice, figures appeared in arched gateways to stare and wave after recognizing the two young women who could only be the daughters of the English banker.

When they reached the summit, Emilie recognized the street along which she'd walked, saw the green patch of park between white buildings, and the imposing solidness of the hospital. Sara sat tall in the saddle and exclaimed over the panorama spread below them.

"Look, we can see over the walls of the casbah!"

"Casbah very nice. Mohamet show *señoritas*." Mohamet displayed gleaming white teeth. But when he set out once more, it was along the avenue that passed the hospital and park.

There were numerous riders about, men on business and women out for pleasure; Arabs in flowing robes moved about on foot, slipping into niches of doorways to let the riders pass. In spite of herself, Emilie felt a tremor dance along her spine as they neared the spot where she'd been yanked from her feet by the horseman. She thanked heaven that Mohamet did not identify the French hospital so that Sara would recognize the spot, but almost as the thought was completed in her mind, several nurses, long grey skirts swishing about their ankles, stiffly starched white aprons and cape glaring in the light, emerged from a courtyard at the side of the hospital and began to walk across the park.

Sara glanced at her sister. Was this where the attempt had been made to kidnap her? Emilie smiled quickly and tried to distract her.

"One almost expects to see nannies and prams."

Sara nodded. "I had no idea it would be anything like this. It's really quite—" She groped for a word.

"Civilized," Emilie said with a laugh. The tension was broken, and the smile returned to Sara's face.

They followed the avenue past the hospital and circled until they were once more descending the mountain. The view was cut off from the most part, and the wind seemed hotter and drier as they lost sight of the sea. But the streets grew more exciting as they became less European. Roads gave way to twisting paths that wound among Moorish buildings willy-nilly. There were many more pedestrians in a variety of native garb, from the white jellabas to colourful skirts and striped robes. The smell of the sea was dominated by more powerful odors of spices, fish and burning aloe.

They came out upon a square and Mohamet flashed his grin and waved a hand as though he had somehow produced the sight for them alone. A long street which began at the waterfront seemed to bisect the city, cutting through the rectangular area which, unlike the park on the Mountain, was cobblestoned and congested, surrounded by small, crowded stalls where natives sat crosslegged, baskets, pots, blankets or other wares hung and strewn at every available inch of space. Several

81

strings of camels and mules milled restlessly as peddlers unloaded baskets, calling out their wares all the while and adding to the din of babbling voices and clanking bells. At one side of the square, a tiled fountain, ornate under a high arch was surrounded by blacks and Arabs drawing water in gourds. Arab women, faces veiled, lifted heavy jars to their heads and glided away like wraiths.

Around the square, a number of modest houses rose like palaces from the confused multitude of Moorish huts. They were the Legations of the various nations, Mohamet informed them, pointing out several by name. It was the same square they'd crossed on their first day, but so different now! The life of the city seemed concentrated here; there were clusters of people everywhere, wealthy Moorish gentlemen surrounded by slaves, gaudily-robed Jews discussing business, attachés of the Legations idling in doorways as they awaited the post from London and Paris, which would be brought from the newly anchored steamer in the bay, and women—the first that Emilie had really seen in any number since their arrival. A dark-skinned beauty, garbed in a sheetlike haik, her veil revealing only huge dark eyes and a glittering ruby set in filigreed gold dangling at the center of her forehead. Two European women, their long skirts and tightly corseted figures a bold contrast to their native counterparts. From an open window of a consulate, the sound of a piano drifted a Brahms melody that was lost amid the raucous shouting and a lamenting chant from the doorway of a mosque off one corner of the square.

Emilie swung down from the saddle, urging Sara to do the same. Instantly, Mohamet was on his feet, grabbing the reins of the three horses in one hand, keeping the other on the strap of his rifle.

"*Señoritas* like visit English Legation?" he asked.

Emilie shook her head. This was the Tangier she wanted to see! Her senses reeled with the excitement of so much at once and the realization that this was a world far removed from the sedate London and English countryside she had known all her life. It was a delving into the past and a portent of the future.

Sara hooked her arm through Emilie's as they walked about the square looking at shops and people. There was a tobacconist, an apothecary, a miniscule café. A group of half-naked street boys swarmed around them, hands outstretched as they cried for coins, until Mohamet drove them off with lashes and screams. A bent figure, the pointed hood of his jellaba dipping like a divining rod, led a laden camel past and vanished into one of the narrow side streets.

"Emilie and Sara Sloane, what a pleasant surprise."

They turned to find Henri Cartier smiling at them. He had just emerged from the French legation, his white linen suit impeccable, his collar and tie fastened precisely as it had always been aboard the *Ophir*. Still he gave the impression of careless charm as he doffed his straw hat and bowed.

"I am pleasantly surprised to find you here in the square. Somehow I envisioned you both sitting quite properly at tea, entertaining and waiting to be entertained." His gaze lingered on Emilie and she saw his amusement.

She tapped her riding crop against her skirt. "I often find it prudent to entertain myself or I should die of boredom."

His brows raised. "You cannot mean that the young gentlemen of Tangier have not already discovered your beauty and charm? Two such lovely young ladies?"

Sara smiled, though she knew he was teasing. She knew too that his remarks were directed at Emilie, and she wondered again about her sister's flirtation with the Count during the voyage from Southampton.

"They have not," Emilie said boldly. "No one has come to call, and it seems we must wait to be introduced to so-

83

ciety properly before we are included in whatever social life the city has to offer."

He frowned and wagged his head. "A pity. Had I known, you can be sure I would have remedied the situation. But I cannot believe your few days here have been boring, from all accounts I hear of marauding tribesmen and gallant rescuers."

Emilie flushed and averted her gaze. She might have known that Dr. Louvel would speak of the incident to Henri! She ignored his remark.

"We've been enjoying the sights of Tangier. I had no idea such a busy square existed. It seems to be the hub of the city."

"I am only becoming acquainted myself," he said, "but it would give me pleasure to accompany you."

"Mohamet is an excellent guide, thank you." She saw Sara's quick sidelong glance at her abruptness but ignored it.

Henri did not acknowledge the dismissal with so much as a flicker of an eye. Instead, he smiled politely. "Then I shall be about my business. I pick up my mail at the French Legation each day, in the event you change your mind and seek company." He bowed. "I've had the pleasure of being invited to the party in your honor to be given two nights hence. I am looking forward to an enjoyable evening." Still smiling, he turned and cut across the square to enter one of the white buildings opposite.

Sara picked at her sleeve. "You needn't be so rude to him, Em. Has he done something?"

Surprised, Emilie felt her face go warm. "Of course not. I—find his company dull. We exhausted all topics of conversation during the three days aboard ship. Besides, Henri Cartier is too impressed with his own charm." She stared a moment at the doorway where the Frenchman had vanished, then signalled Mohamet. "Let's be on our way." The square seemed to have lost its appeal all at once.

The party at the Consulate was a lavish affair by all standards. Emilie and Sara spent the day preparing for it, resting at mother's insistence, then bathing leisurely and having their hair done before dressing. The black girl, whose name was Rachma, was very adept at serving her new mistress, and her nimble fingers twisted and curled the blond hair expertly. She was a silent one, never opening her mouth except to smile or murmur acknowledgement of Emilie's commands, yet Emilie had the feeling that nothing escaped her notice. No instruction ever had to be repeated, no action demonstrated twice. Often during that first week, Emilie counted herself fortunate at having relegated the efficient but dull Jenny to her sister and electing this prize for herself.

The sedan chairs had been delivered that morning, and Roderick Sloane examined them and nodded with satisfaction. He'd seen numerous chairs since his arrival, and these were the finest in workmanship and decoration. Not even the Sultan would have finer; the thought pleased him.

Emilie chose a gown of violet satin with a heart-shaped neckline that set off her flawless complexion. The dress was cut along deceptively simple lines to enhance her slim figure and full bosom, the full sleeves ending just past the elbow so that delicate white lace gloves disappeared under the cuffs. She'd tried several pieces of jewelry and settled finally on a single amethyst on a chain for her throat and an amethyst ring. As she surveyed herself in the long glass, she noted the touch of colour the sun had given her face, despite the frequent buttermilk and cucumber lotions she applied. Still, the glow was becoming against her blond hair and set off her dark eyes. She had grown weary of the bouffant hairstyle and allowed Rachma complete freedom in arranging the soft curls that now framed her face.

When she descended to the sitting room, she noted her mother's approving glance. Father nodded and returned to his glass of claret, glancing from time to time at the pocket watch from his black vest. It would not do to leave too soon and it would be unthinkable to be late.

Sara wore a cloud-light silk dress of moss green, a colour that brought out the depths of her eyes. She was flushed and excited, though she had dozed lightly for several hours during the afternoon and had a tea tray alone in her apartment before dressing. When she saw Emilie's curled hair, she was sorry that she had not instructed Jenny to do something more dramatic with her own, which was drawn up softly with only a small crown of curls at back. Sometimes she longed for her sister's cleverness and ready acceptance of change.

Charlotte Sloane wore blue and looked apprehensive. She had spent the week trying to learn and understand the ways of the place that was her new home. She'd listened to Roderick's descriptions of peoples and places, the banking and government officials she would be expected to meet and entertain. It worried her, but she said nothing. As Roderick's wife, she had been called upon to serve as hostess to many of London's wealthiest and influential families, and she'd manage to do the same here. She was relieved to hear that her own entertaining style would not have to change. The Sloanes would give balls and parties as they always had; Roderick would play polo—there was a field and an excellent club; and she would be welcomed by the wives of ministers and financial tycoons. She had already met several English women at tea with Selina Phelps and they were no different from her friends at home. Still, Tangier frightened her and she longed for the familiar surroundings of London.

They arrived at the Consulate at nine. Since they were the guests of honour, they were escorted to the main ballroom where the Consul-General and several foreign ministers waited to be introduced. The room was crowded, and Emilie noted that not all present were Europeans. There were numerous men in robes and turbans, not the

86

staid white most Arabs in the city wore, but a rainbow of colours that were dazzling under the fine crystal chandeliers hung in a circle from the high domed ceiling. Thousands of candles cast glittering light to flood the room and dance rainbows from the prisms. Somewhere, she could not see where, musicians were playing softly, modern music of violins and piano, soft guitars and harp.

The Sloanes stood in a reception line, smiling and murmuring as people were introduced. Emilie tried to sort the confusion of names, dismissing most since they were persons involved in business or government affairs, contemporaries of her parents who promised to be exceedingly dull. She was impressed with two, however, because the names were already familiar to her from her father's conversation.

Ali Ibn Toumart, the Minister of Finance, was presented by Yusuf Bacali. Ibn Toumart was a small man, with skin the colour of freshly waxed leather, and dark hair that showed at the temples under a magnificent gold cloth turban wrapped in heavy folds about his head. He had a thin mustache and small pointed beard, and his eyes were coal black. His caftan was striped gold and blue satin, and he wore soft, pointed-toed Moroccan babouches on his feet.

"Welcome to Tangier. Fortune visits us with thy presence . . ." He smiled. "May Allah bless *Si* Sloane's business ventures as generously as he has blessed his household."

Beside him, Bacali stood back to introduce a second man. "Ali Ibn Tashfeen, Minister of Foreign Affairs . . ."

Roderick Sloane acknowledged the introduction with a nod. He had already learned that Tangierines did not accept the custom of hand shaking. George Phelps had told him the Minister was invited, but at last word, no acceptance had been received. The man's presence now was a good sign, a stamp of approval on the banking business that had brought Sloane to Tangier. An alliance with the

87

French bank had been a matter of necessity in order to gain acceptance by the Sultan's government, which was already heavily indebted to the French. Additional loans from the Anglo-French bank of Lyon would not only seal English-Moroccan ties but benefit Roderick Sloane as well. If he had the confidence of the Minister of Foreign Affairs, he would be able to keep his finger on the pulse of the economy, and engage in private commercial ventures. And Ibn Tashfeen had come to the reception . . . a good sign.

The Minister of Foreign Affairs was more conservative in dress than Toumart. He too wore a caftan but of muted silvery and white stripes, and his turban was unadorned. He was clean shaven, his skin the colour of well-creamed coffee, his eyes deepset so that he seemed to be regarding each of them from a great distance.

There were other important persons as well. *M'sieur* Augustin, of course. Diplomats of Spain, France and Portugal, consul and wives, junior consuls and viceroys. It seemed the entire city had turned out to meet and welcome the Sloanes. George Phelps took pains to be sure Emilie and Sara were introduced to young people—Darien Melous, a junior counsul; Ian Stavely and Peter Russ, members of the Swiss legation; Martine du Bois, daughter of the director-general of *L'Hôpital Français*; and Doctor Pierre Louvel and his houseguest, Henri Cartier.

Though she had fully expected to see the doctor and Henri, Emilie was caught off guard when Henri bowed and asked her for the pleasure of the first dance. There was no way to refuse politely, and moments later she was waltzing in his arms. A glance showed that Sara had been claimed by Darien Melous, while the young French girl, a dark-haired, not too pretty girl of about seventeen, danced with Ian Stavely. The other two men had disappeared in the throng.

"Are you looking for someone?" Henri asked in an amused tone.

Emilie's attention came back sharply, and she tossed her curls. "No, just interested in my surroundings. I am not yet accustomed to the variety of faces and costumes of Tangier. I find them compelling."

"So much so that you wish to ignore the more familiar?" His tone was soft, almost caressing, and the pressure of his hand at her waist was a bit too intense.

"If that were true, I would have refused you the dance," she said haughtily.

He laughed. "You are so different from the women I know that I find myself fascinated by you, Emilie Sloane."

"If you mean that I am not bowled over by your charm, I consider the difference a compliment."

"Are you sure that it is not exactly the other way around? You do not find me fascinating because you cannot mold me into a pawn for your coquettish game."

Her cheeks flamed. "I find your manner offensive—"

"My manner, or the truth?"

She tightened her lips and looked past him to the other dancers, forcing a smile when her glance met that of Martine duBois, who danced by with the young Swiss.

"You are insufferable," she said at last.

"Do you plan to avoid me throughout our mutual stay in Tangier?"

"I'm sure there will be many functions to which we will both be invited."

"And privately?" His gaze was bold and demanding. "Will you ride with me tomorrow?"

She felt her face warm and she did not answer. Her emotions were swept into turmoil, and she wished the music would end so that she could escape. She knew he was staring and she forced words to her lips. "I'm sorry, I am busy. There are other women who will, I'm sure, find your attentions desirable. I do not."

"Then forgive me, *mademoiselle*," he said with a wry

smile. "Permit me to return you to the arms of your family, and I will not bother you again." The music ceased, and he escorted her to the side of the room, where her mother and several women were chatting. He thanked Emilie and left her standing there.

She was furious as she watched him cross to a pretty young girl she had not met and offer his arm as the music was struck up again. She glimpsed Sara dancing with the young French doctor, and she felt a flood of relief when Peter Russ appeared at her side to ask her to dance. She kept up an easy line of conversation with him, asking dozens of questions about Tangier, his work, his homeland—anything to keep from meeting the gaze of Henri Cartier when they chanced to pass.

The young Swiss was eager to please, though Emilie found him a bit colorless. He was engaged to a young lady at home, he told her, and he hoped to return to Zurich at the year's end, when they would be wed. His fiancée had no desire to come to Tangier, and he confided that, though he missed her fearfully, he shared a reluctance to bring her here.

He realized that his words might be misinterpreted and his face reddened. "Of course, there are many genteel ladies here that would provide her pleasant companionship, but she is a timid girl—" He flushed a deeper shade.

Emilie took pity on him. "I would do the same in her place, I assure you. My father gave us no choice in the matter, and so we are here."

"And I am sure you will enjoy your stay. Tangier is colorful, don't you think?"

They drifted into a discussion of the city, and he mentioned numerous places she had not yet seen. She listened with dwindling interest until the dance finally ended and she was claimed by George Phelps.

Dancing with the French doctor, Sara found it easy to show interest in his description of the hospital and his work. He was a dedicated young man who seemed totally involved in medicine. He was working on a research project on eye diseases, and had a laboratory of mice and guinea pigs on which he experimented. He spoke of the work he had done in Vienna and Paris, and she encouraged him with questions.

"Will you be able to help the Moroccans if you succeed?"

"Eventually, perhaps. I think there will come a time in this country when the rest of the world will force upon them the ways of the twentieth century. Whether that will be good or bad remains to be seen."

"How can it possibly be bad?" she asked, thinking about the ugly, disfigured beggars she'd seen on the streets.

"It can't medically speaking, but along with the acceptance of scientific discoveries the natives will be forced to change the pace of their lives to suit European standards more closely. Modern medicine means forgoing superstition and overcoming ignorance. If I were to find a cure tomorrow for the ophthalmia that causes the blindness prevalent here, what value would it have if I could not convince the people to come for treatment or to be innoculated?"

"But if they knew—?"

He smiled. "It is difficult for us to understand their reluctance because we view them from a different vantage point. Would you be relieved of pain if I were to give you a vial with nothing in it but a bit of paper with verses of the Koran written upon it?"

She shook her head, astonished.

"Yet there are many natives who swear to the relief that such a prescription brings. The strength of mental power in illness is not unknown even in our world. Some doctors devote themselves to studying it today."

"You mean like Dr. Freud?"

He was surprised that she knew of the emminent Viennese physician who had published numerous works dealing with the mind, and one more recently on the theory of sex as it related to human personality and behaviour.

"To an extent," he said, regarding her with interest. "Have you read Dr. Freud's work?"

She blushed. "No, I must profess ignorance. I read a brief article about him in the London *Times* a year or so ago. He was to lecture at the Royale Academy, I believe. Are you interested in his work?"

"Every physician is, although some take issue with his theories. He deals with the mind. I have chosen to devote myself to the study of physical disease and surgery."

"Are there many doctors at the hospital?"

"A dozen, and we've an excellent staff of trained nurses as well. If you are interested, it would be my pleasure to show you about the hospital if you care to visit."

She flushed again and nodded. "I would like that very much."

"We will arrange it soon," he said. Then remembering, he told her he had obtained the artists' names he'd promised and would send the list round to her the following day. She thanked him as the music ended, and they were interrupted by Ian Stavely who asked her for the next dance. Louvel watched them dance off, then walked to the side of the room where long tables had been set up with wine and trays of foods. How unlike her sister she was, he thought. Then, hailed by Doctor du Bois, he put aside thoughts of the girl and launched into a discussion of a difficult surgery they had shared earlier in the week.

When the musicians put aside their instruments after a bit, people gravitated toward small tables which had been set up in alcoves and on several of the cool patios. Waiters in white gauze-like shirts over full silk pantaloons, served trays of sweetmeats, tiny delicate sandwiches, and poured wine. Emilie joined a group of young people on one of the patios, accepting a seat between Ivan Stavely and a smiling young man who was an assistant to the French Consul. She flirted prettily and let the two men compete to keep her supplied with fresh punch and tidbits. Henri Cartier seated himself beside Martine du Bois and chatted, though from time to time his glance swept about the group, lingering momentarily on Emilie.

Sara came out onto the patio with Darien Melous, and Henri rose to offer his chair. Sara looked flushed and excited. She was having a good time, and it pleased Emilie to see that her predications of a new world opening for her sister were becoming fact. Sara had not missed a dance all evening, and now the young junior consul was seeing to her every comfort. Emilie favoured her sister with an almost imperceptible wink that made Sara flush and turn to converse with the French girl seated beside her.

"Dr. Louvel was telling me about the hospital. It sounds very modern and efficient. Your father is greatly respected."

"*Merci* . . . yes, he is quite proud of *l'Hôpital*. It is another world when one considers the rest of Tangier," she said.

"But one must be injured or sick to appreciate it," Darien Melous said with a small laugh.

Martine shrugged. "Medical men would argue that point, *m'sieur*. They see beauty in shining instruments and well-equipped laboratories. Beauty is in the eye of the beholder, no?"

A ripple of appreciative laughter swept the group.

"I have never heard the phrase used in quite that way," Henri said. "Perhaps 'Beauty is as beauty does' would be more fitting."

Emilie felt his glance but did not meet it. Each time he looked at her she was flooded with the memory of his kiss in the passageway of the *Ophir*, of the emotions it had stirred in her. Henri Cartier was a dangerous man—dangerous to her peace of mind, and she turned resolutely from him.

93

"Tell me, Mr. Melous, what sense of adventure prompted you to apply for a diplomatic post in Tangier?"

"You must call me Darien," he insisted. She flattered him with a smile and he went on. "I was the eldest of three children in a literary family that found it advantageous and pleasant to spend a portion of each year abroad. I was bilingual at the age of three, trilingual by the time I entered school. I grew up thinking the purpose of life was to see far-off countries and absorb as much as one could of their cultures. Diplomatic service seemed the most likely profession under the circumstances."

"Is this your first post?"

"Yes." He smiled with embarrassment. "I would like some day to return to Cambridge and study oriental languages in the hope that I may also see service in the far east."

Martine fluttered a pink silk fan and blinked. "Men are so adventurous. I would not have the courage to travel so far. I wept when I heard we were to move here, and it was only because papa promised I could return to Paris if I became homesick that I consented to come."

"And have you? Become homesick?" Sara asked.

Martine shook her dark curls and lowered her lashes. "Not at all. With so many gallant gentlemen about, how could I?" A blush touched her cheeks. "And I spend many hours at the hospital."

"You work there?" Emilie was amazed.

"Not work really, but papa insists in benefits the patients. Many of the women in Tangier come to read to patients, write letters for them or chat. So many of the soldiers are far from home and have no one."

"Dr. Louvel has been telling me about the hospital," Sara said, "and has invited me to see it."

"You must come! Tomorrow several of the ladies will be there, myself included. Perhaps we could have dinner? Mama would be delighted." Martine looked pleased at the prospect and turned to include Emilie in the invitation.

"Do come, both of you. It will give us a chance to become better acquainted."

Sara nodded eagerly and looked at Emilie.

Emilie said, "I think it would be delightful. We shall look forward to it." She let her glance move carelessly to Henri so he would recognize the deliberate lie she'd told him earlier. His expression did not flicker.

"Then it is settled. Late afternoon, say a bit after four? There'll be time for a tour and if you want to talk with any of the patients—" She flushed as she realized she might be coaxing them into something they had no desire to do.

Sara said, "I would enjoy that very much. It must be terrible to be sick and lonely."

Several of the young men moved restlessly and steered the conversation to more pleasant topics. A party was a time for gaiety, and morbid thoughts were quickly banished as the musicians began to play once more. Emilie glanced about the ballroom, seeing her father in conversation with Ibn Toumart and Ibn Tashfeen, his stern face furrowed as he pondered some point one of the men made. Couples began to move onto the dance floor, and she realized that there were at least two dozen Moroccans present, all men, she had not seen a single one of them ask a woman to dance.

She looked about abruptly as she realized Darien Melous had spoken to her.

"I'm sorry, what did you say?"

"I asked if you would care to dance again."

"Yes, thank you." She set aside her punch cup and offered her hand. As they entered the ballroom and began the slow foxtrot, she asked him about the Moroccans not dancing.

"They never do. Their customs are quite different and they do not accept the presence of unveiled women in public readily. Did you know that their own women," he blushed slightly, "wives, that is, are never seen by other men? They must wear veils whenever they venture out, and they never attend functions like this. It's said that a good Moslem woman goes outdoors only twice in her life, when she marries and when she dies."

"How dull for the women."

He laughed. "I dare say, but no one seems to complain, though the ancient customs would seem to work a hardship on both the women and the men."

"The men?"

"Since they do not permit their own women to attend social functions, they have not learned the pleasurable custom of dancing with beautiful young ladies."

"You flatter me."

"Not at all. The entire city is talking of the two lovely English girls who have come to brighten the scene of Tangier. May I dare hope that you will permit me to call some day soon?"

"It would be my pleasure."

"Thank you."

Had he also asked Sara? Emilie found herself hoping he had, for although she was looking forward to a busy social life, she knew that this young man held no special interest for her. He was pleasant enough, but he lacked the spark to hold her attention for very long. He was like dozens of boring young men she'd known in London. She let her mind consider each of the men she had met tonight and realized with dismay that none were as dashing as she hoped. None, except Henri Cartier. And she was afraid of this strange attraction and power he had to make her senses reel. Were her expectations of men unrealistic? She did not like to entertain such a notion. She smothered a sigh as she realized Darien was talking.

"—an incident on the Mountain just the other day."

"What was that?"

He misunderstood her lack of attention and went on with his story. "Not serious, thank heaven, but it could have been. The military were called out and chased the

96

scoundrels a dozen miles into the hills before losing them. A pity they weren't caught. These barbarians have to be taught that they cannot ride into the city to raid and pillage whenever the notion strikes them." He frowned and shook his head.

Her pulse skipped a beat. "There was a raid?"

He looked concerned that he had frightened her. "An attempted one, but unsuccessful. A small band of Berbers rode into a camp where a caravan to the interior was being readied by a French party. Wanted to steal horses, of course, but they were driven off by the guards before they could accomplish it. In a fit of pique, they raised a cloud of dust through a residential area near the French hospital. Screaming and yelping like banshees, they know they strike terror in the hearts of the Romans."

"The Romans?"

"The Moors call all foreigners Romans," he said with a smile that indicated his pride at being able to impart a trivial bit of knowledge that impressed her.

He seemed content to let the story end there, but Emilie was not. She had to know if it was the same incident in which she'd played un unwitting part—and which she hoped was unknown to any but the few persons directly involved.

"They simply rode through?" she persisted.

He frowned. "You shouldn't concern yourself with it, Miss Emilie. I only mentioned the story to emphasize the need for caution when dealing with Moroccans. They seem civilized at times but they are still barbarians."

"Please." She smiled and let her lashes sweep downward for a moment. "Tell me what happened. I promise not to faint away with shock."

He looked concerned a moment longer then smiled. "You are refreshingly different, Miss Emilie. I believe you would not swoon with shock at anything—"

"Then tell me." A smile encouraged him again.

"The Berbers raced through the streets bent on any

devilment they could find. Luckly it was in the heat of the day and most people were indoors—except one poor unfortunate young lady. One of the nurses from the hospital I believe. She was plucked up by a horseman and would have been carried off except Dr. Louvel came upon the scene." He gazed at her. "The young French doctor who was sitting near us a bit ago . . . have you met him?"

She nodded, eyes shining and tongue dry.

Melous warmed to his story. "He was coming out of the hospital and saw the whole thing. Fired several shots close enough to show the Berber he meant business, and then rescued the girl when the man dropped her. Louvel's shouts alerted a guard at the hospital and the man sent for the military at once, but the chase was unfruitful."

"The girl?" She did not recognize her whispered voice.

"Unharmed but frightened."

"Dr. Louvel said it was one of the nurses?"

Melous looked perplexed. "I believe so. I heard the story much later, of course. The girl was not hurt and had been returned to her home by the time the soldiers returned from the chase. The incident was not reported officially except on the military records."

So Pierre Louvel had not revealed her identity! He lied to protect her. She let her gaze sweep the ballroom until it came to rest on the doctor standing near a patio door talking with a distinguished looking man in a cut-away coat with a red, beribboned sash across his chest. Louvel was not as cool and distant as he pretended. She wondered if she would see him at the hospital tomorrow when she and Sara met Martine? She had promised to go only to vex Henri, but now she was beginning to think she might enjoy it after all.

CHAPTER FIVE

Roderick Sloane gave his approval to the project of his daughters visiting the hospital. He had learned much about Tangier in a week's time, including the fact that many important persons of the city undertook charitable work, including the wife of his new business partner, Daniel Augustin. It was considered fashionable, and there were many favours to be garnered through the fact that one's wife passed her time in the company of other bankers' wives. Though the women had no direct knowledge of banking transactions, they came to know bits of gossip that often proved advantageous in arranging business deals. Roderick was determined that Charlotte become involved in worthy projects that he could put to his advantage, but when she begged to be allowed more time to settle into her new life, he reluctantly agreed. He knew from past experience that Charlotte's withdrawing nature was best handled with patience accompanied by a firm hand. The girls, Emilie in particular, would pave the way into the social activities, and Charlotte would follow at a slower pace.

Emilie found riding the black mare exhilarating but she gave into her sister's wishes and went by sedan chair to the hospital the following day. A hand-written invitation to dinner had arrived by messenger midmorning from Madame du Bois, and it was agreed that Emilie and Sara would go to the French family's house directly from the hospital with Martine.

Martine met them at the entrance, chattering pleasantly as she took them on a tour of the building. Neither Emilie nor Sara knew much of medical institutions, since they had both been blessed with remarkable good health. Their few ailments had been tended by a private physician in his surgery, and neither had ever required any kind of a stay in a hospital. They found L'Hôpital Français a pleasant surprise.

It was clean, with only a faint odour of antiseptics and no trace of unpleasant ones usually associated with illness and death. There were tall windows at each end of the long hall and in the rooms. In dark corners along stair-wells, lamps dispelled the shadows and gave a pleasant glow to the white walls. The first floor had several offices at the front and a long room at the rear which was the surgical theater. Martine pointed out the operating table, the medicines and drugs locked behind glass doors and cabinets, a large boiler pan with its own stove beneath where instruments were sterilized before use—a method M'sieur Pasteur had determined effective in killing bacteria.

The second floor was completely given over to wards where rows of beds lined the walls and pale faces peered at them as Martine led them through. Many of the men greeted Martine with enthusiasm; others smiled wanly from their pillows, faces twisted with private agonies. It was easy to see that the French girl was well-known and well-liked. From time to time, she paused to introduce her guests and to speak an encouraging word. Eyes followed as the three moved on. There were several women sitting with patients, reading aloud or writing letters for those who could not manage for themselves.

100

Sara was filled with compassion at the sight of the suffering, and her admiration for the work the women were doing was boundless. The hospital was far nicer than she'd expected, and to spend an afternoon or two a week here would be a welcome task. She asked Martine about it as they emerged from the last ward.

"But of course," the girl said. "All of us would welcome you, especially the patients." Her blue eyes brightened at Sara's quick confirmation.

"Than I shall come whenever you will let me. You must tell me what to do and when is best—"

Martine smiled. "You are welcome any time. I come on Saturday and Tuesdays, and occasionally on Thursdays as well if mama does not require me at home."

"I shall come the same days," Sara declared. She turned to her sister. "Em?"

"Yes, I'll come when I can." She realized it sounded selfish in the shadow of Sara's enthusiasm, but she could not shake off the aura of discomfort that had enveloped her on entering the hospital. She found it disturbing to know that illness and death were so near. She glanced toward a large bright room at the end of the hall and asked about it.

"The solarium," Martine said, leading them toward the spacious sunny area where cushioned wicker chairs and tables of newspapers and magazines were arranged comfortably. Several patients in robes and slippers sat reading or staring out at the grass and flowers of the park that was visible from the windows. A thin-faced man shuffled o one leg and supported himself on wooden crutches as he women entered.

"Please, Paul, do not tax your strength," Martine said quickly.

He shook his head. "The pain of my conscience would be greater than that in my leg, mademoiselle."

"Then allow me to introduce two friends, Sara and

101

Emilie Sloane. They have recently arrived in Tangier."

He acknowledged the introduction with a nod and smile that did not quite erase the pain that was evident in his face. He was young, but his eyes had a haunted look of loneliness and fear that usually marked old age. His thin hair flopped about his forehead umcombed, and his skin was pasty white over sunken cheeks. The crutches nibbled at the floor as his fingers opened and closed around the handles spasmodically.

"Will you read to me today, *Mademoiselle*?" His gaze was intent on Martine's face.

She smiled and answered softly. "I will come back as soon as I have finished showing my guests the rest of our hospital."

He frowned momentarily and his lips tightened to hard line. His gaze did not waver. "Will you read to me today, *mademoiselle*?"

"Yes, very soon. I will fetch the book we began last week." Martine spoke softly as though to a child, and the man's expression relaxed. "Sit and rest now so you will not be too tired to listen." She touched his arm gently and he stepped back, then sank into the chair. His eyes closed and his head fell forward to his chest. Stepping quietly Martine led Sara and Emilie from the solarium.

"Paul was captured by Arabs in a desert fight and tortured most brutally. His mind and body are slow to recover."

Emilie suppressed a shiver as she recalled her own close call at the hands of Arabs, and she questioned Martine with morbid curiosity. "Did they cut off his leg?"

The French girl shook her head and her eyes clouded. "That would have been merciful. No, they hung him from a tent pole and slashed at him with swords. When they finished their games, they tossed him onto a hill of ants and left him to die as they rode off. He managed to crawl an incredible distance to a French army camp before he collapsed. He was brought here, but nothing could be done to save his leg."

"How dreadful!" Sara said.

"It is incredible that such things can still happen in these times, though in fairness I must say that most Moroccans are not savages like those who captured Paul. Still, their heritage is so different from ours that I wonder if they can ever be completely civilized."

They were walking slowly up a wide stairway that led to the third floor. For several moments the only sounds were the gentle swish of skirts, a distant murmur of voices and a soft clatter of glassware.

"But Tangier is a large, important city," Sara said. "With the soldiers of so many nations on hand, surely order can be kept and people protected?"

"To a great extent, but such is not the case in the more remote areas—and that is where our men must fight. Armies of one shereef battle fiercely with those of another, and whichever has the favor of the military seeks aid from our soldiers. One disruption is put down only to have another spring up before the soldiers can return to their garrisons." She grimaced. "I would not like to live in any of the cities of the interior. Safety cannot be guaranteed from one day to the next in many places."

"Do Europeans go there?" Sara asked.

"Some." They were at the top of the stairs and Martine paused in a fragmented rainbow of sunlight that flooded through a stained glass window that crowned the archway of the hall. "The very brave and the very foolish." She turned and indicated an open doorway. "Come let me show you papa's pride—the laboratories."

The doorway led to a large room where four men in white coats and rubber aprons were working at a long table. Strange shaped glassware was filled with bubbling and dripping liquids, and a thin burner hissed a gas flame under a huge flask. The smell of animals and chemicals was strong, and Emilie wrinkled her nose.

103

"They work with mice and guinea pigs," Martine said and pointed to a row of wire cages against an inner wall. Small fat balls of mottled fur stared with beady eyes.

"What do they do?" Sara questioned.

"They test vaccines and new medicines. Did you know that my father knew *M'sieur* Pasteur? They met when papa had a patient who was bitten by a rabid dog. *M'sieur* Pasteur's vaccine saved the child's life! He was a wonderful man, so dedicated and serving." Her eyes shone.

The men turned at the sound of the voices, and one of them came toward them. Pierre Louvel drew off the gloves he wore when handling infected animals, and dropped them into a bin near the door.

"How nice to see you again." His glance touched on Sara, then Emilie and Martine. "I would have thought you all too tired from so much dancing last night to make hospital rounds today."

"Oh, Pierre, you know I always come on Saturday," Martine scolded prettily, and Pierre smiled.

"Yes, you are the most faithful volunteer we have, and I am always delighted to see you. Your medicine is as powerful as those we dispense."

"And now I've brought Sara and Emilie who also want to visit with patients and cheer them. They've both promised to come regularly, and they are so pretty the men will feel better just seeing them."

Pierre Louvel said, "I believe you are right."

Sara noted that Pierre's gaze sought hers and she felt a warm glow. Just as quickly, the doctor smiled at Emilie and the moment passed. Still she found herself hoping that he would show them about the laboratory, but she lacked the courage to ask. She was fascinated by the little he'd told her of his work. Louvel was removing the apron and coat, hanging them on a peg.

Emilie stepped inside the room and glanced about.

"What is all this?" she asked, indicating the apparatus on he tables.

Louvel tilted his head. "Experiments. I suggest you do not touch anything, since we deal with many types of bacteria and it would be unwise to carry such organisms about on one's hands." As though to underscore his point, he stepped to a small procelain sink and turned on the tap, then began to scrub his hands with a dark soap and small brush. While he dried them on a towel, he regarded he women again.

"Have you seen the rest of the hospital?"

"Yes, Martine has taken us through the operating room and the wards—"

"Paul Chaugal was in the solarium," Martine said, and a small frown appeared between her dark brows. "Is he any better? Papa said last week that he might be going home soon."

Louvel's face was serious. "We can do no more for him. In Paris he can be fitted for an artificial leg. Perhaps the ability to walk on his own will will help heal the scars of his ordeal."

Martine looked incredibly sad. "So young . . ."

"I will stop and see him before I make my rounds," Pierre said. "Are you ladies returning to the lower floor? Perhaps you would like to have someone show you about the laboratory? I could ask one of the men—"

"I promised Paul I would read to him," Martine said.

"Then I suggest we go down together." Pierre hung the towel on a peg and pulled down shirtsleeves which had been rolled to his elbows. Deftly he slipped the links to fasten the cuffs, then took his jacket from a coat tree near the door. "I will reserve myself the pleasure of showing you the laboratory another time."

In spite of herself, Sara blushed and quickly told herself that he meant nothing personal in the remark. Emilie was watching him with a curious expression, and it was to her the doctor bowed before standing back to let them precede him from the room.

At the second floor hall, Martine scurried off to find the book she wanted. A nurse, starched white apron over a practical blue cotton dress that was hemmed up to clear sturdy black shoes, rustled past from the solarium, bobbing her head in polite greeting to the doctor and the two women. Pierre entered the sunroom, glancing about instinctively to note which patients were present. Paul Chaugal was still seated near the door; staring with vacant eyes until he heard the footsteps on the parqueted floor. He looked up abruptly with the same frightened expression Emilie had noted earlier. The doctor spoke to him quietly.

"You're looking well today, Paul. Did you rest after lunch as you promised?"

The thin-faced man scowled and stared at Emilie. "Will you read to me, *Mademoiselle*?"

Flustered, Emilie looked at the doctor. "I—"

"Martine has gone to fetch the book you like so well," Pierre said. "She will read to you."

He seated himself in a chair beside the young man and leaned to study the patient without seeming to do so. He asked gentle, probing questions about inconsequential matters, as though simply passing the time of day with an old friend. Paul seemed to have difficulty answering some and Emilie wondered if he was mentally unbalanced. Martine had said something about his mind healing slowly.

She glanced at Sara who was watching the doctor and patient with fascination. It surprised Emilie that Sara would take to charity work so eagerly. Perhaps it would help bring her out of her self-conscious shell. From time to time, Paul Chaugal turned his gaze on one of them. Did he have a wife or girl waiting for him at home? What would she do when she learned that he had lost a leg?

Across the room, another patient was being helped to

106

his feet by a stout nurse with a motherly face. As they neared the door, Sara stepped aside to allow them to pass. As she did, her green skirt brushed the leg of the spindly table beside Paul's chair. The vase of irises toppled, splashing water across the magazines as the table wobbled dangerously. With a cry, Sara grabbed for the vase but it slipped from her fingers and crashed to the floor to shatter in a hundred pieces.

Paul Chaugal screamed and leaped up. Without the crutches, he pitched forward and would have fallen if Dr. Louvel had not been so quick. Jumping to grab the screaming man, Louvel wrapped strong arms about him and held him. Paul was like a wild man, babbling and screeching as though tortured with pain. He lunged toward Sara but the doctor restrained him and forced him back into the chair. A nurse rushed in from the hall, and at Louvel's crisp command, left to bring medication. Emilie drew a pale and shaking Sara away, an arm around her comfortingly. A minute later the nurse was back with a hypodermic syringe. While Louvel still held Paul, the woman injected a colourless liquid into the hysterical man's arm. For several moments, the scene seemed fixed in time, with the doctor clamping Chaugal to the chair, ignoring the inhuman screams that rent the air. Two men appeared in the doorway as Martine hurried in with a book in her hand. She glanced at the broken vase and seemed to understand what had happened, and immediately seated herself in a chair beside Paul Chaugal and opened the thin leather book to a page marked by a strip of ribbon. She began to read aloud; for several moments her words were lost in the wailing cries of the man she was trying to soothe, then the drug took effect. Paul whimpered, sobbed, and at last fell silent. His gaze searched until it found Martine, then went blank.

In the silence, Martine's voice was like a soft bell. 'Where the quiet-coloured end of evening smiles . . ."

Pierre Louvel motioned to the two men, who came for-

ward to lift Chaugal from the chair and carry him out.
The nurse bent to retrieve the crutches, and clucking and
shaking her head, followed the others from the room.

Martine closed the book and dropped it to the chair as
she hurried to Emilie and Sara. "I'm sorry—how awful
for you both!"

Sara stared. "It was my fault—"

Martine frowned, and Pierre Louvel came to take
Sara's hand at once. "Nonsense, you mustn't think that. It
has happened before and despite all we do, it will probably happen again."

"My fault," Sara repeated in a daze.

"Come over here." He arranged pillows on a wicker
sofa and drew Sara to it, seating her then forcing her to
lie back. There were tears in her eyes and she was biting
her lip so hard a tiny fleck of blood appeared under the
white teeth.

"Have tea brought from the kitchen, Martine."

She hurried out and was back shortly carrying a light
blanket which Pierre spread over the shaking Sara. He sat
beside her and lifted a wrist, finger at the pulse.

"Is she all right?" Martine said with concern. "I had no
idea— Oh Sara, I'm sorry!"

The other girl's distress seemed to dispel some of the
shock Sara was suffering. She tried to sit up but the doctor would not permit it.

"I'm all right. It was so unexpected! I've never heard
anyone scream like that. If I hadn't knocked into the
table—"

"It was not your fault," Pierre said firmly. "You cannot
permit yourself to think that way."

"But he was in pain—"

"The pain is in his mind. He remembers the tortures he
suffered and relives them. We have not been able to un-
lock the prison he has created for himself. This time it
was a noise, the broken vase, that set him off. Sometimes

108

it is a word or a figure passing on the street outside. He sees and hears what his mind creates."

A young rosy-cheeked nurse with blond braids tightly wound under her cap entered with a tea tray and set it on a table. Martine thanked her, then poured steaming tea into a cup as Pierre slipped an arm under Sara's shoulders to lift her so he could prop cushions behind her head. He handed her the cup, watching to make sure she could manage before finally sitting back and accepting tea for himself.

The shock was ebbing and Sara was embarrassed by the attention. "Thank you. I'm much better now." She looked at each of them. Emilie was standing a bit apart peering at her with concern. "I'm fine, Em, really I am. It was foolish of me to react so—"

Emilie smiled. "As long as you're all right."

"Yes." She sipped at the steaming tea and felt warmth spread through her. Her hands were no longer trembling and she felt quite recovered, so much so that she wished they would not all stare at her. Especially Pierre Louvel. . . . But then he was a physician and at the moment, she a patient.

"I prescribe a few more minutes rest," he said with a smile. "We shall banish the incident and enjoy our tea." He glanced at Emilie and Martine, and as though tardily aware of their manners, both girls sat.

"I could not forgive myself if you suffered any ill effects of your visit," Martine said. Her face was almost as pale as Sara's.

"No more talk of that," Pierre said firmly.

"You are right," Martine said. Then with an earnest look added, "Is Sara well enough to come to dinner? Mama is expecting us . . ."

"An evening of entertainment is exactly what the doctor prescribes," he said. "But only on the condition that you permit me to escort you to the house. That way I can be sure my patient does not tax her strength."

"Of course," Martine exclaimed. "I'm sure mama will be delighted."

He laughed. "I was not inviting myself to dinner *cherie*. I promised your father I would bring him the notes on my latest experiments."

"But you will be made welcome—"

"I regret I have other plans. Another time, perhaps."

Emilie noted his quick glance in her direction, and she wondered if his plans included Henri. It was no concern of hers, and she pushed away the thought and sipped at her tea. Sara was watching her and when their gazes met Sara smiled.

"You are so silent I am worried that perhaps your shock has been equal to mine."

All eyes turned and Emilie laughed. "Not at all. I am relieved that you are recovered. Once again we are in Dr Louvel's debt." She turned her dark gaze to him. "You seem fated to rescue Sloanes and escort them to safe destinations," she teased.

"It would seem so."

"We must do something to repay you."

"That is not necessary."

"But we insist—don't we Sara?" Emilie flashed a guileless smile.

Blushing, Sara agreed. "Of course." She was at a loss for words as she recognized Emilie's flirtation with Pierre.

"I am told that many Europeans enjoy a promenade along the beach each evening. Father has been so occupied with business he has not arranged such an outing for us. Sara and I would be delighted if you would do so."

Embarrassed, Sara lowered her eyes.

The room was quiet for a moment, then Pierre said, "It would be an honour."

Emilie watched him over the rim of her cup. She could not read the strange expression in his grey eyes. He was unlike any man she'd ever known, and she did not understand why she felt the need to prove anything to him. Or

110

was it to herself? She saw the flush of color on her sister's cheeks. Poor Sara. So conventional. So far, their introduction to Tangier had been the least conventional period in their entire lives. Maybe it was time for many changes.

Charlotte found her days filled with myriad details of settling into a new home, trying to oversee household details that were confusing or did not meet her approval. In truth, she had nothing to do but occasionally instruct Asheema about some minor matter. The Arab woman was extremely efficient and the household ran smoothly and effortlessly under her control. Charlotte's orders were accepted in deferential silence and carried out to the letter, and often beyond. If the mistress of the household indicated a desire for fresh fish on the dinner menu, courses of boiled baby shrimp, oysters on pearly half shells, broiled mackeral in delicately spiced butter sauce, and saffron flavoured white fish would be served. In spite of her resolve to retain every English custom, Charlotte found herself giving way more and more to the housekeeper's silent efficiency. The exotic foods, spicy, fragrant and foreign to the palate, seemed to tempt Roderick and the girls. She would have preferred mutton and boiled puddings to the pigeon pie or strange *couscous* but she was relieved by the fact that at least Roderick was adament about proper tableware. The sight of Arabs eating with their fingers disgusted Charlotte, and she had to avert her glance lest her disapproval be evident to those she dare not offend. They had already been drawn into several business affairs that demanded her presence at social functions, and soon she would be expected to entertain.

Roderick absented himself from the house each morning immediately after breakfast, which he took on a tray in the sitting room of the upstairs apartment. When he returned from the bank at midday, they lunched in the dining room, the four of them at one end of the long table that would easily accommodate two dozen guests. After

111

inquiring the details of their day, Roderick discussed—no
told, for she and the girls merely listened—the progress o
his work, the names and ranks of people he dealt witl
and with whom they would become acquainted. Severa
names came up frequently, and Charlotte gave particula
attention to them. She knew her husband would expec
her to recall all details when she met these persons.

After the noon meal, they retired to the apartmen
where Roderick changed to a dressing gown and slipper
to relax. He had not adopted the Moroccan custom o
wasting the entire afternoon at rest, but he conceded on
hour following lunch, then returned to the bank to worl
at his papers until the business day began again at four
He sat on one of the low-cushioned divans to read th
week-old London Times, which one of his clerks picke
up from the mail packet each day. She sat with a bit o
embroidery, watching him sidelong and looking up atten
tively each time he cleared his throat and rustled the pa
per before reading aloud some item he considered o
interest. And when he finished, he set aside the paper and
reclined on the Moorish sofa, eyes closed, but not asleep
she was sure. She retired to the bedroom and lay upon th
four-poster bed and let her thoughts drift.

She was not unhappy in Tangier. Nor was she happy
she supposed. She had been swept into Roderick's circle
of acquaintances, expected to perform as a prope
hostess. Not that she minded. The social aspects of he
marriage were by far the most pleasurable. She and he
husband had little more in common. The controlled pas
sion that they had enjoyed as newlyweds quickly van
ished, and their actual physical encounters in bed had
ceased altogether by the time Emilie and Sara reached
their teens.

Strange that she always thought of them that way—
Emilie and Sara. No matter Sara was her firstborn and a
tremendous comfort to her . . . so placid and loveable
But any consideration of the two children she'd borne

112

resulted in placing the elder behind her more thought-compelling sister. Charlotte sighed. She worried about Emilie but at the same time envied her. She was so willing to face life, to accept it on many levels and greet it with enthusiasm. She'd been a rebellious child, high-spirited and eager. Many times Charlotte had seen the admiration in Roderick's eyes as Emilie accomplished some new feat; but she had also seen the disapproval when she disobeyed or defied his wishes.

Unbidden thoughts of the incident with the young bank clerk in London came to Charlotte's mind. Emilie had changed after that, and Charlotte was sure there'd been more to it than either Pauling or Emilie told. Emilie had been too docile under the punishment Roderick imposed, and there was a brightness to her eyes that could not mask some inner light. Charlotte had been scandalized by her own thoughts of what might have occurred, and she put them from mind so she would not have to examine them more closely. Emilie's beauty and personality were a source of pride but also of concern. They could easily lead her astray in spite of her upbringing, and the consequences were too terrible to contemplate. It was easier to avoid the matter; and the news of the move to Tangier had effectively erased it.

But Emilie was already showing signs of wildness here. The unescorted outing with its almost disastrous aftermath . . . and Emilie's certainty that her mother and Sara would not divulge her guilty secret. The possibility that Roderick would learn of the incident had worried Charlotte considerably, but with each passing day it grew more remote. She would be vastly relieved when Emilie settled into marriage.

One day during the third week, instead of lying back when he'd finished reading his paper, Roderick stared at Charlotte with a deep frown, his fingers tented in front of his pursed lips. Charlotte forced herself to sit still until he chose to speak.

113

"I have decided it is time to begin entertaining, Charlotte. There is a matter of considerable importance that requires diplomacy and the right contacts. It will be advantageous to obligate certain parties to us socially.

She nodded but said nothing. She could not object; the guest list would be drawn up by Roderick and she would pen the invitations. Roderick would discuss what would be served, what entertainment would be suitable, and she would speak to Asheema who would see to the actual work. How could she possibly object . . . ?

"*M'sieur* Augustin feels that several of the prominent French citizens of the city can be approached to lend support to a number of railroads that will enhance our business ventures. Under the terms of Franco-German conventions, the French cannot undertake any commercial railroad ventures until the line to Fez is completed, and that may be several years, since the project is a difficult one at best. An English owned line would prove most advantageous, though it could not be built without French knowledge and agreement—on an unofficial level, of course." He pursed his lips and tapped a finger against his chin. "It might be very profitable, both to the bank and to us personally, since I plan to invest capital in the venture. But before a word can be said, I must have the assurance that those I approach are in sympathy with my ideas."

Charlotte's lips twitched. "I understand." She did, very well. Roderick was proposing a venture that skirted conventional methods. She knew nothing of railroads or politics, but she knew her husband. He would not inform her of his plans unless she was to play an important part in them. He expected her to listen and observe, to report small reactions that might otherwise go unnoticed. When women sat together at tea or social affairs, it was only natural that their conversation touch upon the business matters that occupied their husband's attentions so fully. And impressions were given, suspicions voiced.

"A dinner party, I think. *M'sieur* Augustin and his

114

wife, *M'sieur* Lemain, the assistant French consul, the Ministers of Finance and Foreign Affairs—Ibn Tashfeen will bring the Shereef of Madawadi—and Henri Cartier, whom we met aboard ship."

She blinked. "The Count?"

He nodded. "He is not a man without influence. His family wields considerable power with the Republic. I've made inquiries." The information he had acquired was impressive enough to make him put aside his misgivings about the man's rakish escapades and reputation. "The chap seemed attentive to Emilie aboard the *Ophir*. I'm sure she will find him pleasant company for an evening."

Charlotte was certain of it, perhaps too pleasant. Was Roderick trying to encourage a marriage between the Count and their younger daughter? It would be a good match in some ways but Charlotte had the uneasy feeling that Emilie would rebel at the idea if she thought her father fostered it. No matter, it was time both girls began enjoying themselves. The past weeks had been spent riding about the city with Mohamet, avoiding prescribed areas which Roderick had detailed carefully to the stableboy, or joining their mother at tea with Selina Phelps or *Madame* Augustin. The young English assistant consul had come to call, sitting stiffly in the parlor making desultory conversation to combat Sara's shyness and Emilie's boredom. Though Charlotte had encouraged him to call again, she did it without enthusiasm. He was scarcely the companion either of her daughters would or that Roderick would approve. Melous's post offered little opportunity for financial advancement.

"When do you wish the party to be held?" Charlotte asked.

"In a week's time, Saturday the eighteenth of June. I will speak to Asheema about additional servants. You may select the menu but I suggest you consult her wishes. She seems extremely capable at arranging assortments of delectable dishes." His gaze wandered to the arched window where silvery leaves of an olive tree rustled. "A remarkable woman . . ."

Charlotte was startled by the gentleness in his tone, and unaccountably her cheeks flushed. Roderick had not spoken gently to her for many years, and to hear him do so now of another woman wounded her in a way she'd believed impossible.

All at once, he was brusque again and she stared at her hands instead of meeting his look. "I had a note at the bank this noon from Dr. Louvel. Seems he is grateful for the visits the girls have been making to the hospital and would like to show his appreciation by escorting them in a promenade along the beach this evening."

For a moment, Charlotte was stunned; mention of the doctor filled her mind with the dreadful incident that had befallen Emilie the day of their arrival. But that was more than a fortnight ago. If the doctor had spoken of it, surely it would have reached Roderick's ears by now.

Roderick mistook her look for puzzlement. "You met the doctor at the Embassy party. He works with Doctor du Bois, director of *L'Hôpital Français*."

She pretended enlightenment. "Yes, of course . . ."

"No reason they should not go. The doctor's reputation is unblemished and I'm sure he can be relied upon to bring them home safely. You might invite him to dinner if you've a mind to."

"The party—?"

"No need to do that. A simple dinner with the family will repay his kindness." He dismissed the subject, sighing heavily as he relaxed against the cushions and closed his eyes. Charlotte sat a few moments, then rose and went to her bedroom.

116

CHAPTER SIX

It had been five days since their visit to the hospital, and Sara was pleasantly surprised by the invitation from Pierre Louvel. She had thought the matter forgotten in the press of more demanding tasks the doctor had. Emilie was both pleased at the invitation and annoyed at the manner of its arrival, though she could not define why she cared. She and Sara had spoken of the doctor several times, and they had revisited the hospital with Martine without seeing him.

The second visit to the hospital had been without incident and Emilie found it a bore. She went because father gave the outing his stamp of approval, and it was a change from sitting about talking with mother and Sara or riding specified paths with Mohamet constantly in attendance. He had not made good his offer to show them the *casbah*—on orders from father, she was sure, but masked by the Rif lad's dazzling smile and his poor excuses: "Too hot this morning." "Too late now, all Arabs go home." "Allah does not smile on this day." And so on until she was convinced he never would.

They had discussed the promenade with Martine, who told them that it was very informal, a time to stroll and

117

gossip or to sit and look out at the sea as it changed colors in the setting sun. It was considered proper for couples or whole families to walk the beach; many men found time to pause and converse with friends or to carry out small business matters that did not warrant more lengthy discussion under formal conditions. The promenade was a social hour for the Europeans of Tangier.

Pierre left the matter of transport to the wishes of the women. Sedan chairs would carry only two passengers but if the ladies would prefer not to walk or ride horseback . . .

"I would like to walk," Emilie said.

When he glanced at Sara, she nodded. She looked lovely in a dress of shimmery green, some veil-like material that whispered softly when she moved. Her chestnut hair was done under a straw bonnet tied with green ribbons and her cheeks were flushed becomingly. Emilie was stunning in a gown of gold silk decorated with small clusters of pink flowers. Her dark eyes seemed an intense amber. Did she consciously try to outshine her sister, he wondered? She was a beauty, and she seemed to be quite aware of it and use it to her advantage. Henri still spoke of her with more than casual interest, though he'd made no effort to contact her to Pierre's knowledge. When asked to join them on the promenade, Henri claimed an engagement, and Pierre did not press the matter. Something had happened between the two, he was sure, but it was not his concern.

The afternoon sun was vanishing beyond the western perimeter of the city, casting purple shadows under the eucalyptus and green oaks that bordered the roadway that descended to the city. The air was beginning to cool, a phenomenon that never failed to amaze newcomers to Tangier. From the heat of midday, the change was welcome and refreshing.

Pierre was amused at Emilie's coy manner. The girl was bold in an enchanting way that he was sure brought many men running to sit at her feet. She was accustomed

118

to attention, and she knew how to handle it with ease. To all appearances she was an innocent child—until a man looked into her eyes. Was that the reason Henri had been drawn to her? Henri was another accustomed to having his way with the opposite sex. At his smile, women were eager to fall into his arms. When they had been at the Sorbonne together, Henri spent more time entertaining women in his rooms than he did at his studies; more than once he had sought refuge in Pierre's apartment when several of his eager young ladies chanced to demand his favours at the same time. And somehow Henri would slide from one affair to another, leaving a trail of broken romances but never lacking for new adventures. Pierre found his friend's escapades amusing but had no time for amorous adventures himself. Medicine was his lover; it had wooed him like a sorceress since his first encounter with a wounded hare on his father's estate in Lorraine. The animal had been caught in a snare and had chewed its leg almost through in an effort to free itself. It stared up at the six-year old boy with frightened eyes and lay trembling to await its fate. With gentle hands, Pierre extricated it from the cruel wire and carried it to a nearby stream where he bathed the bloodied, mangled paw. The bone was laid bare and bore the teeth marks of the hare's strong incisors. Pierre washed away small bits of rotted flesh and cleaned the wound, then used the fine linen handkerchief his nurse had tucked in his sleeve to bind the leg. All the while, the animal watched unwaveringly, eyes glassy with pain and fear. Pierre made a soft bower of leaves and grass under a beech sapling and laid the animal upon it. The hare did not try to escape but rested quietly, as though sure now it had nothing to fear from the fair-haired child who sat and watched until the shadows grew long and leaves rustled a warning of evening. The next morning, the bower was empty; Pierre was haunted by the trusting, pleading eyes of the wounded animal. It was the beginning of an interest in medicine that

119

soon outgrew childish games and became a devotion that consumed his life. There had been several girls who stirred his passion, but none enough to make him consider stealing more than random moments from the mistress of medicine.

He'd thought of both Emilie and Sara occasionally in the past days and even glimpsed them in passing along a corridor at the hospital one day. But the cultures were responding dramatically to the new chemical solutions he'd developed, and he worked day and night, every moment he was away from patients, in the laboratory. He was pressing for a breakthrough, a key to the mysterious, resistant strain of germs that spawned blindness and disfigurement. He'd forgotten completely about the promenade until Dr. du Bois forcibly removed him from the laboratory this morning at dawn and sent him off to rest.

"Not one patient, not one foot in the hospital! It is an order. If you continue this way your health will break and you will lose everything you have worked for."

Banished like a naughty child, Pierre slept several hours and on waking, lay abed trying to clear his mind of work by focusing it on other things he might do for the day. Now, he was surprised at how much he was enjoying the companionship of the two girls.

As they crossed the square below the Mountain, Pierre was aware that many eyes turned on them. Women looked with jealousy, men with envy. Faces turned from café tables, legation windows and knots of men idling as they enjoyed pipes or cigarettes. Men tipped hats, bowed, women inclined their heads. The two young English women were the talk of the city, he was sure. And by nightfall, he would be too. The idea amused him. Emilie was enjoying the attention and said little. Sara continued a steady conversation, asking questions about things she had not seen before. As he answered, he was surprised by her quick grasp of details.

When they reached the *Grand Socco,* Emilie halted as

120

he turned toward the *Rue de la Plage* which skirted the wall and offered a road to the beach without entering the ancient city.

"Let's go this way," she said, indicating the high gate.

"Oh, Em——" There was a quick glance exchanged between the sisters that Pierre did not understand.

Emilie raised eyebrows and studied Pierre's face. "Is it safe?"

"Quite, but most English prefer a more attractive route."

"But we are not 'most English', are we Sara? We've been in Tangier more than a fortnight and have not yet been inside the walls. I cannot bear another day without seeing some of the tantalizing things I have heard and read about." She flashed a captivating smile at Pierre, and he knew he was being challenged.

"Have you been——?" Sara looked questioningly.

"Many times. You may be disappointed."

"I am so bored with proper English manner that I will venture into the old city alone if you two will not accompany me!" Emilie declared.

"No!" Sara was adamant.

"Then let Dr. Louvel take us." Emilie's dark eyes flashed triumphantly.

Sara looked helplessly from her sister to the doctor, who smiled. "It is perfectly safe as long as you do not tempt fate by wandering about alone. We can follow the *Rue des Siaghins* down to the Grand Mosque and circle back to the beach. If you are willing, Sara?"

She nodded. Emilie's daring troubled her, but she felt guilt over her own lack of hesitancy. Her curiosity to see the old city had been piqued by bits of conversation she'd heard. Foreign women seemed to avoid the sector, mainly because of its filth and dark shadowy streets. Men felt free to visit at will, but none encouraged the women to do so.

"Then come this way. I must warn you that some of

the streets are narrow and we will have to pass single file. I entreat you not to become separated." He offered an arm to each of them and they passed through the *Bab Fahs* and into the old quarter.

Emilie was enchanted. The world seemed to change within a few steps, and she was in the Morocco described in the books she'd read. This was the Morocco that offered adventure and excitement . . . mystery.

They started down the rough cobblestoned street. Pierre told them the name of the thoroughfare meant 'street of the goldsmiths', and he pointed out tiny niches that could hardly be called shops, where craftsmen sat crosslegged working their trade by the mealy light of sputtering oil lamps. Emilie would have stopped and watched, but Pierre did not alter the easy pace he had set for them.

At every step, Arab life teemed about them. Beggars in rags were numerous, crippled, deformed, the blind, led by half-naked children who joined the cry for alms at the sight of the foreigners who were fair game to be pursued through the street. The constant babble of voices mingled with the evil grunting of camels and the braying of mules, and several time Pierre drew them aside quickly when a beast stepped too close for comfort. Women glided by like ghosts wrapped in sepulchral shrouds, feet and hands hennaed, only one darkened eye showing above the fluttering veils; many quickly drew the veils to cover all of their faces when they saw the Europeans approaching. Emilie could not help thinking of what Darien Melous had told her of the total subjugation of Moroccan women, and she wondered how they endured it. Was it because they had never known freedom of any kind, taught from childhood to obey without question? Her parents' restrictions on her had an opposite effect and given her the need to rebel.

They came to another square which was obviously a market, though considerably smaller than *Grand Socco*. Stalls opened off the street, tiny cubicles festooned with gleaming copper and brass pots, clay pitchers, bowls and jugs, rainbow assortments of woven cloth spread like peacock feathers. Veiled women sat with their backs to the street, loaves of bread for sale laid out on the stones. Others bent over to examine products and haggle prices. A young Moor, tall and slender, with ebony eyes, turned to stare as they passed, and Emily avoided his piercing gaze. The sweet smell of *kif* drifted into the fading afternoon from a group of men sitting against a wall where a patch of sunlight splashed.

"The *Petit Socco* is frequented by the native populance," Pierre explained. "A market for daily shopping, unlike the *Grand Socco* which attracts the country people to dispose of their produce. It is said that one can find anything his mind can conceive here."

"It seems so primitive," Sara said. "It's hard to believe time has not stopped in some past century."

A burst of high shrill voices heralded the approach of a ragged looking procession. Music, if it could be called that, issued from trumpets, cymbals, pipes and drums, and chanting voices rose and fell in eerie tempo.

"What is it?" Sara asked.

Half a dozen of the group carried banners and in their midst, a very old man with white beard and wrinkled flesh, was accorded a clear space to walk unimpeded.

"A holy sect. The old one is their saint. They are on their way to prayers."

"A saint?!" Sara stared at the tattered old man.

Pierre smiled. "There are many holy men in the Moslem religion. Did you know that the Sultan and all his emirs, shereefs and sheiks are considered direct descendants of Allah? This makes them gods in their own right. Among the poor, the holy are chosen more randomly. If Allah chooses to withdraw a man's reason and keep it a prisoner in heaven, then the man is surely a saint to have such guardianship."

"You are teasing me," Sara said, blushing.

"Not at all. A Holy Fool with his iron scepter is a common sight. The poor offer him coppers, and the rich step aside so they will not be struck or spat upon, but none dares offend him. See how they give him passage, yet flock his footsteps."

The small band of worshippers was almost out of sight down the twisting street. Emilie was aware of the lenghtening shadows as the sun moved toward the sea beyond the city walls. Darkness crooked between buildings and the path was no longer clear. The street narrowed beyond the *Petit Socco* and Pierre was forced to relinquish their arms, warning them again to stay close. The stroll through the ancient city would have been better left for a bright morning, but Emilie would not admit that now. It was too exciting to be wrapped in the aura of the city's colourful tangle of past and present.

The procession surrounding the saint vanished through the gate of the Grand Mosque as Pierre led them across a street that turned east. Against the sky, the small figure of the *muezzin* was outlined for a moment before his evening call to prayer rose, fell and rose again. Everywhere, Arabs sank to their knees and bowed heads to the ground.

"Officially sunset," Pierre said. "If we don't hurry, we will miss the promenade which was to be our destination."

A few minutes later they passed through a gate and descended the steps to the beach road. The outlines of the customs sheds were dark against the glaring red sunset. Several ships lay at anchor in the harbour but there was little activity on the quay. Pierre took them along a path that sloped to the beach dotted with couples and groups, strolling or riding, spaced at intervals as though measured. An English woman on horseback nodded a greeting as a Rif guided the animal at a slow pace. Emilie recognized her as one of the women who had been introduced at the Consulate party but could not recall her name. A French nursemaid herded two small children away from the water's edge, where soft waves lapped the sand.

In the distance, several men with large sleek dogs watched as a servant tossed sticks into the water for the animals to fetch.

"Look at the sunset!" Sara's breath was taken away by the changing colours that stained the sky and water along the horizon. The dusk was pleasantly soft, with none of the threatening shadows that menaced the streets of the old city, and she thought she had never seen a more glorious sunset.

Pierre watched her and marveled at her sincerity. She was unspoiled and eager, and he found her child-like wonder contagious. He had not reveled in a sunset since his youth in the hills and forests of Lorraine, nor had he spent quiet moments appreciating the beauty surrounding him since the morning he chanced to meet her on the hilltop path. He stood a few moments to let her drink her fill of the sight before they began strolling the beach again. Emilie was looking this way and that watching all activities and people.

They came close to three men in frock coats and silk hats and another in a light fawn suit of crisp linen—Henri Cartier. So Henri's engagement had not detained him after all. Instead it had brought him here to the beach where it was a certainty he would meet Pierre and the Sloanes. Coincidence? He wondered.

"Pierre, I did not expect to see you here," Henri lied magnificently, doffing his hat as he took each girl's hand and touched it to his lips. "Emilie. . . . Sara. . . . may I present *M'sieur* Lemaine, the assistant French consul, *M'sieur* Rovan of the International Finance Institute, and *M'sieur* Deloroso of the Portugese legation."

The men bowed and murmured. They were obviously delighted to meet such lovely young ladies, and the conversation turned immediately to how the two were enjoying their stay in Tangier.

"I find it very pleasant," Emilie said quickly. "Pierre has just been kind enough to take us through the ancient

125

city and it makes me feel at last as though I am really in Tangier."

Monsieur Rovan frowned and looked at Emilie in a paternal manner. "I would not think a young lady of your background could endure the squalour and dirt of that sector. It is a dangerous place, and it is not wise for ladies to frequent it, even in the company of gentlemen."

"Come now, Charles, you make it sound as though the Arabs have nothing to do but lie in wait for unwary foreigners. It's not that bad." Juan Deloroso wagged his head.

"He's right, you know," said Paul Lemaine. "It's a fact that danger lurks in unfamiliar places, but the Arabs dare not risk bringing the soldiers down on them by foolish acts against our people. The ladies were as safe as though they carried the King's flag wrapped about them as a shield." He smiled confidently at the women.

Rovan frowned again, but before he could respond, Henri said, "I'm sure Pierre took every precaution for safety. And unless I miss my guess, he was probably persuaded into the adventure by Miss Emilie herself." His smile was so innocent none found fault with his remark, save Emilie, who felt a rising tide of annoyance. He was getting back at her in subtle ways for her refusal to see him, and it pleased her that she had been able to hurt his pride.

"Nevertheless . . ." Rovan was reluctant to drop the subject.

"I know the city well, *M'sieur* Rovan, and chose our route with care. I'm sure that neither Emilie nor Sara would be foolish enough to venture about alone." He did not look at Emilie.

"We have just concluded our discussion," Henri said. "May I have the pleasure of accompanying you? It is not fair that one gentleman should selfishly claim two such lovely ladies. I presume on our friendship, Pierre, to right the matter."

126

With farewells to the three other men, Henri fell in step with Pierre and the women, claiming Emilie's arm. She felt a physical shock at his touch and reminded herself that this man was dangerously attractive. She would show him that she could play his game without falling victim to his charm.

"I trust you have been enjoying your stay in Tangier," she said.

"Not as much as I would if I had the opportunity to see you more often."

She met his bold look. "I have been quite busy."

"Visiting hospitals to engage in charity work?"

She flushed. He probably knew that she and Sara rode with Mohamet each day and that there had been no parties except the dull dinners with the Phelps and du Bois families. Gossip spread quickly in the small European settlement, and any detail was grist for the mill of wagging tongues that had nothing better to do.

"I find the hospital fascinating. I have never before know a physician or a scientist, and Pierre is so devoted and clever. There is scarcely a day that passes that I do not hear of some miracle he has performed."

"You lie very prettily, Emilie."

He was laughing at her. She felt her colour rise and would not look at him. They had fallen slightly behind Sara and Pierre, and when she tried to quicken her steps, Henri clasped her arm firmly and walked even slower. There was nothing she could do without making a scene.

"You have succeeded quite well in avoiding me, but it seems that is to change. The matter has been taken out of your hands."

She raised a puzzled gaze to his face, which was quite serious. "What are you talking about?"

"Only this very afternoon I had word that your father requests my presence at a small diner party to be given next week. Surely his daughters will join their lovely mother as hostesses?"

127

"A dinner party?!"

"You did not know?" He raised a dark brow and looked at her quizzically. "Perhaps I have spoken out of turn. The invitations have not yet been sent, but I was assured of the date and time in order to keep the evening free."

She swallowed her surprise. "I was not aware that you had business dealings with my father."

"I do not, at least not yet. The French minister is a close friend however, and the assistant consul. Since it was *M'sieur* Lemaine who encouraged me to reserve the evening of the eighteenth, I assume it is my friendship with him that makes me worthy of the attentions of *one* of the Sloane family."

Her face warmed again and she turned to look out over the bay. The last golden spikes of the sun were turning brassy in the burnished sky over inky water. So she would be forced to see Henri; the thought quickened her pulse, but at the same time made her apprehensive. She would make certain that they had no opportunity to be alone, no matter how many times father invited him to the house! The very thought of him close, away from prying eyes and public display, almost took her breath away. She tried to rein her thoughts. Similar ones had gotten her into serious difficulties once before, and she would not let it happen again, yet her womanly instincts were aroused and her body filled with a fire that was difficult to control.

"Will you welcome me into your house, Emilie?" he asked.

She detected a note of mockery, and she lifted her chin and turned to him. "I'm sure you will find me quite the proper hostess. I will welcome you as I welcome any other guests my father invites."

"And no more?"

"No more."

His gaze held her a moment. "We shall see . . ." He

looked ahead as Pierre and Sara halted at a large rocky spit.

"The sun is gone," Pierre said. "It is best that we turn back before complete darkness overtakes us." He smiled at Emilie. "Your sister has been very patient with my chatter of experiments and the hospital. I fear I have bored her terribly."

"Not at all!" Sara protested, disturbed that he would even think such a thing. She had enjoyed every account and description he gave, and her respect and amazement for the man and his work knew no bounds.

Pierre smiled indulgently. "Nevertheless, I feel guilty. But we must be getting back. The beach is almost deserted. The time has a way of slipping away when I am pleasantly engaged. Besides, I have your father's permission to take you to the Hotel Cecil for some refreshment before delivering you home. Have you been there?"

They walked back four abreast, the conversation settling here and there like a butterfly on various topics of general interest. Emilie was glad of the diversion to avoid any further personal conversation with Henri, and when they reached the Rue de la Plage, she adroitly managed to maneuver positions so that Henri was forced to walk with Sara while she took Pierre Louvel's arm.

The hotel terrace was set up as a small café and was a popular stopping place for Europeans after the promenade. Light refreshment, often only sweet hot mint tea, offered the chance to pause and continue conversations begun earlier or to chat with those encountered on the evening outing. The dinner hour in Morocco was late, and the Cecil had also become a waystation for those going to dine elsewhere.

Henri found them a table immediately and gave their orders to a red-jacketed waiter who had the dusky skin and eyes of a Moor. Several people at nearby tables greeted them, and Emilie smiled at Darien Melous and Peter Russ, who gallantly rose to bow. At a far table,

Martine and the young French diplomat, Jacques Prigent, who had been so attentive to her at the ball were in earnest conversation. Conversation hummed, eddying and drifting, interrupted by an occasional burst of laughter and the tinkle of glasses.

Emilie was delighted that father had given permission for them to stop. She was even more grateful that Pierre Louvel had invited them to walk! It was the first time she had truly enjoyed herself since the day of their arrival. Father's restrictions precluded most pleasurable pastimes, and she had begun to feel stifled under his watchful eye. Now, sitting on the terrace that overlooked the dark street above the square, Emilie felt caught in the excitement of Tangier once more.

She smiled at Pierre. "I cannot recall enjoying an evening so much, Pierre. I do hope you will ask us again," she said.

"It was a pleasure. It is the first time I have been away from my work for an entire day, and I would not have thought it possible to enjoy myself so thoroughly."

Tea came, and they sipped and chatted, with Emilie devoting herself almost exclusively to Pierre. Let Henri do as he pleased, she would not be drawn into the circle of his charm. He seemed unperturbed and carried on a pleasant conversation with Sara and with Pierre whenever Emilie relinquished his attention long enough. She felt almost giddy with excitement, and she knew she was talking too much. Once she caught Pierre's gaze fixed upon her as though she were a patient with some strange malady, but she did not slacken the furious pace of her chatter. She had to show Henri that he meant nothing to her, that she wanted no part of him. From time to time she glanced at him sidelong and if she chanced to meet his gaze, it was always amused and aloof. What an infuriating man!

When they finished tea, Pierre said it was time to go.

Henri suggested it would be wise to order sedan chairs rather than climb the hill in the dark.

"I was about to do that very thing," Pierre said. "I'll have a word with the clerk." He excused himself and threaded his way along the tables to enter the lobby of the hotel.

"I would prefer to walk," Emilie declared, frowning at Henri. It was not true, but she felt an urge to resist any suggestion he made.

"I think not. *Rue de Fes* is a poor substitute for Picadilly or Knightsbridge Road. Let your evening end pleasantly with a brief ride."

"I do not want to walk," Sara said with certainty, "I do not share my sister's thirst for adventure and daring, and am more than content to avoid these dark streets. I see menace in every shadow!"

Henri laughed gently at her charming naïvete. "And wish you are, at least here in Tangier. It is not a savoury place after dark, and young ladies should be escorted in the proper manner."

Pierre returned, and minutes later two black and yellow sedan chairs, each with the name of the hotel painted in old gilt letters on the sides, were brought around. Emilie tried to maneuver herself into one with Pierre, but to her dismay, he stepped back and allowed Henri to sit beside her. She drew herself to the corner like a trapped animal as the chair was lifted by the brawny slaves, who set off at a slow pace.

"I will not bite."

"Stop making fun of me!"

"What else am I to do when you act like a spoiled child, spank you?"

"You wouldn't dare!" She was scandalized.

He laughed. "Perhaps not, but the thought is tempting. I think it would be enjoyable, but I think once I had you in my arms, I would find far more pleasant occupation for my hands." He stared at her in the gloom of the small en-

closure, and she was more lovely than he'd ever seen he
What a wench! For all highborn airs, she was a temptin
woman—and she knew it! His time in Tangier had n
been spent mooning about her but neither had he bee
able to put her completely from his mind. And now wit
business in the offing with her father, he was looking fo
ward to the prospect of seeing her often. With some luc
he might win the old man's approval to call upon h
younger daughter. The thought amused him and he d
not realize he had laughed aloud until she spoke.

"I find nothing humorous in your suggestion."

"Suggestion? Oh, my mind had already wandered t
other things. Still concerned with you, however." H
moved close and slipped an arm around her shoulders.

"No!"

"The chair maker must have had moments like this i
mind when he designed these conveyances with only on
means of exit. You cannot escape, Emilie." To prove h
words, he drew her close. She struggled and would hav
beat at him with clenched fists, except her arms wer
pinned under his own.

"You have tormented me for three weeks and I am er
titled to some reward for my patience."

"You are entitled to nothing!" She arched her back bu
quickly realized that only pressed them closer, so sat ver
stiff in his embrace.

"You know where Pierre's house is—you have bee
there." He was whispering against her cheek. "Tomorro
. . . I will wait for you."

"No—"

He bent and kissed her, his lips warm and eager on he
tight mouth. His hands stroked her shoulders, her bacl
relaxing the muscles that strained against him. He felt he
quiver then tense again, and he let his tongue play acros
her lips. They tasted minty from the tea, and warm an
soft . . .

Emilie was paralyzed by the sudden surge of desire tha

flooded her. She'd felt the same when James Pauling kissed her, caught in a whirlpool of longing that stirred her entire body. Her mind tried to fight but her flesh cried aloud for his caress. Henri's lips were no longer gentle and she welcomed his tongue between her teeth. She was scarcely aware of his hand at her breast, only of the heat that became an inferno in her body. She was trembling in his arms, and he held her close.

When he released her lips, she buried her face at his shoulder, whimpering softly.

"I will wait for you tomorrow," he whispered. "Pierre leaves for the hospital at eight." He stroked her face gently, letting his fingers trace the pattern of her trembling lips. He could have her this moment, he knew, and though he wanted her fiercely, he knew he had to wait. To attempt getting her away from her family without good reason would certainly raise questions, and her father would clamp his paternal fist around his daughter to imprison her even more than she was already. He glanced about and saw that they were past the consulates, already on the tree-lined road where the Sloane house stood. He brushed his lips to her cheek, then released her and sat back to give her a few minutes to compose herself.

Shame filled Emilie, shame at the knowledge that she had enjoyed his kiss and his caresses, shame at the awareness that she wanted him—as she had wanted James Pauling.

Sara settled into the sedan chair with a pleasant feeling of peace mingled with sadness that the evening was drawing to a close. She had enjoyed it immensely, and as Pierre Louvel took the seat beside her, she knew it was mostly because of him. It had not been the walk, the beautiful sunset, the quiet tea . . . it had been these—but because Pierre was there to share them. When she'd claimed interest in his work, it had been the truth. She never tired of listening to him describe experiments or special medical cases that he had treated. He spoke of his work with near-reverence, and she found it humbling to know that a man could be so dedicated.

The sedan chair swung into motion and for a moment she was off balance and fell against him. His quick strong hands caught her and lingered a moment on her arm even after the chair swayed in steady rhythm.

"It has been a delightful evening for me. I thank you for making it so, Sara." His face was a pale blur in the dim light that splashed from houses along the route.

"It is I who must thank you."

He laughed. "We could become a vaudeville routine if we continue to thank each other." He reached and took her hand. "Let this be the end of our mutual gratitude, then." He bent his lips to her fingers, then released her hand and sat back.

It took her by surprise, and for a moment she was too flustered to do more than smile. His touch had been casual, but she felt a deep inner trembling that she had never experienced before. She was far more comfortable when he was talking about his work.

"Have you contacted any other artists yet?" he asked.

She blushed, though he could not see in the darkness. "I have not done so, though I do thank you for sending the names around to me. It seems such a frivolous pastime that I hesitate to pursue it."

"Nonsense," he said, peering at her. "You have a talent and you should develop it."

"It is a useless talent at best. I shall never be good enough to be a serious artist."

"How can you tell until you try? Many great careers begin with a casual interest which, when developed, becomes deeper. You might surprise yourself if you spent more time at your painting and drawing."

No one had ever encouraged her this way, and she did not know how to respond. There was no argument against his logic, and she was forced to search her own mind for he truth. "I suppose it is just that I am too lazy to work diligently and face the possibility that I may not have as much talent as my dreams permit. To play at work is quite a different matter from actually doing it."

Her answer surprised him. "That is a wise observation, but perhaps you should consider risking the consequences and also the chance that you will succeed. You seem to me a very determined young lady who knows her own mind."

"I?!" She reacted with genuine surprise. It was the kind of thing that was usually said about Emilie but never about her. She felt herself flushing again and fussed with her shawl.

"Has no one ever said that before?"

She shook her head, and he laughed softly. "You are a delight, Sara. I had not thought there was a woman so unspoiled, so refreshing, left in this world. I may be forced to rethink some of my outmoded ideas about females . . ." His smile lingered, and Sara did not want to break the spell with mere words.

The rode the rest of the journey in silence, comfortable and companionable. When the sedan chairs reached the house, Pierre declined to come in but walked her to the door. Emilie had hurried in as they approached, and a silent Henri leaned against the arch of the outer court, cupping a match to light a cigarette while he waited for Pierre.

Pierre took Sara's hand and held it. "I hope that we can walk again another evening."

"I would enjoy it." She had difficulty meeting his gaze, and when she did, he too looked away.

"Goodnight, Sara."

"Goodnight, Pierre, and thank you . . ."

He stood watching as a male servant, properly English in black cutaway and wing collar closed the door after Sara entered the house.

135

CHAPTER SEVEN

Emilie slept fitfully, tossing and twisting until the bedclothes were hopelessly tangled and she rose and walked
out to the gallery to stare at the pale moon riding the
night sky. The breeze was cool on her fevered flesh as she
leaned against the post supporting the roof trellis, her fingers idly plucking a bougainvillea leaf and crushing it between nervous fingers. She would not go to him, it was
out of the question. She sighed and hugged her arms
across her breasts. Did all women have such longings? It
was not the kind of question one could discuss with anyone. Sara or her mother would be shocked at the thought
of her allowing Henri Cartier to tempt her in so senuous a
manner.

Frowning, she recalled how ill at ease mother had been
when Emilie began to ask questions about her own body
and the process of birth. Her mother had not been able to
bring herself to speak of such matters and delegated the
task of imparting information to the stiff-bodied, stern-
faced governess who taught the girls until their teen years.

Miss Veronica had spilled out words in short spasms
as though each pained her. Natural cyclic menses. . . . an
indication that a girl was no longer a child but ap-

proaching womanhood . . . a burden to be endured but never discussed. Miss Veronica had even gathered the courage to show the girls the soft knit napkins that they would use when their maturity demanded it, but when Emilie persisted in asking further questions, the governess turned scarlet and tight-lipped.

"Time for a girl to know about such things when she is married, not until." The subject was dismissed. Emilie knew now, of course, that Miss Veronica had undoubtedly never lain with a man, never felt the passionate touch of male flesh in her body or the sweet breath of desire on her lips.

And mother? Had she been merely an instrument for father's pleasure or had she known the tormented emotions of need? It was difficult to picture mother in that role of womanhood, just as it was impossible for Emilie to talk to her about her own confused feelings.

When at long last she returned to bed, it was to toss again and wait for the morning light. Her resolution wavered and was renewed a dozen times before dawn finally chased the darkness and the distant *muezzin's* call announced sunrise. When Rachma came with her breakfast tray, Emilie barely touched the food. She ordered a bath and luxuriated in its soothing silkiness until the water grew tepid. Rachma helped her dry and dress, her huge eyes like glistening coals, and Emilie saw in them a wisdom of womanliness. She had never considered the girl in any way but as the excellent servant she was, but watching her move about the room, Emilie was keenly aware of the smooth rhythm of the black girl's motions, the sensuousness of each step, each turn.

"Rachma . . ."

The girl turned. Emilie had learned over the weeks that she spoke some English, not as much as she understood, but sufficient for them to engage in sporadic conversations.

"Are you a virgin?"

137

The girl's eyes showed she did not understand. Emilie frowned and tried again. "Have you ever slept with a man?"

Rachma hesitated, then said, "Yes, miss . . ." Her voice was soft as the flutter of a bird's wing.

"You are not married."

The black head moved from side to side, then realizing the implication of Emilie's question, Rachma lowered her gaze. "I am a slave."

"You were taken against your will?"

The puzzled look returned, and Emilie grew impatient with the disparate backgrounds that made it so difficult for them to communicate. She persisted. "The man with whom you slept—did he force you against your wishes?"

"I am a slave," Rachma said. "The wishes of the master of things are my wishes."

"Your master took you?!"

Rachma's face was passive. She saw nothing unusual in the situation, obviously. Emilie recalled Yusuf Bacali mentioning that Rachma had been bought from the house of a rich Moroccan.

"Was he the only one?"

"No, miss."

"Who then?"

"Ali Hailit, son of the master, found me pleasant to look upon, as did Ussi, the master's house servant."

Emilie chewed at her lip. "And you, Rachma, did you find any of them pleasant to look upon so that you enjoyed being a woman with him?"

"Ussi very good to me." She smiled and her eyes became alive, remembering.

"Where is he now?"

"He has not been sold."

"How long has it been since you have seen him, lain with him?"

The girl's eyes masked, and Emilie realized that as a slave in the household of the Sloanes, she was probably

138

orbidden to leave the grounds or entertain in her quarters.

"I will not tell my father," Emilie said softly. "I speak to you as a woman to a woman. Do you see him? Do you lie with him and find pleasure in your body?"

"Yes . . ." So softly, it was scarely a sound, but Rachma's eyes spoke more than the word.

Emilie turned and let Rachma fasten the sprigged dimty gown, holding herself straight so the material would ease under the girl's nimble fingers. The few words with Rachma told her more than the painful halting conversation with Miss Veronica. A woman *could* enjoy, a woman *did* enjoy! It was only the hampering bonds of convention that kept most from realizing themselves fully. A man was free to enjoy pleasures of the flesh with no more reprimand than to be called a rake, and even then such a reputation made him enticing to other women! But a woman was expected to save herself for the marriage bed and the hope that somehow marriage and excitement would become synonomous. Try as she would, she could not picture her father rousing her mother to heights of passion as James had roused her, or as Henri was promising to do if she acceded to his invitation. The thought made her body tingle with suppressed excitement, yet she could not conciously make the decision that would end her torment.

She wandered about the house, looking in on Sara who was sitting at the window sketching the gnarled olive tree in the garden, and who declined the invitation to walk or ride, and on mother, who was at the desk in her sitting room penning invitations to the dinner party Henri had spoken of. She was so engrossed in her task, she nodded absently and did not look up when Emilie spoke to her.

"I'm going riding, mother."

"Yes, dear."

She considered returning to her rooms to change into a more suitable gown, but was impatient to be away from the house. She ran down the stairs in a swirl of soft dimity, holding her skirts up so her slippers would not catch. She would ride only to the top of the hill, no farther. She needed to feel the wind on her face and the heat of the sun. Realizing she'd forgotten a hat, she paused at the foot of the stairs, then shook her head and hurried out the door.

"*Señorita* ride?" Mohamet scrambled to his feet from the shade of the stable where he'd been sitting polishing a leather halter. His eyes made a quick survey of her dress but his face showed no surprise.

"Yes, saddle the mare at once."

"*Merci* . . ." The leather was hung over a peg, the polishing cloth thrown to the ground as he scurried into the stable.

Emilie paced, listening to the gentle nicker of the mare and the slap of leather as the animal was readied. Very shortly, Mohamet led two horses into the sunlight.

"It is not necessary for you to accompany me. I am only going to the top of the hill."

"Mohamet like ride." His smile was broad and his face looked guileless.

"It is not necessary."

"Mohamet like ride."

She sighed and let him help her onto the mare. He had his orders, and she would not be able to dissuade him. Father had probably threatened his job or even his life if he disobeyed.

They rode up the narrowing street to where the hill crested and afforded a view of the city below. The sun was dazzling and the white buildings gleamed like sparkling wash hung out to dry on the side of the hill. The sun was hot on her head, and she wished she had gone back for a hat; the never-ceasing *levante* whipped her hair from its loose pinnings so it fluttered about her face and twisted tendrils at her neck. Along the horizon, fat clouds rolled out of the sea and piled into murky balls of gray. They were the first blemishes on the sparkling clarity of the sky Emilie had seen since their arrival in Tangier, and she watched in fascination as the clouds gathered into a boiling mass.

"Storm comes," Mohamet said. "We go back."

She shook her head, watching as the sky darkened and the wind carried the clouds toward land.

"Rain soon. Get wet, *señorita* . . ."

"Go if you want, I shall stay!" She spoke sharply, and the boy's eyes swept the horizon momentarily.

"Rain wash Mohamet feet." He grinned.

Annoyed, Emilie nudged the mare and headed along the road leading to the small park near the French hospital. It would be more sheltered among the buildings than on the exposed hilltop, she told herself, refusing to think that she might have other motives. The wind was much stronger all at once, and the darkness that had been concentrated over the sea encroached on the bay and the lower city. By the time they reached the park, the dampness of the wind had collected in large drops that spattered thumbprints in the dust. Irises swayed and bent, stems straining, as the wind slashed across the park and flattened the grass to a shimmering carpet. Emilie felt several cool drops on her face and bare arms, a few soaking through her gown. Then in the sharp gust of wind, the storm was upon them, pelting rain in torrents as though the sky had opened directly overhead.

Mohamet's voice was carried by the wind. "*Señorita—*"

She peered at him as he pointed hopefully to the hospital and surrounding buildings. She nodded and headed for the house where Pierre Louvel had taken her after the incident with the marauding Arabs. Sensing her destination, Mohamet hurried to grab the reins of the mare and lead the way to the steps of the building, slipping from his horse and holding out a hand to help her down.

The door was open before she touched the ground, and Henri Cartier pulled her inside, motioning to the boy to

141

take the animals around to the back. The door was closed and Henri was looking at her with a pleased expression.

"I was watching at the window and saw you on the ridge."

Water dripping from her sodden clothes, Emilie pushed back her rain-slicked hair.

"You are drenched. Here, come along to the parlor, I'll light a fire."

"That's not necessary—"

"It is if you do not wish to catch pneumonia. Then you would once more be Pierre's patient instead of my guest."

"I was about to turn toward home when the storm caught me unaware."

He cocked his head and studied her.

She shivered and frowned. "Mohamet should have warned me . . ." The feeble lie sounded lame to her own ears, but he did not challenge it.

He took her arm and led her along the hall. Instead of turning to the left where Pierre had tended her, he led her to a stairway of polished mahogany. She looked apprehensive and hesitated.

"My apartment is upstairs. I've a fire laid."

His hand was firm at her arm and she let herself be propelled into motion once more. The house seemed very quiet, and she wondered if the servants were about. She shivered again, and he slipped his arm around her.

"You're cold. Here—" He opened a door at the right of the stairs and led her into a comfortable apartment. It was richly furnished, with several very fine French pieces in the style of Louis XVI, tufted and covered in rich brown satins and velvets; there were also several excellent Moorish sofas, stacked with downy pillows brilliantly striped in brown, black and gold. It was definitely a man's room, yet it carried every appointment needed to make it comfortable and attractive. At one wall, a fireplace was built into the thick stone, its gracefully arched opening screened by brass mesh in the shape of a proud peacock,

142

il feathers spread. Henri knelt and touched a match to he kindling, and it sprang to flames. In moments, the warmth penetrated the room and he drew her close to the hearth.

"I am glad you came. I hoped you would."

"It was accidental . . ."

"I think not. I felt your response to my kiss last night. Was that accidental too?"

"Why must you always tease me?!" She was angry at herself but wanted to shift the blame to him. Her pulse was pounding in her temples and despite her sodden clothing, she was so warm she felt fevered.

"Do you want me to order a sedan chair to take you home this very moment? Mohamet can bring the horses when the storm ends." He regarded her with a piercing stare until her gaze fell nervously.

She studied the leaping patterns the fire threw across the thick Persian carpet. Beneath her shoes, small damp circles spread on the gold and black pattern.

"I am ruining your carpet," she said.

He stepped to her, tilting her chin so he could look at her face, but she did not raise her eyes. His hands began to work at the fastenings of the wet dress, skillfully undoing them as he turned her back to the fire so that its warmth brushed her flesh. He slid the dress from her shoulders and she made an unconscious attempt to cover her breasts as the garment fell in a puddle at her feet. The silk chemise was damp and clung to her skin. Gently, he bent to rescue the dimity gown and shake it out before hanging it over the back of a chair. His thin face was serene, his eyes bright, as he knelt before her and rolled down her stockings then removed them with her slippers which he placed on the hearthstone to dry.

Again he stood before her and raised her face to him. This time her glance fluttered and faltered and her eyes closed as he took her into his arms and kissed her. His hands scorched her flesh through the thin chemise and she

143

was scarcely aware of his slipping the straps from her shoulders, loosening the garment so it fell past her waist then to the floor.

Slumbering desire came alive. She was in his arms giving her lips willingly, welcoming his hands on her body. She shivered with rampaging emotions that left her dizzy.

"Emilie . . . Emilie . . ." He kissed her neck, the hollow of her throat. His nostrils were filled with the fragrance of her body, and he felt the quickening of his own passion at her willing acceptance of his kiss.

She moaned as surging passion consumed her. His kisses were heady, his touch tormenting. She was filled with desire that left her trembling helplessly in his embrace. His hand found the high curve of her breast and was impossible to breathe past the fire in her throat.

He brought her to the settee, drawing her down as he marvelled at the sight of her lovely breasts, the slim, taut body with a velvety thicket of hair where thighs met. She was as beautiful as any woman he'd ever seen, and he was filled with the power of his desire. She lay with eyes closed, breath fluttering in erratic bursts. He gazed at her as he undressed quickly.

She watched him from under half-closed lids, ashamed of the pulsing need that entrapped her and the intoxicating excitement that filled her as she viewed the tight curl of hair on his chest, the lean, hard belly, his magnificent male organs. She felt no fear, only ready desire.

He came beside her and touched her shadowed face, bending to kiss her full red lips, gently at first then greedily as his flesh came against hers. He let his fingers explore intimate places until she shivered and bit her lip to keep from crying out. He put his mouth to her breast and took the nipple while his hand stroked her thigh and moved between her legs. A long shuddering sigh escaped her lips, and he looked up.

"You are incredibly beautiful . . ." He moved over her then, slowly and gently.

She opened her eyes to see his face close. His body was warm, his maleness probing to find the haven of feminine flesh that welcomed him eagerly. She was aware only of the intensity of the pleasure that grew as he entered her slowly, letting his weight down so that the delicious warmth consumed her. Then she was crying out, meeting the desire that fused them together and swept her into a tide of passion from which there was no escape except in ultimate release. She felt his flesh under her hands and was dimly aware of holding him close, moving with him and adding to her own pleasure by encouraging his. Her mind was a kaleidoscope of emotions, impossible to sort or define, until at last they exploded in a whirling climax. The sound of her own breath roared in her ears, her voice cried out to him, and she felt the instant rush of his fulfillment.

Dazed and trembling, she lay in the circle of his arms, letting him hold her close in the aftermath of their intimacy. She felt as if floating on a cloud, light and drifting, but more vitally alive than ever before in her life. She smelled the heat of his body, and the faint odour of cologne, musky and masculine, mingled with her breath which at last quieted. Her mind was oblivious to anything but the sensation of warmth and well being that pervaded her body. It seemed an eternity since she had experienced the first intimacy with James which had been so quickly followed by guilt and self-recrimination; she was in no rush to rouse herself from the present euphoria.

Henri lay thinking more practical thoughts. He was pleased with the outcome of events, glad that he had been forced to wait so long to enjoy the delight of Emilie's body. As he'd guessed, she was not unfamiliar with the ways of women with man, and he suspected, no virgin. Still she had the freshness and delight in her own sensuality that made her coquettish game believable—and made her the more desirable for it. She had come to him of her own accord, pretending fate had driven her to seek shelter from the storm, but he knew better. Hadn't he watched her from the window as she sat her horse atop the hill, the Rif lad with her pointing out the coming squall that could have been outrun had she agreed to go immediately? He smiled and inhaled the sweet smell of lemon verbena in her hair. Emilie Sloane was a passionate and desirable woman, and she could no longer hide behind a façade of innocence. His stay in Tangier would be all the more pleasant now. . . .

At last he stirred and pulled back to look at her. Her golden hair was damp at her cheeks, curling like pale fingers on her sun-kissed skin. He brushed it back and lifted her face to kiss her gently.

"You have surprised and delighted me beyond words, Emilie."

Her sooty lashes fluttered but she did not open her eyes. He smiled and petted her face gently.

"No need to fear being a woman, cherie. We shall speak to no one of this pleasant interlude, and you will come again, eh?"

Her lip trembled and she caught it between her teeth.

"Here now, open your eyes and look at me." He held her chin until she did his bidding. Her eyes were unfathomable pools, dark and mysterious. "Was it not pleasurable for you as well as for me?"

For a moment she could not answer. She was torn between truth and the slow return of guilt. Before all courage fled, she said, "Am I wanton for enjoying it so?"

He laughed and kissed her cheek. "Do you expect some terrible fate to fall upon you for coming alive as you were meant to be?"

She sighed. "No one has ever explained. Girls are brought up in ignorance, you know, at least proper English girls with parents like mine. No matters of personal nature are ever discussed. Where was I to turn to for information?"

"No friends—girl talk?"

"Hints and blind guessing. The ignorant pretending to instruct the ignorant." She thought of Miss Veronica's blushing countenance and the quick end of the discussion when it became too uncomfortable. And the girls at Miss Dreyfus's Academy had whispered and giggled but had known nothing.

"You learn very quickly, my pet."

She looked at him to see if he was making fun of her, but his smile was gentle. Did he know that she was not a virgin? Did men have ways of knowing such things? James had guessed her purity, but perhaps that was more worthy of notice.

"Do you think less of me for what has happened?" she asked.

He looked genuinely surprised. "Less of you? *Sacre Dieu*! Do you believe me a fool? Don't you understand that I have been waiting and hoping for this moment since I first met you? I wanted you, and now that I've had you, I can only want you more. Will you come again?"

The specter of James Pauling rose to cloud her thoughts. But he had crudely suggested that their meetings would continue, there had been no gentleness in his manner. He'd been quite impersonal, almost coarse. Henri was treating her with respect, easing her over the guilt that would have filled her if he acted differently.

"Please, say you will," he coaxed.

"Yes." It was what she wanted, she could not deny it.

He took her in his arms and kissed her again, lingeringly with spent passion. When at last they drew apart, she gazed at the window and was amazed to see the sun bright outside. She sat up with a start.

"The storm is over! Mohamet—"

He drew her back into his arms. "Mohamet will remain in the servants quarters until he is summoned."

"But I am expected home for the midday meal. Father—" Her face suffused with colour at the thought of her father.

147

"Father . . . all right, I suppose I must let you go, though it would not take much to stir the embers of my desire." He sat up. "The bath is through there."

She climbed from the divan and ran across the room, conscious of his gaze on her naked body but remarkably free of shame. It was only when she saw her reflection in the huge glass over the wash stand, saw the high colour in her cheeks, the brightness in her eyes, that she realized how totally pleasurable the past hour had been. She splashed tepid water on her face and washed quickly, then used Henri's tortoise shell comb to right her tangled hair.

When she returned to the sitting room, he was dressed and had shaken out her chemise and gown, which were dry from the heat of the fire, though badly wrinkled. He handed them to her.

"The best I can do without calling a servant to press them."

"No!" Her quick look of alarm made him laugh, and she giggled at her own frightened reaction. She dressed as he lighted a thin cigarette and sat watching her from the sofa. And when she was ready, he escorted her downstairs and sat her in the formal parlor across the hall from Pierre Louvel's study, while he went to instruct Mohamet to bring around the horses.

Their leave-taking was quite formal, and as she rode away she stared steadfastly ahead. The streets were empty and she prayed feverently that no one had seen her leave the house. She was still breathless with excitement, her body tingling and vibrant with its new-found joy. Henri had been gentle and considerate, and she hugged to her heart the memory of his flesh against hers.

When they neared the junction of el *Kabir* and *Rue de Fes*, she realized that neither she nor Henri had spoken of love. She smiled. Love needed no words. . . .

CHAPTER EIGHT

The preparations for the dinner party went so smoothly that Emilie and Sara were scarcely aware they were in progress. Unlike parties in London which caused all manner of stirring and preparation, this one seemed accomplished by a feat of magic, undetectable until it had been done. One moment the dining room was vacant, the next the table was set with sparkling crystal, delicate Spode china, and gleaming, heavy sterling. There were no kitchen sounds, or aromas, since all food was prepared in the rear buildings, apart from the house itself.

Charlotte spent the entire day in her rooms, bathing and relaxing so she would be able to greet her guests with fresh spirit. Roderick spent a few hours at the bank but did not return after lunch in order to prepare for the party. Sara was content to sit for several hours in the garden with her sketch pad. Only Emilie could not give herself to idleness, and she was up early, riding the sleek black mare along the ridge and through some of the closeby valleys that interrupted the hills before they became the mountainous barrier that sealed Tangier from the desert. She'd ridden every day since she'd gone to Henri but had not summoned the courage to stop at the house again. She expected a note from him, some word, but none had arrived. She gentled her mind with the assurance that he was discreet not to risk having a message intercepted.

And she would see him tonight. She sat her horse atop the ridge where she could overlook the park and hospital street, staring at the house where he might be this very moment, her heart fluttering with remembered ecstasy and new longing. Would there be an opportunity for them to speak alone tonight? She prayed father would not monopolize the men so completely that she and Sara would be only ornaments to decorate his party. He was completely oblivious to the wishes or interests of young people, it seemed to her, and she and Sara were expected to smile and be charming to all the dull people his business demanded he entertain. She was heartily sick of banking talk—all manner of business affairs. What would it be like to dine alone with an interesting man . . . with Henri? She closed her eyes and dreamed a candlelighted table, touching fingers and whispered words . . . .

Behind her, Mohamet's horse snuffled and pawed the ground, disturbing her reverie. Sighing, she nudged the mare and headed back along the hill.

She lingered at her bath, letting Rachma lather her hair and rinse it with warm water from the pitchers, then wrap her head in a soft towel while she continued to soak in the perfumed water. She lay back against the blue tile, her breasts supported by water, the nipples taut, as her thoughts returned again and again to Henri and the hour they'd shared. She was strangely free of guilt, though it cropped now and again when she realized what her father would do if he were to discover the liaison. The thought brought colour to her cheeks. She would be branded wanton, probably shipped back to London to Rothingale's or some other rigid, private academy that would be a prison. She tightened her lips and determined never to let such a thing happen. She was not a child . . .

150

how well she knew! Yet father would treat her like one as long as she was under his roof.

She paused with hand in midair as she scooped a cluster of frothy bubbles from the surface of the water. Father would never see her in another role until she created one for herself, one quite independent of him and the household in which she'd been brought up. She would not be a child when she married and had a home of her own!

The idea seemed so startlingly simple that it quite took her breath away, yet she was able to accept it without reservation. Somehow, the idea had been on the perimeter of her thoughts all along. *That* was why she felt no guilt in her affair with Henri! She *did* love him. Hadn't she lain content in his arms, enjoying his caresses and murmured words? Hadn't she reacted with pure joy to his suggestion that they continue to see each other, to meet secretly and enjoy the pleasure they had discovered in each other? It had been different with James Pauling, who had filled her with guilt and revulsion as soon as the deed was done, where there had been no warm desire lingering after the physical act.

She gave the matter of love considerable speculation and somehow imagined it would strike her with more impact that she felt now. Perhaps the physical joy of being with a man was love it itself. But no, she had found physical joy with James but nothing to follow it past the first encounter. With Henri, it was different. She wanted to see him again, wanted to be with him, wanted to have him hold her. Yes, she was in love. She laughed softly, and Rachma gazed imperturbably until Emilie ordered the girl to scrub her back. The soft-bristled brush reminded Emilie of Henri's gentle fingers on her flesh, and she hugged her arms across her breasts and prayed for the hours to fly until she saw him again.

She selected a gown of saffron linen, a cloth so fine that it was silky to the touch. It was one of the few she'd had made by the local dressmaker, an adaptation of the colourful gowns worn by the slaves of wealthy families, loose skirt swirling about her ankles, gathered at the waist and topped by a daring snug halter style bodice that was kept from immodesty by a short bolero that covered her shoulders. She studied her reflection in the glass and was pleased with what she saw. Rachma arranged her hair in a crown of loose curls that seemed random and very fetching. She pinched colour to her cheeks and touched a dab of rouge at her lips. Turning, she surveyed the image again and saw Rachma come up behind her. The girl held out a small green bottle with a glass stopper.

"A touch . . . to stir the passions of the man you desire."

For a moment, Emilie was taken aback at the slave's knowing look, then she unstopped the bottle and moistened her fingertips with the delicate oil, touched it to the hollow of her throat and the back of her neck. It was a sweet aroma Emilie could not define, but Rachma smiled.

The first guests arrived promptly at nine; M'sieur Daniel Augustin, father's partner in the Anglo-French Bank of Lyon, and his wife Janine. They were a middle-aged couple, as typically French upper class as the Sloanes were English. M'sieur Augustin bowed over the women's hands, brushing his lips and pencil-thin mustache in a brief courteous gesture. His wife was an attractive woman, her dark hair touched with grey that she did not hide, knowing full well it gave her an air of distinction and enhanced her patrician features.

They sat in the drawing room, with Hawley passing a tray of apertif glasses, and talked of general matters. Within minutes, Hawley ushered in Paul Lemaine, a squat heavy woman who was his wife, and Ali Ibn Toumart, the Moroccan Minister of Finance. Introductions were made round, though everyone had met with the exception of Lucille Lemaine. Emilie recalled the small, dark Arab from the consulate ball; he wore a flowing *jellaba* of brilliant hues and a red turban the colour of gazelle blood.

He bowed and kissed hands, murmuring mixed greetings of English and Arabic to the ladies. His dark eyes took in the striking dress Emilie wore, and she saw approval. The other women, Sara included, were garbed in conventional European gowns, which though quite lovely, could not compare with the garment that floated around Emilie like an African sunset. Even her father, who first frowned at the unfamiliar fashion, had complimented her on her choice. Now she could not wait for Henri to arrive.

Father apparently believed the young Frenchman would arrive with *M'sieur* Lemaine who was his close friend.

"He urged us to come along without him since he feared he would be slightly detained. He is much in demand at all local gatherings, both business and pleasure, and he could not avoid a late tea with friends of his father's." The assistant French consul winked broadly. "They have a daughter who would not hear of excusing Henri from his promised call."

Emilie's chest tightened with jealousy and it was difficult to keep her smile from fading. She forced herself to chat with *Madame* Lemaine until Hawley once again appeared in the arched doorway to announce additional guests.

Both men were garbed in flowing robes, their feet slippered in *babouches* which clicked softly on the tiles.

"Ah, *Si* Ibn Tashfeen, welcome to my home." Roderick Sloane went to greet his guest, bowing in return to the Arab's low sweep.

As at the Consulate party, he wore conservative dress, muted colours and an unadorned turban, yet his presence was commanding. The man with him was tall and straight-backed, his wide shoulders undisguised by the green and gold striped robe. At one shoulder, the cloth was gathered under an egg-sized glittering emerald; a smiliar stone only slightly smaller was set in the center front of the green turban wound about his head. His face was deeply tanned, with strong features that gave him a bold handsomeness, and he wore a small mustache. His dark eyes seemed to take in the room at a glance.

Roderick Sloane was eager in his welcome, and Emilie realized that the two guests must be very important indeed. The Minister moved in an approximation of a bow.

"*Si* Sloane . . . may I present His Excellency, the Shereef of Madawadi, Taleb al-Mu'min." He presented his guest with a flourish.

Taleb al-Mu'min accepted Roderick's bow but did not return the gesture. His carriage was so straight that he might have been a statue, except for the intensity of his eyes that moved from person to person as Roderick introduced him to the other guests. Emilie stared in fascination as the shereef's gaze lighted on her momentarily; she imagined she saw a flicker of interest in it but it was veiled immediately.

Taleb al-Mu'min chose a low divan and sat crosslegged with the utmost ease. It was extraordinary that he could assume so formal a pose while seated so comfortably, and Emilie decided it came of a lifetime of practice. Pierre Louvel had said that shereefs were considered holy men, direct descendants of Allah; Taleb al-Mu'min was very rich then and very powerful. And quite aloof. He was not unaware that he was an important guest in the Sloane household and he accepted it as his due. Emilie wondered what business her father had with the intriguing Arab.

Hawley did not offer the apertif tray again, which puzzled Emilie though she knew there must be some very good reason of which she was not aware. Her mother looked nervously around the assemblage and began to converse with the two French women about London. The men slid immediately into talk of business affairs. They spoke of money loaned to the Sultan's government, and of a new railroad spur to aid travel in the interior. Unfamiliar names and places were mentioned, and Emilie wondered if they were connected with the distinguished Arab

154

guest, thus accounting for his presence at the dinner party. The shereef was silent for the most part, looking disinterested except for his keen eyes which did not miss a flutter of motion or an expression. Once when the Minister spoke directly to him, he nodded slowly as though he had already given his answer grave thought. Emilie watched her father and knew that he wanted the shereef's goodwill—his desire for it was almost a tangible thing in his expression. She had never seen him quite so anxious to please.

"The Pendash Company can be the instrument of peace among your people," he remarked to the shereef.

Taleb al Mu'min said nothing.

Roderick nodded sagely. "A railroad spur right to your doorstep, so to speak, means a steady supply of food and other commodities."

"The valley of Madawadi is fertile enough to grow every crop my people need."

Roderick looked flustered. "Quite so . . . quite so. Machinery to harvest the crops . . ."

"Progress will overtake my people eventually, it is so." The shereef regarded the banker solemnly.

"And military protection," *M'sieur* Augustin said. "A railroad can bring soldiers and arms to your aid in the event of an uprising. Even now there are rumours of a revolt in the making. Strong military power in the interior is good for your people, is it not so?"

Al Mu'min seemed to shrug, though he did not move. Emilie had the feeling that *M'sieur* Augustin's remark displeased him, and she wondered why.

Henri arrived then, and new introductions were made. Henri apologized profusely to his hostess, and he held Emilie's hand at his lips a trifle longer than necessary, so her heart raced. Father showed no sign of annoyance at his tardiness but welcomed him and motioned Hawley to bring a drink.

So it was the Moroccans who did not drink. . . . But

155

Emilie's interest was centered on Henri now, and she concentrated on not letting her emotions show. It was difficult to be in the same room with him and not touch him. She wanted nothing more than to be in his arms and— She reined in her thoughts.

Henri was far more in command than she. He fell into easy conversation with Roderick Sloane and the others.

"We were speaking of the troubles in the province of Shaweea and along the Algerian front," Roderick said.

"And the need for additional railroad tracks," *M'sieur* Augustin added.

Henri nodded, glancing at the French banker. "A wise move. The concession of administration of public works makes it possible for work to move ahead swiftly. I'm told that materials for rails and roads are already being brought in."

Taleb al Mu'min's gaze shifted to Lemaine. Without change of expression, he said. "The railroad to Fez is not yet laid down."

"Of course," the French assistant consul said quickly, "but the work will go rapidly. Believe me, your Excellency, France is most anxious to carry out its promises to your people."

"Your promises concern those who choose to follow the leader you have put on the throne."

Lemaine cleared his throat and pursed his lips nervously. "Moolay Hafid's revolt against his brother was an action in which the French had no part."

"To indulge a man's whims in order to create a debt he cannot pay is a move more deadly than a military attack. Moolay Hafid enjoys your protection because he cannot pay the debt he inherited along with the throne. And my people pay the price of his folly." The Arab's face was impassive, but an undercurrent of tension swept the room.

Henri leaned back and sipped the apertif. "The protection of the French benefits all your people to some measure. Your own affairs prosper markedly."

156

For an instant, the Arab's eyes flashed, but when he answered, his tone was even. "We are a simple people, Si Cartier. The ways of your world dazzle and confuse the mind. If we can no longer he left in peace, then we must learn to deal with the foreigners on their level."

"But your country has not been at peace during its entire history," Roderick offered. "Tribe against tribe, brother against brother."

"*Inch'allah. . . .*" the shereef murmured, his gaze lowering but not before Emilie saw the small angry spark in it.

"The railroad will bring progress," Lemaine declared. "The city of Fez will prosper, as will all of the interior."

"Prosperity is not always measured in terms of Roman wealth," the shereef said.

"Our heritage gives us a different viewpoint from which to see life," the Minister of Foreign Affairs said smoothly. He seemed eager to improve the strained atmosphere that was growing within the room. He smiled at the shereef, then at the others. Allah gives us time, and all things come as Allah wills them."

Heads nodded and the moment was passed. The brief silence among the men created a sounding board for the shriller voices of the women who were discussing an upcoming polo match for which grandstand seats were being constructed for comfortable viewing.

"—proper stadium, though the plans are in the making," Lucille Lemaine said. She looked about suddenly as she realized her voice dominated the room. Her husband smiled reassuringly.

"Have you had the pleasure of attending any of the polo matches, *M'sieur* Sloane?"

Roderick said he had not. "But I am looking forward to it. I do not play myself. Such active sport is better left to the young chaps, eh?" He glanced, smiling, at Henri. "I am told you instruct the art of fencing at St. Cyr, *M'sieur* Cartier."

157

"I spent a year at it, though I doubt that I will return to the post. My family wishes me to devote more time to business in Paris."

Hawley appeared in the doorway with a silent signal that dinner was ready. Roderick Sloane got to his feet, offering his arm to the wife of the French assistant consul. "Shall we? Dinner is served."

There was a general milling, with *M'sieur* Augustin taking Charlotte's arm and Henri bowing with a devilish smile at Emilie.

"*Mademoiselle* . . . ?"

She felt the pressure of his hand at her fingers as she let him escort her to the dining room. Sara followed with Lemaine, the others close behind. The shereef walked beside *Madame* Augustin but did not take her arm. In the dining room, there was some delay as each guest sought his name on the small porcelain place cards which Charlotte had written with crayon in delicate script. The importance of the Moroccan guests was evidenced by the fact that the two Ministers were accorded seats next to their host, with the two French women at their sides, then Henri beside *M'sieur* Augustin and Emile next to him. Opposite, the shereef sat between Madame Lemaine and Sara, while the French assistant consol and Roderick's business associate, Augustin, were seated at either side of their hostess.

Emilie was delighted to be beside Henri, though it was almost impossible to keep the tide of emotion in check. How could he be so casually proper when her own heart was racing and straining? As he held her chair for her, he managed to whisper, "You are a lovely vision, pet . . ."

It made sitting through the meal more difficult. Each morsel of food she put to her mouth seemed to catch and refuse to pass down her throat. She wanted only to look at Henri, to touch him, to hear his voice speak gentle words.

Conversation eddied about the table in a mixture of topics, none as serious as those that had been set forth in the drawing room but touching peripherally on business matters, the social life of Tangier, and news from London and Paris.

Sara was kept entertained by the young shereef who sat beside her. Her first impression had been that he was a hard, cold man, ruthless perhaps, but now his tone was gentle as he divided his attention between her and *Madame* Lemaine. He spoke of his people, the countryside around Fez where he lived and inquired pleasantly into their feelings about Tangier, almost giving the impression that if something displeased them he would see to it personally that the matter was corrected. From time to time, he spoke across the table to Emilie or to Henri, and the winking emerald in his turban caught the light and shattered it into brilliant shafts that sparked in all directions. He was perfectly at ease in the European setting, a man obviously accustomed to dealing with non-Moslems.

Asheema had arranged a meal of banquet proportions, with course following course, palatable combinations of Moroccan delicacies and less spicy English fare. A variety of wines were poured by servants Emilie had never seen before, undoubtedly engaged for the occasion or who were otherwise relegated to the hinterlands of the house. They glided about on slippered feet soundlessly, knowing exactly what was expected of them and performing admirably. From beyond the arched doorway to the patio, soft strains of music threaded through the hum of conversation.

"It would give me great pleasure to show you the facilities of our bank, Your Excellency," Roderick Sloane was saying to the shereef.

Taleb al-Mu'min's eyes went to his host. "I am only in Tangier for two days," he said.

"Our business is about concluded, your Excellency," the Minister of Foreign Affairs said. "Perhaps we can arrange time on the morrow?"

"*Inch'allah*," the shereef murmured, lowering his gaze momentarily.

"Excellent, excellent." Roderick was pleased. "We will await your convenience," he said, glancing at *M'sieur* Augustin who nodded quickly and looked triumphant.

Emilie was bored with chatter of financial affairs and longed for the meal to be over. They would, she knew, return to the drawing room . . . perhaps there would be opportunity for her to slip into the garden with Henri. Thank heaven father was so preoccupied with his own affairs that he had little time to notice her. She was afraid her excitement must surely show; from time to time she caught Sara's questioning glance in her direction.

When at last the meal was over, the men retired to the library with cigars and brandy to talk business again, while the women crossed the cool patio garden to the music room. At her mother's insistence, Sara sat at the spinet piano and entertained with several selections. Emilie wandered to the door and stared into the dark garden, lighted only by four torches set in iron holders at the corners of the gallery. She could see shadows in the library and hear the low throaty sound of the men's voices. Then as she watched, a figure detached itself from the shadows and emerged under the canopy of the gallery, pausing to hold a match to a slim cigar.

Glancing around to make sure her mother and the others were absorbed in Sara's playing, Emilie slipped from the room and ran along the covered walkway, staying to the shadows until she reached Henri. He took her arm and drew her beyond the reach of the mealy torchlight. She was in his arms instantly, pressing to him and lifting her mouth to his. Their kiss was heady and searching, and Emilie trembled.

"I have been in agony all evening with you so close . . ." he whispered. His words were sweet music, and she never wanted to leave the tight circle of his arms. "When can I see you . . . ?"

160

"Anytime—soon—" She clung to him with a desperation born of the surging emotion.

He stroked her cheek, touched a finger to her quivering ps. "Will you come tomorrow morning?"

She brought her lips to his so there was no need for vords. Her body was weak with desire and she felt his ard maleness press against her thigh.

"You are a wonder of beauty tonight, and I am consumed with jealousy every time another man's eyes linger on you." One hand found the edge of the saffron bolero nd slipped beneath it to touch her bare back. She smothered a whimper of delight and gave him her lips again as he brought dizzying torment to her flesh. All thought of her own jealousy at his lateness and *M'sieur* Lemaine's eference to a young lady who claimed Henri's time was orgotten. If he had suggested they sneak from the garden hat moment, she would have agreed, heedless of the consequences.

But he did not. He separated himself from her gently. "We cannot remain here. Someone may come from the house." His smile gleamed in the pale glow of the cigar as he brought it to his lips. Smoke curled lazily in an aromatic trail. "I will wait for you tomorrow," he said softly. "Go now before your mother or sister inquires for you."

She turned unwillingly back along the gallery toward the music room. The final movement of the Chopin polanaise drifted into the garden, and she glanced back. She saw the pinpoint of Henri's cigar, and imagined she could detect its aroma even at this distance. She paused in the shadows, to catch her breath and smooth a hand across her hair before entering, then slipped into a chair near the windows. Her mother gave her a brief glance and returned her attention to Sara.

When the song was finished, the women applauded and begged Sara to play again. Blushing, she declined and was rescued by Hawley's arrival to say that the gentlemen had

gone to the drawing room and would like the ladies t
join them.

Roderick looked very pleased with himself, and Cha:
lotte knew that the business discussion had gone well. Sh
did not know its precise nature, but Roderick had cau
tioned her to pay special heed that the shereef was mad
comfortable, though what in the world he expected her t
do mystified her. She was glad she had given Asheema
free hand with the dinner menu, since the Arab gentleme
seemed to enjoy the special dishes set before them. Stil
she couldn't help wondering what it was Roderick sough:

Now as they sat for some final minutes of conversatio
before the party ended, she wondered if she should offe
permission for the Arabs to smoke their sweet-smellin
pipes. No, they had undoubtedly done so while the other
had cigars and brandy. And with Roderick looking s
content, she decided to follow a more cautious path an
say nothing.

The shereef was inquiring politely if the girls had see
the city.

"Scarcely at all," Emilie said, smiling and deliberatel
not looking at Henri for fear her emotions would be to
clearly exposed. "We have ridden about the Mountai
and through several streets, but only once have we bee
fortunate enough to be taken within the walls of the ol
city. That is the heart of Tangier, is it not?" She wa
aware of her father's gaze but she did not meet it.

"Tangier is many things. The *casbah* is the oldest sec
tion and the hub of native life, but most Europeans d
not find charm in its narrow streets and crowded quarters
The palace and mosques are quite magnificent and worth
of attention." She was struck with the intensity of hi
gaze, though his face was serene and his expression di
not change.

"I would love to see both," she declared with enthusi
asm, looking about the room as though for agreemen

162

om the others. "I have never been inside a Mosque or a
alace and would find it exciting."

The shereef's lips curled to a ghost of a smile. "It is
rbidden for unbelievers to enter a Mosque, but perhaps
can be arranged for you to visit the palace. I would
ish that pressing affairs did not demand my quick return
 Fez," he said, completing the smile he had begun ear-
er. "On my next visit I would be honoured to escort you
 the palace." His head dipped in the familiar bowing
ose.

Emilie wondered if he was sincere or merely getting out
f an awkward situation.

"I'm happy you can find time to stop by the bank to-
orrow, Your Excellency. I think you will be impressed
ith the progress we've made in just a few short weeks,"
ockerick said.

"It is so, I am certain," the shereef said without enthu-
asm.

Roderick understood the matter was no longer an inter-
sting topic of conversation, and he dropped it. It was
nough that the shereef had agreed to come by. Ibn
ashfeen was the man to impress now; his influence with
e shereef would cement relations and assure cooperation
ecessary for the venture into the interior. The bank had
e money, Cartier and Lemaine had the knowledge of
roposed railroad routes, and with the cooperation of the
linister of Foreign Affairs and the shereef, a railroad line
om Fes to Meknes and swinging westward to Rabat
ould put the Anglo-French Bank of Lyon—and Roder-
k Sloane—in an enviable financial position. The bank
ould prosper from the interest on the loan, and he
ould prosper as the major stock holder of the company.
 pleasant contemplation, most pleasant indeed.

He made a mental note to have Daniel find out when
e shereef would be in Tangier again. Another dinner
arty might encourage the Arab chieftain to fulfill his
xpressed wish to show Emilie and Sara some of the city.

Any expedition of that nature would pave the way fo
comfortable business dealings. Roderick did not underest
mate the value of two beautiful daughters in holding th
attention of those he wished to court in business. In th
meantime, he was pleasantly surprised and pleased b
young Cartier's request that he be allowed to call c
Emilie and take her to the polo matches and to dinne
He'd have a word with Emilie so that she didn't take
notion to refuse the invitation when it came. Headstro
child, but he was determined in this instance that she c
nothing to upset his carefully laid plans.

CHAPTER NINE

Emilie left the house early the following morning, too impatient to listen to the chatter between her mother and sister about the success of the party. Henri had not mentioned a time, and she dared not appear at the house before the doctor had left on his day's business.

As always, Mohamet brought his own horse as well as hers. She instructed him that this morning she would ride along the beach, and he nodded and would have set out down *Rue Belgique*, except that she held back and demanded that there must be another route through the city. The Rif looked surprised but nodded, then led the way east until they came to another street that sloped to the sparkling bay below. On the hardpacked sand where the tide had gone out, Emilie kicked the mare to a gallop and rode with her face uplifted to the wind until some of the restlessness dissipated. Slowing, she questioned Mohamet about a narrow trail that turned inward over low sandhills. He replied that it went to the hill of Shaf. At her insistence, they followed the trail and came to a splashing river which they forded easily, thence to the shade of a large hill where Mohamet reined his horse. Beyond the hill, the river curved and widened and the land

165

became a flat plain which would be a sea of mud in rain, she was sure. In the distance, she could see sma patches of what looked like gardens fenced by aloes an prickly pears. It was a tranquil sight that helped sooth her troubled spirit.

She wanted only to be with Henri, yet she wa frightened by her own lack of guilt or fear. Perhaps i was because father informed her last night that Henri ha asked permission to call and that it had been given Emilie would, her father was sure, accord him the respec his position and title demanded. Left unsaid was that Car tier was a vital link in the chain of a financial empir Sloane was forging; her father's manner gave Emilie t understand that he was interested in maintaining th young Frenchman's goodwill, and that any part she coul play in doing so was expected. She'd scarcely been able t hide her surprise, knowing the reservations her father ha voiced aboard the *Ophir* when Henri's reputation was th subject of gossip. But she welcomed the change of atti tude, since it would make life considerably simpler. Sh hadn't dared ask how soon Henri would call for fear o seeming too eager; and in actuality, she found the secre rendezvous this morning heady and exciting.

When at last they turned back toward the city, Mo hamet led her along a road that approached the hilltoj from the far side. They walked the horses at a leisurel pace, passing half a dozen streams that washed dow from the hillside and wound among rocks to dig crevice: in the sandy soil. Green grass sprouted, fed by the recen rain, and white narcissus nodded in the growing heat Emilie squinted at the sun and judged it was past ten surely late enough for her clandestine visit. Mohamet gav no sign of surprise when she turned the mare toward the French hospital and stopped before the doctor's house He led the horses around to the rear as Henri opened the door.

Henri took her in his arms at once and found her lips

166

His touch was eager and her passion surfaced instantly. His embrace fanned the fire to flames, and she clung to him with growing desire.

"You smell of sunshine and the wind," he murmured.

"I have been riding aimlessly to make the time pass more quickly."

"Then come, I have waited too long already." With an arm about her waist, he led her upstairs. There was no need for a fire on such a pleasant morning. The room was cool, the curtains drawn across the arched windows so the light was muted. He took her hat and placed it on the table, then reached for her hand and drew her to the bedroom. She had only glimpsed it on her first visit, since they had never gotten past the comfortable low divan near the fireplace. The bedroom was pleasantly furnished and as masculine in decor as the sitting room; a large bed with heavy mahogany frame and russet coverlet stood against one wall, a carved-legged table at each side holding polished brass lamps and candleholders, two matching chests with brass-handled drawers were against another wall, while a comfortable velvet-upholstered chair and ottoman occupied the space at one side of the double windows which overlooked the park. A writing table, with ink well, pens and paper laid out, stood at the opposite side. Henri went to the window and drew the drapes, masking the day to a dusky, intimate light. When he turned to look at her, he smiled and inclined his head.

She felt a rush of colour to her cheeks, a mixture of uncertain reaction to his scrutiny and her own turbulent emotions. He came toward her, his hands out for hers, which she gave willingly. His flesh was warm on her icy fingers as he drew her toward the bed. As he pulled back the coverlet, the satin sheets rustled softly. He was smiling as he began to undo the buttons of his shirt, watching her until she busied herself at the fastenings of the blue dress. Her fingers fumbled and she realized her hands were shaking.

167

Why? Was she pretending a sophistication she did not feel? She had been here before and let him bring her delight . . . why should it be different now? She concentrated on loosening the dress and slipping it off, then hanging it carefully over the chair.

His arms came around her, pressing at her hips and belly, rubbing the silk chemise over her flesh in a way that was intimate and rousing. Her breath caught and she stood very still as his hands moved upward to her full breasts. His fingers searched for the nipples that grew taut under his touch. She let her breath out in a long sigh as he pulled her close and turned her about. He was naked, his clothes tossed to the floor, and the heat of his flesh seared as he took her into his arms. Deftly he removed the chemise and claimed her naked flesh to his maleness.

"How is it possible for a woman to be so desirable, so beautiful?" he whispered.

She could not answer. Need left her trembling and breathless, weak in his arms as he led her to the bed and lifted her onto it. He sat beside her, feasting his eyes on her perfection, letting his own desire grow more urgent. Her lips moved in silent plea, and he smiled. Then they were together, bodies uniting and drawn into the fire of passion. Emilie gave herself to him completely, searching for pleasure and discovering it as his body became part of hers. She cried aloud, wordless sounds that were unmistakable demand, as she felt the hot rush of his powerful maleness.

She clung to him when he would have moved from her. Again her body had given her such exquisite delight that her mind was stunned. She was afraid to look at him for fear the glorious moment would be shattered, yet she wanted to see his sharing of her joy. She raised her face.

He was lying with eyes closed, a half-smile on his lips, his face utterly relaxed. How handsome he is, she thought, and how lucky she was to have him love her. She ut her lips to his cheek. He opened his eyes and turned azily.

"You are a wonder," he said.

She buried her face in his shoulder and hugged him close so she could twine her fingers in the sparse, dark hair of his chest. She found it exciting to touch him and o feel the residual pleasure in her body. He turned and petted her, and she was pleasantly surprised by the ingling sensation.

"I have received your father's permission to call on you, *cherie*."

"Yes, I know." She let her hand move downward on his lean body.

He laughed softly and caught her hair so that she was orced to look at him. "He has told you?"

She nodded and tried to put her lips to his but he drew out of reach with a puzzled look. "I see . . ." He spoke more to himself than to her, then smiled quickly and gave her the kiss she wanted. "That will make our tête-à-têtes more easily arranged."

"Would you have stopped seeing me otherwise?" she asked.

Smiling, he stroked her cheek. "I think perhaps you are a wanton wench after all, not the innocent I mistook you or."

She knew he was teasing but she persisted until he answered.

"Nothing could keep me away from you, my pet. But it s good to have parental approval, even though your papa might disapprove violently of your appearance and mine his moment."

She flushed and looked pensive until he drove the uncomfortable thoughts from her mind with a tender touch of fingers here and there upon her body. In moments, her preath quickened and she looked at him with surprise. She had believed her passion spent . . . and his . . .

"You look like a doe caught unaware by the flutter of

169

leaves in a lonely glen . . ." He saw her tremulous smile, and her fingers tensed on his flesh.

"I did not know—"

"You do now, eh?" His hands were arousing her once more, rekindling the fires that had been smouldering under the surface of her emotions.

"Yes . . ." She was eager for him and did not try to hide her feelings. She offered her lips, her body, and welcomed him when at last he moved over her. She sighed as his heat entered her, and then she was soaring to new heights to meet his demands. The ecstasy was prolonged and heady, a gathering storm of passion that gripped her and tossed her in an emotional sea which swallowed her totally. When at last it released her, she lay spent and sated.

Henri rose and absented himself to the bath, returning some time later wearing a dressing gown of black brocaded silk. He looked down at her, enjoying the sight of her magnificent body which had delivered promised pleasure. She made no move to cover herself, and he smiled. She was enough to drive a man mad with wanting her—and with having her. He crossed to the writing table and took a thin cigarette from the silver box, striking a match and holding the flame close. He inhaled deeply as Emilie stirred and opened her eyes.

"Are you expected home for the noonday meal?" he inquired lazily.

Startled, she sat up. "I'd forgotten!" All at once she scrambled from the bed and rushed to pick up her clothing.

He laughed and shook his head. "There are a thousand excuses one can give for tardiness."

She looked at him and had to laugh when she saw the expression on his face. "Yes, I suppose. But I might find it difficult to mask my feelings if mother or father were to question me closely."

"I am pleased that I have discovered such passion in

170

ou . . ." He took her in his arms briefly, holding her
lose and kissing her gently.

She sighed and one of her shoes slipped from her grasp
o clatter to the floor unnoticed. If only she could stay
. . He kissed her more lingeringly and she felt the rush
f her pulse, the warm radiance of love.

"Henri . . . how I long to be with you always. . . ."

He did not answer, but even his silence was comforting.
She felt secure in his arms, and very loved. When at last
he released her, she retreated to the bath.

Sara continued to spend afternoons at the hospital with
Martine, and she found the visits enjoyable. They also
gave her a feeling of accomplishment, something she'd
never had before. It seemed her life had been empty
until now, unproductive, a waiting time that was filled
with inconsequentials. Now, though she realized her efforts were small, she was rewarded by the smiles of
bedridden patients, cheerful greetings from the men who
had come to know her and wait for her visits. She was especially pleased with Paul Chaugal. The incident of the
broken vase seemed completely forgotten, and he accepted her reintroduction into his small world with a
ready welcome. He asked her to read to him and sat quietly as she continued the poems of Browning that Martine
had begun. The soldier's attention span varied; sometimes
he tired quickly and fell asleep in his chair; other days, he
would not let her leave until one of the nurses or doctors
came to take him back to the ward. Sara was always patient, speaking in quiet tones, and she began to hope that
his private nightmare was easing.

One afternoon, when Paul had fallen asleep in the
chair, his chin on his chest, Sara closed the book and
slipped from the solarium. There still might be time to play
a game of chess with Marcel Duran, an old soldier who had
been blinded in one eye during a battle with a band of
Berber tribesmen. They had played before, and Marcel,

171

who quickly caught on to her ruse of letting him win, challenged her.

"To lose honestly is not defeat," he said solemnly, and he extracted her promise that thenceforth she would play to the best of her capabilities.

She stopped at the room where a kettle was kept boiling so that nurses and doctors who had time might pause for tea. At one side of the room was a table of games and writing materials; a small bookcase held a dozen books which were the property of Martine and others but kept on hand for patients who enjoyed reading fare beyond the periodicals and newspapers that were delivered to the hospital. Sara slipped the leather-bound volume of Browning into its space and gathered up the chess board and box of onyx chessmen. She heard the whisper of the door and turned to find Pierre Louvel smiling at her.

"You have become one of our most faithful workers," he said.

"I enjoy it."

"I only regret that our paths so seldom cross. Do you have time for a cup of tea?"

She was about to refuse, thinking of Marcel Duran, then reconsidered. She had not had an opportunity to talk with Pierre since the evening of the promenade and their chat during the ride home.

"Yes. Here, let me fix it." She set aside the chess game and busied herself with the kettle and a small blue onion patterned tea pot. "You look tired," she commented as he lowered himself into a cushioned wicker chair with a long sigh.

He shrugged. "I suppose, but there is so much to be done."

"Doctor du Bois says you push yourself too hard."

Pierre's sandy brows lifted. "Have you been discussing me with the director?"

She smiled. "Not discussing, but we have spoken of

you. He is full of praise for the work you do in the laboratory and for your skills as a surgeon. He claims the hospital has made tremendous strides in reputation since your arrival. He hopes too that you do not take a notion to find an easier or perhaps more rewarding practice elsewhere."

Pierre leaned forward to accept the tea. "I enjoy my work too much to consider leaving—and I suspect Doctor du Bois knows that." He smiled and some of the tension disappeared. "I have seen you here several times but have not been able to catch you before you vanished. Tell me, how is it you are willing to devote so much time to this work? Are you not kept busy with social engagements?"

She hesitated. "None that takes precedence over my desire to share time with your patients."

"You do very well with them. Paul Chaugal shows marked improvement since you have begun visiting. I am told that you read to him often."

"He enjoys it so . . ."

"And it is very beneficial. There has not been another attack such as the one you witnessed on your first visit."

"Does that mean he is well?"

He sipped the fragrant mint tea. "It is too soon to make any claim of cure, but the longer the span between flares of violence, the better his chances of complete recovery. It is impossible to know what goes on within his mind, but time may heal what medicine cannot." He sat back and closed his eyes as the tea relaxed him. He was tired, and it was pleasant to pass a few minutes in pleasant companionship. He was still surprised at how at ease he was with Sara; often he was not with women. He hoped he and Sara would become freinds. She was so different from her sister. He wondered if Sara knew that Emilie was seeing Henri. He supposed so—Henri had the father's permission, and they walked and rode often. If only his own work were not so demanding, he might enjoy such pleasant pastimes with Sara. Thinking about it made him sigh.

173

"What is it?" She'd been watching the strain ease from his face, but all at once it returned in full measure and he sat up.

"I am due on my rounds. I must go." He finished the tea. Getting to his feet, he stood gazing at her a moment. "Will you join me for tea at the Hotel Cecil this evening? I finish my rounds about six—if that's not too late for you? Perhaps you are expected home?"

She smiled. "I can send a note to mother so that she will not be concerned. I would be delighted to have tea, Pierre."

"Good. I shall meet you here at about six. I can call a sedan chair—"

"I would like to walk if you're not too tired."

He laughed. "I could not be so tired that I would not enjoy a leisurely stroll with a pretty young lady. At six then?"

She nodded and he was gone. She stood staring at the door several minutes before she rinsed the tea cups at the small sink, then took up the chess set and headed for the ward.

He was late by a quarter hour, full of apologies which Sara brushed aside.

"I have only arrived myself. I've been playing chess with Marcel Duran and find him a formidable opponent."

"So he has maneuvered you into competing with him. Crafty devil."

"He lulled me into thinking he was a mediocre player, now he keeps me at my wits end," she said, tying the bonnet strings beneath her chin and letting Pierre place a lacy green shawl over her shoulders.

"His mind has not given the slightest way to the illness that ravages his body."

"Illness? I thought his problem the loss of sight—?"

"True, but he also suffers from a recurring malady of the chest. We have performed surgery, but there is little

174

we can do to halt the malignancy. He knows and accepts his condition but does not like to speak of it. If it helps to make his last weeks pleasant, it is a small wish to grant."

She felt suddenly defenseless. How little she knew! She had accepted Marcel Duran's cheerfulness and good humour at face value, talked with him of going home and the life he would live. She was unaccustomed to pain and misery—or to bravery. It was disturbing to think how fragile life was, how delicately balanced between pain and pleasure.

"I've made you frown," Pierre said. "I am an idiot to speak of such matters when we are embarking on a pleasant afternoon. Come, I promise not to broach another somber subject—upon my word." He took her hand and they left the hospital to walk down *Rue Belgique*.

They sat at a table near a wrought iron railing from where they could see the crenellated wall of the ancient city against the western sky and the shifting designs of sunlight and clouds as the day drew to an end. Despite his promise, Pierre could not keep from discussing his work, and he did not realize that Sara skillfully led him to do so with her quiet questions and penetrating interest.

"How is it you never went into nursing?" he asked. "You have a natural aptitude, I think."

"It never occurred to me," she said honestly. "I was not brought up with thoughts of a career."

"So you let talent lie fallow?"

She blushed. "That is the second time you have accused me of that fault."

"Not accusation but observation."

"I sent a note around to *M'sieur* Prichard as you suggested. He has invited me to a small exhibition of his paintings and is willing to discuss the matter of lessons."

"Excellent, excellent. You will go, of course?"

"I would not be permitted without an escort and father—"

"I shall take you myself! When is it to be?" He was as excited as a child.

"The last Sunday in July."

"I give you my word that nothing will prevent me from attending, though I shall probably have to leave notes all about the house and hospital for myself. My memory is notoriously bad." He took a pad from his pocket and scribbled with a stub of pencil he unearthed from another pocket. He put them away. "I am delighted that you took my advice and I am sure you will find *M'sieur* Prichard an excellent instructor. He has an international reputation."

The sun disappeared beyond the horizon and redcoated waiters moved about the café lighting lamps that cast a soft glow. The time had passed so quickly Sara could not imagine where the evening had gone. It had been the most pleasant she had ever spent, and she was sorry to see it end.

Emilie found her life so changed that she wondered if she were the same girl who had come from London. She saw Henri at least twice a week, riding with him among the hills south of the city—blessedly free of Mohamet's watchful scrutiny, since father considered the young Frenchman proper escort and was privately assured by Henri that he carried a pistol at his belt whenever he ventured out. Henri took her to a polo match at the wide field laid out on the hill overlooking the Straits of Gibraltar, and they sat on a thick blanket Henri brought to cushion the crude benches. Emilie found it difficult to concentrate on the game with Henri so close, but she listened dutifully as he told her that the sport had originated in Persia and had more recently been copied by British officers in India who brought it to England and the continent. He was knowledgeable, explaining rules, chukkers, handicaps and the extensive training required to ready ponies for the game. Henri's interest in sports was obvious and when she inquired if he planned to play polo while in Tangier, he shook his head, smiling, and squeezed her hand.

"Not when I can spend my time so pleasantly with you, *cherie.*"

Whenever they could steal a moment away from prying eyes he held her hand or dared to kiss her in promise of what was to come. Their private times grew more relaxed as Emilie lost her fears and let her heart rule her head. Though she was still extremely circumspect about their meetings, she came to Henri whenever he asked, lying in his arms in the shaded bedroom of his apartment and learning the ways of love for which her heart and body yearned. She murmured against his warm flesh, declaring her love, and he held her close and whispered her name.

July passed in a lazy swirl of days that became a pattern of real and anticipated pleasure. When she was not with Henri, Emilie's mind was filled with thoughts of him, counting the hours or minutes until she would be with him again. When she was obliged to accompany her family to some affair or other where Henri was not present, she was bored and restless, and only the knowledge that she would see him soon kept her content.

The change in his daughter was not unnoticed by Roderick Sloane. Had she met a man at last who could tame her wild spirit? She was seeing Cartier often, and Roderick hoped the friendship would blossom into romance. Henri Cartier had not yet committed himself in the matter of the Pendash venture. Roderick and Daniel Augustin had made the financial arrangements, and the Minister of Foreign Affairs assured them of the cooperation of the young shereef through whose lands the tracks would be laid. Roderick spent considerable time with Lemaine and Cartier, but the two continued to delay in finalizing the plan. Their backing was vital to assure that the French would not hinder development of the planned spur line that came dangerously close to being a violation of the agreement with the Sultan. If he could entice young Cartier to put capital into the scheme as well as his political support, he would safeguard his own investment doubly.

And if Emilie married the chap, there would be little chance of Cartier withdrawing support at a crucial stage.

CHAPTER TEN

Sara looked forward to the exhibit at *M'sieur* Prichard's gallery on *Rue des Vignes*. When out on an errand one day, she had ridden past the building expecting to find a gallery similar to the ones she knew in London, discreet windows, an oil or two on easels draped with velvet. She hoped to acquaint herself with the artist's style so that she could talk with him when the opportunity presented itself at the show.

The first time she rode past, she was sure she had the number or street wrong, since there was nothing that remotely resembled a gallery or proper shop. The street was a mixture of typical Arab houses with blank walls facing the narrow street, and an occasional European building to break the monotony. She actually hesitated before a low Spanish villa, convinced that despite the name lettered on the gate, it must be the artist's house, and that his gallery and studio were incorporated in his living quarters. But there was no indication of the painter or his work, and she rode on in disappointment.

When the day of the exhibit finally came, it began with a dazzling sunrise that blushed the sky pink before the heat blanched it milky blue. At midmorning, clouds rolled along the horizon, gathering over the sea to roil and sweep inland on a cool breeze as a storm drenched the coastline and settled the dust. It lasted less than a half hour; when it passed, the sky was brilliant in its wake.

Sara watched from the window, her face lifted to the cool breeze. She had come to enjoy the quick violent storms, the sudden changes of nature that marked an unchanging land. She had spent considerable time these past weeks at her drawing, studying her own work with a critical eye, trying to determine if she really possessed a talent worth notice. Not on a professional level, of course; she had no delusions about following her interest to that extent. But if she was to take lessons—a prospect she had not yet broached to father—she wanted to be sure the money would not be wasted, no matter how small the amount.

She had never shown anyone her work except the few instructresses of art that school had offered. Emilie had seen it, of course, and mother and father, but none of them evidenced more than polite interest. Only Pierre Louvel had remarked on her ability and encouraged her.

She smiled thinking of him and the outing they would share this afternoon. She recognized that her feelings toward Pierre had grown beyond friendship these past weeks. She looked forward to seeing him at the hospital or their occasional chance meetings in other places. She returned often to the spot on the hill where she had met him while sketching, not admitting it was with the hope of seeing him, but he did not come by. He had taken her to tea only the one time, but she realized how busy his schedule was. She was content to share a few minutes in the lounge or solarium at the hospital with him when she could, and to idle spare moments with thoughts of him.

She brought herself from her daydreams and began to ready herself for the afternoon. The exhibit would begin at four, as soon as people began stirring. Pierre had promised to take her to dinner afterwards at a very pleasant café in the ancient city which, he assured her, served exquisite food that delighted the palate.

She dressed with care, choosing a light gown of fine linen the weight of a cobweb and the colour of pale forget-me-nots beside a stream. It flared gently at her hips and fell in loose folds at her ankles. There was only one layer of crinoline at the back so the gown followed the natural curves of her body, including the snug bodice ornamented with tiny embroidered violets. The neckline was rounded, low enough to be cool without being daring, and the sleeves were short and full at the shoulders. She chose a small black straw hat that perched atop the bouffant hairdo from which Jenny plucked a single curl at each side to fall in front of her ears. Jenny insisted on a pale lavender parasol and lace gloves to complete the outfit, and Sara agreed with a willingness that surprised her. She had never before taken such pains to look her best, and when at last she surveyed herself in the glass, she was pleased.

"You look lovely, Miss Sara," Jenny said, eyes wide and hands clasped before her like a child viewing an unattainable toy displayed in a shop window.

"Thank you, Jenny."

Pierre was punctual despite his fears. His Sunday schedule was light, with only emergencies to upset the routine of ward rounds and consultations.

Asheema let him into the drawing room, and Sara appeared moments later. She was beautiful in a wispy lavender gown that accented her fair colouring, and he smiled and took her hand.

"The afternoon is warm so I have taken the liberty of bringing a sedan chair. If you prefer to walk later, we can."

"I can't tell you how excited I am at meeting *M'sieur* Prichard. I've been working at my sketches . . ." She pulled on her gloves.

181

"Here, let me carry your portfolio." He took the folder from her and tucked it under his arm.

"I am embarrassed to show my work."

"No need to be. He will like it, I'm sure."

She appreciated his thoughtfulness and reassurance, and realized again how much she enjoyed his company. She'd never known a man like him and never felt the way she did now. She reined her thoughts as they left the house and entered the sedan chair at the arched gateway. Pierre had never spoken of his feelings, and she was sure that he considered her no more than a casual friend and a pleasant companion when his work permitted him a few moments. Martine declared Pierre had never shown as much interest in any woman before . . . yet Sara dared not hope.

The ride to the gallery was brief and they sat in companionable silence in the gently bobbing chair that rose and fell with the running pace of the bearers. The morning storm had washed the city clean, leaving it dazzling in the sun; the pounding feet of the slaves raised no dust on the damp road. The fragrance of jasmine drifted from English gardens along *Rue de Fes*, and the soft rustle of greenery whispered to chattering birds. Each time Sara traveled here she was impressed by the contrast between the lush foliage that defined the foreign sector and the starkness of the native houses where no trees, no growing plant showed outside the white walls.

The runners slowed as they approached the curve of the *Rue des Vignes* where Sara had looked in vain for Prichard's studio. To her surprise, they stopped before a building crammed in a row of identical structures, flat walls facing the street with only alleyways between to give access to what lay beyond. Pierre paid the men and helped Sara from the chair.

She stared at the building and Pierre smiled. *"M'sieur* Prichard's . . ."

"He is French . . ."

"He prefers to live in here in order to capture the essence of Tangier."

He led her under an archway and through the narrow alley that turned twice before opening suddenly into a garden that was a riot of colours and fragrances. A twisted fig tree at one corner spread its leafy arms to shade half the terraced garden, which fell away to a squat white house on the hillside. The house was not large and seemed to angle in all directions as though the builder had been unable to make up his mind. A path of flat white stones cut randomly through beds of flowering cacti to the door.

The sound of tinkling glasses and laughter floated from open windows where curtains had been drawn back. People milled about inside, coming into view momentarily, then disappearing into the shadows to become disembodied voices.

As they entered, a tall thin man with white hair and a pencil-thin mustache turned to greet them.

"You are Sara Sloane . . ."

"Yes." She was surprised at his knowing her name.

"I am delighted that you could come. Pierre, good to see you again. You have been remiss in paying social calls to old friends."

He had not told her they were friends . . . She smiled nervously, and was quickly reassured by Pierre's easy manner and the artist's warm welcome.

"I see you have brought some of your work. Good . . . good . . . Let me take it. I will look at it and we can discuss it before you leave. Now, please, make yourselves at home. Pierre, you know your way about . . ." Smiling, M'sieur Prichard left them as a middle-aged couple arrived and he greeted them.

A waiter in scarlet coat and pantaloons, gleaming ebony face topped by a white turban, bare feet twined with gold cord about the toes and ankles, offered a tray of apertifs.

183

Pierre took two, handing one to Sara with a smile. "How one is expected to drink and walk about to view paintings at the same time disturbs my sense of orderliness. Women are always more proficient at these things . . ."

She sipped the delicate, sweet wine as they walked toward the first of the paintings hung on the wall near the entry hall. It was a striking oil of a magnificent white stallion ridden by an Arab in flowing white robes. The shadowed contrasts in the painting were more perfectly executed than any Sara had ever seen, and she was impressed with the excellence of *M'sieur* Prichard's work.

She was equally impressed with the house. She'd never been inside a true Moorish house. She'd supposed they were similar to her own, but she realized now that the Sloane residence had been considerably modernized along European lines.

The entry was a spacious hall, the floors tiled in dark mosaics, the walls white except for the row of tiles along the ceiling coping which blended orange and blue beneath an intricately carved ceiling. At one end of the hall, a recessed alcove contained a low sofa and cushioned chairs with a silver coffee service on a low table of inlaid mosaics. People were milling about, glasses in hand, chatting in small groups or moving toward the room beyond where easels had been set up and paintings hung along the walls for display. The room was large, with carved pillars and demi-arches. Several divans were grouped around Persian rugs which covered a woven floor matting; heavy brass candlelabra stood on tables at the corners, and a chandelier of several dozen candles was suspended in the center of the room and could be raised or lowered by a heavy black chain caught in a bracket at the wall. Other than the gallery of pictures hung along the east wall, the remaining walls were bare except for one fine tapestry so delicately done it seemed to be the work of an expert calligrapher.

The entire assemblage was European, which surprised

Sara. She would have thought wealthy Moroccans might patronize the well-known artist and would certainly be invited to the exhibit. She glanced about wondering if she knew anyone but did not. Several people moved on and a space cleared, and she became absorbed in a painting on a tall easel. It was even more dramatic than the first, and she studied it. The canvas showed a street in the native quarter, narrow and crowded with people who seemed to spill from the canvas. Veiled women, eyes downcast, robed men, a slave leading a reluctant camel. That Prichard had been able to fill a canvas so well with teeming life amazed Sara, and as she continued to admire it, she became aware of details that had escaped at first glance. The colours were muted in the shadows, brilliant in the shafts of sunlight where it fell between houses.

"Do you like Serge's work?" Pierre asked.

"It is marvelous! I am ashamed to ask him to waste time on my pitiful attempts—"

He shook his head and would not let her finish. "No more of that. We will let Serge be the judge of your talent. Now look, here's one quite different . . ." He put his hand to her arm and moved on to the next painting, a landscape that showed the desolation of the arid region beyond the city, a rocky hillside and windswept plain.

From time to time as they made their way around the room, Pierre paused to introduce her to someone—a doctor from the hospital, a Spanish diplomat and his wife, two nurses who had recently returned from furloughs at home. They also met several English and French consulate members and a M'sieur Augustin, her father's business partner. He looked surprised to see Sara.

"I did not know you were interested in art, mademoiselle, else I would have made arrangements for you to meet some of our local artists before this." He looked at Pierre, frowning to remember his name. Sara supplied an introduction and *M'sieur* Augustin bowed. "Of course, we

185

have met before. Is your father attending the exhibit?" he asked Sara.

"No, he is at the polo matches."

"Please give him my regards . . ." The little man drifted away, taking a full glass from a tray carried by a striking black girl. Pierre watched him with a strange look.

"Does your father do business with *M'sieur* Augustin?" he asked.

"They are partners. Why do you ask?"

Pierre looked away from the Frenchman with a quick smile. "Curiosity, nothing more."

She was completely enchanted by the exhibition, about twenty-four paintings in all and two pencil sketches that were almost hidden in a small alcove at the far end of the room. When they had seen them all, Pierre led her to a room which was obviously the artist's studio.

It was bare except for a large easel on which a partially finished canvas stood. Pots, brushes, cleaning cloths and a palette cluttered the top of a cupboard stained with multi-hued dribbles and spatters. The room was at an angle to the gallery so that it caught the north light through high arched windows, and though the ceiling and arches were richly carved, the room had a stark look as if the artist wanted nothing to intrude on his creativity. Almost unnoticed in one corner, an alcove held two Moorish divans of somber colours. Near it, canvases were stacked against the wall.

"The crowd is beginning to thin," Pierre said, "Serge will be along shortly. You don't mind waiting a few minutes?"

"Of course not."

"Good. Would you care to sit?"

"I'd like to look around, that is if you don't think *M'sieur* Prichard would mind?"

"Not at all." He watched as she moved about the room, glancing at the work on the easel, tilting her head

186

to study the picture of a camel caravan crossing the desert, though the suggestion of the animals was just beginning to be formed. She looked so intent, Pierre had to smile. With the light behind her, her hair took on a coppery glow. The small hat created shadows across her face that gave her a pensive air. She was quite beautiful, he thought, and at this moment he almost wished his work were not so demanding.

She moved away from the easel and glanced from a tall arched window to the garden outside. There was no view of other houses; the studio might be isolated in time and place from the rest of the world. Sara had not felt so at peace since leaving England, but when she tried to examine her thoughts, the peacefulness gave way to a disturbing awareness of the man who stood across the room from her. As he watched her, her emotions gave fuel to imagination, and she drew herself up short. Pierre had consented to escort her for the afternoon, nothing more. She must not read unspoken—unbelievable—meaning into his actions. She smiled and turned back.

"There is no view from the window. *M'sieur* Prichard must do his sketching elsewhere."

"It is forbidden by Moslem law that any Moroccan window overlook another's house."

"Really? How odd . . ."

He smiled. "Just as it is forbidden that the human form be depicted in art. Have you not noticed that no Moroccan house contains pictures of people or animals? They confine themselves to geometrics and calligraphy."

"So no Moroccans are at this exhibit!"

"Precisely, though I am told that some of the wealthy modern men depart from custom enough to invest in the works of great masters. There's a persistent rumour that the Sultan's palace contains a room filled with western art works valued at millions of francs."

"Do you believe the rumour?"

He shrugged. "I have never given it much thought. I

187

believe the Sultan is as much concerned with his own wealth and welfare as he is with that of the people he rules. He is manipulated by foreign powers and cleverly used to promote outside interests in the name of his own people"

"I do not understand," Sara said.

Pierre sighed. "My country's government disclaims any intention of interfering in the internal affairs of Morocco, yet it occupies the whole of the Shawiya district and extracts interest on monstrous debts that the Sultan can never pay. England and Germany are no better. Each wants a slice of this poor country that has not asked for, nor I suspect wants, the help pushed upon it."

"How long can Morocco exist in the old way? The twentieth century is one of modern factories and transportation. This country cannot grow until it, too, develops these."

"And what will Morocco do with its railroads and factories? How will it produce without technological aid from foreign powers? So you see, to faster progress, Morocco must let us help, and we lend money that makes it impossible for the country to act independently because we must watch over our investment. Is it Morocco we are interested in, or the profit to be made on their ignorance and easy maneuverability?" He saw the concerned look on her face and realized that he was, in essence, condemning the system that had brought her here. "Forgive me, I meant no disrespect to your father or to his work. It is not an individual deceit but a national one we play. Many of my own countrymen do the same or worse, including some of my close friends. But enough chatter of subjects that dim the light in your eyes. We came to enjoy the afternoon and I am spoiling it. Ah, here is Serge."

The artist came into the room carrying Sara's portfolio. The strings were untied and he had obviously been looking at the sketches and watercolors.

"The last guest is leaving," he said with a smile. "I

suppose if one intends to earn a living from his work, he must endure these exhibitions but I am always relieved when they end. I much prefer to be at peace in the world of my canvases." He indicated the alcove. "I've ordered tea. Please seat yourself comfortably, Sara. I may call you Sara?" At her quick nod, he smiled again. "Good, good . . . I think we will be friends."

Sara still found it awkward to manage the low cushions but she tucked her legs under and settled back. Pierre sat at her side while Serge Prichard took the opposite corner of the divan so that he was facing them. He opened the portfolio and went through the pictures slowly, inspecting each, turning them so they caught the light, sometimes holding one off at arm's length for a better view. He pursed his lips and once he frowned.

"You have an excellent eye for colour and your perspective is good." He nodded, turning to yet another sketch. "Yes, quite good. Have you studied at all?"

"Only at the school I attended where the art mistress was more academic than artist. She encouraged and seldom corrected."

"I see. Well, I think you are right, Pierre. This young lady has a talent worth developing. If she is willing to work hard." He gazed at Sara.

Amazed, she looked from Serge to Pierre and felt her face warm. "I don't know what to say—"

"Then say you will work," Pierre said. "When can she begin, Serge?" Pierre was quietly efficient, taking Sara's agreement as a matter of course. He saw she was pleased with Serge's appraisal of her work and his admiration. She looked like a child who had just been given a sweet. He laughed gently. "Sara?"

"Yes, of course I will work. I cannot tell you how honored I am—"

Serge said, "I am a hard taskmaster and I demand the best you can give. Ah, here is our tea."

A black girl dressed in peach muslin set the tea tray on

189

a low brass table and busied herself with the pot, crushing fresh mint leaves and pouring boiling water from a long-spouted kettle. The girl sat on her haunches to arrange delicate glass cups on tiny saucers while the tea steeped.

"I suggest one lesson a week to start," Serge said. "Would Wednesday be convenient?"

"Yes, of course."

"Good. I'll expect you about one. The light is best then and we can escape the heat by working indoors." He was silent as the girl passed cups and offered a tray of tiny pastries. Serge popped one into his mouth and chewed, talking the while. "No need to bring brushes or canvas, I've enough to get you started. Make a list of supplies you have at home, so we can supplement them from my own stock or when I next place an order in Paris."

When she tried to protest, the artist waved off her words and she was silent. Pierre smiled reassuringly to tell her she had nothing to fear, all details were arranged.

"Now tell me where you have been keeping yourself, my friend," Serge said to Pierre. "And what of the journey to Fez? Are you still bent on that foolishness or have you given up the idea?"

Pierre shrugged. "I am too involved at the moment to leave my work but I have not abandoned the idea totally. Perhaps next year."

"Madness." Serge looked at Sara, who was confused by the conversation's abrupt change of course. "Our medical friend is a slave to the notion that he must carry his work to the ends of this beautiful but forsaken country, and he wants to go to the interior to establish a hospital!" He shook his head and looked paternal. "A clear case of talent taking over the man. Madness and genius are closely akin, eh?"

"No need to bore Sara with my work," Pierre said. "I'm afraid she is much too patient a listener and allows

190

me to prattle endlessly. I would prefer to talk of other matters. Was the exhibit successful?"

Serge let himself be drawn back to the subject of art. "I sold six canvases. Enough to keep me in materials and food for another year. I can hardly ask more." He drank some tea and popped another pastry into his mouth.

"When are you going back to Paris to exhibit?"

Serge frowned and licked a crumb from his lip. "I am not ready. I do not feel I have completed my work here. I have many more pictures I wish to do."

"But you've done so many wonderful canvases," Sara said.

He shrugged. "Let me show you my real work." He drained the cup and returned it to the tray then rose from his cross-legged position in a fluid motion to cross to the stacked canvases in the corner. "Come here."

Pierre helped her to her feet. The artist was drawing out several canvases from the stack and propping them along the bare wall. "See, I have merely begun."

The paintings were of a mosque, one of the colnnaded court dotted with figures of men bowed in prayer, heads bent to prayer mats; another of a minaret outlined against the sunset, with the small figure of the *muezzin* calling his message from the parapet; still another of a veiled woman in a shadowed doorway opening onto an opulent harem.

"Tangier is so many things it is impossible to put them into a single canvas, so I must keep working until I have captured life in all its facets."

"But you have!" Sara was aghast at his depreciation of his own work.

Pierre smiled mockingly. "Madness and genius . . . blood brothers."

The artist threw back his head and a laugh rolled from his throat. His humor was infectious and Sara could not suppress a smile.

"Yes, my friend. We are all a bit mad and perhaps the world is a better place for it." He sighed heavily. "Can I

191

request the pleasure of your company for dinner this evening? My housekeeper makes a passable pigeon pie."

"I have already asked Sara to dine with me at the Café Royale."

Serge's brows were white arches almost reaching his hairline. "Then I shall not intrude."

"You are welcome to join us," Pierre said.

"No . . . enjoy yourselves and I will relax with a carafe of wine and a pipe of *kif*. Another time. Thank you for bringing so charming a guest to grace my studio, friend." Turning to Sara, Serge took her hand and pressed it to his lips. "A pleasant evening, Sara, and when you come on Wednesday, I promise you I will be far less charming and put you to work at once. If your father is concerned about the reputation of so young and beautiful a daughter spending hours in the company of an artist, feel free to bring along a chaperone. I accept the idea of being considered a danger to any young lady, since it is flattering despite my years." He squeezed her hand and then walked with them through the gallery, empty now except for the faint odor of cigarette smoke.

"Good day, Sara, Pierre. Until we meet again."

Throughout dinner, Sara proclaimed her delight at being able to study under Serge Prichard. She was sure father would permit it; he need only investigate the man's reputation to know what a wonderful opportunity it was for her. She had asked nothing for herself since their arrival in Tangier—or for many years, as a matter of fact. Surely he would agree to this simple request. With a start, she realized she had not discussed the cost of the lessons with the artist. Stricken, she questioned Pierre.

He shook his head. "I think he is delighted to have a hand in the molding of a fine artist. His fee will be modest."

"Father will insist on proper payment for the lessons."

"Then your father can make arrangements with Serge.

ow, what will you order? The chicken here is especially
licate."

They dined and talked of many things, and when at last
erre helped her from the sedan chair at the gate of the
ouse at *el-Kabir* road, Sara could not recall a day so
easantly spent in her whole life.

CHAPTER ELEVEN

On a beastly hot day in August, Emilie spent the mornir
at home trying to escape the oppressive heat that cradle
the city in winds born of a furnace rather than the se
There had not been a cooling shower for almost a for
night, and the air was dry and dusty, settling a gray fil
over the city. In the ancient quarters, processions of tl
faithful wailed pleas to Allah to send the grace of rain.

When father returned from the bank at noon, he brol
his usual routine by going upstairs to bathe and chan;
suit and shirt before descending for lunch.

Emilie would have enjoyed a quiet meal that left her
her lethargy and thoughts of Henri. She was to see him t
morrow, and the anticipation almost equaled the actualit
She would have gone to him every day if it were possibl
but Henri declared there were other matters that d
manded his attention—the business venture with her f
ther, for one. So she had to content herself with seei
him once or twice a week, but the heady intoxication
these hours carried her through the other days.

As soon as she entered the dining room, she knew h
wish was not to be granted. There was an air of expecta
cy in the room. Father looked up from his place ar

eeted her with a smile instead of his usual indifferent
ance.

"Be seated Emilie. Asheema, you may have the girls
rve now."

Emilie took her place and glanced at Sara who gave an
mperceptible shrug and a puzzled look. She too had noted
he change in father's manner and wondered at its cause.
harlotte sat looking at the girls and at her husband, her
yes bright but with a tiny crease across her brow. It was
bvious she had some hint of what was to come.

Roderick waited until they had completed the first
ourse, fresh oysters nestled in half shells laid upon a bed
f ice, before he introduced the topic of conversation.

"Taleb al Mu'min has returned to Tangier," he said,
oking at each of them to be sure they recognized the
ame of the shereef whose cooperation was so necessary
o the success of the Pendash Company. "I had not ex-
ected him until after the Fast of Ramadan, but other
usiness has necessitated an earlier visit. He was kind
nough to stop at the bank this morning to pay his re-
ects."

Emilie wondered if they were to be subjected to a dis-
ussion of business through the entire meal. She recalled
he shereef distinctly, handsome to a fault but disdainful
nd remote as though he really was a descendant of the
loslem god he claimed by birth.

Roderick inspected the salad set before him and
odded approval to Asheema, who stood at the doorway
pervising the two girls serving the meal. The salad lay
n a bed of fresh green lettuce, crisp vegetables cut in
ny slivers and tiny shrimp with a delicate dressing of oil,
ream and spices.

"The shereef has been kind enough to recall his
romise to escort you to the Royal palace and to the *cas-
ah*," Roderick said, glancing at his daughters before he
icked up the fork and tasted the salad. "You will meet
im at five this afternoon at the palace. It is all arranged."

195

Emilie recovered from her shock first. "Meet him at the palace?"

"He will send bearers and a chair. He regrets that the Sultan is not in residence, but you will have his personal escort through as many rooms of the palace as are open for visitors."

"And the *casbah*?" Emilie asked, still scarcely believing the words coming from her father's lips. They had been forbidden to venture anywhere inside the walls, forbidden to see the *casbah* even with escort until now. The shereef's goodwill must be very important indeed to bring about so sudden a change in father's attitude.

Roderick cleared his throat and sampled the cool salad again before replying. "Since it was your wish to see it, I find this the perfect opportunity. The shereef is an influential man who is always surrounded by numerous servants and bodyguards. You will be in no danger while in his company."

The line on Charlotte's brow deepened but she stared at her plate and said nothing. Roderick had informed her of his decision and the matter was settled. Her fears were of no interest to him.

Emilie glanced at Sara, still stunned by the announcement. How like father to simply announce that he had made plans for their day. Sara had been at the hospital all morning, and Emilie knew her plan had been to return when the midday heat had passed.

Sara blinked and tendered a small smile. "It sounds very pleasant, father. Let us hope the day cools a bit by then." She offered no resistance since she knew it would do no good. She would send a message to Martine not to expect her.

"Not many English or Europeans have the honour of seeing the palace in such distinguished company. I'm sure you understand the importance of the shereef's hospitality. You have my permission to have dinner with him if such an invitation is forthcoming."

Surprise compounded surprise. Father had never before given a blanket permission for anything. Emilie felt a tide of annoyance that he would humble himself so completely to Taleb al Mu'min.

The heat had not eased by evening, and Emilie wore a dress of pale yellow dimity with lavender ribbons at the rounded neckline and very short puffed sleeves. She chose a wide-brimmed, natural straw hat and comfortable soft kid slippers with slender heels. She wore only a single petticoat and a batiste chemise underneath, in the hope that she would not swelter before the evening was over.

Sara wore a lightweight gown of pale green linen, and a white organdy hat with a cluster of green flowers at one side. She wore white lace gloves and carried a green purse into which she tucked several linen handkerchiefs to use to wipe her face and hands. It seemed impossible to stay spotless in the unrelenting heat and dust.

The sedan chair sent for them was spectacular in every way. Neither had ever seen such a grand conveyance since arriving in Tangier. Roderick, who remained at home to make sure his daughters were punctual, was extremely pleased. The shereef had obviously sent a palace chair, purple and crimson in colour, with finely tooled engraving on the wood inlaid with beaten gold that caught the sun's rays and splintered light in a hundred directions. Two runners dressed in white pantaloons with yellow sashes, brilliant red shirts with high collars and gold buttons, preceded the chair carried by four burly slaves in purple pantaloons and black sashes, barefooted, naked chests glistening with sweat. Each runner carried a stout whip to clear the path as they raced ahead.

The ride was as smooth as a railroad carriage in London. The slaves moved in perfect rhythm so the riders were not jostled nor tossed about in the slightest. Both Emilie and Sara were too surprised to do more than gape as they were carried along, first through the tree-lined European sector, then along the *Grand Socco* and through *Bab Fahs* into the Street of the Goldsmiths. Shadows were already beginning to creep along the narrow streets, and the ragged outlines of the *casbah* were visible only at odd moments as they were lost in the labyrinth of the ancient city. The runners screamed and whipped at man or beast who had the misfortune to block the way, and the procession did not slow its pace as the cobblestoned streets became steep and twisting.

Emilie tried to see everything but each view rushed by in a kaleidoscope of color and smells. There were places where the street seemed so narrow she worried the chair would not negotiate the sharp turns, but somehow the slaves managed the trip without incident. Some were no more than passages with many arches and some sort of sheltering roof of sticks and vines. Emilie leaned to see better, wishing they might stop and inspect some of the intriguing cubbyhole shops, or the hidden recesses beyond the stone facade that lined the street. Only the smell was distracting, a mixture of waste and rotting foods, mingled with heavy spices and smoky fires.

They were through another gate then, and the palace, its many towers reaching into the indigo sky, was before them. The slaves raced up the broad marble steps. The runners had already entered, and in a moment a dozen brightly clad servants were at the doorway, holding aloft torches to dispel the gentle dusk and light the way for the guests. A guard of honour formed along the stairs, military-stiff in red jackets rimmed with gold braid, fluttering white breeches over black slippers with gold tassels at the pointed toes. Two black-skinned women bowed almost to the ground and walked sedately before Emilie and Sara as they entered the palace. They stepped aside as other servants, olived-skinned, eyes darkened with kohl, their slim bodies supple in flowing yellow silk, folded their hands prayerlike asking the two to follow, please.

198

The palace took Emilie's breath away. It was lighted by thousands of candles and brass lamps swinging on chains from rounded arches, wall sconces and niches. The flames wavered and danced softly in the flow of air from the central courtyard where a fountain, supported on the backs of a dozen stone lions, splashed and trickled. Gold inlaid columns ringed the court and led gracefully up to ornately carved ceiling arches that glittered and winked in the soft light. The effect was that one had stumbled into a room of pure gold, a treasure house of oriental splendor. The floors were marble, polished to a luster that sent back reflections; along the side walls, recessed fountains done in intricate tiles were flanked by benches and pots of greenery.

The two servants led Emilie and Sara around the court and through another arch leading to a room slightly smaller than the one they'd just left but just as splendid. The air was cool, a breeze billowed gauzy drapes drawn over hidden windows. The tiled floor and walls were geometric rainbows, with half a dozen arches leading to dimly lighted courts. A tangle of fig branches, twining vines and shrubs could be seen, and white-stoned paths disappeared into the darkness.

At one side of the room, a corner had been arranged with a rich Oriental rug surrounded by a circular divan in front of which was a low table. Taleb al Mu'min was seated on the divan, and he glanced up as the servants bowed before him. He smiled and indicated Emilie and Sara should sit, taking no notice that their European gowns made this difficult. Emilie felt a tic of annoyance at his grand manner, then quickly reminded herself that their cultures were vastly different, and his did not call for a man to rise or show homage to a woman. Quite deliberately, she lifted her skirt and tucked feet beneath her to sit in the Arab fashion on one of the red velvet cushions. Sara sat more sedately with legs bent to one side, skirt covering the tops of her shoes.

199

"I am delighted that you could come," Taleb said. "My visit was unexpected so I could not pay the courtesy of inquiring in advance of your availability."

"It was very kind of you to remember," Sara said.

His glance met hers. "The promise of a shereef is not like the wind in a cage. Once made, it is kept."

Emilie could not remain annoyed even for a moment. She was too excited about being here and having her first real glimpse of Moroccan life without a veil of European propriety. She gazed about, openly admiring and exclaiming at the richness of detail everywhere.

"The Sultan has great wealth," Taleb said.

She turned to see if he was teasing but there was no smile on his face. She asked, "Does he give you free run of the palace? Are you staying here?"

"The Sultan is in Rabat, but were he here I would be his guest. Since we are both sons of the Prophet, it is written that the door of my house is the door of his, and his mine."

A servant glided in with a tray which she set on a carved-legged table, knelt and began crushing mint leaves into a silver pot. While the tea steeped, she arranged tiny bone china cups with a pattern of raised gold scrollwork and a small pot of honey. Another dish held small dark bits of cake that seemed made entirely of fruit and nutmeats. When the tea was ready, she poured three cups, flavouring them with honey scooped from the pot with a gold dipper. She passed the first to the shereef, never lifting her downcast gaze, then one to each of the women before sitting back on her heels and bowing her head until she was needed again. Taleb paid no more attention to her than if she were part of the furnishings.

"We shall enjoy light refreshment then I will show you the palace." Taleb raised his cup and watched the two over the rim as he sipped slowly.

"I must confess I am ignorant of the ways of your

eople," Sara said. "Does the Sultan have a palace in Ra-
at as well as here?"

"And in Casablanca and Fez. Whenever he must see to
he needs of his people, it is fitting that his life not be dis-
urbed in any way."

"But he can only be in one place—"

"The palaces are kept ready for his arrival. Those de-
cended in the family of the Prophet are permitted to
hare the abundance of Allah's wealth, though the Sul-
an's personal quarters are never entered by any other."

"The palace is huge," Emilie said.

"It was built many centuries ago when it was necessary
or the Sultan's armies to protect against raiding Berbers
nd those who would unseat him from his throne. His
rmy lived close at hand."

Emilie sipped the sweet tea, enthralled at being in the
iidst of such luxury that the shereef took for granted.
Iow strange these people were, and how exciting. She
ished they would tour the palace now, but Taleb made
o move as the servant refilled the cups. The shereef
alked in a soft voice about the history of his people and
ie country's ever-shifting politics. His tone was evenly
leasant, but Emilie detected an underlying note of rancor
henever he mentioned the French or British. She sensed
is strong will and suspcted that no matter who con-
rolled his country, no one would ever control this man.

They sat through a third cup of tea, the custom, Taleb
xplained at Emilie's attempt to refuse it, thus settling the
iatter firmly. When the last of the tea was served, the
irl rose from her knees and backed from the room still
owed, gaze averted from the master's.

The palace was even more enormous than Emilie or
ara imagined. They were led through room after room,
uge reception areas that might host a ball four times the
ize of any either had ever attended, cathedral-like sitting
ooms, and dozens upon dozens of living suites, with huge
edchambers, balconies, courtyards and sitting rooms. All

furniture was uncorrupted by European influence, low di
vans and beds indistinguishable one from the other excep
for the lavishness of covering. Tapestries of the fines
threadwork covered walls, and draperies were heavy with
gold embroidery and tassels. Taled pointed out the *iya*
or women's apartments, and explained that most Euro
peans called the rooms by the Turkish name "harem."
When Emilie responded that the same was true of Moroc
cans classing the English with all others as "Europeans"
instead of by their proper designation of "Britons", Taleb
favoured her with one of his rare smiles. The women'
beds were splendidly decorated with rich, dark red cu
velvets and coverlets of lace, the walls covered almos
completely with hangings so that no stone showed. Net
ting draped from poles over the beds could be draw
closed, and carpets covered the glowing mosaic floors.

Taleb was an excellent guide, pausing long enough fo
them to see everything yet moving at a steady pace s
they could cover as much as possible. Even so, it was im
possible to see the entire palace—that would take man
hours, it was so huge. He did not show them his ow
apartment nor that of the Sultan. Emilie wondered if the
could be any more elegant than those they'd seen.

When Taleb took them through a court, both girls ex
claimed aloud. The gardens were lighted by flamin
torches set in wrought iron holders along paths and
hundred or more oil lamps that swayed gently fron
branches and among thick shrubbery. The effect was
dusky daylight that lent an exotic air to the romanti
gardens. Paths curved among flowerbeds, tiny jungles o
overhanging trees where birds chattered at their disturbed
sleep, around small courts where fountains splashed
softly. There was a small zoo stocked with animals
brought from the desert and far reaches of Africa: ele
phants, monkeys, panthers, lions, caracals, lynx and ga
zelles. Birds with rainbow plumage squawked and rustled
on perches of an enclosure that resembled a miniature

orest but gave them room to fly in caged freedom. Taleb ointed out the magnificent stables where sleek gleaming orses pawed the straw-covered ground.

For the first time in many weeks, Emilie was engrossed nough to have no thoughts of Henri. Her mind was filled ith the splendour of what she saw and the realization hat *this* was Morocco. She wondered at the aloof manner f the shereef; his background obviously made him disainful of women, yet he had made a point of inviting hem and playing the part of guide, a task he might easily ave delegated to a servant. He was a puzzling man, and he wondered that her father found it possible to do usiness with him.

When at last they returned to the room where they'd aken tea, Taleb left them seated while he excused himelf, saying he would return shortly. Puzzled, they sat and aited, whispering over what they had seen. The palace eemed very quiet all at once, as though the two forigners were alone in its vast caverns. A drapery at the indow fluttered and from a nearby mosque, the *muezin*'s call rose and fell.

"*Acha*," Sara said. "The final evening prayer."

Their host returned some minutes later, his religious bligations having been tended in private. Emilie wonered how he had been able to forecast the time so accuately; there was not a clock or watch to be seen.

"We shall go to the *casbah* now." He inclined his head. You will find it quite a change from the palace, but if it , your wish—"

"Oh, yes!" Emilie declared before Sara had a chance to oice any doubts.

"So be it," he said. "We shall dine at a restaurant here the owner can accommodate us with a private oom."

They went on foot, followed front and rear by a retinue f armed guards and burly slaves, one carrying the hereef's banner in the lead. People fell away from the pro-

cession as the guards cried out. Taleb strode with hea
high, his caftan flowing and snapping in the breeze wher
ever he turned a corner or drew up abruptly to answer
question put to him by one of the women. There was littl
to see save the squalour of filth of the street, and the tin
niches lighted so that merchants might sell their wares
The streets were so narrow that often the group had t
proceed single file. When this happened, Taleb strode ou
in front with no pretense at western chivalry but com
manding the position of respect due him. It was enoug
that he had agreed to be seen in public with the two, an ac
tion causing many whispers and exclamations from me
huddled under arches or crowded in coffee houses. But h
was the shereef of Madawadi, and he would do as h
wished, *inch'allah*.

He led them along streets too numerous to count
showed them tiny courtyards from which servants scurrie
to hide as the powerful man appeared. He pointed ou
wealthy, unveiled Jewish women who dressed like gypsies
and had clanking gold bracelets and necklaces to ador
their bodies and small pillbox hats that were richly orna
mented with silver. They were not confined to a *mellah* i
Tangier, Taleb told them, and once again Emilie detecte
a note of disdain in his voice.

Sara and Emilie were quite breathless when they ar
rived at last at the restaurant. It was a large sprawling
house set among tiered gardens, hidden from view behin
a high wall. They barely glimpsed the spacious publi
rooms which combined secluded, Moroccan-style alcoves
with European chairs and couches around low tables. The
rooms were separated by columns and tiled partitions tha
sprouted thick greenery to soften the expanses of tile. The
odor of flowers and aloe burning in carved pots mingle
with the indistinct aromas of spices and cooking meat
The private room was as elegant as the palace they'd jus
left. Taleb and the girls sat in a comfortable circle
Moroccan style, and were served by a retinue of slaves

who never needed a command. The proprietor knew his distinguished guest's desires and saw that they were met amply. It was an honour and a pleasure to entertain the shereef in his humble establishment, and he praised Allah a hundred times over for his good fortune.

They ate with fingertips, Taleb selecting the choicest portions of each dish for his guests before taking his own. He watched with a glint of humour, and Emilie was sure he expected them to be rude or ignorant enough to ask for tableware, but she and Sara merely exchanged conspiring glances. Each dish was a subject of intense curiosity, and they asked a dozen questions on what the foods were called and the ingredients. There were dishes of chicken, fish and game in sauces that varied from delicate to so strong that Emilie could not hide a grimace of distaste or force down more than a token swallow. A leg of mutton was broiled on a spit over a charcoal brazier at one corner of the room, sliced and served directly from the fire. Skewered bits of lamb and vegetables were also cooked as the meal progressed and served after a light, palate-clearing course of fresh vegetables boiled in faintly spiced water. Between courses, slaves brought bowls of warm water and towels so that hands could be washed and faces wiped. Wine was poured with each course, but only for the women.

Throughout, Taleb was a charming host, telling stories to amuse them. He never spoke of personal matters, but it was evident that he was drawing his tales from experience and his own background. When the last meat course was cleared, a golden melon was removed from under the covering of damp straw where it had been cooling and cut in generous wedges. Three musicians appeared in a secluded courtyard at the side of the room and began to play. One had a mandolin, another a small drum, the third a lute-like instrument, which in response to Emilie's question, Taleb identified as a theorbo. The strange haunting music,

205

a mysterious lament, provided a perfect background for conversation.

When the meal was over, a pipe was brought for Taleb and he relaxed against the cushions as tea was once more prepared and served.

Sara sighed. "I don't know when I have eaten so much. I shall not be able to swallow a morsel for days, I am sure." She smiled at the shereef.

"It gives me great pleasure that you are not disappointed after such high expectations." He looked at Emilie as though waiting for her affirmation or denial.

"I share my sister's delight," she said. "I would burst the seams of my finest gowns if I dined this way often."

"European women find pleasure in starving themselves to remain slim. It is not so in my country. Plumpness is desirable in a wife or concubine."

"Do you choose your women by weight then?" Emilie asked mischievously. "Do you have a wife or harem?"

Sara cast a quick disapproving glance at her sister's lack of discretion.

"I have not seen fit to take a wife."

His frank gaze unsettled Emilie, and she plunged on heedlessly. "So you have only concubines?"

For a moment, Sara thought the shereef had been pushed beyond patience by Emilie's rudeness. What in the world had gotten into her to delve into such personal matters?

"Yes, and none dares displease me or she is quickly banished. The fahs teem with comely maidens who would live happily in the palace of the shereef."

Unaccountably, Emilie felt her face warm. Sara seized the opportunity to steer the conversation to safer ground. "Is your palace as magnificent as the Sultan's?"

He shrugged, his face impassive. "Adequate." He inhaled the pipe and let the sweet smoke of the hashish soothe him. He was not sure why he had followed the impulse to invite the two Englishwomen to join him for an evening that might have been spent with the comeliest of the Sultan's maidens—or any other woman he desired. No . . . that was not quite the truth. He had not been able to put Emilie Sloane from his thoughts since first seeing her. Her beauty, yes, but more. The passionate awareness in her eyes, the subtle sensuousness of her movements. She was a girl to remember a long time when out of sight, and thoughts of her left him with a hunger that the women of his *iyal* did not erase. But he was the shereef, and she was a foreigner. His real interest lay in the dealings with *Si* Sloane and his plans for a railroad into Madawadi. The daughter was nothing to him. . . .

CHAPTER TWELVE

The summer passed with hot, windy days only occasionally relieved by showers that drenched the parched ground with water quickly evaporated or soaked to subterranean depths. The European sector was an oasis of green in the dusty town, since foreigners instructed slaves to carry huge pitchers of water to pour over grass and flowerbeds to keep them from dying. In Arab quarters, only hardly succulents survived, and the Moroccans shook their heads in wonder at the wasted industry the Romans spent coaxing unnatural blossoms. The hills around the city took on an arid look, with dry, wild grass disintegrating to dust under the feet of horses and runners. Numerous caravans were outfitted to depart for coastal cities or the interior, and the travelling camp at the southwestern edge of the city became a dustbowl under stamping feet of camels and the constant putting up and tearing down of tents and camp equipment.

Sara enjoyed her lessons with Serge Prichard. Father had agreed after learning that the artist's reputation was excellent and that the man considered Sara talented. He saw little point to the lessons, but no harm either. She went once each week, accompanied by Jenny, staying most of the afternoon to diligently absorb whatever knowledge the artist imparted.

He smoothed her sketching technique, showing her tricks of the conte crayon and the charcoal and urged her to be more direct in enclosing space with a line or with shadows. He made sketches beside hers to point out where he had emphasized this or that or modified another feature. He talked of economy of line, and at the same time taught her not to be too easily satisfied with a first effort but to reach beyond it, and once he rubbed his hand over a charcoal sketch of a still life, saying it was not good enough.

Mortified, she sat perfectly still, fighting back the tears, almost outraged that he would come and blot out her drawing. Then slowly she forced herself to try to see what he meant. Why wasn't the sketch good enough? Had she missed something? The more she studied it, the more she decided he was wrong. It *was* good, she was sure! With stubborn determination, she leaned forward and began to pick out the almost obliterated lines and put them in as they had been, working with a mixture of anger and intensity as the sketch took form again.

She looked up suddenly and found Serge watching her with a tiny, almost imperceptible curl of a smile at the corner of his mouth. He nodded slowly.

So she was right! He'd been testing her to see if she could discern good from bad. The realization gave her enormous confidence all of a sudden.

Usually they were quiet except for the dialogue necessary to their work, but sometimes he insisted she take tea with him after a long session, and then he often spoke of famous names in the art world, his own hopes and aspirations and, occasionally, of Pierre. They'd known each other some years before coming to Morocco. Pierre's father was the son of a noble family who was a patron of the arts. It was he who had encouraged and made possible Serge's career by purchasing some of his earliest

works, thus giving the artist money to continue hi
studies. The elder Louvel had been surprised by his son'
decision to enter medicine but accepted and supported it
According to Serge, Pierre Louvel was talented, dedicated
and highly respected in his field. He might have had a
chair at the Sorbonne or a post in any of the great clinic
of Paris or Vienna, but he chose to work among peopl
who needed him most. Whenever Serge spoke of Pierre
his expression was openly admiring.

The more she learned of Pierre, the more Sara admired
him . . . and the more her emotions slipped beyond the
restraints she tried to put on them. Each time they met a
the hospital, she felt growing pleasure at being in his com
pany, though they did little more than chat or occasion
ally take tea in the lounge near the solarium. Once when
he was leaving the hospital early, he asked if she would
like to ride with him, and she accepted eagerly. They
went south of the city, beyond the ridge where caravan
were assembled and readied for journeys to remote cities
A caravan had departed that morning, he told her, look
ing wistfully toward the vast desert beyond the hills
Stream beds were muddy, many dry and caked from lacl
of rain and the summer's heat, and the wind whipped
sand into undulating waves along the slope of the hill. Al
tracks had already vanished, the caravan swallowed up
by the desert.

They sat their horses in silence except for the sighing of
the wind as it carved its mark on the sand. She sensed his
respect and awe for the majesty of the land, yet she shud
dered inwardly at the thought of passing beyond the ring
of security that surrounded Tangier. She wondered if
Pierre was thinking of his hope of travelling to Fez, but
she did not intrude on the beauty of the moment with
words.

For Emilie, the weeks rushed by in a dizzying turmoi
that exploded into hedonistic passion when she was with

Henri. They met several times a week, often forced to spend part of their precious time together at public affairs, such as polo matches or hunts or attending parties that were expected of them, yet they always managed to steal an hour or two alone to fall into passionate embrace. Though Emilie worried about being seen entering or leaving Pierre Louvel's house so often, Henri chased her fears with his kisses and his lovemaking.

In her father's presence, Henri was courteous and slightly aloof. Often when Henri called for her for an evening's outing, she came downstairs to find the two men in an earnest conversation that came to a quick end at her appearance. Neither her father nor Henri ever spoke of the business dealings they had and Emilie did not inquire into them. Father seemed pleased with himself of late, so the venture must be progressing well. As long as it gave her added opportunity to see Henri, she was happy. Taleb al Mu'min's name was mentioned occasionally, but he did not come again to the Sloane house, nor did Emilie and Sara receive any further invitations from him.

By October, the heat of the summer had not broken; there had been no rain for several weeks so that dust covered everything with a grey film and the breeze from the sea was no longer refreshing. The entire populace seemed affected, and the foreigners closeted themselves indoors as much as possible to sit about well-watered gardens and sip cool drinks, closing off the Arab world beyond the green hedges. The natives moved at a slower pace and lengthened the afternoon solitude until the sun went down.

At home, Emilie wore loose caftans that permitted some movement of air around her body and steadfastly ignored her mother's pleas for more suitable garb. Only when she went out did she select gowns from her growing wardrobe, and these the lightest weight, the palest colours and loosest fit she could manage. Many of the women of Tangier did not go out at all, but Emilie was too restless

211

to be cooped up without adventure. She rode each morning at dawn before the sun climbed over the eastern Rif then bathed leisurely on her return. She had given up visits to the hospital with Sara in favor of seeing Henri though she departed the house with her sister to avoid questioning by her mother. On the first occasion, Sara frowned and was reluctant to take part in the deception.

"There are women at the hospital who see mother regularly. Word will get back to her, perhaps even to father."

Emilie waved off the sobering thought. "I shall worry about that *if* it happens but not until. Oh, Sara, I have never felt this way about any man before. We must be together whenever we can manage it!"

"It's not right to see him secretly, especially at his apartment." Sara spoke not out of prudery but from genuine concern for Emilie's welfare.

"It's the only chance we have to be alone. I cannot give up the precious moments we share, so do not ask me. You needn't say anything at all, and if mother or father learns the truth, I shall take full blame."

"I worry about *you*," Sara said.

"No need to. I love him, Sara, and he loves me."

"Has he spoken of marriage?"

Emilie hesitated, then smiled. "It would hardly be proper to announce an engagement after three months. Besides, there is his family to consider. They may wish the wedding to take place in Paris."

In truth, Emilie longed to hear Henri speak of marraige, but he had not done so. They whispered intimate words, and when they lay together, she could not doubt that destiny meant them to be together always. Her own desire found complete satisfaction with him, and when they spoke of the future it was always on short terms . . when they would be together again, when she would come to him.

By the middle of the month, the unrelenting heat had brought activity to a standstill. There were fewer and fewer social affairs among the Europeans, even though nights began to bring a small measure of relief from the heat with cool dews. It was as though languid evenings were required to revitalize bodies that had been drained by the blazing sun of the days.

When she joined Henri one morning, she sensed a listlessness in him that did not dispel until they lay in the wide bed. Even then, their lovemaking lacked some spark that had always been present before, and Emilie felt an uneasy disappointment.

"What is it, love?" she asked, her head nestled against his bare chest as he lay smoking a cigarette.

"I have been thinking about Paris."

She looked up with a start. "Paris . . . ?"

"Yes. Some matters there require attention and would be best handled by my return."

"But you can't—" The thought of being without him left her desolate.

He raised his head and glanced at her as he reached to snub out the cigarette. "It would only be for a short time. A month, perhaps. My business will bring me back quickly, I assure you." At her crestfallen look, he kissed the tip of her nose. "And you, of course, my pet. How can I stay away from you very long? Will you miss me?"

"Oh, Henri, I cannot bear the thought—" Tears scalded her eyelids and she buried her face at his shoulder so he would not see them. Her voice was thick and her chest seemed suddenly constricted.

"A month will pass quickly," he said, petting her hair and trailing his fingers over her naked shoulder.

"When will you go?" she whispered hoarsely.

"Next week. There is a ship on the twentieth."

She bit her lip and fought the tears. Less than a week . . . five days . . . She took a deep breath and cast aside the last shreds of her pride. "Take me with you, Henri. We can be married in Paris—or before we go."

His hand fell from her shoulder and he stared. For a

213

moment, surprised accounted for the strange look on his face, then Emilie became aware that it was more than that. Shock, disbelief. She sat up, leaning so her breasts brushed his chest.

"You do want to marry me, don't you?"

For what seemed an eternity, the room was silent. Outside, cicadas shrilled tuneless notes. Henri's gaze was unswerving, and it was Emilie's that faltered.

"I am not ready to settle into marriage, my sweet. I thought you knew that—"

She stared. He could not be serious. He was teasing, making a joke that would soon be pushed aside with a kiss, an embrace. . . .

He reached to extract a cigarette from the silver box, pulling himself up so he leaned against the headboard of the bed. As he struck a match, he focused his gaze to the cigarette a moment, then blew smoke.

"Marriage has been the furthest thing from my mind."

She could not believe what she was hearing. "You never intended to marry me?" She drew back, impatiently pushing aside the flaxen hair that was in complete disarray about her naked shoulders. His face was calm, his eyes serious.

"Did you think I would just because I found your body desirable? If such were the case I would have been guillotined for polygamy long ago, I assure you. You have been the most enjoyable of lovers and, but for you, I might have tired of Tangier long ago. Perhaps some day . . ." He reached for her and she drew back as though burned. His eyes went wide and a smile curved his lips. "Don't be a child, Emilie . . ."

She stumbled out of his reach and from the bed. She stood glaring at him, her hands clenched and her lips quivering.

"Come back here . . ." His tone was gentle.

She shook her head, wanting to run but unable to

214

move. His naked body in repose was both compelling and disturbing, and she turned away with a sob.

"You wanted a lover and I wanted you. Is that so terrible a thing to admit?"

She whirled. "I wanted no such thing! You seduced me!"

He laughed and smoke curled about his dark head like a small evil cloud. "You came to me willingly. You were as eager for my caresses as I was to sample your charms."

"Sample!" Fury choked her and she stamped a foot and rushed at him with beating fists. He grabbed her and pulled her across his naked body, pinning her to him. For a moment she struggled wildly but could not free herself, and she collapsed in tears. His cigarette fell to the coverlet and she watched a ring of charred cloth form around its glowing tip, spreading like ripples in a pool after a stone has been tossed. The wispy smoke became acrid as the feather stuffing of the quilt ignited and sent up a spurt of flames. Her mind reeled with hatred for the man who was holding her and with the sense of danger the fire instilled, yet she said nothing. Henri's face was turned away from the flames, his lips pressed at her ear as he tried to rouse desire in her and make her forget his cruel words. Her relaxation had lulled him into thinking the fight was gone from her, and he loosened his grip on one arm and began to stroke her breast.

"We are two of a kind, Emilie. No denying we have passion enough to delight for a lifetime. Do not spoil our affair by trying to tie me with bonds of matrimony."

She breathed in shallow gasps, staring at the spreading flames in horror-struck fascination, listening to Henri's words with a numb mind. All at once the flames leaped like macabre dancers and a burst of smoke mushroomed in her face. She coughed.

"What the—" Henri tried to leap up, but Emilie tensed suddenly and gripped the bedclothes to hold him under her. Tears stung at her eyelids and burned along her

215

cheeks from the smoke and from her rage. The fire singed her hair and she closed her eyes; she could not breathe but nothing seemed to matter. She was aware of Henri's cry, a forceful thrust which sent her sprawling as he leaped up. For a moment, hot pain engulfed her and she realized she had fallen upon the flaming bedclothes. Suddenly she was pulled roughly up, adding new pain as hands slapped at her hair and body. She screamed an agonizing cry, then sank to the floor as unconsciousness claimed her.

She was aware of the antiseptic smell before she opened her eyes. Dull pain throbbed in her head which seemed so heavy she was sure she would not be able to move it. She lay listening to unfamiliar sounds that defied recognition, yet she knew she should be able to place them. She drifted reluctantly from a foggy grayness that offered comfort and oblivion, yet her mind would not focus memories or reality.

She felt different somehow, and she tried to define the feeling without opening her eyes. Somehow her fuzzy thoughts related reality to danger. She was not at home, her bed was far more comfortable than the stiff sheets she lay upon now. And she was not in Henri's bed—

Memory rushed to fill the void, and her eyes flew open.

The fire—! She jerked and tried to sit. Instantly a figure came toward her and put restraining hands on her shoulders.

"Lie back, Miss Sloane . . ."

She stared at the woman in blue dress and crisp white apron, a white cap perched atop her gray hair like a fluted halo. A nurse. Emilie sank back, exhausted by the spurt of motion, and looked about. She was in a high bed with stiff sheets drawn up to her chin. Her arms were trapped at her sides and her neck was stiff with bandages. Two screens, shirred cloth gathered in metal frame, curtained the bed in a small alcove. There was a window near the head of a bed—she could see the shaft of light that fell from it, but when she tried to turn her head, pain shot through the numbness in her neck.

"Please lie still," the nurse repeated. "I'll tell the doctor you're awake." She disappeared past the screen.

The hospital . . . How had she gotten here? She tried to remember but could not. Only Henri's degrading words, her rage, and then the fire. She closed her eyes which felt puffy and tired, and did not open them until she heard footsteps.

Pierre Louvel stood beside the bed, pulling back the sheet so he could pick up her wrist and hold his finger to her pulse. He said nothing until he lay the arm atop the cover.

"Your sister is most anxious to see you. I will allow her a few minutes." His grey eyes seemed to search her face and she looked away. He started to leave but she called him back.

"Doctor—"

"Yes?" He came close to the bed so she would not have to strain her voice.

"I—I don't recall what happened. How did I get here?"

His eyes narrowed and his lips pursed thoughtfully. Then, quite calmly he said, "Henri brought you. There was a fire and you were overcome by smoke. Your burns are not serious though several will take a few weeks to heal properly." His tone was briskly efficient, without sign of condemnation or compassion.

"Henri . . .?"

"He was not injured."

She closed her eyes because she did not want Pierre to see the angry emotion that filled her. Henri was not injured. Not his body, not his pride. Only she would suffer.

"If you are tired, I will tell Sara to wait awhile longer."

She opened her eyes. "No, I want to see her."

He nodded and vanished around the screen. A few mo-

217

ments later Sara walked softly to the bed, her eyes worried and full of pity. "Em, how do you feel?"

"I'm not sure."

"Pierre says the burns will not scar."

She knew . . . Emilie could see it in her expression. Sara and Pierre Louvel knew she had been naked in Henri's bedroom when the fire occurred.

"What time is it?" Emilie asked.

"A bit past three."

"Father?"

Sara shook her head. "I was here when you were brought in and have not gone home. I wanted to make sure you were all right, to talk to you."

Emilie sighed and her lashes fluttered. Sara was offering her a chance to invent a story that father and mother might believe. It would only be possible with Pierre Louvel's consent and cooperation . . . and Henri's silence. She had little to fear from Henri, she was sure.

Sara closed her hand over her sister's. "You must not upset yourself, it will be all right. No one knows—" She left the sentence unfinished. Four persons knew: Emilie and Henri, who had been in the fire, and Sara and Pierre to whom Henri had rushed her. "But I cannot delay telling father and mother any longer."

Emilie felt a surge of tears and blinked rapidly. "I am a fool."

"Hush." Sara's hand was comforting. "Pierre says the burns on your back and shoulders will heal quickly. They can be covered with light dressings." She gazed at her sister. Poor foolish Emilie. She had suffered enough shame without father knowing her disgrace.

Henri had quickly put out the flames that consumed the bedding, then pausing only to don his trousers and shirt, wrapped Emilie in a blanket and ran with her from the house to the nearby hospital. Her face had been covered by the wrapping, and none of the nurses who assisted in the emergency treatment knew who the patient was

218

hank heaven Pierre had been on duty! Had it been any ther doctor, the entire hospital, if not the city, would now Emilie's identity by now—and the fact that she had rived naked, carried by Henri Cartier.

Pierre summoned Henri at once, admitting him to the urgery while he treated Emilie's burns. Henri blurted out is story, pacing the small antiseptic room and clapping is hand to his head in anguish.

"*Mon Dieu*! I did not believe she took our affair seri- usly. It was a pleasant interlude for both of us but—" Ie shook his head and looked at Pierre who was com- letely occupied in cleaning the blistered flesh at the back f Emilie's neck.

"No affair is ever serious to you," he said, his voice uriously flat.

"She believed I would marry her and take her to aris," Henri said. He looked at Sara for understanding. Your sister is a very desirable woman but—I swear, I eant her no harm! It was an accident . . . the cigarette . . she said nothing until the flames were everywhere!"

Sara felt a knot in her chest. She could not condemn Ienri; and she was filled with compassion for Emilie. oor dear Emilie . . . so eager for living, so easily swept ato loving.

She smiled at Emilie now. "Are you in pain?"

Emilie shook her head and winced as the bandages raped raw places at her neck. Sara was instantly solici- us.

"Lie still—"

Emilie closed her eyes and sighed.

"Emilie?" Sara's voice was gentle and Emilie looked at er through the tears that were forming. "There is no eed for father to know the details of the accident."

Emilie blinked.

"Pierre has already cautioned Henri, and the servants an be relied upon to be silent. There is a travelling camp nly a few miles outside the city, or at least there was un-

219

til this afternoon. The caravan set out a short time ago
It's customary for departures to take place in the morn
ing, but this one was delayed because of a sick chil
whom Pierre was called to tend. There were no French o
English in the group, only a German family and Arat
merchants headed for Casablanca." The words did no
come easily. Sara was not good at fabrication, but sh
would do anything to ease this painful time for her sister
She and Pierre had talked it over, examined every detail
closed all loopholes where questions might be asked. Now
she laid out the story for Emilie. The three of them ha
ridden to the camp, and while Pierre tended his patient
Sara and Emilie wandered about watching the prepara
tions for departure. An unseen object caught Emilie'
foot; she fell—close to a campfire, her hair, the burns ac
counted for. At Pierre's insistence, she was brought to th
hospital and would remain until he was sure there was n
infection.

Emilie could not contain the tears that spilled over he
lashes. She moistened her lips with the tip of her tongue
"You would say this for me?"

Sara took her hand and squeezed it. "You are ver
dear to me. I could not bear it if you were sent off t
Rothingale's." She was finally rewarded with a tremulou
smile. "Then it is settled. I shall go to the bank and te
father myself. He will undoubtedly come to be sure I hav
described your condition precisely, and of course he'l
want to talk to the doctor." She brought Emilie's hand t
her cheek and held it close. "Now you must rest. Pierr
has given you a sedative and you must let it do its work."

Alone, Emilie closed her eyes and drifted quickly into
hazy unreality that was comforting to mind and spirit
When thoughts of Henri tried to intrude, she pushed then
aside agonizingly. The memory of his laughter, his crue
words haunted her, and she longed for peace.

Her recovery was rapid but Pierre insisted that she re

main in the hospital until most of the dressings could be removed. Emilie did not argue; she was in no hurry to go home and be forced to face her father. He'd shown no emotion when he came to see her, though Sara declared he'd been upset on hearing the news. He spoke briefly to the doctor, then to Emilie, but did not insist on a repeated account of the story. Apparently, Sara had convinced him, and Emilie was relieved. Still, she suspected father believed the accident was in some way her fault, that she was not entirely blameless, even if only for clumsiness that could have been avoided.

Mother came too, tearful and wringing her hands, bringing books and a needlepoint sampler that lay untouched on the bedside cabinet. It was easier to deal with father's disapproval than Charlotte's consternation and sympathy, and Emilie pleaded fatigue so that she did not stay long.

At dusk, Sara returned to say that Henri was outside and wished to see her. Emilie turned her face to the wall and bit her lip.

"I will not see him!"

"He wants to assure himself that you are all right," Sara said gently. "He has been distraught since—"

Emilie jerked to face her sister, unmindful of the searing pain. Her pale lips quivered. "I will not see him! I cannot!"

"I understand . . ." Sara kissed her cheek and pretended not to notice the tears that traced a silvery path on her sister's cheek. "I will tell him."

Alone, Emilie let the tears flow unchecked. It was difficult to search her heart and to admit her foolishness. Henri had never spoken of marriage; he had scarcely used the word "love" except in the heat of passion. It was *she* who had professed her love over and over, she who had assumed that his physical love included deep emotion, as it had for her.

Pain wrenched her heart. She had believed herself in

221

love with Henri. She had allowed ecstasy to create dreams of a lifetime with him and had given her body willingly to his caresses, casting aside awareness of Henri's reputation for roguish escapades and romantic involvements. She believed only what she wanted to believe.

When at last her tears were spent, she stared at the darkness outside the window. She could see no buildings, only the dark shadowy thickness of the trees in the park, but she was aware of the presence of Henri's apartment as though viewing it. In rational thought, she supposed it was a blessing the house was so close to the hospital or she might have fared worse.

Had Henri returned to the apartment? She wondered how much damage the fire had done and hoped it was not extensive, since it was Pierre Louvel's house, and she wished him no inconvenience. She found it remarkable that he was willing to twist the truth to protect her reputation. She barely knew him, yet he showed more concern for her than Henri, with whom she had been foolish enough to believe herself in love. How could she have been so stupid? She shuddered as she considered the tragic consequences the affair might have had, and she silently vowed never to make such a mistake again. No man would ever have her again except as wife.

Pierre allowed Emilie to be up and about after the first day. In the robe and slippers Sara brought, she walked the hospital corridors, sat in the solarium and occasionally chatted with other patients. Some of the men remembered her from the visits she'd made with Martine, and they were delighted at the chance to talk with her again, and most solicitous about her injuries. She avoided such discussions at first, then became accustomed to the lie that had been invented to account for them and accepted the inquiries and sympathy. The physical pain was gone in a short time, but Henri's perfidy was a raw wound that would be a long time in healing.

The screens were removed from her bedside and a comfortable chair brought in. It was not a large room, one of the few private rooms the hospital offered. Most patients were in long wards, and most were men. The few women were surgical patients or seriously ill, and Emilie made no attempt to become acquainted with them. Pierre came each morning on his rounds to inspect the burns and pronounced them healing well. He often stopped again late in the day to look in on her.

He was pleasantly polite and his brisk, professional manner gave way to the casual friendship they had known before the accident. He did not speak of Henri or the circumstances that brought her here, and she was grateful.

On the third day, Emilie heard footsteps at the door as the light was beginning to fade beyond the hills. She enjoyed sitting in the dusky evening, and tonight she had taken pains to brush her hair until it gleamed and lay soft about her shoulders. She turned with a smile, but it was not Pierre Louvel who stood in the doorway but Henri! Her heart raced erratically and the blood pounded in her temples.

"Emilie, I had to see you." He stepped toward her, one hand extended in an offering of compassion.

Her body stiffened and it was difficult to control the trembling anger that coursed through her.

"I do not wish to see you. Please go."

He tilted his head as though to see her more clearly in the dim light. She grew uncomfortable under his gaze but met it defiantly.

"I only wish to say that I am sorry. It pains me to see you injured."

His words were like salt rubbed into an open wound. Fury surged and exploded. "I have never meant anything to you but a few pleasant moments when it suited your fancy!" Her hands gripped the chair and it took great effort to refrain from shouting.

He was silent a moment. "Perhaps at first."

223

"And the last time we were together? Was I so dear to you then that you found my emotions laughable? Was I so dear that you could not bear the thought of marrying me and taking me to Paris?" Bitterness engulfed her and she could not control the angry words. "Don't speak to me of caring! You care for no one but yourself!"

"Must marriage and caring be synonomous?" he asked gently.

"To a woman, but you cannot understand that. You find it too easy to have women fall into your bed and play the game according to your rules, and when you tire of one, another is readily at hand to take her place."

"I would quarrel with your choice of words," he said softly. "And I would contest the idea that I played a game in which I made the rules. Aboard the *Ophir,* you were eager for my attention as long as I paid court along the lines you defined. Then it was you who came to my apartment, *cherie.* I did not force you, though God knows I wanted you badly enough."

The colour that flamed in her cheeks was hidden by the growing dusk. She could not win a battle of words with him. He was too clever at manipulating the truth to make her feel guilty, and guilt left her angry and tongue-tied.

"Please go," she whispered.

"Emilie—give me time to adjust to the idea. I have never felt about another as I do you—"

"Please go . . ."

His reply was caressing. "My ship leaves in three days, but I will return. A month will seem a long time without you."

Eyes blazing, she whirled. "You will have no trouble filling your bed, *m'sieur*! Do me the courtesy of leaving now and not troubling to see me when you return!" She turned back to the window, determined to force him from the room and her thoughts. When he touched her shoulders, the shock was so violent she cried aloud.

"Leave me alone!"

He was startled by her outburst.

"Go away and leave me alone!" She jumped to her feet, her eyes burning with tears she would not shed in front of him. Her breast heaved as she choked back sobs, gulping air and pressing her lips between her teeth.

As he retreated to the door, he collided with Pierre Louvel, who had been coming along the hall and quickened his steps at the sound of Emilie's cries.

"What is this?" Pierre demanded.

Henri was more shaken than he cared to admit. "I did not mean to upset her."

"You were told she did not want to see you. Have you no regard for her feelings? Please go at once."

"Yes, of course. *Adieu, mon ami.*" Henri hurried down the corridor.

Pierre went to Emilie and put his arm about her shoulder. She was sobbing uncontrollably, and he let her distress wear itself out.

"It is all right, no need for tears. He is gone and I shall inform the staff that he is not to be admitted again. You must not upset yourself further."

She sniffed and accepted the handkerchief he held out. She was aware of his comforting arms as she covered her swollen eyes and dried her tears.

"That's better," he said. "Would you like to go to bed? I will order a mild sedative."

She dabbed at her nose and shook her head. "It's not necessary."

"You're sure?"

She nodded and looked up. "Yes. I am all right now."

"That's better. Now, is it anything you care to discuss or shall we close the matter forever?" He led her back to the chair and sat her gently.

The remnant of a sob caught sharply. "There is nothing to discuss."

"Sara has promised to return this evening to sit with you awhile."

225

"She is the kindest sister anyone ever had."

He nodded, his smile seeming to shift with the shadows that fell across his face. "Shall I light the lamp?"

"No, the darkness is pleasant." There was enough light from the hall so that the room was not in complete darkness. She did not want him to see her tear-streaked face. "Please, doctor, don't leave me yet."

He drew a small wooden chair close. "I can only stay a moment. I have other patients I must see before the dinner hour."

"You work very hard."

He shrugged, and his thin face looked solemn, his eyes unreadable. "It is my profession."

"I have never known a man who enjoyed his work so much, or who devoted himself so totally to it."

"There is much to do."

They were silent a moment, then Emilie said, "I have never thanked you properly for what you've done."

"No need."

She shook her head and clasped her hands in her lap before looking at him. "Twice you have rescued me when another would have left me to my fate."

"I think not," he said, smiling. "You are much too charming to be ignored or abandoned in danger."

"I was not speaking of physical rescue." She lowered her gaze, then glanced at him once more. He looked puzzled but there was a touch of smile at the corners of his mouth. "You have saved me from my father's wrath and from public shame. There is no way I can thank you sufficiently for that kindness."

The smile lingered. "Then do not try. I am only glad that it was possible. And I am glad that your injuries are not more serious. Your sister has been very concerned."

"Sara is a jewel. I do not know what I would do without her." She sighed. "Sometimes I wish I were more like her."

"Why?"

226

The question startled her and she glanced at him. He was framed in the soft glow of the light from the doorway. "Because she knows what she wants from life. She is not driven by need for adventure."

"Is a desire for adventure bad?"

She frowned. Somehow she had expected this quiet man to agree readily that a woman should be more docile. "It seems to lead me into trouble more often than not." She felt colour rise in her face as she thought of Henri, and she turned her gaze to the window in spite of the darkness.

"Perhaps your judgment is not always wise, but you should not fault your adventurous spirit. Life would be very dull if we were content to accept only the hand dealt by fate. There would be no science, no medicine, no travel—no progress at all."

She looked at him curiously. "I have never thought of it that way." She was amazed at his lack of condemnation. He knew she'd had an affair which, by most standards, placed her in a category of women not generally accepted. She had never known anyone like him before, and she felt her respect and admiration grow. With a smile, she said, "Still, I owe you a debt of gratitude."

"The invention of the story was Sara's idea."

"You consented to it." ·

He smiled. "Yes, and I hope this is the last time I find the need to bend the truth for your mistakes, Emilie." There was no rancour in his tone. "Now I must go, though it would be pleasant to linger." He got up and lifted the chair back to its place. Looking down, he said, "Are you sure you do not require a sedative?"

"Yes, thank you."

"Shall I send a nurse to help you back to bed?"

"I prefer to sit."

"Then goodnight, Emilie. Rest well."

CHAPTER THIRTEEN

November rushed across the city in a clash of warm winds from the Mediterranean and the cool *Gharb* from the west. The days were pleasantly warm except for occasional bursts of raw, disagreeable dampness that sent women scurrying to dressmakers for heavier gowns and wraps. Summer was gone, and the European sector of the city came alive once more.

In the weeks that followed her release from the hospital, Emilie was bored and listless. Father forbade her to venture away from the house without his approval and without proper escort, and his stern gaze warned Emilie not to disobey. He had not questioned the story of her accident, but he wanted no repetition of similar circumstances.

Darien Melous called with flowers and an eager smile, but Emilie did not encourage him to come again. Martine and Sara sat with her and tried to make the time pass pleasantly, but even their efforts did not dispel Emilie's gloom.

Pierre came to the house often to see her. The burns at her neck were still red, but the soft, downy hair was beginning to grow back, and he was pleased that the hair roots had not been killed.

Emilie took shears to the singed ends and cut the straggly, uneven lengths. Giggling at her image in the mirror and at Sara's expression, she snipped until the golden hair barely covered her ears. She had no idea it would curl so and, delighted, she fluffed it to a soft halo.

Pierre commented on its attractiveness, and she was pleased that he noticed.

"I thought you only noticed burns and wounds, not the people behind them," she teased. Her admiration of Pierre had grown immensely, and she could never forget his gallantry. Each time he visited, she coaxed him into staying for tea, or if he protested that time would not permit, she walked with him through the patio garden where it was cool in the dappled shadows. She looked forward to his visits, and when he probed at her injuries, she pretended pain so that he would not dismiss her as a patient.

"You do me an injustice," he replied. "I would have to be blind not to take notice of one so lovely."

"You do not think my bobbed hair too daring?"

He laughed. "Perhaps on anyone else, but on you it is enchanting. I suspect you will go through life being different from most women, Emilie."

She glanced at him sidelong. "You yourself told me that it was a good thing to be adventurous. If I am adventurous, then I should dare to be different."

"I cannot argue the point, and I certainly cannot find fault with the lovely new hairdo. Besides, as a doctor I must commend it because it does not interfere with the healing of your wounds."

They were strolling through the patio, and he stopped at the arch leading to the outer garden. "I must go."

"Will you come tomorrow?"

"I think not. In two days I will remove the last of the dressings. The skin has grown nicely and can be left uncovered."

"I will miss your visits." She grinned impishly. "Would I be too adventurous in asking you to call when I am not a patient? I know that you cannot work every minute of the day. You escorted Sara and me on the promenade one evening, and you ride." She tossed the golden halo of curls and watched his face. "Will you ride with me one day?"

His grey eyes flickered for an instant. "I would be delighted."

"I consider it a promise that I will not allow you to forget. Now, I suppose I must not detain you but I shall look forward to seeing you in two days. We will celebrate the removal of my bandages with a ride into the hills." She took his hand and pressed it a moment, then turned toward the house.

For the duration of several breaths, he stood watching her, wondering at her boldness but pleased by it at the same time. She was a very attractive woman, and a man would be a fool not to enjoy her company. Shaking his head, he walked through the rear garden to where his tethered horse was cropping sweet grass that had sprung up with the cooler weather. Swinging into the saddle, he found himself humming a gay tune.

He came late in the day on Saturday. Emilie was dressed for riding, a bottle-green velvet suit with black lapels and piping. She'd left off the jacket, and the collar of the white satin blouse, tailored except for the frilly jabot at the neck, was open.

"There is nothing further I can do," Pierre said, dropping the discarded bandages into the pan Rachma held for him.

"Should she use a salve?" Charlotte asked. She was always present when the doctor treated her daughter, along with Rachma who fetched anything the doctor required.

"A bit of cream morning and night to keep the skin soft, nothing more," Pierre said.

"We are fortunate to have such a competent physician available," Charlotte said. "Sara tells me that one of your experiments at the hospital has caused considerable excitement among your colleagues . . . some new discovery?"

Pierre showed surprise that Sara knew. "A small breakthrough in isolating a strain of bacteria. We are far from victory." He had seen Sara earlier today but had not had time to talk with her. He rarely did lately, and he made a mental note to seek her out and inquire about her lessons with Serge.

"I think you are too modest," Charlotte said with a smile.

"Pierre spends too much time talking about his work, mother. Today he has promised to ride with me, and now that the medical call is finished, I'm eager to be on our way. Pierre?"

He rose and took Charlotte's hand to bid her goodbye.

Emilie buttoned the neckline of the satin blouse, then let Pierre hold the jacket as she slipped into it. The green velvet was taut over her firm breasts, accenting her figure, and Emilie saw Pierre's admiring glance. She settled the jabot at the neck of the jacket and crossed to a mirror over a small marble table to put on a small black velvet hat. She studied her image and fluffed several yellow curls, pulling them forward to lay like wisps of smoke in front of her ears. She saw Pierre's gaze upon her as she turned, smiling.

"Shall we be off?"

He let her slip an arm through his as they went through the patio to the stables.

They rode south of the city, following *Rue Belique* and *Route de San Francisco* to *Rue Sidi Amar*, the road Pierre told her went to the lighthouse at Cape Spartel. When Emilie exclaimed that she had never seen a lighthouse and wished to do so now, Pierre shook his head and said it was several hours' ride and could not be accomplished with such a late start.

"Will you take me another time, then?" she demanded smiling to show she meant the request in a most complimentary way.

"If I can spare an entire day—"

"You must not work every moment. It is not good for you."

"Are you the doctor now and I the patient?"

"Would you not give a patient similar advice?"

He laughed. "I suppose I would."

She grabbed the reins of his horse suddenly and jerked the bit in the animal's mouth. "I will race you to that distant olive tree—"

His horse shied, rearing, then snorted as Emilie kicked the black mare and raced along the path. With a shout Pierre slapped at the animal's flank and was in pursuit galloping at a mad pace as though the devils of hell were after him. He could hear Emilie's laughter floating with the wind, and he laughed aloud. It had been years since he'd ridden with such abandon, years since he had shucked all restraints and let himself feel the freedom of being alive.

She reached the tree and slid from the saddle as he reined in and jumped to the ground.

"I beat you!"

"You gave me no warning!"

"Two seconds were lost, no more, yet I won handily by at least five!" She clapped her hands and whirled like a gleeful child. "Admit that I am the better rider!" Dizzy, she fell against him and his arms caught her.

Still laughing, she threw back her head and looked at him. The laughter stilled and her brown eyes became pools of dark intrigue. Her red lips glistened with the dew of invitation, and Pierre closed his arms about her. Then he was kissing her, swept into an intoxicating whirlpool of emotion stirred by her closeness. Her body molded to his,

232

soft curves warming him with a surprising intensity that brought stirring to his loins. He drew back, but her lips claimed his again, and he did not resist.

Emilie savoured the kiss, the warmth of Pierre's embrace, and the pressure of his body. How good it felt to be held close . . . For several minutes she gave herself to complete enjoyment, not letting any thoughts intrude. His lips were firm, yet gentle, eager but not greedy, and when at last his mouth released hers, she sighed and stood with eyes closed, not willing to shatter the fragile moment.

Pierre looked at her with pulse stirred and breath quickened. It was easy to imagine how Henri, or any man, might be drawn irresistably into wanting this woman. His own desire left him tense and suddenly wary. He had sat in judgment on his friend for taking advantage of a young innocent creature, now his own maleness was assertive enough to follow the same path. Gently, he released her.

She opened her eyes.

"Pierre?" She wondered if he was angry. He could not be. He had enjoyed the embrace as much as she—his lips had told her that. She put a hand to his arm gently.

"Are you sorry?" she asked softly.

He turned to stare at her. "Sorry? *Mon Dieu*, no!" He was astounded.

Smiling, she reached for his hand and drew him to sit beside her on the hard ground, their backs to the gnarled bole of the tree. For several moments they were silent, glancing at each other sidelong from time to time until their eyes met and Emilie burst into laughter.

"We are still friends?"

"Of course! How could you imagine otherwise?" He caught her hand and held it, his face serious. "I am not a man to enter into an affair lightly—" He broke off at the stricken look on her face and the sudden tensing of her body.

"Do you think that because we shared a kiss that I am

233

ready to fall into bed?" Dark lights danced in her eyes. Before he could answer, she pulled her hand free and scrambled to her feet. "Just because I made a mistake with Henri does not mean I am a woman of loose virtue."

He was at her side instantly, holding her when she would have mounted her horse and left him standing. "Stop it this moment!" He was using the same voice he did with hysterical patients, and it had an instant effect. She blinked and stopped struggling.

"I meant no accusation, only an admission of my own weakness. I meant only that I would treasure your friendship or your l—"

His gaze wavered, but she knew he had been about to say *love*. He was attracted to her then, she had not imagined it. Soberly, she tried to examine her feelings about him but they were too vague to be dissected. She enjoyed his company, and she had enjoyed his arms around her, but she felt no emotional tide of desire.

"I understand," she said contritely. "Now, since we are friends, let's ride again. It seems a long time since I have enjoyed a day like this." Smiling, she let him assist her to the mare, then watched him swing into his own saddle.

"The sun will soon set," he said. "It is best we head back. The hills are not safe after dark."

They rode in companionable silence, only occasionally commenting on some bird that scurried up from their path or the crimsoning sky above. When they arrived at the house, he dismounted and walked her to the garden archway.

"Thank you for a most enjoyable time, Emilie. Your prescription of a day's outing was exactly what I needed."

Her eyes twinkled. "Then I prescribe repeated doses, at least once a week so the symptoms of overwork will not appear again."

"On condition the repetitions are with the same charming companion."

"Of course!" She laughed and blew him a kiss from her fingertips as she ran inside.

Emilie raced up the back stairway and hurried along the gallery toward her rooms. As she passed Sara's door, she stopped on impulse and poked her head inside.

Sara was seated near the window, a Queen Anne chair drawn close to the table on which a lighted lamp stood. An open book lay in her lap. She smiled.

"I've been riding with Pierre," Emilie said, dropping onto the sofa and pulling off the velvet hat.

Sara nodded. "Mother told me."

"Did you enjoy your day at the hospital?"

"Yes, very much." Sara's glance fell to the book and her fingers toyed with the thin ribbon used to mark her place.

"He's very nice." When Sara looked up with a puzzled expression, Emilie said, "Pierre, I mean."

"I know who you mean. It only surprises me that you are just discovering it. I have been impressed with him since we first met."

"That's not what I mean," Emilie jumped up and wandered about the room, lifting a picture here, a book there. "I mean he's *nice*. Different than I expected."

"In what way?"

"Well, he's considerate and gentle and yet, I don't know, strong, I suppose is the right word." She whirled and ran to her sister, kneeling before her and looking up earnestly. "He is a gentleman. Even after he kissed me he didn't try to take liberties."

Sara felt her throat constrict. "He kissed you?"

"Yes. It was not planned, it just happened." She smiled, remembering. "But it was extremely pleasant."

Sara was silent as she struggled against the astonishing pain of jealousy that welled. The joy in her sister's face gave agony to her heart, even though she quickly told herself she had no claim on Pierre. They'd shared pleasant hours and talked of things of mutual interest.

235

They'd sat close, walked together, leaned heads over café tables—but he had never kissed her.

Emilie completed another restless turn about the room and stopped before Sara's chair, hugging her arms across her breasts and rocking on the heels of the black kid riding boots. "He has promised to see me again."

Sara glanced up. "Be careful, dear Emilie. Don't be swept into anything—"

Emilie stamped a foot. "If you refer to the matter of Henri Cartier, you can be sure I shall never make that mistake again! No man shall ever bed me unless he marries me first!"

Pain gripped Sara and the blood drained from her face, but Emilie was too wrapped in private joy to notice. She sighed and picked up the black velvet hat she'd dropped on the sofa.

"I am going to have a hot bath before dinner. Has father said if we are to have guests?"

Numbly, Sara nodded. "Some business associates." Her voice was a tortured whisper.

"Oh, bother! I am heartily sick of father's business and talk of railroads and investments!" She bent to kiss her sister's cheek. "Thank you for listening, Sara. I do not know what I would do without you." She opened the door and was gone.

Sara realized her hands were clenching the book in her lap so tightly that the leather had curled and several pages folded. She forced herself to relax, then carefully smoothed the pages before closing the book and setting it aside. She sat staring from the window until Jenny tapped at the door and inquired if she wished to get ready for dinner.

In the next weeks, Emilie picked up the threads of her life as though Henri Cartier had never unraveled them. She rode with Sara and Ian Stavely and Peter Russ, accepted invitations to consulate parties, which she found dull but offered an opportunity to spend evenings away from home. Though she flirted and was greatly admired, no young man captured her attention for more than the interval of a dance or two. Henri, of course, had gone, and when his name was mentioned she closed her ears and heart resolutely.

Pierre did not attend the parties, and no amount of coaxing on her part could convince him to take more than an occasional day away from his work to be with her. Even these outings were limited to rides that lasted only an hour or two, or sometimes tea at the Hotel Cecil or dinner at one of the small cafés sprinkled throughout the European sector. On bringing her home, they paused in the garden, and Pierre took her in his arms to kiss her; each time she was filled with glowing pleasure and anticipation, but he always released her and withdrew, leaving her to want and to wonder. She found it flattering that he cared enough to consider her self-proclaimed virtue and infuriating that he was able to resist so readily. She longed to re-experience the stirring passion that had marked her encounters with Henri, but was glad at the same time for its absence. Pierre was comfortable to be with. She sometimes wondered what marriage to such a man would be like, but they never spoke of it, though at times she discovered Pierre gazing at her as though he wondered similar thoughts.

Roderick Sloane spent considerable more time at home of late, bringing business associates with whom he closeted himself in the library for lengthy discussions. The three most frequent visitors were the Moroccan Ministers of Finance and Foreign Affairs and Daniel Augustin. The discussions concerned the railroad lines being constructed by the newly formed Pendash Company, financed by the Anglo-French Bank of Lyon and personal funds from both Sloane and Augustin. The line to Larache was already laid, and work was progressing on the portion that would connect with Petitjean. There were several short spurs along the coast, built by the French, but these could not be connected until a line to Fez was completed. In the meantime, Roderick and his allies in the Pendash venture would lay tracks in several directions from Petitjean, like the spokes of a wheel, so that when the French commitment was met, they could connect to existing lines to form a major network crisscrossing the desert. The first company to close the gap between the coast and the interior would hold a strong hand in commerce, potential power and wealth. Though the Pendash venture did not technically violate the French-Moroccan agreement, it came dangerously close, and without the cooperation of several chieftains of desert tribes, the project would fail.

Henri Cartier returned from Paris shortly before St. Andrews Day and was immediately invited to a conference with Roderick Sloane and Daniel Augustin at the bank, a conference which was continued into the evening by an invitation to dinner. Emilie knew nothing of Henri's presence until she descended the stairs and joined the family in the sitting room. She had not expected guests and had dressed casually in a soft wool jersey gown of coppery brown with long sleeves and a high neck that hid the fading scars at her neck. She had been riding with Pierre earlier in the day and the crisp, invigorating air had brought rosy colour to her cheeks and a brightness to her eyes.

She stopped short in the doorway on seeing Henri, feeling both a quick shock of surprise and a heady surge of guilty emotion. Henri rose at once and came to take her hand.

"How delightful to see you again, Emilie. I would not have believed it possible but you have grown more beautiful."

She extracted her hand as quickly as possible and barely answered his gallant greeting. If she had known he was here, she would have pretended an indisposition that would excuse her from dinner, but there was no escape now.

Sara appeared, and Henri greeted her with the same chivalry. Sara murmured politely how pleasant it was to see him back; etiquette dictated she be polite to her father's guest, yet she felt a lingering animosity toward the man who had been the cause of Emilie's injuries and her consequent involvement with Pierre. The past weeks had been a strain. Seeing Pierre at the hospital, then listening to Emilie's detailed recital of each outing with him with their stolen kisses, were knife wounds to Sara's troubled heart.

Pierre had said nothing of Henri's return, and Emilie wondered if he knew. It seemed likely; perhaps he had not wanted her to know. Was Henri staying with him?

She reined her thoughts quickly. She would not see Henri, no matter what. She could do nothing about his business dealings with her father, but she would not encourage him in any way. She deliberately chose a seat a distance from him and turned her attention to conversation with Daniel Augustin, asking him endless questions about his wife and daughter, monopolizing his attention until dinner was served. Since the dinner was informal, she chose her own seat, beside Augustin, leaving Sara to sit beside Henri, whose dark gaze lingered on Emilie questioningly. After dinner, when the men retired to the library to continue their discussion, Emilie pleaded a headache and went to her rooms.

Preparations for Christmas seemed strangely dispirited in the mild climate of Africa, despite the array of festivities the Christians of Tangier planned. Doors and gates were hung with wreaths of cedar or pine twined with red ribbon, candles in windows of the villas cast their cheerful glow to passersby. Moroccan style houses sported garlands of bougainvillea and palm around archways and shocks of pine boughs in pots at entries. Dozens of parties were planned, and though an air of gaiety prevailed thoughts were of home and other Christmases with frosty cold winds, shopping expeditions and hidden gifts. And family.

A few were fortunate enough to secure leave and return to England or the Continent for brief stays. Among these was Peter Russ, who glowed with the prospect of seeing his fiancée, and Doctor du Bois, his wife and daughter, who were to enjoy a month's respite in Paris and the southern coast of France before returning.

The thought of a trip to England never crossed Roderick Sloane's mind. He was barely aware of the passing of months, the change of seasons and the coming holidays. He left the preparations to the women; he was completely occupied with the Pendash Company. With Henri Cartier's return, the last of the monies required for the venture were secure. Ali Ibn Tashfeen had once again made contact with the Shereef of Madawadi. The money paid him by the Anglo-French Bank of Lyon enabled the shereef to placate his people with new wells, food and horses. Arabs with full bellies and tents were not as anxious to revolt against foreigners who crisscrossed the vast desert with iron tracks and stream-belching locomotives. Taleb al Mu'min was agreeable to the idea of a council of tribal leaders to deal with the Pendash Company and assure the safety of its projects. The shereef was returning to Tangier shortly to conclude the necessary agreements and receive additional payment for his efforts.

He was, of course, invited to a lavish holiday party being given by the Sloanes.

It seemed half the populace of Tangier was invited. The house buzzed with activity for days in advance; Charlotte fussed and inspected every detail of the preparation. Asheema patiently and willingly followed instructions, but the Christian holiday spirit was markedly lacking among the staff, and she thought her mistress slightly deranged when the table decorations had to be redone a third time because the colors of greenery were not quite right.

The doors between the reception room and the rarely used reception hall at the front of the house were opened so there would be ample room for dancing, dining and conversation groups. An alcove at one corner was reserved for musicians, a small band of excellent players who had been imported from France for the holiday season, assured of numerous parties and excellent income as well as their passage. Tables of food were set along one wall of the reception room where most of the furniture had been removed and replaced by a variety of chairs. Charlotte insisted on borrowing chefs from half a dozen households to prepare the platters of meats and fish, salads, nutbreads, tiny openfaced sandwiches with sprigs of watercress specially grown, and a variety of cakes and biscuits that seemed enough to feed all the country rather than the forty-six invited guests.

Emilie insisted that Pierre Louvel be invited, and though his name was not included on Charlotte's original list, she acquiesced. She could hardly do otherwise after all the doctor had done for Emilie, and he was a pleasant enough young man, a bit intense but cultured so that he would be at ease among the guests. She was too busy to give it thought beyond penning the invitation.

Guests began arriving at nine and were escorted directly into the reception room by a bevy of servants dressed in purple and green caftans with silver corded sashes and tiny tinkling bells on their toes. Asheema had been permitted to handle arrangements regarding additional servants, and there seemed an endless supply of new faces and willing hands. Trays with wine glasses and punch cups circulated constantly, and every time a guest sat, a slave appeared to offer an array of foodstuffs. The musicians tuned their instruments and played the newest waltzes, two-steps and faster tempos.

Emilie added to the holiday spirit in a breathtaking

gown of scarlet velvet with pine green lace ruffles across
the lowcut bodice and at the edges of the sleeves that
came to her wrists. The skirt was full cut for dancing, and
with her golden curls set with tiny bows of green ribbon,
she was the embodiment of Christmas. Every man who
spied her raised an approving glance which she answered
with a smile.

Her gaze swept the room in search of Pierre but did
not find him. Henri Cartier was present and gazing at her
with frank approval in his eyes. When their glances met,
she lifted her chin and turned away with a disdaining
look. Henri hid his irritation with a smile. He found her
amusing—and still most desirable. He'd been pleased at
the lack of outcry over the incident in his apartment.
Pierre said little beyond the exchange at the hospital
when Henri had gone to see Emilie, and his friend's
silence was more rebuking than words. Since his return to
Tangier, Henri had taken a house found for him by *Monsieur* Augustin. He knew Pierre was seeing Emilie from
time to time, and it disturbed him because his own feelings
for her had not lessened; she was not an easy woman to
forget, he'd discovered. He saw Sara at the other side of
the room and crossed to ask her to dance before any of
the other young men could capture her.

"You are as lovely a Christmas vision as I have ever
seen," he said. It was true. She looked charming in a
gown of pearl white satin that set off her chestnut hair
and hazel eyes. Though she was not as beautiful as her
sister, she carried herself with a grace and bearing that
gave her a regal look. She had been unfailingly polite to
him since his return, but he sensed a reserve and admonition in her manner. She had not forgotten nor forgiven
him for the episode of the fire. In her eyes, he was a
seducer, he was sure.

"Thank you, Henri." Though he had been at the house
several times since his return, they had had little time to

alk, since he'd been swept off into conferences by her father. "I trust your trip to Paris was pleasant."

"Quite, though the weather was a bit cold."

"I would find it invigourating after the warmth here. I sometimes long for the snow and crispness of England in December."

"Perhaps if your father's business ventures go smoothly, you will soon return."

She looked up, surprised. "Has he indicated such a possibility?" She thought her father well ensconced in the bank and his work here.

"I was merely surmising. Most English and Europeans stay only a short tour of duty. For all its charm, Tangier lacks the amenities for a completely satisfying life."

"Then you plan a return to France eventually?"

"Of course. I would have stayed this trip except for the business that brought me back." He fell silent for a moment, then asked, "I have not wished to upset your sister, but I have been most concerned that she is fully recovered from the accident. Pierre gives me a physician's platitudes."

Sara regarded him solemnly. "Perhaps as I do, he finds it difficult to believe your interest is not to encourage my sister into further foolishness. Isn't it enough that she brought herself to the brink of disaster? It would be a kindness to leave her alone."

Unlike Pierre, she placed the blame on Emilie as well as him. This surprised him and gave him pause to think on the wisdom of the girl in his arms. "You have my assurance that I mean her no harm and will not force my attentions on her. I have always been honest with your sister, though she thinks otherwise," he said.

Sara met his gaze for several moments. "Yes, I believe you were. Set your mind at ease, Henri. Emilie is completely recovered from her ordeal both physically and mentally. There are no scars."

He smiled and they danced in silence for a bit. The

243

floor of the smoothly tiled hall was crowded with couples now, and it was difficult to hear the music over the laughter and chatter.

"I would have thought Pierre would be here," Henri said. He had not spoken to his friend for several days, but such an invitation would be natural under the circumstances. Unaccountably, Sara flushed but her voice was steady when she answered.

"He is invited." She glanced about the crowded room. "I have not seen him yet."

"Time is unimportant to Pierre when he becomes involved in his work. He has been known to forget many social events. But I am sure he will arrive soon." Just as he was sure Pierre was bedazzled and unaware that he was being swept into Emilie's web of ensnaring charm.

Emilie was claimed by one partner after another. Laughing and chatting with each, she kept looking for Pierre and grew more annoyed and impatient when she did not find him. He had promised, and he had spoken of the party to Sara when she was at the hospital this very morning. But she did not let his tardiness spoil her fun. Parties were meant to be enjoyed, and she danced every tune until at last the musicians put up their instruments and retired to another room to refresh themselves.

Jacques Prigent asked if he might bring her some tidbits. She nodded absently, not caring about food or drink and weary of Jacques' steady chatter about Martine, who was away for the holidays. With a glance toward the reception room where people milled about the tables, Emilie stepped through the arched doorway and out into the patio. She shivered in the cool breeze after the warmth of the dance floor but inhaled deeply and walked away from the doorway. She had no desire to have Jacques join her and spoil the peaceful solitude. She strolled to the archway leading to the street, then turned back impatiently when she realized that Pierre would ride to the stables at the rear where a dozen lads tended the horses

nd sedan chairs. Well, she would not search him out in
ae servants' quarters. How infuriating he was to be so
te. Doubtless some crisis claimed his attention at the last
noment; even so, it was inexcusable after his promises.

She crossed the garden along one of the sheltered paths
eneath the olive tree and leaned against a gallery post,
ghing and staring up at the blanket of stars that pierced
ae black sky. The noise of the party was muffled by the
ick walls of the house, though she could see people
assing before the archways.

Henri Cartier was clearly visible near an open window,
is head bent as he talked with a pretty girl who looked
p at him with undisguised admiration. Emilie's heart
ghtened and for a moment her breath was fire in her
reast. How clearly she remembered his eyes, his arms
bout her, his body . . . She closed her eyes and buried
er face in her hands to smother a wrenching sob. She
ated Henri Cartier and wished she need never see him
gain! And she hated herself for the desperate need her
ody felt, the trembling desire that left her breathless and
ade her toss and turn alone in her bed each night. Her
ind could erase Henri Cartier, but her body would not
lease the memory of his caresses and the union of their
odies.

She sighed and raised her head. No good to stand and
eep for the past. She thought again of Pierre, and how
fferent he was. Sometimes she wondered what he felt for
r. He said little, yet she knew he cared. She saw it in
s eyes when they were together, and she felt it in the
essure of his touch in unguarded moments when they
ere alone, and she found it in the kisses they shared.
ven though there had not been another moment like that
ae on their first ride, a time when he was taken by sur-
se and could not disguise his desire. And each time he
ft her, she re-examined her feelings and wondered if
ey could be defined as love.

Suddenly she was aware of the sweet aroma of Turkish

245

tobacco and looked about. The torchlight did not disp
the shadows under the gallery and she could barely mal
out a robed figure. She uttered an exclamation of surpris
There was a rustle of sound as the man stepped towar
her.

"Forgive me," Taleb al Mu'min said. "I did not wish
disturb your reverie."

Once again, his flawless English surprised her. "I ha
thought myself alone," she murmured, aware of his pen
trating gaze. She had not seen him inside, but then sl
had been occupied with dancing, a pastime he did not f
vour. His face was a dusky blur beneath the pale turba
She could not read his expression but she felt a blus
stain her cheeks. He had told her once that an Arab d
not look upon a woman unless he wished to have her.

"Have you been in Tangier long?" she asked.

"I arrived two days gone. Because *Si* Sloane's hou
was being readied for the Christian festivities, we conduc
ed our business at the bank, much to my regret, since
deprived me of seeing you."

"You flatter me." She let her gaze fall, then looke
back toward the party.

"I think not. You are accustomed to honeyed wor
from the mouths of men."

"I would not think a shereef considered such thin
worthy of his notice when so many maidens are at h
beck and call." His manner irritated her. He was alwa
so sure of himself, so maddeningly aloof!

He was silent though his gaze did not shift. It was sl
who looked away again. The winking jewel in his turba
was like a huge eye that pierced the darkness and the d
fenses of her mind.

"You no longer find the Frenchman's company enjo
able."

Her cheeks flamed. "I do not think that any of yo
concern!"

His infuriating, unsmiling face taunted her, and sl

moved to flee along the gallery, but his hand caught her shoulder. His grip was like steel but the touch managed to remain gentle. She was aware of it to a degree that disconcerted her.

"The ways of the English are foreign to my mind, and I regret if I have spoken out of turn." His voice softened slightly, but he did not remove his hand. "In my country a man speaks the truth as it is revealed to him."

She felt compelled to pursue the matter. "Truth and opposition are two different things."

He was unaccustomed to bantering with women, and the girl's temper amused him. Her tongue spoke words for their own sake. He had seen with his own eyes that she avoided *Si* Cartier, had not danced with him a single time or paused to speak with him. A lovers' quarrel? No, more, he was sure. This female would duel with words until a man's patience vanished and he swept her into bed to silence her. He felt her warm skin beneath his hand where the edge of the dress crossed her shoulder. The gown was provocative with its curved neckline that showed a crescent of pale flesh and the swell of her bosom. He had been unable to forget her since his earlier visit, though he reminded himself that she was an infidel who could mean nothing to the shereef of Madawadi. But she was also a woman full of promise, and he was drawn to her.

"I remain in Tangier twelve days. Will you come to the palace to dine with me?"

His request was completely unexpected and for a moment she was speechless. She was tempted to refuse because of his attitude, but she realized that such petulance would hurt no one but herself. She enjoyed the evening she and Sara had spent with him, she could not deny that. Instinctively, she knew if she refused his request now he would not ask again. There was something compelling in his carriage, his unwavering gaze. The hand at her shoulder had not twitched, yet she never lost her awareness of it.

"Yes," she said finally and simply.

"Tomorrow? Or is it one of your holy days?"

She shook her head. "No." Christmas was five days off.

He lowered his hand. "I am to see your father and the Minister at ten in the morning. I will come for you as soon as we conclude our talk." He inclined his head, and she acknowledged with a quick nod. "Until then . . ."

He stepped back into the shadows and walked around the gallery toward the reception room. He was framed in the light of the archway for a moment, his tall figure imposing in the crimson and gold robe and blue turban. He did not look back.

Emilie watched until he melted into the crowd, as a strange pulsing excitement filled her. What an extraordinary man. She couldn't have been more surprised by his invitation, or more delighted. Several minutes passed before she made her way back to the party.

"Ah, there you are. *Mon Dieu,* I have searched every where for you—" Jacques Prigent looked foolish balancing two crystal punch cups and a bone china plate of tiny cakes and sandwiches.

"I'm sorry. I felt the heat and stepped out for a breath of air."

He was concerned immediately. "You are all right now?"

"Fine, thank you." She accepted a cup and sipped the punch while he found chairs where they could sit with their refreshments. She scarcely listened to his chatter; her mind was fully occupied with the shereef. She watched him across the room where he stood with her father and several other men. He was taller than most, and she was struck by his handsomeness. He had not included Sara the invitation . . . She forced her attention back to Jacques nodding to some question she had not even heard.

248

"Ah, here is Pierre. He seems to be looking for you," Jacques said with a sly wink.

"Excuse me." She put aside the cup and rose to greet Pierre. "You are late," she scolded.

"Am I? I lost track of the time."

"Another patient, I suppose." Her tone was more petulant than she intended.

He studied her a moment, then nodded. "Yes, I am truly sorry." He looked about the crowded room as the musicians who had returned to the alcove struck up a lively tune.

"Well, you are here now, and that is the important thing. I would like to dance. Come." She took his hand and led him to the floor. "Will you be forced to work on Christmas? I have been hoping that you will join us for dinner. Mother has planned a magnificent feast of roast goose and plum pudding, a traditional English Christmas."

He smiled at her enthusiasm, wondering if it was the party that had brightened her cheeks so much or the upcoming holidays. She was like a child in anticipating happy events.

"You mother has not invited me."

She frowned. "Only because I promised to find out if you were free." It was not strictly the truth. The thought of including him in the party her mother was planning had only occurred to her this moment, a fact which flushed her with guilt. There were a dozen or more people invited, one more would be easy to accommodate.

"I regret I have already made plans. Several of the doctors and nurses at the hospital have arranged to dine with patients who are able to be up and about. Had I known—"

"Surely you can be excused!" she said, scowling at him. "You devote too many hours to your work. You should not spoil Christmas by spending it at the hospital."

"I do not think it spoiled."

"Oh, you are hopeless! All you think about is the hospital and your work!" She was angry though he had done nothing, and she knew that he would not give in to her demands. She had learned long ago that Pierre would not be pushed into anything.

"Would you enjoy a ride on Christmas morning? I am not due at the hospital until noon."

She tossed her head and soft curls of gold danced about her face. "I expect we will be busy opening gifts and—" Then, she sighed and smiled. She could not stay angry. "I would love to. About ten?"

"Perfect."

"And you are forgiven for being late and leaving me to dance with so many dull young men."

He laughed. "I suspect you have not missed a single dance and have enjoyed every moment of the evening."

"Am I so transparent?"

"So enchanting that men would not leave you standing alone very long."

She basked in the compliments and was sorry when the music ended and he led her from the floor, refusing to dance every number though she would have liked it. She pouted momentarily then danced off with a young English soldier.

The party lasted well into the morning, with the trays of food on the tables being replenished steadily and servants moving among the guests with fresh offerings of wine. Several of the men grew a bit boisterous after hours of imbibing, and wives began leading them toward the stables and home. Pierre looked very weary and Emilie did not have the heart to beg him to stay when he took his leave with several others who were heading toward the hospital. Henri was already gone, Emilie had not seen him leave, but the shereef was talking with the elder Sloane and Ali Ibn Tashfeen in an alcove at one end of the reception room.

At last the musicians packed their instruments, and the party was over. Charlotte, Sara and Emilie bade the last guests goodbye amid dozens of compliments on the success of the affair. Charlotte beamed. Roderick would be pleased, and she had enjoyed herself immensely. She had not been looking forward to the Christmas season away from home, but now some of her fears were laid to rest. Invitations had been extended and accepted, and the season would rush by in a flurry of activity, so there would not be time for boredom or homesickness.

Roderick walked to the gate with the Minister of Finance and the shereef, saying last goodbyes and thanking them for honouring his house with their presence. The shereef seemed more friendly than before, and Roderick considered that a very favourable omen.

CHAPTER FOURTEEN

Emilie changed outfits several times before deciding a last upon a peach colored linen that showed to advantag the tan she had acquired in spite of bonnets and parasol to shield her from the sun. It was cut on simple lines, wit an immodestly low neckline. The dress had a short jacke which she buttoned against the chill in the air. The da had begun bright, but a raw wind sprang up and cloud scudded along the western sky like a grey shroud outlir ing the crenellated wall of the ancient city and the tawn hills to the south. The temperature was comfortable ex cept for the wind, and Emilie decided on a light cape c blue wool in case of rain. When she descended to th drawing room, her mother looked up in surprise.

"Where are you going, dear?"

"The shereef has invited me to the palace."

"The shereef?! Does your father know?" Roderick ha said nothing . . .

Emilie studied her reflection in the mirror-like surfac of a lacquered vase, puffing her hair so the curls sprar loosely.

"I'm sure the shereef spoke to him. They were togeth a great deal last night and they had another meeting th

orning. I think the shereef is too important for father to
efuse his wishes."

"What a dreadful thing to say, Emilie. Your father
would not agree to anything simply to curry favour."

She would argue that point but did not want to upset
er mother. "Has Sara been down?"

"I believe she's gone to the hospital, though I would
ave thought her exhausted from the party. It was a
uccess, don't you think?"

"Yes, mother."

"Mrs. Phelps said it rivalled the finest Embassy
ffairs."

"You did an excellent job, mother. I know everyone
ad a wonderful time. It will be the talk of the city for the
ntire holiday season."

Charlotte was pleased by the compliment from her sec-
nd born, and she tried to banish her misgivings about
milie's outing. Roderick was so involved lately, he
eemed to care less about domestic matters. He had per-
itted both girls to visit the palace and the *casbah* with
he shereef once before. She saw no reason to forbid it
ow.

"You will be careful? I do not like to think of you
mong all those Arabs," she murmured.

Surprised, Emilie laughed. "Mother, you simply can't
nagine the respect which Taleb al Mu'min is treated. I
ssure you, I am safer than here in the drawing room with
ou."

A bell tinkled softly, and Asheema appeared to an-
ounce that the shereef had arrived. At the doorway, two
alace servants formed a guard at either side of the arch
s Taleb entered.

"*Lella* Sloane . . ." he smiled at Charlotte. "I must
ompliment you again on the pleasant evening just past
nd thank you for the invitation."

"Oh . . . I'm so glad you enjoyed it. It was a lovely

253

party, so many nice people." Charlotte flushed and fe
silent.

Emilie hid a smile. Her mother had no idea how ex
traordinary the show of European manners was. She wo
dered what had prompted them, knowing that Taleb wa
not a man to do the expected merely because it was ex
pected. He looked at her.

"If you are ready?"

"Yes. Goodbye, mother."

"Goodbye, dear . . ."

Taleb nodded and they turned, one of the servan
scurrying ahead, the other falling in step behind as the
went through the courtyard and gardens to where he ha
left a magnificent white stallion with silver-studded ha
ness and bridle and tooled leather saddle. Behind it wa
the fine sedan chair that had been sent for Emilie an
Sara on their first visit to the palace. When Emilie rea
ized he meant for her to ride in it alone, she shook he
head.

"If you are to ride, I will ride also. Please send one
the servants to the stable to have my mare brought."

Taleb regarded her curiously for a moment. "You are
strong minded woman," he said without reproach.

"You have done me the honour of calling for me pe
sonally," she responded. "I would enjoy riding in you
company."

"So be it." He spoke sharply to a slave who ran towa
the stable.

"You are very different from the foreign woman I ha
met."

"Have you met so many?"

"Enough."

The slave returned with the black mare, with Moham
still tightening the cinch as the animal walked. The sla
knelt in the dust to make a stepping block for Emilie, an
Taleb offered his hand. His fingers were warm as sand u
der the hot desert sun.

They rode slowly up the hill, circling the European sector along the summit, then crossing along a route Emilie had never followed before, which bordered the cliffs overlooking the sea and approaching the ancient city from the west. The view of the ocean was spectacular; the *Gharb* whipped along the cliff with biting sting of salt spray and mist, making Emilie draw the blue cape close. She raised her face to the wind, throwing back her head to let the power of it flow through her. They had been silent, but now Emilie twisted in the saddle and called out.

"I want to ride, Taleb!" Without waiting for an answer, she slapped the reins against the mare's flank and kicked into a gallop, turning on the path and rushing past the shereef and servants heedlessly. She heard a quick clatter of hooves as Taleb wheeled his horse to follow. Laughing aloud, she coaxed power from the sleek mare, glancing over her shoulder to see Taleb smile as the powerful stallion closed the gap. Then they were side by side on the cliff-top path, cloak, skirt and robe flapping like sails. Emilie's blue velvet riding hat was whipped from its pins and flew away but she did not notice. The blood sang in her temples as her heart pounded with the joy of freedom.

As they raced past the road that had brought them to the summit the path narrowed and was less defined, but she did not slow the horse. She glanced sidelong and saw Taleb's steady gaze upon her, as though his mount needed no guidance. He would ride as long and as far as she, she was certain. She laughed again and saw his answering smile.

Breathless, she finally slowed the mare and stopped under a stunted cork oak. Taleb reined in beside her.

"You ride excellently but impulsively," he said. He was not the slightest short of breath, and Emilie realized that in spite of his apparent life of ease, he was in excellent physical condition.

"Is it impulsive to ride as the wind?"

"Only if the trail is unfamiliar to you."

255

"Would you have let me go if it was not safe?"

"I would not have stopped you."

That surprised her and she studied him curiously. "Yo would let me ride into danger?"

"I would allow you the decision. You have alread shown you are not conventional, by your own countr men's standards nor by mine. You demand freedom spirit and none should try to rob you of it, least of all I."

His eyes were inky pools whose hidden depths sh could not read, yet she found no disapproval in his gaz She had challenged him and he had met her on her ow terms. He had not felt the need to show his superi horsemanship by giving the stallion its head and makir the ride a race, which he would have won easily. And I credited her ability without flattery.

She tossed windblown blond curls and her eyes dance For a moment, they sat looking at one another, gaz locked in sensuous awareness. How different they wer yet how similiar. At long last, Emilie thumped a he against the mare's flank and started back along the pat Taleb rode beside her without speaking. One of the slav had recovered her hat and held it out to her, but she r fused it with a wave of a hand as the wind gusted ar caught her cape. A thunderous cloud roiled and lightnir rent the sky in a jagged slash. Still Taleb did not brea the pace Emilie set, and when rain began to spatter the dusty trail, it was she who urged her mount to a bri canter so they might reach the palace before being caug in a deluge.

They entered the walled city by the *Bab er Raha* ar rode the horses up the palace steps. Alighting, they hu ried inside as the horses were led away.

She gave her cape to a servant and shook the dampne from her hair. The rain, which had barely begun, no pelted down in a grey screen. The warmth vanished all once, and Emilie shivered. The shereef spoke in Arabic a Moor in gold livery as he led Emilie around the court

256

a room where a fire had been laid in a large circular pit recessed in the wall. Cushions were strewn about the outer edge of the circle over a luxurious carpet.

She moved to the fire, holding out her hands to warm herself and rubbing her arms under the peach-coloured linen. Charcoal glowed under leaping flames; the fire had been started much earlier to chase the chill from the room. The soft click of *babouches* made her turn. Four servants entered carrying braziers of red-hot coals which they set at the corners of the carpet, thus completing a circle of warmth around them. Taleb indicated the cushions nearest the fire. She sat, tucking her feet close so that she half reclined on the cushions. Leaning back, she stared into the flames.

"I have never known an Englishwoman before," Taleb said unexpectedly.

She looked up. "Are there none in Fez?"

"Perhaps, but I have not made their acquaintance."

"You must know many in Tangier. My father says you have many business dealings with the Minister of Foreign Affairs. You are invited to all manner of social functions."

His gaze did not shift but she had the impression that he had looked away. "To see people is not to know them. Allah has written that the face shown to the world masks the man inside who waits to escape."

She frowned. "Do you believe that? Am I different than I seem? Are you?"

"We are each many things. We expose only that portion of ourselves we wish others to see."

The fire had warmed her and she was quite comfortable, even with the unusual conversation. Again she thought how different he was from any man she'd ever known, and she felt a stirring respect and admiration. She shifted on the cushions, sitting with knees hugged to her body as she used to do as a child when listening to the wind rustle autumn leaves while she dreamed fantasies of escaping the boredom of her life. The firelight behind her made her hair a halo and her cheeks glowed with the heat.

"Do you think we display parts of our nature much the way we would a collection of jewels?"

He settled himself where he could look at her, and waited until a slave set down a tray and began preparing tea. He still wore the white robe but now he reached up to remove the voluminous turban and set it aside. She had never seen him without it; his hair was black as pitch and curled back from his forehead and ears softly. He looked younger, but it was impossible to guess the age of the face with eyes aged by wisdom.

"The analogy is not totally unacceptable, except that the display often is made without conscious thought. We act from habit once a pattern is established."

She shook her head impatiently. "I do not agree. Even habitual actions take deliberate thought, and it is quite possible to alter a pattern on a moment's notice. Did I not do that when I chose to ride along the ridge?"

"Even a changing pattern is part of a pattern."

"I do not understand. Do all Arabs think in so convoluted a manner?"

He took a cup of tea. "We are taught to ponder all particles of dust as material for clay to build strong houses."

She sighed and sipped her tea, puzzling over him. The silence lengthened and he did not break it. He seemed at ease simply sitting and looking at her, communicating without words. With anyone else, it would have become awkward, but she felt no compulsion to disturb the intimate silence. She did not understand his remark, yet she felt as though she were absorbing it unconsciously.

When they finished tea, lunch was served before the fire, a meal as exotic as the one they'd taken in the restaurant on her first visit. There were fewer courses and smaller portions but still enough to feed a dozen people, far more than Emilie was accustomed to eating at midday. Yet everything was delicious and she could not refuse any plate. Taleb sat beside her, taking each bowl the servant put down, and when deeming it fit, selecting the choicest portions for her before taking his own. They ate with fingers, washing with hot towels after each course. They chatted or were silent by turn, according to their mood. Outside the arched windows, the storm spent itself and blew out to sea, leaving the sky washed clean. When Taleb asked her if she would like to stroll in the gardens, she agreed eagerly.

The gardens were quite different by daylight, and the shereef took pains to answer her constant flow of questions about the names of strange plants, flowers and shrubs. She wanted to know everything, to fill her mind with physical details of the world in which Taleb lived, the world that molded his mind and manner. She was irresistably drawn to him. Excitement stirred her deeply, and though quite different from the arousal she felt with Henri, it was no less sensual. Taleb did not touch her, had not since helping her to mount her horse. Still, his presence was overpowering.

The sun passed overhead and the city quieted for the afternoon solitude that was observed even though the cooler winter weather no longer demanded it. Taleb escorted her to a room at one end of the *iyal* where a bed had been readied for her. She protested she needed no rest, but he left her with a promise to return in an hour's time. She gave in meekly, reluctant to argue with him.

She saw him every day after that. In the mornings, he came to the house and they rode among the hills to the west and south of the city, sometimes fording the river and traveling miles into the outskirts of the desert before turning back. Each outing was an experience that Emilie savoured, hugging it to her and examing it over and over in an effort to discover why she felt as she did. They never spoke of personal matters, only of philosophical thoughts which were often riddles to her mind, though he

259

seemed to find them lucid. Some evenings, Taleb sent a chair to bring her to dine at the palace with him, always in private. The sultan was still at Rabat; Taleb seemed to have the entire palace at his disposal. Occasionally, Emilie saw robed figures at a distance but no one ever joined them. And there were never any women but the slaves and servants who catered to Taleb's every whim. His life was far more elegant than Emilie had ever seen; even the richest families in England did not employ such huge staffs nor enjoy such lavish lifestyle.

Emilie lost track of the days which passed all too quickly and would have been mourned except that each new one brought Taleb into her life once more. She scarcely saw her family except at lunch, and then did not listen to conversation that had no meaning for her. Her father was pleased by her friendship with the shereef, since it strengthened his own position in the Pendash Company's dealings with the Moroccans. The fact that he did not discourage her from seeing Taleb was all that mattered to Emilie. Charlotte was puzzled by her husband's attitude but said nothing; Sara watched her sister with a growing sense of foreboding. The shereef was unfailingly polite, but Sara was convinced that the gap between his culture and their own was too wide to bridge. She was made uneasy by the spark in Emilie's eyes as she dressed for dinner with the shereef, or the quick smile with which she met him when he came to ride. Sara had not talked confidentially with her sister since before the party, the beginning of her involvement with Taleb al Mu'min. There were no more rapturous tales of her romance with Pierre; he seemed forgotten in a matter of days.

On Christmas morning, Sara woke early as she always did and enjoyed breakfast before a warm bath and dressing. She had purchased gifts in the *socco* and several shops in the square: a silk scarf for her father, an intricately drawn-thread shawl for her mother, and a beautiful tooled leather purse for Emilie. Each was packaged in bright paper, ribboned and bowed, and laid on the table near the door of her rooms. On the desk near the window lay another package, flat and thin in white tissue paper. It was for Pierre. Beside it, a string shopping bag of the type servants used for marketing was filled with presents for patients at the hospital. She had promised to join the staff and patients briefly in their Christmas celebration after dinner, and she'd collected a few tokens to distribute to ease the loneliness of those who had no families to share the holiday.

The day was pleasantly warm, without threat of rain. When the family gathered for Christmas breakfast and the exchange of gifts, it seemed odd to hear the song of nightingales outside the open windows. A champagne Christmas breakfast had been tradition since the girls were small, one that had been eagerly awaited even as they grew older, since father always seemed less stern. He was particularly jovial this morning as he distributed gifts, and on opening packages, exclaimed and thanked the women for each present. His own gifts to them were lavish, an indication of how pleased he was with their adaptation to life in Tangier and his own success. To Charlotte, he gave an emerald necklace of perfectly matched stones, selected by the Minister of Finance's personal jeweler and set in a fine filigree of gold, handwrought by a mastercraftsman in the *Rue des Siaghins*. To each of the girls, he gave a pearl necklace with a ruby center stone the size of a sixpence coin.

Emilie put hers about her neck and worked the clasp. "It is beautiful, Father!" She had never owned anything so magnificent, and she fingered the cool stone against her flesh. She had chosen a dress the color of wine, and the ruby matched as though designed especially for it.

"Thank you, Father. It's the most wonderful gift I have ever had," Sara said with a smile. She lifted her hair so her mother could help with the fastening.

261

"There are no finer stones in Morocco, you can be sure," Roderick said, beaming. "Some larger of course, but they belong to the royal families and are not on the market. I trust all of you will wear them in good health." He lifted his champagne glass.

"We must toast the success of the venture that brought us here," Sara said with a smile, still holding aloft the glass. "To the bank and your new company, Father. May they prosper."

Charlotte and Emilie murmured and they drank again, then they settled to a true English breakfast, thanks to Colleen who had deigned to enter the kitchen and take matters into her own hands so that Christmas would be Christmas. There were kippers, tiny sausages, scrambled eggs and a rasher of bacon. Hot rolls, cinnamon buns and sweet, fresh, dark bread replaced the flat Arab loaves that had become commonplace, and coffee, rich and strong in aroma, with thick cream and sugar.

Taleb arrived as the Sloanes retired from dining to the sitting room. Roderick was especially glad to see him, wishing him great felicitations even though he did not observe the Christian holiday. Taleb wished them all well but refused the glass of sherry Roderick offered. He had come to ride with Emilie, and if she was ready—?

She looked to her father, afraid that he might object on Christmas day, but he did not. He expressed hope that they would enjoy the ride and pleasant weather. He was considering an outing himself a bit later, he said. Charlotte had learned to ride passably well under Mohamet's patient instruction, and they might venture along familiar streets to pay calls on some of her friends.

Realizing that Sara was left out, Taleb graciously invited her to join them but she refused. She did have plans, she said. Taleb let the matter drop. He had discharged the token courtesy he felt bound to offer.

Sara was alone when Colleen entered the sitting room, her head cocked in surprise. "The young doctor is here,

Miss Sara. He says he's to ride with Miss Emilie, but she's already gone. What shall I tell him?"

Sara was on her feet instantly. How like Emilie to forget! She went to meet Pierre who was standing near the twisted olive tree that shaded the patio.

"Pierre, how nice to see you."

"Sara . . . merry Christmas."

"Merry Christmas to you. I am afraid Emilie has been thoughtless and gone off. She will be angry with herself for missing you, I am sure."

He frowned. "I should have sent a note so she would be sure I had not forgotten," he said. "I am late, and I'm told that appointments made with me are not held in sacred expectation. I tend to be careless of time."

"The fault is hers if the appointment was made, no matter how long ago." She would not let him blame himself for Emilie's discourtesy. "I hope it does not inconvenience you."

"We were only to ride." He looked at her. "Would you consider taking her place? I have not seen you except for odd moments for some time. I am eager to hear about your lessons with Serge and what you have been doing."

Sara hesitated. More than anything she wanted to ride with him, but she feared meeting Emilie and an awkward situation. No, she told herself. Emilie would simply laugh it off without regard for Pierre's feelings. "I would love to," she said. "If you will give me a moment to fetch a hat . . ."

"Of course. I will wait in the garden and enjoy the sun."

When she returned, she had changed the green gown for a riding dress of brown linen with velvet lapels and cuffs, though how she managed to change so quickly amazed him. She carried a small velvet pouch which she looped over the pommel before mounting her horse. They rode away from the city toward the hills in the southwest, a route that would take them to the hillside spot where he had first seen her sketching. He selected the route because he enjoyed the quiet scenery away from the city and the natural wildness of the trail. When he asked her preference, she was willing to leave the choice to him.

They talked of her work with Serge Prichard, how much she was enjoying it and how much she was learning. She sounded far more confident now, and he was glad. She also mentioned that Serge had told her Pierre exhibited artistic talent which, despite encouragement, he had never pursued.

She chided him. "You were the one who said it was wrong to waste a gift."

He laughed. "True, but mine is so mediocre that it was not difficult to choose between it and my love of medicine."

"You might still work at it as a leisure pastime to relax after a busy day."

"I prefer to sit with my journals or newspapers if I have time."

"You are incorrigible," she scolded.

He glanced along the rocky, wind-swept hills, greening now with the winter rains. Of late, he had taken more hours off than ever from his practice to spend with Emilie, who made him laugh and feel happy enough to forget all else.

They came to the spot where he had first seen Sara sketching, and she drew rein. With a smile, she dismounted and unfastened the velvet pouch to carry with her as she walked to the level place that commanded a view of the city and bay. As he joined her, she unfastened the strings of the velvet bag, drew out a small white package tied with green ribbon and held it out to him.

"Merry Christmas, Pierre."

He took it, watching her the while. He had not thought to buy a gift for her, and he certainly never expected to receive one. He felt at a loss for words.

She sensed his discomfort and smiled. "It is a token of appreciation for all you have done for me."

"I have done nothing—"

She would not listen. "You introduced me to Serge and you let me come to the hospital. I have never been so happy in my lifetime, and it is you who set me upon the path that makes me so."

He could not answer and busied himself with the ribbon which fluttered in the breeze until she caught it and twined it around her fingers as he unwrapped the paper.

It was a painting, a small oil done with clear strong strokes; the picture was the scene that lay before them at this moment. The miniature canvas managed to capture the drama of the white buildings, gleaming minarets and mosques, flags above the legations snapping in an unseen breeze, against a background of the calm but powerful Mediterranean with sunlight slashing golden rays across its azure depths.

He looked up. "It is beautiful and very well executed. Sara, how can I ever thank you?"

"By enjoying the picture. I ask no more."

He smiled, slipping the canvas back into its paper, then into his pocket so he could hold out his hand to her. "Come, let us enjoy a ride as far as the river before I return you to your family and your Christmas dinner."

Emilie and Taleb rode along the Cape Spartel Road. Taleb ordered the slaves and guards to stay at a distance so there was no feeling of being watched. He never went anywhere without a full complement of armed men, and she wondered if he considered himself in danger from marauders or from the foreigners. When she asked, he waved away the answer as of no consequence and said it was the will of Allah.

Winter rains had made swamps of many low areas, and they followed an upper road where the steady *Gharb* dried the ground almost as fast as the heavens watered it. On one spot, they saw a herd of sheep and goats grazing on new sweet grass, while the herder sat crosslegged beside a scrub bush, his eyes closed, his palms turned up on his lap in order to receive any blessing Allah might visit upon him. On the other side, they glimpsed the sea between gray crags.

When they came to a jagged cliff, Taleb motioned his people with a sharp gesture and they dismounted and went down the steep hillside on some preordained purpose. Taleb reined his horse and swung from the saddle in a sweep of yellow robe. He helped her dismount, then started down the cliff, still gripping her hand in his own powerful one.

"Where are we going?"

"I wish to show you a place no Christian has ever seen. Have no fear, I will not allow you to fall."

It was the first time he had indicated any concern about her inability to meet his pace, but before she had time to wonder about it, she understood the reason. There was no path, save that which the slaves and guards had made moments before by hacking at tenacious shrubs and clearing loose stones that might catch an unwary foot and tumble her into the sea below. The path grew narrower with every step as it cut between huge boulders and skirted those that were impassable. Several times, Taleb tugged at her arm to show they had to duck some rocky overhang. Ahead, she could hear the steady swish of scimitars and occasionally see the bobbing white turban of a slave. The ground levelled all at once, and the slaves were standing before a natural arch in a rock. Taleb stooped to make his way through the opening; with a sense of excitement, Emilie followed. For a moment, all sound of the wind and sea was cut off by the thick walls of stone. Then they emerged from the narrow, damp pass into a vaulted hall in the heart of the rock, dimly lit from above by rays of warm, golden light. It resembled the interior of a magnificent cathedral. The drip of water from hidden springs tinkled like crystal bells, and shafts of light played upon the glistening rocks to create designs of silver, red and gold.

Emilie stared in ecstatic wonder as Taleb gently urged her forward. She became aware of a low rumbling sound which broke into a hoarse roar as they neared the far end of the room where a pointed arch opened straight to the sea. Waves crashed and funnelled through the opening with a furious rushing sound, as though the dragon of the deep hurled itself into the cavern. Taleb guided her along a ledge at the side of the cave, and they were looking down at forthy, eddying water which had worn the lower rocks smooth as glass. It churned in a spraying mist, then retreated in a hissing whisper to gather force for the next onslaught. The cave was quiet until another wave crashed.

"It is the most beautiful sight I have ever seen," Emilie whispered in the interval of silence that followed.

"There are many caves such as this along the coast. Time and the tide accomplish what no human hand can." He fell silent, but she knew he was watching her.

"You say that no Christian has been here before . . . Why did you bring me?"

His gaze held hers while another roaring wave tumbled at their feet and retreated. "It pleases me to see your beauty in this setting. A rare jewel should be surrounded only by the finest precious metals so its beauty is enhanced."

She was accustomed to compliments, but she felt her cheeks blush and her gaze wavered. His words were like a silken caress that made her pulse race. She felt a shock of pleasure as his hand tightened on her arm. For a moment, she dared not speak or move. Another wave spent itself and echoed the pounding of the blood in her temples.

"I do not wish to return to Fez alone." Taleb said quietly.

She stared at him, confused by the heavy emotion that filled her so unexpectedly.

"Your eyes are dark pools in a grotto, and your lips are glistening rubies dampened by the mists."

267

Her heart hammered and she trembled as he raised gentle fingers to her cheek to trace the line of her jaw, then touch her lips. "I am unaccustomed to making requests of women. Must I utter the words?"

She was paralyzed with the throbbing desire that was awakened in her. Finally she managed to whisper, "Yes . . ." Her brain reeled, and though she sensed his desire, she could not sort her thoughts to understand his intent. Was he asking her to share physical pleasure? He said he did not want to return to Tangier alone. Surely he did not expect her to travel with him to warm his bed?

"I wish you to become my wife, to return to Fez with me and remain with me always."

"Your wife?!"

He scowled. "Have I said the words wrong? If I were dealing with your parents I would pay whatever price they asked and take you away. Is there some custom in asking a woman herself that I am unaware of?"

Numbly, she shook her head. "It is only that I am so surprised. I did not expect . . ." Words failed her.

"We have spent sufficient hours together to know that our lives are destined to be one."

She wanted to feel his arms about her, feel his lips on hers, be swept beyond confusing thoughts and decisions. She wanted him as lover, she could not deny it. Her body cried out for the touch of his flesh, and her knees went weak with the thought. But they had never spoken of intimate matters, never declared feelings, yet he was offering her not an affair but marriage. Marriage . . .

"You are silent, but the trembling of your flesh tells me you share the passion I feel. I have followed the strange custom of calling on you at your home, riding, and dining with you. Is there more ritual to be observed before I can speak the passionate words that fill my heart?"

"I—I don't know what to say—" Confusion swept her again.

"Curse Satan!" he swore softly. His eyes were as black

268

as the shadowed rocks of the cave. He pulled her into his arms and kissed her, his lips hungry and demanding. All resistance, all doubt, vanished and she clung to him with reckless desire. His strong arms held her close, and she felt his hard, lean body against her soft curves. His hands moved at her back, her waist, her neck, leaving fiery trails that seared her flesh. She wanted him as she had never wanted any man before, a need so fully born in an instant that she would have welcomed his lovemaking on the hard floor of the cave. Her senses reeled and her body tensed with desire.

He held her at arm's length and stared into her eyes. "You share my desire."

"Yes."

"You will marry me?" When she did not answer immediately, he peered at her in the misty light. "Would it please you instead to be a concubine in my harem?"

In spite of herself, she had to laugh, and he caught her in his arms again and kissed her, tongue capturing hers to smother the sound. Her pulse became a roar to match the crashing waves. Yes, she wanted him. Yes, she would wed him! Had she not sworn that no man would have her again without marriage? Taleb was asking it as his right to fulfill the huge passion that gripped them, a passion she could not deny, nor wanted to.

She clung to him, burying her face in the cool folds of his *jellaba*. "I will marry you."

"Allah has written it . . ." He stroked her hair gently as one might a child. "We shall live in his bosom." When she looked up at him, he smiled. "In paradise . . ."

He kissed her with controlled passion, then led her back along the ledge and through the cave to the steep path. He did not release her hand until they were once more at the top of the cliff and she was on the black mare.

CHAPTER FIFTEEN

The shereef and Roderick Sloane were closeted in the library for more than an hour when Emilie and Taleb returned. Taleb would not consider waiting until the following day, a suggestion made by Emilie in an effort to pull herself together and prepare her family for the unexpected news. It seemed cruel to spring such a surprise only two hours before the house would be filled with guests invited to Christmas dinner, but Taleb saw no need to observe such nonsensical whims.

Emilie avoided her mother and sister, unwilling to answer questions she was sure her agitated state would cause. She paced her rooms, stepping out to the gallery to stare down at the library where she knew the two men were discussing her future. Though she listened intently, she could not hear their voices. She half expected father to rage loud enough to inform the entire household what his discussion with the shereef was about.

The library was at the rear corner of the house, with an entrance through the hall or directly from the gallery. Father and Taleb would undoubtedly come out through the gallery, and she would be able to read father's expression instantly.

270

Too nervous and impatient to stand still, she went inside again, only to return to her post when the suspense once more became unbearable. What were they saying? Let father say yes, she prayed silently. And if he didn't? She knew she would go off with Taleb anyhow. Nothing mattered but being with him. In the bosom of Allah . . . in paradise. She tried to imagine the lifestyle that would be hers but could not. It did not matter, not as long as she was in Taleb's arms.

When the heavy carved oak door finally opened, Emilie shrank back into the dappled shade of the bougainvillea. The two men walked side by side, staring straight ahead, faces solemn. Her heart skipped then thundered. She had never seen her father look like this. Neither pleased nor angry; ominously stern . . . and something else, something unreadable. When they passed below and reentered the drawing room, Emilie scurried along the upper hall and down the stairs, skirt flying, slippers slapping the tiles. She paused at the newel, clutching the rail to draw several deep breaths before walking along the hall to the drawing room. She paused again at the door, and almost collided with Asheema who was coming out.

The Moorish servant bowed her head. "*Si* Sloane desires to speak with the daughter of the house."

Taking another nervous breath, Emilie walked in, shoulders back and hands clenched to hide her shaking. Her father and Taleb were standing near the Queen Anne sofa on which Charlotte was seated. Behind her, Sara stood with a hand on her mother's shoulder, her face pale, her eyes wide. Charlotte looked as though she had just heard the voice of God announce the world was to end. The room was so hushed Emilie could hear nothing but her own heartbeat. She waited for her father to speak; she glanced at Taleb who stood as easily in his yellow robe as he always did, his impassive expression telling her nothing. Her father glanced at the doorway to be certain the servant was gone, then he looked at her.

271

"Taleb has asked for your hand in marriage, Emilie, as you are aware."

"Yes, Father." Her lips formed the words but no sound came out.

He cleared his throat and his gaze flicked to the carpeted floor for an instant. "Is it your wish to wed him?"

She forced words past the constriction in her throat. "Yes, Father." Her nails were cutting into her palms, and she concentrated on the pain.

Mother whimpered, and Sara's hand at her shoulder was quickly reassuring. Emilie dared not look at either of them.

"Harrummph." She had never seen father nervous, but there was a small tic at the corner of his eye and he had difficulty with his words. "I have given my permission."

Her breath rushed out in a sigh, and she looked at Taleb. His expression did not alter, but she saw the triumphant gleam in his eyes. He had won his prize. She was his. The thought quickened her breath and made her quiver inwardly. Even her mother's stricken gasp could not diminish her joy.

"Thank you, Father."

"Harrummph. . . ." Roderick walked to one of the gilt chairs and sat, crossing his legs with deliberation in order to gain time he needed to collect himself. "Taleb wishes the wedding to take place as soon as possible, since his responsibilities demand his return to Fez almost immediately. Your mother would, of course, prefer more time to arrange matters. A proper wedding—" A glance at Taleb aborted his words abruptly. "There are things to be settled."

Emilie could not contain her joy another moment. She ran to her mother to sit and fling her arms about her and kiss her impulsively. "I do not want to wait, Mother. I want to marry Taleb so I can go to Fez with him. This is not England where we must consider family and lifelong friends. I will marry in the church if the rector is willing."

She turned to Taleb. "You will grant me that small request?"

He nodded and said nothing. It was as though he could afford to be generous in his victory, and such details were of no consequence.

Roderick seemed to sigh, though he made no sound. "Very well. I leave the plans in your hands. When will you leave Tangier?"

"In four days."

Charlotte sobbed and pressed a scrap of silk handkerchief to her mouth. Her eyes were wide and frightened.

"I must return to the palace now," Taleb said, inclining his head to the women. "This is your holiday, and I know you look forward to your celebration."

"Are you sure I cannot persuade you to stay to dinner?" Roderick said as though the matter had been gone over and already decided. Charlotte grew paler and her hand trembled.

"No, but I thank you *Si* Sloane. I must attend to matters at once."

Roderick was on his feet, saying goodbye then. Emilie leapt up. "I will see you out, Taleb."

No one tried to dissuade her, and she walked sedately beside her fiance with breathless excitement, silent until they were away from the house and at the yard where the slaves stood with his horse.

"I cannot believe it. Too much has happened so quickly—"

He gathered her in his arms, not caring about the servants who were statue-like and expressionless. His kiss stirred and filled her with desire.

"Four days will seem forever," she whispered.

His fingertips caressed the nape of her neck. "Forever begins when you are mine."

She watched until he had ridden beyond the fringe of trees, horses' hooves clattering on the hard ground and raising dust in spurts. She glimpsed his yellow *jellaba* be-

273

tween green branches. Then he was gone, and she turned to stroll back to the drawing room, pausing to pluck a leaf from an oleander and twirl it in her fingers dreamily. Four days. . . .

She heard father's voice and mother's weeping the moment she opened the door. She would have escaped in order not to spoil the beauty of her thoughts, but her mother spied her and drew her into the dispute that had erupted the moment Emilie and Taleb left the room.

"How could you do such a thing, Emilie?" Charlotte cried. She was weeping openly, her eyes red and puffy, the silk handkerchief a sodden mass in her clenched fist. Her pallor had been replaced by a blotchy redness that was alarming.

"That will be enough, Charlotte!" Roderick commanded. "I will not have you carrying on in this disgraceful manner. The matter is closed."

"My baby—"

Emilie had never heard her mother so pathetic and would have been moved by her tears except for her own joy and the knowledge that she and her mother had never shared any intimacy of affection.

"Emilie is a grown woman and has made her decision. Taleb is a wealthy and powerful man, she will lack for nothing." Roderick did not look at his daughter while he spoke.

"But he is a barbarian—!" The words rushed out before she could stem them.

Roderick pounded his fist on the mantle. "Taleb al Mu'min is an educated, civilized man. He is concerned with the welfare of his people and chooses to live among the tribes he rules. That does not make him a barbarian. He sees fit to support Daniel and myself in our endeavours, keep that in mind, dear Charlotte. I have invested my entire capital in this venture—which is succeeding because a man of the shereef's influence backs it." He paced the length of the room angrily, hands clasped be-

274

hind his back. When he turned, his look clearly indicated the matter was closed. "Go upstairs and collect yourself. We will not speak of this again, except to help Emilie make plans for her wedding." He drew a gold watch from his pocket and flipped open the case. "I think we will all benefit from an extended siesta today. It is Christmas and we are expecting guests. Charlotte, Sara . . ."

A curt nod brought them to their feet, and Sara, who had not said a word, helped her mother from the room. With considerable effort, Charlotte ceased crying but her face showed the strain.

Emilie started to cross the room on impulse, went instead to where her father was still standing by the fireplace.

"Thank you, Father. I love Taleb and we will be happy." She stood on tiptoes and kissed his cheek, something she had not done since childhood, then ran from the room.

They would be happy—they would!

Upstairs, she flung herself on the cushioned divan and savoured the turbulence that filled her. This morning she'd had nothing more important on her mind than enjoying Christmas. Now she was about to be married and be swept into a new life! She jumped up and went to the chest where she had put the magnificent ruby and pearl necklace father had given her. She held it at her throat and stared at herself in the glass, turning this way and that so the stone caught the light and winked like the sunlight in the cave where Taleb had taken her.

He'd said her lips were glistening rubies. . . .

Would she have jewels as the wife of the shereef? Of course. Taleb himself had a splendid array which he wore proudly. She tried to imagine what being married to Taleb would be like but could not. She knew, though, that at last her passions would be met, her love returned. A guilty thought of Henri and the almost forgotten James

275

Pauling crossed her mind but was banished quickly. A new life, no room for the past.

A tap sounded at the door and she ran to fling it open.

"Sara! Oh, I am so happy I think I shall burst!" She pulled her sister into the room, shutting the door so that their voices would not carry. She had no wish for father to enforce the declared siesta.

Sara's brow creased with a worried frown. "Everything has happened so quickly, Emilie. Why did you not tell me about Taleb?"

"I did not know myself until this very day." She sighed and danced a mad whirl about the room, coming back to take Sara's hands and pull her to the sofa. "We have been riding, but I did not realize he was courting me. He's been such a gentleman, not so much as held my hand before today!"

"You have never spoken of love or the future?"

"No. I was totally unprepared for his proposal—it took me quite by surprise."

"Didn't you ask for time to consider the idea?" Sara's voice was curiously flat.

Emilie sighed and hugged her arms across her bosom. "When he kissed me, I did not need time. I knew I wanted to be with him forever. Oh, Sara, be happy for me! I have been searching for true love and now it has come. Don't scold me for my haste to grasp it."

Sara moistened her lips with the tip of her tongue, then forced a smile as she hugged Emilie. "Of course I am happy for you, though I must admit you could not have surprised us more. Don't be upset by mother's tears. She is concerned for your welfare. Father might have shown a bit more diplomacy in his announcement to ease the shock."

Emilie giggled. "I was terrified he would refuse."

Sara said nothing to that. She suspected father's motives might be quite selfish, but it would do no good to air such thoughts.

"Your life will change drastically, Em. Are you sure—" he checked the question. Emilie's decision was made, it was too late for warnings of caution. Sara still had difficulty believing the news. She did not dislike Taleb; in fact, she admired him and accorded him considerable respect, but at the same time she did not believe Emilie could merge her life with his with any degree of ease. Was Emilie being carried away by a romantic notion as she had been with Henri? She was foolish and headstrong, with romantic ideals that had swept her to the brink of disaster once. Sara prayed that it was not happening again.

"I am sure."

"Then you have my blessing as well as father's. Be happy, Emilie." She kissed her cheek. "Goodness, four days! How will you ever be ready?! There is so much to do!"

The church was persuaded to permit the ceremony, and a license was granted by the bishop despite reluctance to permit a marriage between Christian and Moslem. The wedding would take place in the rectory of the Anglican Church, performed by the rector, but no Moslems other than the groom would be permitted to take part in the ceremony. Emilie agreed readily, as did Taleb. She wanted only for the marriage to be accomplished, and had no interest in the formalities. She was to be Taleb's wife, and that was all that mattered.

Charlotte wept privately. It was wrong, she knew it as surely as she had ever known anything, but she also recognized that Emilie and Roderick would never be persuaded to change their minds; to pursue the matter would accomplish nothing but bring Roderick's cold anger upon herself.

Emilie wore a gown of white batiste, cut and sewn by a half dozen seamstresses in two days time. It was fitted at waist and bodice, with a scooped neckline that curved

277

over her full breasts, with only a ruffle of lace to make ï
modest. The long sleeves were cuffed with lace, the skir
fuller than the current style yet not overly done. The en
tire gown was dotted with tiny snow white silk bows, and
a long veil was held to her hair by matching silk bows a
sides and crown. Around her throat, she wore the pear
and ruby necklace father had given her for Christmas
and on her right hand, a dazzling pearl ring which Tale
had sent on Christmas night. She'd seen him only onc
since the conference with her parents and the announce
ment of their plans to wed. He came to the house to in
quire her wishes in the matter of the wedding ceremony
When Taleb kissed her as they said farewell in th
garden, the fires of her longing were ignited.

She stood beside Taleb in front of the altar which wa
draped in white with a gold cloth laid over, an open Bibl
atop. Emilie was oblivious to everything but the man a
her side, and the room swam in her vision as she concen
trated on Taleb's face. His eyes darkened momentaril
when the rector requested them to kneel, and for an in
stant, Emilie thought he would refuse. At her quick, ner
vous smile, the darkness in his gaze masked, he swep
white robes aside with an imperious gesture and fell to hi
knees beside her. He was handsome in stark white cafta
over white *serouals*, a white turban wound round his head
in heavy folds, its only ornament a winking diamond o
enormous size. The white enhanced his deeply tanned
face, jet eyes and the small moustache. She had neve
seen him more handsome, and she believed herself th
luckiest girl in the world—and the happiest. She glance
nervously as the rector intoned the sacrament of marriag
in singsong cadence. She was conscious of Taleb's gaze
and the room seemed to grow unbearably warm. I
swirled in a hazy blur as Taleb slipped a diamond-studde
ring on her finger and the rector pronounced the word
that made her Taleb's wife.

Her parents and Sara stood behind them, but she ha

nvited no one else. Both Charlotte and Roderick were
villing to accede to her wishes in the matter, though they
tad invited several dozen people to a reception at the
touse afterwards. It was as though the wedding marked a
:hange in all of their lives, a passing from a family unit to
t separation best accomplished in private. Sara had
telped Emilie prepare for her wedding day, listened to
ter sister's happy chatter and expectations, and said little.
Vhat was there to say? It had all been said, and Emilie
vould listen to nothing but the singing of her heart.

Taleb took Emilie's hand as they rose, holding it in his
own as they turned to face the Sloanes. Roderick smiled
ts Charlotte rushed forward to embrace Emilie and kiss
ter cheek.

"A married woman . . . it hardly seems possible . . .
oh, dear—" She sniffled and reached to the sleeve of her
olue gown for a lace handkerchief.

Sara kissed her sister and smiling warmly at Taleb. "I
shall miss Emilie. She is very dear to me."

"And to me," he said solemnly but with a twinkle in
tis eye that lightened Sara's heart.

Emilie could not contain her joy. She gazed at Taleb
with her heart swollen with pride, and her body tingling
vith suppressed desire. She longed to be alone with him,
o be in his arms, to know him fully . . . She sensed his
desire, felt it in every touch.

"Our guests will be waiting," Roderick said.

Taleb nodded, and they proceeded from the rectory to
he sedan chairs. Taleb had arrived on horseback, but a
palace chair had been brought, and he and Emilie entered
t now. The moment they were settled, four ebony slaves
garbed in white pantaloons and gold turbans, lifted the
poles and set off.

Taleb smiled at her. "And so your Christian ceremony
s done. Are you happy?"

"Yes . . ."

He drew her close, pushing aside the veil impatiently

and claiming her mouth greedily as he crushed her to hi
bosom. She felt his strength and the tension that spoke o
burning desire held in check. She gave her lips willingly
her breath breaking in ragged patterns as her body cam
alive. She was his, and soon she would know the total jo
of union with him. And she would know it in his world
not in a chaste bridal bed in her father's house. The
were to leave for Fez this very night.

Breathless, she clung to him and savoured each stroke o
his hand at her cheek and throat. He tilted her face upward and looked deep into the deep pools of her eyes
Quite suddenly, he released her and sat back against the
purple velvet cushions.

Amazed, she could not hide her dismay. It was so apparent in her face, Taleb laughed gently.

"You look like a startled gazelle. Would you have m
take you as my wife here in this tiny cubicle?"

She shook her head, cheeks flaming.

"Then use the few minutes of the journey left us to
compose yourself. The little I know of English customs
leads me to believe your guests will expect a chaste brid
to appear before them. Is it not so?"

Still blushing, she nodded.

"I have waited many suns and lonely moons," he said
"I will endure these last hours until we can become one."

Her hands trembled as she righted the bows and vei
and smoothed the bodice of the gown. They were alread
at *Rue el Kebir* and would reach the house soon. She
could not quiet the fluttering of her heart, though she
breathed deeply and clamped lips between teeth. Tale
reached across to lay his fingers at her cheek.

"This is a day of days, little shereefa, and the hour
will pass quickly. I have informed your father that we de
part at dusk. We need only spend an hour or so with you
guests before taking our leave."

"Mother will be disappointed—"

His face darkened. "You are my wife now, not he
280

ttle one. My caravan has already delayed its departure.
We will ride to meet it so the morning sees us on the
desert." He smiled. "Tonight you will lie in my arms, and
Allah's blessing will rest upon us."

Her uneasiness vanished as quickly as it had appeared.
He was right; she could no longer view her family the
way she always had. She was no longer a child but a wife.
Taleb's wife.

The sedan chair was carried through the garden
directly to the doors of the reception room, which had
been flung open to accommodate the people who waited
now for a glimpse of the couple. The news of the wedding
had shaken the European sector to its roots, and tongues
wagged about little else the past days. Women sighed
dreamily at the romantic story but also shivered at visions
of dusky harems in far-off places. They whispered daring
guesses of what Emilie's life would be like, and they were
frightened and envious. The men, young and old alike,
were stunned that Roderick Sloane would permit his
daughter to enter into such a union. It wasn't as if Emilie
did not have her pick of eligible men—she left a trail of
mooning swains wherever she went. But an Arab? Good
Lord, what could the girl be thinking? Or her father?
There had been some intermarriages between Christians
and Arabs in which brides had gone off and never heard
from again. One or two marriages had been successful to
a measure, notably that of Miss Emily Keene who had the
foresight to insist on a marriage contract drawn under Islamic law. But Emilie Sloane was rushing headlong, and if
there was a contract drawn, no word of it reached the
ears or tongues of those eager for gossip.

There was a murmur as the couple entered the room,
Emilie with her arm through her husband's, her face radiant and flushed. Aware of stares and admiring glances,
she held her head high as she stood beside Taleb and her
parents in a reception line as guests offered eager felici-
ations.

281

"Congratulations. . . ."

"Our wishes for a happy life. . . ."

"Such a lovely bride—"

"Every happiness. . . ."

Taleb did not shake hands, though a few of the men made tentative gestures, forgetting the Arab custom o perhaps thinking that the shereef would change his way now that he was married to an English woman.

Henri was in the line . . . and Pierre.

Henri frowned deeply and his voice was low. "My ver best wishes. I pray you find a rich and satisfying life to gether." He bowed his head in deference to Taleb, an took Emilie's hand to press to his lips.

She felt her face warm and it was an effort not to pul away from his grasp. She forced a smile to tight lips "Thank you. I am sure we will."

He moved on, and Pierre stood before her. With start, Emilie realized she had not spoken to him since he engagement to Taleb. She had completely forgotten he promise to ride with him on Christmas—everything! Sh smiled and took his hand eagerly.

"Pierre—how glad I am you came!"

"My warmest wishes, Emilie." His eyes were strangel sad, though he kissed her hand.

"Thank you. I am so happy—" She turned a beamin face to Taleb, who smiled indulgently. "Taleb and I are t live in Fez, did you know?" She was like a child, eage for his approval.

"I have heard. I hope you find the interior country t your liking. Again, my warmest regards and wishes fo your happiness."

As Pierre moved away, Taleb watched him curiously The look in his eyes spoke of love, longing unfulfilled He, too, was in love with Emilie. Did she know? Her eas manner denied it, though she must have provided som encouragement to earn such devotion and cause suc pain. The other Frenchman was another matter. His lool

282

oke boldly and intimately; he had shared passion with milie and wanted her even now. Taleb disliked the ealthy young count. In dealings with Sloane and Ali Ibn ashfeen, Cartier had an air of aloofness that bordered on oldness. His disdain stemmed from the certainty that his oney gave him a power, and his financial backing was of rimary importance to the Pendash Company, just as aleb's wealth and power among the tribes were. Someday, eir wills would clash, and the Frenchman would be a ormidable opponent, but one who could be beaten, Taleb used. One victory had already been gained in winning milie, others would be just as easy to achieve.

Charlotte had rehired the French musicians to provide usic as guests milled about drinking champagne and ibbling biscuits and petit-fours, iced in pastel colors and ecorated with tiny rosebuds of sugar. There had not een time to plan more elaborate refreshments, even if milie and Taleb would have permitted it. Charlotte was ecidedly uncomfortable in Taleb's presence, though he as unfailingly polite and very quiet. And now she was ncomfortable among her own friends, who said all the ight things, but could not completely mask their disaproval. Only Selina Phelps had voiced her concern the ay after Christmas when Charlotte, weeping, had told er the news and begged for help.

"Roderick is a fool to permit it, Charlotte, you must peak with him."

"He will not listen—"

"Your daughter's life may be at stake. This is not England where a girl can return to her parents' home if she nds married life disagreeable and needs time to adjust. he shereef is a powerful man who will not brook disoedience from servants, slaves or wife!"

"What can I do?" Charlotte wailed, burying her face in er hands and weeping copious tears.

"The bishop?"

Charlotte looked up with tear-swollen eyes. "Roderick

283

has already approached him and received permission. Besides, I believe Emilie would agree to a heathen ceremony if the church did not agree. Her mind is set."

Selina sighed. "Then you can do nothing but pray."

Charlotte gasped and began weeping again, and her friend put a comforting arm about her shoulders. "It will be all right. There, there." In face of total defeat, Selina changed her tactics completely. "There are many very civilized Arabs among those who deal with Europeans. Perhaps it is not as bad as we think. After all, Emilie is not a stupid girl. She is aware of the drastic change that will take place in her life, and I'm sure she and the shereef have discussed the matter fully." But when Charlotte had left, Selina had a very long, earnest conversation with her husband, imploring him to do something to prevent the marriage, a move he agreed to in principle but could not implement even as Consul-General.

At the reception, Charlotte's tear-brimming eyes were noted and laid to a mother's natural emotions. The women did not ask the questions they longed to have answered, nor did they voice the fears concerning the success or wisdom of the marriage, except in hushed whispers when none of the Sloanes were close enough to overhear. The men drank champagne and were either silent or talked too loud and fast to cover their awkwardness.

Sara found Pierre in the patio, his champagne untouched and growing warm. She was pained by the grief in his eyes. Emilie's abrupt change of heart had wounded him, and he still looked bewildered, as though he could not grasp the truth of what was happening.

"I know Emilie is pleased that you have come," she said gently.

"I can only stay a bit. I must get back—" The words came heavily.

"There is solace in work," she said.

He glanced at her, surprised that his feelings were so apparent, and he tried to smile.

"I have discovered that truth many times in the past. And you? Do you accept your sister's marriage without reservation?"

She hesitated. "It would be useless to do otherwise now that the ceremony is done. I would find it very difficult to live in a style so foreign to my own, but Emilie and I are quite different, and I hope the adjustment will not be impossible for her."

He nodded, reading more into her words than she uttered. It was not only his pride then that bred worry. He sighed and tried to put aside memory of the desire he felt for Emilie, desire which he had not expressed to her or demanded fulfillment of.

"Will they live in Fez?"

"I am told the shereef's palace is not within the walls, but several miles across the desert. I know nothing—" She shook her head.

"There is a small European settlement in Fez," he said, suddenly shifting roles and becoming the comforter. "I think Emilie will not lack for companionship. She now holds a position of considerable importance and many will be anxious to make her acquaintance."

"Will she be permitted? As the wife of the shereef, she may be expected to remain apart from others."

He frowned. "Taleb al Mu'min has already defied the customs of his people to a major extent. I expect he will be lenient with Emilie's wishes." No man could refuse her much, he thought, and what she was refused she might take anyway. He prayed that the Arab chieftain was wise enough to give Emilie more leeway than he would an Arab woman.

"Pierre?"

"Yes?"

"I know so little of the Moslem religion. Is it true that

285

a man can take more than one wife?" Her lips were pal
under the touch of color she'd put to them.

He set the champagne glass on a bent branch of the o
ive tree and took her hands. "Yes, it is true, but it is n
always practiced. Hasn't Emilie discussed this with him?"

Sara shook her brown hair which was done in a ne
bouffant and highlighted by yellow ribbons to match h
gown. "I do not think so. She's said nothing. Oh, Pierre,
am frightened. I wish she had given it more consideratio
She scarcely knows him."

"Nothing can undo what has been done."

"I suppose I am foolish to worry. Emilie is so happy.
have never seen her more radiant."

"I must go," he said, dropping her hands. "Will I se
you at the hospital soon?"

"Tomorrow."

"Good. And I must thank you again for the painting.
hangs in my office and each time I view it, it reminds n
of the lovely woman who gave it to me. I would enjo
seeing more of your work one day if you have time."

She felt a warm glow. "Of course."

"Good. And now, *adieu*. I will not bother your fami
with farewells when the party is just beginning. Plea
make my apologies." He strode through the garden ar
went through the archway.

CHAPTER SIXTEEN

[Ta]leb spoke briefly to Emilie as shadows began to fall [ac]ross the patio and the sky turned crimson and indigo [ab]ove the twisted olive tree. She slipped upstairs, changed [fro]m the white wedding gown to a riding dress of brown [sil]k, with beige cuffs and collar, brown calfskin boots that [bu]ttoned snugly across her ankles, and a beige hat with a [co]pious veil that could be tied under her chin to keep it [fro]m being unsettled by the wind. Her portmanteau and [se]veral trunks had already been removed to the travelling [ca]mp, and she had only a small leather satchel of per[so]nal items to carry with her now as she slipped down the [re]ar stairs to where Taleb waited under the gallery. There [wo]uld be no goodbyes, no tearful partings. She'd bid her [fa]mily farewell earlier, promising to send frequent letters [wi]th caravans destined for Tangier or with military [po]uches moving between the garrison here and the one at [Fe]z. They spoke in vague terms of visiting each other, but [no] plans were made.

Taleb led her through the rear arch, his hand at her [ar]m urging her to match his quick pace. The palace sedan [ch]air had been dismissed. Taleb's stallion had been [br]ought about; beside it stood another magnificent horse,

almost a twin to Taleb's except it was a mare a hand
two smaller in size. It was fitted with a soft woolen sadd
blanket of crimson edged with gold braid, a pale saddle
hand-rubbed leather, and the most elegant trappin
Emilie had ever seen. The leather was soft and supple, o
namented with delicately scrolled tooling and studde
with rubies, emeralds and pearls that winked and gleame
in the day's dying light. The horse nickered softly a
tossed its head with a flash of creamy mane.

"Oh, she is beautiful!" Emilie exclaimed.

"A wedding gift. The mare is called *Bent Chitan*
daughter of Satan. My own stallion is her sire. You w
find her spirited enough to ride when you wish to race t
wind, yet gentle enough to bring you back safely to me."

Emilie turned, her eyes dancing. "I shall never ride a
other animal! It is the most wonderful gift I have ev
had!" She stroked the mare's cheek and let it nuzzle
her outstretched palm.

"*Inch'allah*," Taleb murmured with a smile, then ga
his hand so Emilie might climb the mounting block a
swing into the saddle.

She felt the horse's power under her, impatient to be
motion. Taleb spurned the block and leaped into t
saddle of the stallion, his white robe billowing like
cloud. How she loved him! Her heart thudded wildly
the knowledge that they would soon be alone to discov
the ecstasy she knew would be in his embrace. Her bo
and mind had been tantalized by his kisses, his touch, a
now she would know him. . . .

As soon as Taleb was astride, four servants rode out
formation. Outside the walled yard, they split, with tv
riding ahead, two a respectful and watchful distance b
hind. Taleb set an easy pace that enabled them to e
change words as they rode.

"How powerful the mare is," Emilie exclaimed, leani
over to stroke the horse.

288

"My personal servant broke her to the saddle. No other hand has touched her."

She smiled, thinking how little she knew about him. A personal servant . . . she'd never seen anyone but the few palace slaves. How thoughtful he was to give her such a magnificent gift. The horse was a magnificent specimen, and she felt a glow of pride. Each time she looked at Taleb, a shiver of excitement warmed her.

"Is it far to the encampment?"

He shook his head and the veil-like hanging beneath the turban fluttered. "Less than an hour. We shall reach it by dark."

His words were an intimate touch, full of desire. She longed to gallop the mare but knew that no animal could maintain so fast a pace for an hour's time. So she contented herself with the steady walk, with an occasional brisk canter when the ground leveled for a stretch.

They went by the same route they had taken on Christmas morning, along the Cape Spartel Road to the upper road that followed the sea. When they passed the cliff where the dark grotto and cave were, they smiled knowingly at each other. They turned inland then, across a flat grassy plain, a row of low hills that flattened to a shallow depression which glittered with light. They had reached the encampment. Emilie saw at once why Taleb elected this spot in preference to the one nearer the city where other caravans began. The site was well protected by hills all around where sentries could be posted with a view for miles in each direction. The plateau was flat and circular, with a crescent-shaped sector where the animals were tethered for the night, and sweet grass provided ample food and a thin ribbon of a stream reflected pale moonlight. The tents were set up in a circle, each with a flaming torch stuck into the ground before it. Most of the tents were of a size, except for a very large one in the center. It was circular, its tentpole half a dozen feet taller than the rest, with a blazoned flag of crimson, yellow and black flapping from its top. The canvas was boldly stripped like the gown of a gaudy female. Two black slaves garbed in silvery material that shimmered in the breeze, stood near the covered entrance, long pikes held so ends rested in the sand and points aimed skyward. They stood so still they might be statues.

A cry went up around the camp as the front guard rode in, shouting and waving to rouse everyone to the fact that the shereef had arrived. Servants rushed forward—grooms to take the horses, women to light incense and lamps as tent flags were pulled back and men formed a line of escort. Taleb dropped from his horse in a symmetry of motion and came to lift Emilie down then pull her arm through his own as he proceded toward the large tent. A hundred eyes watched, but there was no sound save the whisper of the wind in the trees and the gentle hiss of flaming torches. A carpet had been spread on the ground for them to walk on, and the moment they entered the tent, the flaps were lowered to close them in.

The entire floor of the huge tent was laid with exquisite carpets, Persian and Oriental in design, deep and rich in colour. Laid over the grassy plateau, the effect was as though walking on a cloud, so soft were they. Draperies were hung along the inside of the tentpoles to soften the stark lines, these of many hues, some plain, others elaborately embroidered. Brass lamps swayed gently from hooks, their small flames casting mealy light to the farthest reaches of the circular tent. In the center, a scarlet mat was surrounded by cushions, and a table was laid out with covered dishes kept warm on a brazier of glowing coals. Steam hissed from a kettle, and teapot and cups stood beside dishes of sugar cubes and mint leaves.

At the back of the tent, draped white gauze completely surrounded the bed, except at one side where it was drawn back by a gold cord. Tall tapers in brass candlesticks at either side of the plump mattress disclosed silk sheets, pillows in a rainbow of colours, and embroidered coverlets as elegant as tapestries.

There was not another soul in the tent. At this moment, Taleb wanted no servants fawning. He wanted only Emilie. He turned to her now, enjoying the amazed expression on her face as she saw the interior of her bridal chamber. She had the same startled look as when he'd asked her to marry him, and again he marvelled at her innocence. Did she think he would take her to some filthy tent such as the Nazarenes set up? He reached to untie the veil under her chin while she stood watching him with huge dark eyes that stirred his passion.

She could not control the desire that filled her. His touch was so gentle, she was hardly aware of it until the hat pulled away from her hair and his fingers moved to her face, stroking cheek and ear, lingering a moment before combing a path through her crushed curls. Then she was in his arms, tight against his hard, muscular body, feeling the quick rise of his passion and responding to the demand of his kiss. Her lips parted to welcome his tongue as their breaths mingled. All sights and sounds were swept away and they were alone in a hurricane of need. Emilie was consumed by the raging fire, and her body curved against him in urgent demand. Her tongue spoke against his.

He tore his lips away savagely and pulled her across the room to the veiled bed. Without a word, he took off his turban and threw it aside as he began to undo his robes. The wide sash released the caftan where it had been held tight at his waist. He seemed to shake his body free of the cloth, and it slithered to the carpet. Transfixed, Emilie's fingers worked at the fastenings of the riding boots and dress unconsciously. Beneath the robe, Taleb wore a transparent shirt that came almost to his knees, and under that, loose white trousers gathered and tied at his ankles. She could see a tangle of dark hair at his chest, and her pulse quickened. His eyes were devouring her, urging her to discard her garments so they might feast on her flesh. Her pulse throbbed wickedly, and the odour of incense was more intoxicating than champagne.

"Shereefa." The single word laid his claim to her, as she worked loose the last hook that held the bodice and skirt and let both fall at her feet, unworthy of notice. She slid the straps of the silk chemise from her shoulders, hesitating a moment with arms crossed over her breasts to catch the garment. He reached out to free it so she stood naked in his scrutiny as he removed his shirt and untied the drawstring that held the trousers in place. She drew a quick breath of astonished delight as his maleness sprang into view.

Then there was no time for thoughts. She was in his arms again, pulled to the mattresses in eager embrace, their bodies fused in a white heat of desire. He kissed her lips, her throat where a pulse pounded, her breasts where nipples grew turgid instantly. His hands explored her body and his burning flesh caressed her. Each touch made her shiver with expectant delight. Her entire body tingled with sensations that went beyond any desire she had ever experienced. Her hands grasped eagerly for him, searching the taut skin at his back, finding the tangled hair at his chest and moving downward until she encountered the warm thicket and his throbbing male organ. She closed her hand about it and felt his surge of desire.

Their gazes locked in understanding as he moved over her quickly, tasting her lips as he lowered himself into the welcoming haven of her thighs. Then there was no need for guidance, and he entered her with a quick thrust as her arms went about him to draw him close. Her hips rose to meet him, and she cradled him between the warm flesh of her thighs. Their union was a symphony of perfection, her body accepting, then making its own demands. They soared in harmony and murmured love sounds of their claims. All ecstasy she had known before paled in comparison to what she felt now. She was con-

sumed by her need and by his strength. His hands slipped
under her waist and his fingers dug into her heated flesh
as they were caught up in an incredible moment of rapture. She cried breathlessly as pleasure surged and exploded, and he breathed words of passion at her ear as he
spent his orgasm.

She lay very still, afraid to shatter the sensation that
she was suspended in a glass bubble that floated on his
breath. She slowly became aware of her surroundings . . .
The sighing wind outside the tent, the gentle crackle and
spit of the charcoal in the braziers, the silk sheets beneath
her naked body, the canopy over the bed. The smell of
the incense filled her nostrils, and she smiled as Taleb
moved to lie at her side with one arm carelessly claiming
her breasts.

"And so, my little shereefa, the fulfillment exceeds the
promise. You have shared with me the greatest pleasure
and made my waiting worth the time."

"I am still dazed . . ." She went weak when he gazed
at her and bent to kiss her trembling lips. His very touch
renewed desire, and she turned to press against him. He
offered no reprimand, but held her gently and continued
to caress her so that her pleasurable feelings were not quieted but brought to life once more. He knew the most intimate spots, the hidden places which triggered passion
and brought her to pulsing need. She lost track of time;
desire once more merged with fulfillment as he took her
again, slowly but with no less passion than before. And
when they were done, they lay in each others arms for a
long time before Taleb stroked back the damp curls and
raised her face.

He said, "And now, shall we partake of our wedding
feast or does lovemaking sate your appetites?"

Laughing, they rose, and he wrapped her in a luxurious
silk robe from a carved cedar chest behind the bed. It fit
perfectly, the amber and cream stripes cascading over
breasts and hips to touch her toes. The material was

feathery in weight and whispered with every motion. The silk caught the lamplight and radiated its warm glow.

From the chest, he pulled a pair of yellow babouches which she slipped on her feet, again a perfect fit. He indicated a second and third chest. "You will be more comfortable without the restraints of English garments."

She saw they were filled with robes, caftans, slippers—a king's ransom in exquisite clothing of Moroccan style. She lifted a caftan, a hooded robe similar to the *jellabas* men wore, a tunic, a cloak. Eyes shining, she whirled in delight. Taleb slipped on a robe that matched hers in colour and style, and he watched her with amusement.

"They are lovely—how in the world were you able to do it in so short a time?!"

"The palace tailors began working on them four months ago."

"Four—?" She stared.

"I decided that you would be mine that evening you and your sister came to dinner. My slaves have excellent eyes for size and colouring. It required only a word to have you appraised and measured."

She dropped a gossamer red overblouse and gaped at him. "You decided four months ago?! You did not even know me, other than having seen me at my father's house!"

"That was sufficient."

"How could you know I would come to love you or entertain the thought of marriage?" His manner was infuriating and she could not believe any man would take so much for granted! Her eyes blazed and she felt her temper rise.

"*Inch'allah*," he murmured, still smiling as though there was nothing more to be said.

"Allah has no control over my heart!" she fumed.

He laughed aloud then and took a long stride to grab her into his arms, lifting her off her feet as he drew her into a fiery kiss. She tried to struggle against him but his arms were like a vise. All the while, he nibbled at her tight angry mouth until her lips relented and became moist and eager to accept his domination. Her anger ebbed and she embraced him with ardour. When he finally released her, there was no fight left in her, only warm, secure love.

"Now, let us enjoy our wedding feast. I am famished," he said. He took her to the cushions on the scarlet mat in the center of the tent, and they sat crosslegged, side by side. Taleb clapped his hands sharply; immediately two slaves slithered through the tent flaps and knelt at either side of the couple. One produced a flat brazen dish and a pitcher of warm water. Following Taleb's example, Emilie held out her hands so they could be washed and dried before the meal began. The other girl readied a bowl and uncovered the first of the dishes on the brazier, a fragrant stew of fowl garnished with olives and flavoured with saffron and pine nuts. From another dish, she produced small loaves of fresh bread which she broke before handing to them. Taleb broke off a piece, dipped it in the stew and put it to Emilie's mouth.

"This food of life is a gift from Allah to our marriage . . ." He broke another piece, dipped it and ate, watching her. The slaves sat on their haunches, eyes downcast, patient as Taleb showed Emilie how to break off bits of chicken and pick the most delectable olives and nuts. After a time, Taleb dismissed the plate. The washing ritual was repeated, and another course was presented. Tiny crabs, cracked from their shells, shrimp and pearly onions in a delicate sauce. In time it was replaced by mutton boiled with almonds and apricot kernels.

Emilie had not been aware of hunger, but now she ate with an appetite to rival Taleb's. He smiled and coaxed tidbits to her lips, insisting on presenting her with the choicest portions of each dish set before them. There seemed an endless array—*couscous*, a forequarter of lamb, a compound of green vegetables mashed together and boiled in oil, cakes of paste and honey to dip in orange marmalade with cinnamon; and finally bowls of fruits, tiny sweet tangerines, oranges, persimmons, and deep red, juicy pomegranates. With the final washing of hands, bowls of rosewater were brought and sprinkled lavishly on the couple and about the tent. The slaves extinguished most of the lamps, lighted new incense in the burners, then retreated to leave them alone once more.

Taleb offered his hand and drew Emilie to the bed. They made love almost savagely, as though they could not fill themselves. And when at last they slept, Emilie lay close to Taleb amid the silence of the vast desert.

She woke to unfamiliar sounds of shouting and the grunting of camels, startled for a moment until she realized she was still in Taleb's arms. He was awake and watching her, a smile playing at the corners of his mouth as she came awake, blinking and rubbing her eyes. He pulled her close for an eager kiss, but when she would have begun love play to rekindle the fires that burned so brightly the night before, he rolled from her and got up. His naked body was perfection, and she could not take her eyes from it.

"We break camp in an hour's time. Shall I summon one of the slaves to help you dress?"

She shook her head, stretching luxuriously. "A bath?" she asked, not attempting to cover her naked breasts as his gaze went to them with hunger and admiration.

"That is a luxury you must forego until we arrive at the first oasis, and then you must tend to such lengthy matters at night. We leave with the rising sun each morning so that the trip can be accomplished in five days. I will send a girl with water for you to wash." At her expression, he laughed gently. "Then I will return to take breakfast with you—provided you do not dally so long that my hunger overtakes my wish to be with you." He clapped his hands and before she could scramble from the bed into a robe, a black girl entered with a pitcher of water balanced on her head. Taleb was through the tent flap before it came to rest.

Sighing, Emilie washed in the warm water, which was scented with crushed flower petals. She felt totally rested and vitally alive. Her flesh tingled with the knowledge that she was Taleb's wife, that this was the first day of a new life . . . and that his physical love met every hope she'd ever cherished. Taleb had not remarked on her eagerness in bed, though she was sure he was aware of her lack of virginity. No doubt he suspected her affair with Henri since he had troubled himself to observe and comment on its end. If Taleb was able to close a door on that part of her past, so would she. She vowed never to allow memories of Henri to intrude on her happiness, or let guilt assail her.

The slave laid out garments from the trunk, and Emilie dressed quickly. The girl was already scooping up the bed linens and removing them. Other servants entered with trays, steaming kettles and the paraphernalia for making tea. By the time Taleb returned, breakfast was laid and they sat to eat quickly and almost in silence. He was preoccupied with some matter or other, though she was certain none of the responsibility of striking the camp fell to him. Still, she thought it best not to chatter at him, and she refrained from reaching out to touch him and hold him according to the dictates of her heart.

When at last they relaxed over tea, Taleb regained his good spirits and explained the procedure for the day.

"We will ride out with escort as soon as you are ready. You will find it more comfortable to cover yourself with a *jellaba* so the hood can be pulled to shade your face and keep out the wind. It grows hot as we cross the plains."

"Will we ride all day?"

"We will pause for a midday meal and rest, and to allow the pack caravan to overtake us and go ahead to select the encampment for the night. By the time we reach our first night's camp, food and a comfortable bed will await us." His eyes sparked sensuously.

In spite of herself, Emilie blushed, and there was a quickening of her pulse.

"It has been my observation that most European women spend an inordinate amount of time readying themselves for a journey on which they will not be seen except by servants or perhaps a lonely carrion circling overhead. Have I married such a woman?"

She laughed. "I shall be ready in ten minutes time—less!" She scrambled to her feet and threw her arms about him impulsively. "I shall be ready at a moment's notice anytime you call . . ." She kissed him, and his arms held her against a body that was strong as steel. When he let her go a moment later, his smouldering gaze showed that his passion was as alive as her own.

"Tonight, my little shereefa," he whispered, then he was gone.

She hurried, humming a gay tune as she pulled on the riding boots and *jellaba*. The garment was made of exquisite, soft camel wool, the colour of a newborn fawn, with only a gold braid at the edges of the hood and closures to accent its plain lines. She stretched out her arms and turned in a lazy circle, admiring the way the robe fell in soft lines over her body. She still marvelled at how perfectly everything Taleb had ordered fit, and she wondered casually where her own trunks were. She made a mental note to ask him as she gathered up a pale kidskin *couffir* into which she put handkerchief and a small jar of cream for her lips.

Outside, the air was still cool as the sun began its morning climb at the eastern horizon beyond the row of sandy hills. Taleb was giving instructions to a thin, bearded man who wore a dark striped *jellaba*, the hood of which lay back and showed a brown turban covering his hair. He did not look like a servant, though she supposed he must be. Taleb had not mentioned any other travellers who would accompany them on the journey to Fez. His gaze slid to Emilie momentarily, but his attention did not waiver from what Taleb was saying. The rush of Arabic, harsh and guttural on any other tongue, had a musical lilt on Taleb's. When he spied her, he concluded his remarks to the man, who salaamed and backed away.

Taleb came to her with a smile. "An English woman who means what she says. I have found a remarkable pearl indeed. Come, my dove, the horses are ready."

He led her across the compound to where the Arabians were saddled and slaves stood ready to assist. Seated in the high vantage point of the saddle, Emilie gazed about the camp. She had not seen much of it last night in the dark and in her total preoccupation with Taleb. It was a remarkable sight. Much larger than her first impression, with more than a dozen tents in a circle, some of which were already being struck, the poles laid, canvas wrapped, ropes coiled. Taleb's banner lifted in the breeze over the largest tent which was already being dismantled. Beyond, camels were being loaded, and a string of mules with huge panniers that almost obscured them brayed and chattered complaints as additional weight was placed upon them. It was a scene of great bustle and excitement, but one quite remote from Taleb, who tugged at the stallion's reins and set out. Emilie drew the mare's head about and caught up with him. The sun crested the rim of the hill and sent spiky golden shafts dancing over the sand, like a great star beckoning them toward their destination. How wonderful she felt! Her heart was filled with joy, and she looked at Taleb lovingly. He have her an indulgent smile, then turned his attention to the journey at hand.

She had not noticed until now that he wore a sword and dagger at his waist. She'd never seen them before; the scabbard was silver, tooled with a design that seemed an inscription of Arabic characters. The hilt of the sword was encrusted with jewels, sparkling rubies and emeralds and small pearls. The handle of the dagger was similarly decorated but with the stones set in what seemed to be gleaming gold; she could not see the blade which was hidden beneath the folds of his robe.

She enjoyed the ride, though the wind seemed to gain in intensity with each mile. At the onset, they followed the coastline but could no longer see the sea, only smell the salt spray in the air. By midmorning, that was gone and a biting sting of sand replaced it as they turned inland. It seemed to Emilie that they traveled hurriedly, in spite of the fact that the horses maintained a steady plodding gait which was easy to accommodate oneself to. There were fourteen riders in all, eight of whom were on mules and soon outdistanced the slower horses. Taleb explained that the servants would choose a sheltered spot where the noon meal could be prepared and eaten and the party could rest before continuing the journey. If she tired before then—

No, she insisted that she would match his pace and ask for no concessions, which made him smile. He did not tell her that he had already slowed his normal pace considerably for her comfort. She was determined to prove herself strong and capable, and the idea amused him. How feminine she was in spite of her headstrong ways. That had attracted him to her in the first place. He had seen the strength, as well as the passion in her eyes. He bided his time until her infatuation with the Frenchman wore itself out. And now she was his. He felt pride equal to the glow after a victorious battle.

Soon after the sun passed its zenith, they came to a small clump of fig trees; wispy smoke from a campfire and braziers was carried by the wind to assail them with the aroma of cooking. They had been riding almost five hours by Emilie's reckoning, and she was more tired and thirsty than she cared to admit. Gratefully, she let a slave help her from the horse. In the shade of a date palm, a small tent had been erected, its opening away from the force of the wind, the flaps tied back to permit circulation

300

of air. Taleb led her inside and they sat on cushions strewn on the carpeting that covered the sand.

"I am dying of thirst!" Emilie declared. She had not asked for a drink as they rode, since she had been given no goatskin of water and saw none at Taleb's belt.

Taleb pushed back the hood of his burnoose. "It is better not to drink until the night encampment."

"Not to drink? That is impossible! I am already as dry as the sands we cross." She smiled to take the peevish tone from her voice. "Tea. Yes, I'll have tea."

Taleb instructed one of the slaves to fetch tea for the shereefa. He contented himself with the small pigeon pie and flat round bread which was brought. Emilie picked at her food and filled herself with the sweet quenching tea, which revived her spirits and strength.

When the meal was cleared and hands washed, Taleb left the tent. Emilie unfastened the *jellaba* and slipped it off before laying down on the soft carpet and cradling her head with a pillow. Outside, she heard a chanting lament of voices and sat up. Curiosity impelled her to the tent flaps and peering out, she saw Taleb and four other men on their knees on mats that had been unrolled on the sand a few paces away. They were bowed, foreheads touching the mats, and the wailing rose and fell in cadence. They were praying, Emilie realized with a start. The Islamic custom of *Fajr* to *Acha* was observed even here. She drew the tent flap almost shut and watched. On his knees, Taleb was indistinguishable from the servants with whom he knelt, except for his carpet having been placed ahead of the others as they faced east. She studied his bent figure, thrilling to its strength and feeling the longing stir within her. She would learn about his ways, she told herself, she would learn and adapt herself as much as she could without foregoing her Christianity.

When the chanting ended and the men rose, she ducked inside and laid down on the cushions once more. Taleb entered a moment later, removing his turban, weapons and *jellaba* before lying beside her. She came into his arms instantly, eager for his caress.

"The afternoon ride is hard, Emilie. You will need your rest."

"I prefer you—"

"Hush—" He kissed the words away, savouring the taste of mint on her lips. "You will rest now, for soon we ride again. And tonight we will lie together in the bliss of the second of our seven fig days."

He held her against his chest, stroking her hair gently, and she sighed. "What is that—seven fig days?"

"The English call it 'honeymoon'?"

She smiled. "Seven fig days . . . very well, my husband, but you need not think I will always give in so easily to your wishes," she said dreamily; weariness overcame her and her eyes closed.

He said nothing but continued to stroke her head gently. In moment she was asleep.

When Taleb shook her awake, two hours had passed and it was time to be underway. She rose and readied herself quickly, taking time to rub cream on her dry lips. When she emerged from the tent, the rest of the camp had already been dismantled and packed; there was only the tent to be tended, and they would not wait for that. With the six riders who accompanied the horses, they set out once more. The heat seemed more intense, and Emilie pulled the hood of the *jellaba* across her face to shield it. She'd noted the long wool scarves the slave women wrapped round and round their faces and necks, and decided she would ask Taleb for one for herself. It would be a help in keeping out the wind and the sand.

They were underway an hour when Emilie began to feel a wicked thirst that surpassed any she'd endured on the morning's travelling. She tried to ignore it but it grew to monumental proportions until she thought her throat would seal itself off for want of a drop.

"Taleb—"

He turned instantly, though her call was carried away by the wind so that it was a mere whisper of sound.

"I am so thirsty—"

He drew rein and let her horse come abreast of the stallion. "I warned you it was unwise to drink at midday."

"But surely the servants carry water. To pause long enough to slake my thirst would not delay us." She was irritable at his reluctance to grant her so small a wish.

"To drink now would make matters worse, for you would require more shortly, then more, and more. And the heat would exhaust you so that you would not be able to ride."

"That's ridiculous—"

He turned the horse's head and did not look back as he rode on. The matter was finished and he would not duel words. She would soon learn that he knew the ways of the desert, and she would learn to heed his advice.

Emilie bristled in unchecked fury, then kicked her horse to catch up with him. Before she could open her mouth to chastise his ungentlemanly behaviour, he reached across and grabbed the noseband of the mare's bridle. His eyes were glowing coals in deep pits.

"Do not trot the horse. Do you wish to exhaust the animal as well as yourself?!"

Taken aback by his outburst, she blinked and choked off the words she had been about to utter. She had never seen him angry, and she sensed that it would not be a pretty sight or experience. Her own anger would accomplish nothing in the face of it. Furiously, she jerked the horse aside so she could ride free of Taleb's restraining grasp, though at a leisurely walk. She felt his eyes on her but she would not turn. She would not be treated like a child, nor would she give way to what seemed like weakness in his eyes.

They rode the remainder of the day in stoney silence. Once or twice, Emilie almost relented to ask a question about some plant or bird, some struggling wild flower that had pushed up near a hidden spring, but each time she clamped her lips and was silent. As the day progressed, the heat intensified along the sun-scorched camel track, and Emilie's thirst became a monstrous clawing thing in her throat. Her tongue was a swollen lump of leather, and it would have been impossible to speak even if she tried. The tears that stung her eyes were dried by the relentless wind bfore they could fall.

When at last they came in sight of the night camp, she was near exhaustion as Taleb had predicted. Knowing him right did not improve her temper or her disposition, and she fell into the arms of the servant who lifted her from the horse. She could barely keep on her feet as two slave girls came forward to escort her to the large tent in the center of the encampment. She collapsed on the bed, her tongue thick at her swollen lips. One of the girls set to brewing tea immediately, while the other left the tent, returning a moment later with a small silver cup which Emilie grabbed eagerly. The girl would not let go of it; she shook her head, her eyes full of sympathy and determination. She allowed several drops of the cool liquid to pass Emilie's lips before she withdrew the cup. The dampness teased Emilie's palate and she begged for more, but the girl allowed only another sip. In rage, Emilie tried to take the cup, slapping out with open palm to strike the black girl full across the face.

"Give it to me, I say!" Emilie cried, tugging and spilling the precious water onto the front of her *jellaba*.

The girl was frightened but would not relent. Emilie sobbed and tried to grab the cup which might still offer a drop.

Suddenly Taleb was standing over her, and the slave scuttled backward without rising. When he took the cup from the girl's hand, she vanished instantly, fleeing the tent.

"Zamita is slave to the Shereef of Madawadi," he said

slowly. His gaze fixed on Emilie with dark intensity. "Like all others, she does *my* bidding and has no will of her own. Until such time as you acquire sufficient knowledge of the ways of your new life, it would be wise not to attempt to exercise authority that countermands mine."

His tone was without rancour, but she felt as rebuked as she had when he'd grabbed her horse in a momentary flare of anger. She was caught in confusion between the knowledge that he was right and her refusal to be dominated.

He sat beside her and put an arm about her. "Now drink, but very slowly so that you will not become ill. When the tea is ready, your throat and belly will welcome it." He put the silver cup to her lips and she swallowed gratefully, making no protest when he removed the cup after one sip, waited, then offered it to her again.

Gradually she began to feel better, and her anger and resentment passed with the wicked thirst. By the time the girl brought the tea tray, some of Emilie's good humour had been restored and she was able to smile at Taleb.

"The tea will revive you," he said. "And then dinner. Would you care to hear some music while we dine?"

He was being so solicitous, she could not hold any remnant of anger. "It would be nice," she said.

They drank the mint tea, then sat upon the scarlet carpet and sampled an array of foods that rivaled the feast they'd had the night before. How the cooks had managed so far removed from civilization was a mystery, but Emilie did not question it. Taleb entertained her with stories or bits of information about Fez, and they listened and watched as drummer, tambourine player and lutist performed lively tunes and two girls garbed in filmy veiling that scarcely covered their naked bodies danced sensuously. They were as supple as snakes, bending and twisting, arching and gyrating in a centuries-old dance of the desert. Taleb watched with muted interest, but his gaze strayed often to Emilie. When she became aware of

305

it, she smiled to show him there was no longer any disharmony between them.

She enjoyed the dance but could not help thinking of the gasps of disapproval it would bring from her mother. Except for the inherent beauty of motion, the dance might be considered obscene, or at the very least, suggestive. The two honey-skinned girls personified sensuality, each movement designed to arouse and tempt. Emilie supposed the dance was primarily for the entertainment of men, but she found it exciting and it was not long until she also felt her desire for Taleb rekindled. She cast covert glances in his direction and longed for the entertainment to be concluded so she could be alone with him.

As soon as the meal was cleared, the dancers retired and Taleb drew Emilie to the bed, his hand gentle at the fastenings of her loose garments, undoing, slipping off the *jellaba* and caftan, smiling when he saw that she still wore the foreign undergarment that clung to her high breasts and the gentle swell of her hips. She let him slip the straps and bare her flesh, and lay shivering with anticipation as he fondled her body, cupping each mound lovingly with warm hands, rubbing her flesh with gentle sensuous motions until her breath came in quick gasps and her eyes showed a fire that could not be hidden. He extinguished the lamps and disrobed to lie beside her under the silken sheets, and welcome her warm eager body pressed so quickly to his.

She murmured his name as a prayer of desire, and he moved into her with fevered gentleness. The misery of the day faded from thought, from memory, and there was only the singing of their bodies in desire and fulfillment.

CHAPTER SEVENTEEN

The days that followed were patterned after the first, with long morning and afternoon rides, broken only by the short interval of rest at the first oasis to be sighted after midday, and marvelously happy nights that passed too quickly as Emilie slept in Taleb's arms. She never tired of his lovemaking; indeed, she found new thrill each time he came to her, and her body grew in sensitivity to his so that they were in perfect harmony. She learned too that it was best to listen to all advice Taleb offered, no matter how casually given. She never insisted on drinking at midday again, and to her surprise she rode more comfortably the rest of the day for the sacrifice. It was as if putting a small amount of liquid into the body gave fuel to the thirst that could not be quenched, while depriving oneself meant only minor discomfort and a healthy thirst by evening. She learned, too, that the sun was merciless, and she wrapped her face in a long woolen scarf Taleb gave her, with only a slit open at her eyes. In truth, she rode much of the time dozing in the saddle, letting the horse have its head; it followed the others devoutly and never wandered off the track.

After the first day, the scenery became more monotonous. They travelled huge expanses of desert for hours without sighting another living creature outside their own party. Twice, they made night camp near the outskirts of tiny villages, where the villagers rushed out and, at recognition of the shereef, swore to protect the band from any harm during the hours of darkness. When Emilie questioned Taleb, he smiled and said there was no danger except from the villagers themselves, who would cheerfully rob any caravan they were "protecting" if they believed they could do so without being caught. But he quickly assured her that none would dare attack the caravan of the shereef. And so it was.

When she and Taleb rode off each morning with their personal slaves, cooks and guards, the camp seemed in a hopeless mess as tentpoles were pulled down, supplies stacked and animals laden. Yet at some point during the day, the retinue overtook those who had gone on ahead and preceded them to have night camp ready when they appeared. She supposed it came from practice and the ready obedience of so many slaves, but it was a marvel nevertheless.

One night when they reached a camp ground before the long shadows of darkness crossed the desert, Taleb told her that he and several of the men were going out to hunt partridge, and he invited her to join them. Delighted, she girdled her *jellaba* with a lemon yellow sash, tied a silk scarf about her head, then set out on horseback with the five men. The camp was near an olive grove, and one of the Moors led the way across open, down-like country where the riders spread out and suddenly spurted to a fast pace that sent birds winging up from the tall grass of a wash. Rifle shots cracked sharply, and half a dozen birds fell to the ground in seconds. The riders wheeled, raced through the depression again and managed to scare up several laggards who were easy prey for the quick guns. In all, nine birds were killed before the flock was hopelessly scattered. Laughing, Emilie rode at Taleb's side and glowed with pride at the two birds felled by his shots. He was adept with the long gun, and she marvelled at his skill. She would have thought sword and dagger more appropriate weapons for the primitive culture in which he lived. Still, guns had been around a very long time and Taleb's men were certainly proficient in the use of them.

The partridge appeared with the evening meal, roasted with onions and sage, thyme and curry flavouring, as delicate a dish as she had ever tasted. Maybe it was having accompanied the hunt that made it seem so.

On the fourth day they came into a valley that was miraculously green after the dry sands. Along the rising ground that bordered it, white villages dotted the hills and horizon, but the caravan did not pass close to them. Emilie asked Taleb why they did not stop, and he merely shook his head and said the peasant villages were unworthy of their notice. They entered a narrow, rocky gorge and came out to a small plain which seemed the stopping off point to undulating hills that stretched as far as the eye could see, with a ragged mountain peak looming over them indistinctly in the distance. Across the floor of the plain, a silver river trickled and splashed over rocks; the noon camp was already set up at its banks. The sky had turned grey but the heat had not diminished. Instead it was like a heavy blanket weighing upon them, the air burning. When they'd eaten, Emilie and Taleb lay together, motionless as they listened to the chirp of grasshoppers and the soft strum of a guitar played by one of the guards. "Will we be there soon?" Emilie asked.

"We will see Fez shortly after sunup tomorrow," he said. "Are you tired, my little shereefa?"

"No, only anxious to have the journey over so that I may be with you other than on these wretched horses. My bottom will be blistered by many more days in the saddle."

He laughed gently. "Then I shall tend your wounds and nurse you back to health with love."

She giggled, then sighed comfortably against him.

"You have ridden magnificently," he said. "I would not have believed any woman so capable and determined."

She glowed with pride. "I have learned much with so able a teacher." She lifted her lips to his face and kissed him. "And I have much to learn, but I will make you proud of me, Taleb, I promise."

He regarded her solemnly. "I am already proud of you, my sweet. And now, sleep, the day is hot and we have several hours to ride before nightfall."

When she woke, she was damp with sweat. The air was muggy and oppressive, and she sat up to push back her unruly hair and fan the loose caftan about her body. She was alone in the tent, the rug beside her empty, though the pillow retained the impression of Taleb's head. She saw that a pitcher and basin had been left for her convenience, and she rose to wash in the tepid water. As she finished, she was aware of how quiet the camp was. She rummaged in her *couffin* to draw out the ornate silver watch that had been a gift from her father on her sixteenth birthday. She had not worn it about her neck as was her custom because of the heat that caused metal to feel like molten lead against the skin. She could not accustom herself to the Arab manner of guessing at the time by the length of shadows or some mysterious instinct which told them when to tend to their daily prayers.

It was late; she had slept long, yet no one had wakened her to set forth on the afternoon ride. Puzzled, she peered out the tent flap and saw that no preparations were being made to break camp. The cooks were dozing under a large palm, backs against the rough bark, legs outstretched in an awkward circle like some deformed scorpion. Slaves were at the river's edge, bent at some task Emilie could not discern. Taleb and the guards where nowhere in sight.

310

She took advantage of the lengthened respite to find her brush and patiently unsnarl her tangled hair. It was beginning to grow out a bit, and she fluffed curls over her ears to lay on her shoulders. A bother . . . perhaps she would snip it again. Its bobbed style did not offend Taleb. More than once he had commented on its golden beauty, and often he raked his fingers through it in moments of passion, claiming it his golden prize.

When she finished brushing, her hair was like spun gold in a halo about her head. She changed from the damp caftan to another of lighter weight and a deep salmon color, and longed for a glass to view herself, knowing full well that she would look as pretty as she ever had. She took pains with her skin these days, creaming it at night to soothe it against the dryness caused by the desert sun. When she'd complained to Taleb that her lips had become sore and cracked, he commanded a slave to bring a special balm. The tiny pot of pink, pasty substance had the delicate scent of roses, and when Emilie applied it, her lips felt better immediately.

She was brought from her reverie by the sound of voices outside and quickly donned the fresh *jellaba* that had been brought while she slept, an afternoon ritual. One of the voices was Taleb's, and she saw him seated in the shade of a clump of palm trees. He was not alone. The man with him was vaguely familiar and it took a moment for Emilie to recall where she'd seen him. It was the man to whom Taleb had spoken in the travelling camp the first morning, the one she had supposed a servant, but whom she had not seen again throughout the trip.

The two sat crosslegged, their heads bent in earnest conversation. She hesitated, knowing that she should not interfere in her husband's affairs, but boredom and curiosity overcame her and she approached with a smile. Taleb did not register surprise at seeing her.

"You had a good rest, my little one?"

"Excellent. The heat saps the strength." She glanced a the leaden sky. "Will it rain, do you think?"

"A brief shower before dusk." He was amused by he boldness in approaching men discussing matters that di not concern her, but he did not reprimand her. He ha overlooked many of her indiscretions and would continu to do so as long as they were of a minor nature. He'. known what upheaval his life would undergo when h chose an Englishwoman for a bride. She had not bee: brought up in an *iyal* to learn a woman's place and duties yet he had been so attracted to her that he had been un able to put her out of his heart. No matter that he coul have any woman in Fez, a dozen if he wished. He wante. Emilie, and now she was his . . . but she would be a lon time relinquishing her English ways. Like a spirited horse she would learn more quickly if allowed some freedom.

His companion sat with eyes lowered so as not to be hold the unveiled woman. Omar ben Hadj had spoken hi opinion openly when Taleb confided his plans to wed.

"It will weaken your strength among the people of ou tribes. You above all must hold fast to the laws of Mo hammed," Omar had said.

"It is not forbidden to take a wife," Taleb answere. patiently.

"You should choose her from our people!"

"I am descended from the Prophet himself and h speaks through me. I will choose my wife according to m heart and desires, and the union will be blessed, and th people will accept the shereefa and pay homage to her! will impart my *baraka* to her, and it will be so."

That ended the discussion; Omar said no more, but h was still uneasy in the presence of the Christian woman.

Taleb invited Emilie to seat herself beside him with pat of hand to grass. "Omar ben Hadj, my chief *caia* brings me news that there has been a revolt in Algier: All the cavalry of Fez were sent against the rebels and ar only now returning."

312

Emilie looked startled. "Cavalry—? I do not understand." Fez suddenly seemed very remote from the peaceful comforts of home; it disturbed her to hear of revolt and soldiers.

"The French lead an army of Moors to keep our land safe from intruders," Taleb said with a note of irony.

Emilie studied him but his face was impassive.

He went on. "Heads will hang over the gates of Fez today."

"Taleb! Do not say such a thing even in jest!" Emilie shuddered.

Omar traced a pattern in a sandy spot with a fingertip. Taleb merely shrugged and murmured, *"Inch'allah."* Then he said, "Omar has brought me word that matters require my attention in the city before we journey to Madawadi. We will spend a day or two there while I tend these affairs." He smiled. "It will be arranged for you to meet your countrymen who make the city their home. I am sure you will find the company of women entertaining after so long a journey with no one to talk with but me."

She blushed, ready to say that she would be happy with him alone forever, but the prospect of seeing another English face, chatting about feminine things excited her. And seeing Fez! With Taleb to guide her, she would not be sequestered from the sights and sounds of the native sectors.

"And now, we go on to our final camp," Taleb said, rising and dismissing Omar with a spate of Arabic to which the man nodded, salaamed and retreated without looking at Emilie. Taleb took her arm. "Come, we are ready to ride."

"But the camp, not a thing has been readied!" She looked to the river where the cooks were still leisurely wading and chattering, cooking pots washed and stacked on the bank.

"Because we have no further need of them. They will ride directly to Madawadi. Tomorrow we shall enjoy our

midday meal in the comfort of a walled garden within o
own house." His hand tightened momentarily at her wa
and his eyes were possessive.

After two hours' ride among broom-clad hills, th
came to the vast table-land of Fez, encircled by mou
tains and hills. Emilie's breath was taken away at tl
magnificence of lush fields and rich earth that Taleb sa
produced huge amounts of grain and produce. Here ar
there, sprinkled on the hillsides, were *duars* comprised
black tents, which resembled boats with their keels in tl
air, twenty to thirty in number, set in parallel rows li
the sides of a large square. Between the rows, robed fi
ures moved like insects, and around the outskirts, a fe
cattle and sheep grazed lazily.

The valley was split by a sparkling river, splashir
banks swollen by the winter rains. Flocks of cranes, wi
geese, doves and pheasants flew over it and gave the a
pearance of a vast, luxurious garden. She had not expec
ed anything like this after so many days of drea
landscape, and she was disappointed when Taleb sa
they would ride on so as to cover most of their journe
before nightfall. They rode along a well-travelled pa
and were no longer alone. They encountered numero
caravans coming from the city, families returning fro
market with laden camels. They had to ford the river, ar
again Emilie chose to ride *Bent Chitane* rather than l
carried above the swirling water. She was soaked, exce
for her boots which she removed and fastened about h
neck to keep dry.

By the time they reached the last camp, an exquisi
sunset stained the sky crimson and gold, and Emilie sle
in the peaceful knowledge that they would reach the
destination the next day.

At dawn when they rose, Taleb took her outside ar
turned her toward the sunrise. "Behold Fez," he said, ci
cling her with his arm.

314

The city lay in the morning haze, its crenellated walls ark against a golden sky that had not yet turned blue. It eemed a forbidding place, shadowed and somber, with one of the light-hearted European atmosphere of Tanier and none of its whiteness. Yet it was compelling . . . ps of minarets and domed tombs could be seen, and ocasionally a splash of green where trees towered above ae walls.

"It is magnificent!" she exclaimed, laying her head to is shoulder and enjoying his closeness. "I have never een happier than I am now, Taleb."

"*Inch'allah*," he murmured, and kissed her head. "Alah has written it over you that you are mine forever, and gives me joy that you are pleased. You will like Madawadi as well, little shereefa. The palace is comfortble and the gardens beautiful. There are no finer horses han those in my stables and no more devoted slaves than hose in my service. You will lack for nothing."

She turned a smiling face to him. "I am happy because have you. The other things are nothing so long as you ove me . . ."

They kissed lingeringly and her sense of peace was eeply renewed. Slowly, they returned to the tent to take heir meal before riding the last hours into the city.

An ever-lengthening line of the wall revealed itself as hey neared the city, until at last they were riding directly inder the towering stone mass, so high that Emilie had to rane her neck to see the top. A section of wall seemed to un at right angles from the rest visible ahead, where lue-grey kestrels hovered, heads into the wind, wings eating, as they watched unseen prey below, and rollers umbled about in their morning acrobatics to greet the ew day. Behind the wall, Lombardy poplars raised vertial green fountains to the sky.

There were dozens of people moving languidly as they ntered or left through a great gate which offered access

315

to the city. The breeze carried a stench that made Emili
reach for a handkerchief from her *couffin*. Not far fro
the gate, she spied a huge mound of animal carcasses ro
ting in the sun, with carrion feasting on the decaying fle
and flies droning like locusts. She turned from t
ugliness. They had acquired a company of guards, an
though Emilie could not be sure where they had con
from, they seemed known to Taleb and were undoubted
in his service. They were afoot and on horseback, all wi
rifles slung over their shoulders, forming a solid rin
about Taleb, Emilie and the horsemen who had accomp
nied them from Tangier.

She expected to see rows of houses once through t
gate, but they were still between walls topped by towei
At on side, a green-domed tomb, shaded by palms, w
crowded around with robed figures, who had come to pr
at the holy place. They passed through a second gate an
Fez lay before them, houses piled in irregular rows on t
side of the hill to the bottom of the bowl. The stree
were steep and the horses plunged downward with a sur
footedness that Emilie found remarkable. She gripped t
pommel and leaned to keep her seat, so engrossed in t
precarious descent that she scarcely noticed her surroun
ings for a bit. She was vaguely aware of narrow stree
cutting off at all angles, tall houses, and the deafenii
noise of the horses hoofs and clamouring shouts as the wa
was cleared. The streets afforded less passage than tho
in Tangier, and often they were forced to ride single file.

Then quite unexpectedly, they were passing through a
archway to a sweet-smelling, green garden. The air w
cool and fresh, scented with jasmine and aloe; the groun
beneath the horses' feet was smoothly raked, slight
damp from watering that held the dust down. From t
outer garden, they passed through another gateway an
came upon the house, set like a jewel amid tall trees an
walkways and patios with splashing fountains. It was
princely mansion to equal the sultan's own palace! Tl

illside was terraced so the house below was reached by
means of a path that wound through a small grove of
range and lemon trees. At the final level, another wall
arpeted with trailing vines shielded the house with pri-
ate gardens.

They dismounted at massive, carved wooden doors
hich were opened by salaaming servants and flanked by
x soldiers in scarlet pantaloons and billowing white
irts, each holding a polished rifle at ready across his
hest. The soldiers who had accompanied them the final
g of the journey vanished, yet Emilie sensed they had
ot gone far. Was Fez so dangerous that Taleb needed
any men in attendance at all times?

"We have reached our destination. Does it please you?"
aleb said, taking her hand to lead her through the door.

"Oh, yes!"

He laughed gently at her child-like exclamation. "Then
ome and let me show you your quarters. You will wish
bathe and change."

She followed him, staring at the rich appointments of
e house. It was built around a court, with a gallery sup-
orted by twelve white pillars joined by arches, each so
tricately carved that it seemed a work of art. The pave-
ent of the court was a splendid mosaic, the arches paint-
1 in arabesque. There was a carved openwork balustrade
rrounding the upper gallery, and from it several hanging
pestries added grace and harmony. In the middle of the
urt was a round fountain with water splashing swiftly in
steady stream; at a side wall, a recessed fountain echoed
murmuring trickle.

There were servants everywhere; they semed to hover
doorways in anticipation of any command from Taleb
at would send them scurrying to do his bidding. Black
aves, turbaned Moors with gleaming white *gandourahs*
d tunics, soldiers with wicked scimitars at their waists
d rifles in their hands.

Taleb led her along a passageway past several cham-

317

bers that were cool dim retreats. They went up a wid tiled stairway, then along the gallery and finally into huge chamber. The walls were veiled in gauze and tape tries of the most delicate colors, the floor covered with thick, soft carpet that resembled an exotic meadow. huge bed, low and multi-cushioned and screened by ne ting tied back with silver chains, was at a wall betwe two arches that opened to a green patio. At another wa a multitude of garments hung from a wooden po screened by curtains, caught back now to show a rainbo of colours that fluttered and whispered in a gentle bree that stirred the air.

"It is fantastic!" she said, turning to Taleb with a war smile. "It is so large I shall become lost, I am sure!"

"There is not a corner of the house or grounds which I cannot find you, my love . . ." He studied h face and was moved by the warmth of the love in h eyes. She watched him with parted lips, breath rushi with excitement. He had never seen her lovelier, despi the riding clothes and a smudge of dust at her chin. H bent and kissed the full red lips that tasted of sunshi and were eager for love. It would be easy to spend t day here with her, but he forced himself to release her.

"There is a bell." He showed her a handwrought silv bell on a table in the center of the room. "If the slaves not understand your wishes or fulfill them, this will bri Hadra. She speaks English and will set matters right."

"Who is Hadra?" Emilie asked almost dreamily. S was still savouring the kiss, wishing Taleb did not have go.

"She has been in my house many years and knows r ways."

Emilie nodded, not really caring and sure that it wou be impossible to find anything wanting in this magnifice place. "And you?" she teased. "Will you serve me fait fully?"

"The shereef serves no one but Allah . . ." His to

318

as soft and his eyes amused as he took her into his arms and kissed her fervently.

Once more, Emilie was swept into the compelling tide of desire, so much so that she quickly forgot the bud of annoyance she felt at his unwillingness to respond in kind to her teasing. It was difficult to adjust to his seriousness in moments that should have been carefree.

"And now I must see to affairs that demand my attention. After your rest, we will dine, and I will arrange for you to visit with the English Consulate. He has been informed of your arrival and has arranged for you to meet the English ladies of the city so your time can be passed in pleasant company."

Smiling, he left. Instantly, as though they had been waiting the cue, three women appeared from a curtained doorway. One bowed and spoke her name to the new mistress of things.

"Zohra . . ." She smiled, and Emilie nodded to show she understood.

The woman spoke softly to the two slaves, who immediately reached to begin unfastening Emilie's garments. They meant to undress her, Emilie realized, and she would not be expected to unfasten so much as a single tie. She was unaccustomed to such service but did not protest. It seemed a great luxury indeed, and she knew that the slaves were following orders and had been trained well in their work. Taleb would tolerate nothing less than perfection.

She heard the quick chatter of surprise when the *jelaba* and *tunic* were removed and she stood in her chemise. Obviously, they had never seen such a garment and found it cause for some amusement. Emilie let them examine it minutely. One of the girls held it up against her own body as she pirouetted; the other two clapped hands to mouths to suppress giggles. Finally, the undergarment was put aside. Then to Emilie's utter surprise, the slave who had held it, a slender, pretty girl whose fea-

319

tures had none of the heaviness common to her race
quickly removed her own clothing and slippers. For a mo
ment Emilie thought the girl meant to try on the chemise
but she merely stood in ebony splendour, her full breast
firm and high, her waist slim above well-rounded hips
Giggling and chattering, the naked girl pulled back a cur
tain and coaxed Emilie through an arch toward a court
yard. Emilie shook her head furiously, trying to cover he
breasts with her arms. If she could get to the bell on the
table, perhaps Hadra could make them understand that the
new mistress did not walk about outside unclothed! Bu
the other two had a firm grip on her arms, and her pro
tests fell on deaf ears.

The air was warm, the breeze cut off by the high wal
and hedge around the courtyard. Emilie stared in wonde
at the scene before her. In the center of the court, onl
several yards from the doorway, was a huge shallow poo
with a fountain in the center. On the tiled stone surround
ing it mats and pillows were arranged for reclining, som
in the sunlight, others in dappled shadows of a smal
grove of trees and shrubs along one wall of the court. Th
pool was built on two levels, the lower one closer to th
house. The far end of the other section was lost in a
garden where two fawns perked ears and paused momen
tarily in their drinking to stare at the women. Around th
lower pool, several large pitchers and dippers were place
within easy reach. The naked black girl stepped into th
water and scooped water in a dipper, then poured a slov
stream over her black shoulders. The water beaded an
caught the sunlight, and the girl flashed a dazzling smil
at Emilie as she held out the dipper.

A bath! This magnificent pool was her bath! Emili
stepped into the tepid water, taking the dipper the blac
girl offered and spilling the cooling liquid over her body
She shivered delectably, then moved into the pool so sh
stood in water to her knees. One of the fawns lifted it
head, and its nose twitched in curious surprise.

The slave waded close, pausing to pick up a jar of sweet-smelling oil with which she began to rub Emilie's skin. The fragance was jasmine, the oil soothing and cleansing. Emilie stood like a water nymph, her face held to the sun as she was rubbed and scrubbed. When the slave motioned her to rinse, Emilie lowered herself into the water and moved arms and legs languidly. She scooped water in her hands and splashed her face, then sat preening in the sun while the slave washed and rinsed her hair. The steadily moving water from the upper pool carried away the lather to hidden drains so that the water about them was always clear; Emilie marvelled at the ingenuity that had planned such a wondrous bath.

When at last she tired of the water, she stepped out to be engulfed in a large soft blanket, patted dry, then encouraged to lay upon one of the mats in the sun. She had never felt more pampered, and she giggled at an image of her mother's horrified expression were she to see her daughter lolling nude at an outdoor pool! Poor mother would be scandalized.

Emilie closed her eyes and thought about her family for the first time since she'd left Tangier. Could it have been only five days ago? She realized with a shock that she had not seen another European in all that time! Even more shocking, the lack had not bothered her. She had been completely absorbed in her devotion to Taleb and his powerful mastery. His love more than made up for the grueling journey, the heat, the discomforts she'd endured. Recalling that first day when she had disregarded Taleb's warning and consumed water at the noon stop, she knew that she had much to learn about life here, but she felt pride that she had not slowed the caravan, nor complained or begged Taleb to ease the strain of the daily riding.

She sighed and opened her eyes, shielding them with a hand. The girl who tended her bath had vanished, but the other was kneeling now beside her with an open jar of oil.

Without a word, since they had no language in common, the girl began to rub the oil on Emilie's skin, gently covering her entire body with the delicate balm. Zohra brought a soft brush and stroked Emilie's hair to dry it. Afterwards, Emilie returned to the chamber where the bed had been readied; as soon as she laid herself upon it, Zohra dropped the curtains and the room fell silent as the three women reclined on cushions nearby to take their rest with her.

Emilie stared at the canopy of netting. The bed was most comfortable but also lonely. It was the first time she had slept without Taleb since leaving Tangier, and she longed for his comforting presence. She'd grown accustomed to it and felt strange without him. Frowning, she thought back over what Taleb had said when he escorted her here . . . *your* quarters. Would he not share them with her? She sat up, drawing back the curtain so she could peer out. The hanging clothing was all female, the slippers laid in neat rows below the hanging garments all of a size for her dainty foot. *Her* quarters. . . . she was to sleep here alone.

Piqued, she slid from the bed and crossed the room. Zohra was alert instantly, hurrying to reach the wardrobe before her mistress. She shook her head and pointed to the bed.

Emilie was adamant and reached for a blue caftan. "I do not wish to rest," she said impatiently.

Though she did not understand the words, Zohra could not mistake the tone of voice, and she quickly removed the garment from the hanging rack and held it for Emilie to slip into. It was a silky material, almost transparent, and the taut nipples of Emilie's breasts were outlined clearly. Scowling, she pointed to a yellow embroidered tunic and motioned that she wanted to don it also. Zohra's face was impassive as she followed the unspoken command. Satisfied, Emilie let the slave place soft blue slippers on her feet as she snatched up the hairbrush and pulled it through her curls once more. Zohra pointed to a tall, narrow looking glass in an upright gilt frame. Emilie crossed to look at herself. The tunic and caftan hung loosely, and when she spanned her waist with her hands, Zohra darted to the wardrobe, returning a moment later with a satin sash of midnight blue to tie about her mistress' waist.

That was better. Emilie dismissed Zohra with a wave of her hand and left the apartment. She stood a moment on the gallery, looking along its length in both directions to orient herself, then set out toward the stairs she and Taleb had ascended. On the lower floor, she was not at all sure which direction to turn. They had crossed here . . . or was it there? It made no difference, since she had no idea where Taleb might be. She started along the corridor to her left, pausing to look into chambers, until she at last heard a murmur of voices from one not far from the tall entrance doors. She could not distinguish words, but she recognized the deep timber of Taleb's tone.

At the doorway, she stopped. Taleb had claimed pressing business, and if she were to interrupt him, he would not be pleased, she was sure. She was a fool to rush out of her quarters so impetuously, and she certainly could not broach the subject of sleeping arrangements in front of a guest! She turned to go, then halted again as she realized Taleb and his guest were speaking English, not Arabic—and there was something familiar about the other voice. Her curiosity would not subside, so she ventured close to the open door, thankful for the soft velvet slippers that did not betray her presence.

"—a man who speaks with the truth of the Prophet!" Taleb was saying.

"The prophet does not require the merchandise I have to offer, my friend. I force nothing upon you. If you do not wish to buy, there are others."

"Curse Satan!" Taleb said savagely.

Emilie frowned and concentrated on the other voice.

323

"I must return to Beldeen before sundown, so the matter must be decided at once."

Clipped, self-assured . . . *Herr* Muller! But it couldn't be! He had long ago left Tangier to return to his work in Rabat. What was it he did? She frowned, unable to recall details of the German couple she'd met aboard the *Ophir,* and certain now that it could not be the same man. Perhaps another German; most had accents.

"I need time to assemble the gold."

"I have knowledge of your *makhzen* here at the palace as well as the one in Madawadi. You are trying to buy time, my friend, time that you will put to use in attempting to steal the guns and ammunition which my men guard at Beldeen. I warn you, such a scheme will fail. If I do not return by sundown, my emmissary aboard the train will carry the news of your treachery to those in Rabat and Tangier who will pay handsomely for such loyalty."

"*Balek, Herr* Muller, I am not a Nazarene to be threatened." Taleb's voice was dangerously cold.

"If you believe I make idle threats, it is your privilege—and your mistake."

They were silent, and Emilie held her breath lest she betray her presence. She did not understand the full meaning of what she was hearing, but it was apparent that Taleb was not pleased with his dealings with Muller.

"My decision is made," Taleb said. "I will pay the price, though it is three times the amount agreed upon."

Muller's voice was heavy with triumph. "Good, good. You will find the guns of highest quality and very accurate. You may wish to order additional—"

Taleb left no room for doubt in his tone. "Once a man has broken his word to me, I do not conduct business with him again." He clapped his hands sharply. Before Emilie could duck out of sight, a slippered Moor appeared behind her, glancing at her with a startled look as he entered the room.

Emilie was torn between the desperate desire to flee

324

and the knowledge that the servant would tell Taleb that she had been listening. Taleb had said his servants were devoted—they would surely tell him of unusual behaviour on the part of his English wife. The matter was settled for her by Taleb's sudden appearance in the doorway. His eyes were blazing and his lips tight. He looked at her without speaking. She felt colour flood her face and she stammered a half-hearted explanation.

"I—I did not know you were engaged. I realize now my intrusion—"

"Can it be—" *Herr* Muller poked his round head at the door. "Is is! *Mein Gott!* Emilie Sloane, what are you doing here?!" Muller was so astonished that he stared open-mouthed, his glance taking in the flowing Moroccan garb, her slippered feet.

"We have concluded our discussion," Taleb said to Emilie in a tone of complete ease. "*Herr* Muller, Emilie is no longer the daughter of *Si* Sloane, she is my wife, shereefa of Madawadi."

Muller could not have been more thunderstruck had Taleb slashed him with a rawhide whip. He looked from one to the other, mouth still gaping. With concerted effort, he smiled.

"Then I must offer my congratulations and every hope for your happiness," Muller said, his face suffusing.

"I will have the chest carried to your caravan." Taleb was dismissing him.

Muller nodded, looking to Emilie again. "Goodbye, Miss—"

"Goodbye, *Herr* Muller, and thank you for your good wishes. Please give my kindest regards to *Frau* Muller. Is she in Fez with you?"

He shook his head. "I travel on business . . . alone." He glanced at Taleb. "*Auf wiedersehen.*" He bowed and exited as a slave opened the tall doors.

For a moment, Taleb's displeasure was a tangible force between them. Determinedly, Emilie lifted her chin and faced him. "I'm sorry if I interrupted, Taleb. I could not rest and thought to explore the house, or better, to have you show it to me." She smiled, hoping to win him over.

His dark eyes regarded her somberly, and when he spoke his voice was perfectly controlled. "Your stamina constantly amazes me, little one. I would have thought you exhausted after five days on the desert and ready to sleep all afternoon. But as long as you are up, come, I will show you the house." He took her arm and walked with her, leading her through little courts and corridors, chambers of such grand elegance that they took her breath away. Walls were hung with gold embroideries, intricate candelabra and Moorish lanterns hung from arches and ceilings. Emilie exclaimed over each new discovery, and Taleb patiently answered her questions. He did not refer to the matter of *Herr* Muller, and Emilie was determined not to bring up the matter for fear of dissipating his good humour.

The upper floor of the house was devoted to apartments, each with its own court and pool, and none so elegant as hers except for Taleb's. Seeing it, she turned to face him questioningly.

"As husband and wife I expected we would enjoy a mutual bed. I do not wish to be away from you." She smiled winningly and caressing his arm.

"It is the custom for women to enjoy their own quarters. Are your rooms not satisfactory? I can arrange—"

"That is not the point! I want to be with you, as we were during the journey." She looked at him through lowered lashes.

"Do you think that I will find you less desirable because you are the distance of a minute away?" He smiled as though to banish her fears. "There is a passage from my apartment directly to yours. Come, I will show you . . ."

They crossed the room, with Emilie gaping at the lavish appointments; the apartment was larger than hers and more sumptuous, with only slightly darker colours and an array of male wardrobe to give evidence of its masculine nature. Slaves stood at either side of a doorway through which Taleb led her, and she wondered about them but did not have time to ask as Taleb rushed her along almost conspiratorily.

"Behold!" He waved with a flourish. Emerging from the passage they were standing in her own chamber. The passageway let out behind a screened doorway that she had not noticed earlier. Taleb took her in his arms. "So, my little one, you see how quickly I can be with you." He stroked her hair and took her lips. She clung to him eagerly, chasing all doubt that clouded her mind. "And now I will have your meal brought. I regret that my presence is required elsewhere and I cannot enjoy a leisurely midday meal in the garden as I promised, but I will make it up to you this evening. I have already arranged for your escort to the house of the Consul. Is it your wish to go attired in Moroccan dress, or do you prefer to make your introduction in stiff, proper English style?"

He was teasing her, but she did not mind. Her good humour restored, she tossed blond curls and smiled devilishly.

"I am shereefa of Madawadi. I will wear the garments my loving husband has so lavishly provided."

"So be it. Need I ask if you will ride or if you wish a chair."

"Taleb!"

"*Bent Chitane* will be ready at the front gate in an hour's time. And now, I must attend to things. I will see you on your return, and we will dine and spend a most pleasant evening together." He kissed her again, and she wished the afternoon were already gone so that she might stay in his arms.

CHAPTER EIGHTEEN

When she left the palace, she was accompanied by six armed guards from Taleb's private army, two black slaves, and two women, veiled faces shrouded beneath the hoods of *jellabas*. She protested but Taleb was insistent that she would do his bidding in this matter, since there were many in Fez who would delight in harming the house of the shereef. She would never venture a step from the palace without proper protection, he told her.

As she rode through the narrow streets of the city, she was assured by the presence of the retinue. Whatever her reservations about the European quarter of Tangier had been, Emilie could put no such blame to Fez. There was no foreign influence in architecture to be seen, no neat Victorian houses or familiar gardens, no square dominated by the flags of legations. The streets were barely lanes, and houses turned bleak walls to them. Low archways indicated entrances, but sharp angled walls cut off all view of what lay beyond, except for an occasional burst of green treetops. Fez was entirely Moorish in character, an ancient wise man blind to the new century.

The British Consulate was no different from other buildings at first impression, but when they had passed the wall, Emilie was delightfully surprised by a mill and mill pond, water gurgling through the race, that stood beside the stables. Two Moorish soldiers rushed forward to take over the horses, and Taleb's guards walked with Emilie as she traversed a passage, angled to screen the house from the outside. It led to an arcade that went around three sides of a shaded patio where a fountain played gently in a graceful, octagonal basin. The house was two-storied, built against the hillside, with a flat roof and parapet, over the top of which a grove of trees could be seen.

Emilie was ushered into a study at one corner of a wing. A small, balding man with pinched brows and a leathery skin rose and came around the desk, his quick smile showing yellowing teeth.

"My dear—Emilie, is it?—welcome to Fez. I trust you had a tolerable journey. You look none the worse for the trip."

She let herself be led to a worn, comfortable looking sofa near a low table. The room was neat but almost shabby, the furniture a conglomerate of pieces that had undoubtedly been handed down over years of consulate service . . . the sofa, a large Morris chair with fresh antimacassars that looked comically out of place, a battered desk with a heavy brass paraffin lamp, a cabinet stacked with papers either waiting to be filed or for which there was no room in the drawers, and two tables, the oak one near the sofa and a gate-legged Queen Anne under one of the windows. The walls of the house were thick and the fact that it was built into the hill gave it a touch of musty dampness.

"Now, some tea." The consul reached for a bellrope near the door and tugged it sharply. Apparently the order had already been given, for a servant appeared immediately with a tea tray, which he placed on the table.

"I am Douglas Gregory. I cannot tell you how delighted I am—we all are—to have you here. It is the first time that an English woman has come to Fez in such an honoured capacity. Shereefa . . ." He shook his head in wonder. It was obvious he was consumed with curiosity but dared not voice his questions.

"I am looking forward to becoming acquainted with your city, Mr. Gregory, and to meeting my countrymen here."

He bobbed his head. "It is already arranged but I claimed for myself the privilege of taking tea with you before allowing the ladies to have you. We received word only yesterday that you were arriving. A surprise, most pleasant, most pleasant."

Emilie's brows raised. "Who informed you of my coming?" Taleb had only mentioned last night that they would stop in Fez before finishing the journey to Madawadi.

"One of the shereef's deputies—" He frowned then smiled quickly. "*Caid* Omar ben Hadj. Not directly, of course. The shereef does not deem it necessary to notify anyone of his arrival save his staff. But the women have a way of hearing the gossip." He smiled again, then sat back as the servant poured the tea and passed a cup to each of them. Emilie was very surprised to discover English tea rather than the familiar mint she had grown accustomed to. The servant held out a china saucer on which thin slices of lemon lay in a circle.

"Tell me about the women," Emilie said. "Are there many? I do hope there are some close to my age." She sipped the tea and declined the biscuits he offered, which were obviously from a tin.

Gregory hid his momentary surprise. Surely she knew—"I am sorry to say that there are none, unless you consider the daughter of the Italian military engineer, and she does not speak a word other than her native tongue."

Emilie held the tea cup in tight fingers. "*No* young ladies? Wives? Daughters?"

He sighed. "None. I expected you knew that the British
330

colony numbers only eleven. The entire non-native population of Fez is less than fifty."

She stared, unable to believe what she was hearing. Eleven English . . . fifty Europeans . . . ?

He pursed his lips in and out as though trying to think of some way to ease her shock. "I am, ahem, not married, nor is my assistant, Mr. Link. Dr. Madden has a wife and two small daughters. She has asked to have you brought round—they live not far from here. I'm sure you will enjoy her immensely. From Essex, I believe, charming woman. The children are so—" He held a hand about three feet from the floor to indicate a size. "Their governess is Swiss, a spinster of some forty years, I would judge." He was relishing the information as much as Emilie's mother might a tidbit of gossip. "And, of course, we have three missionary ladies. Misses Martingale, Drew and Charing. Miss Charing also serves as the postmistress."

Emilie had recovered from the stunning news and found it wryly amusing. So she was to have no confidantes, no women with whom to form friendships. A doctor's wife with two little ones, and three missionaries! She almost laughed aloud but managed to restrain herself.

"I'm sure I will enjoy Mrs. Madden's company and that of the missionaries."

"To be sure . . ." But his eyes asked if they would accept this beautiful young woman who dared to flaunt convention and make her first calls in native garb! None of the other women, English or European, had accommodated themselves to that dubious comfort.

Gregory discussed the other Europeans, detailing their status, abodes and ages. Consuls and assistants, several military men, two merchants and a French photographer and his wife who, being Jewish, chose to live in the mellah. Emilie scarcely listened as he chattered on. When she had professed undying devotion to Taleb and his way of life, she had believed the contacts with her own world would not be so completely severed. Missionaries and the wives of doctors and government men sounded very dull. She sighed inwardly.

Gregory relished his role of informant and went on to scatter bits of information like grain before a bird. Social life in the European Fassis was limited to occasional dinner parties, playing bridge or whist, or riding out along the river to hunt ducks or partridge—the men of course—while the ladies watched.

It sounded too dull for words, but Emilie listened politely, smiling and nodding at intervals. Finally, the Consul got around to prying for information.

"I'm told your father is with the Anglo-French Bank of Lyon?"

"Yes. His appointment to it brought us to Tangier."

"Ahhh." His head bobbed. "There are rumors that the French hope to establish a protectorate in the near future. I am not sure it would be wise."

"I know nothing of political matters," Emilie said. "My father's business was quite apart from our personal life." Not precisely true, since it had brought her and Taleb together, but she knew nothing of French military plans.

Gregory pursed lips in and out. "The railroads," he said, tenting his fingers and tucking thumbs under his chin as he peered at her.

"I do not understand," She was weary of the conversation and longed to escape. Hinting, she rearranged her skirt as though preparing to rise.

"If the railroads are completed, the French will find it an easy matter to bring in guns and supplies to enforce their beneficence. I fear the Moors will not take kindly to such persuasion."

She thought of the conversation between Taleb and *Herr* Muller. Guns . . . Taleb was already purchasing some. "It is my understanding that the French have a treaty concerning the railroad from Tangier to Fez." Bits of conversation between her father and others formed an indistinct picture in her mind. "No other railroads can be built until it is completed."

"Just so, just so, but there are those who would circumvent the agreement by readying spur lines that do not violate the strict rules of the treaty but are most useful in bringing contraband within a few hours journey of the city."

She regarded him with a guarded stare. "Where is the nearest railroad?"

"At Beldeen, three hours journey from here. Of course it goes only as far as Meknes, but from there other spurs link to the coast."

She was irritated by his cat-and-mouse game and faced the issue head on. "Do you think my father has some connection with these matters?" she asked haughtily.

He retreated instantly. "I meant to imply no such thing. Dear me, dear me . . . not at all."

She had called his bluff and now he was afraid. Of whom? Her father? Not likely. Taleb?

"My father's connections with the French are of long standing. The new bank at Tangier has the approval of both the French and British government, Mr. Gregory. I am sure that any transaction in which they engage has been carefully considered and will be in the best interests of both countries, as well as Morocco."

"Quite so, quite so." Did she imagine it, or had he coloured under the deep tan? "In my next despatch, I plan to send regards to your parents through Mr. Phelps, our consul in Tangier—you know him, I'm sure."

"Yes." She would not help him end his embarrassment.

"If you care to send a telegraph message to let your family to let them know you have arrived safely, I will see that it goes off with the evening despatches."

"A telegraph? I had no idea—"

He smiled, comfortable that the conversation had shifted to neutral ground. "Yes. We have one, and the mails are quite reliable, though not as fast as we are accustomed to at home. Now, I have detained you long enough. Mrs. Madden will be furious with me for keeping you so long. Please come again to visit anytime. It delights an Englishman's heart to chat with one so young and beautiful."

"Thank you, Mr. Gregory. I will be in Fez only a short time, but I will come again soon, I'm sure. You've been most kind in welcoming me. And I most certainly would appreciate the use of the telegraph—"

He rose quickly, crossing to the cluttered desk and unearthing a pencil and tablet, which he handed her. She wrote a brief message, signed it 'Love, Emilie,' and handed it to him as she got to her feet.

"Thank you again, Mr. Gregory."

"I will have one of the men lead the way to the Madden residence. It is only a bit down the lane but you'll want to take your horse, I imagine." He walked with her to the door, smiling and bowing as she departed and Taleb's guards, who were waiting directly outside, escorted her back to the stables. She glimpsed a young Englishman peering at her from behind the drape of another doorway but he was gone a moment later. The curious junior consul, no doubt, too shy to ask to be introduced.

The section through which they rode was entirely residential, and though houses were well screened behind high walls, it was obvious that they were large in size and had extensive gardens and orchards. The scent of citrus trees clung to the winter air, and green leaves showed above whitewashed walls partly mottled from the winter rains.

They entered an archway and came to a gate which was securely bolted. When the Consul's servant rapped, a panel was drawn back and a face appeared before the bolt was slid back and the gate opened to allow them entry. The house and grounds were more elegant than the Consulate, yet not as grand as the Sloane house in Tangier. Mrs. Madden was at the door to greet Emilie as she dismounted.

"How good of you to come," the doctor's wife said with a smile, but not before Emilie noticed the quick glance of surprise at the caftan and tunic.

"I am pleased to be invited," Emilie said, extending her hand to the woman's warm grasp.

"The others are waiting—come, they are most anxious to meet you." Mrs. Madden led the way through a wide hall and along a corridor. The house was not built around a patio but in the shape of an ell, with a terraced garden falling away along the hillside and several stairways leading to the upper rooms and roofs. Still it was a charming house, and well furnished with wood and brass pieces that were Moorish in character. Emilie suspected that the house belonged to a wealthy Moor who let it to the foreigners.

The sitting room faced directly on the garden, and four other women sat about a tea table. Their expectant smiles froze momentarily, then quickly thawed as introductions were made. Like Mr. Gregory, Mrs. Madden stumbled over Emilie's name settling at last on calling her by her newly acquired title, the Shereefa of Madawadi.

"Please, call me Emilie and we will all be much more comfortable," Emilie said, accepting a chair. Mrs. Madden resumed her place and poured tea. A plate of delicate honey cakes were passed, and Emilie accepted one with a polite smile.

The three missionaries varied in age from late thirties to indeterminate, grey-haired, thin-faced agelessness. They were so much alike that Emilie found it difficult to recall which was which only moments after the introductions. The Swiss governess of the Madden children, Hilda Weiss, was ill at ease, and it was obvious that although included in the social gathering, she was well aware of her place. She was a plain woman, hair severely drawn and caught at the nape of her neck, thin lips and grey eyes un-

335

der pale brows. Colourless . . . and well past her fortieth birthday, hardly the type to inspire Emilie with any hope of camaraderie.

Mrs. Madden was plump and looked older than her thirty-odd years. She had undoubtedly been a pretty woman in her younger years, but marriage and life away from the luxuries of home had robbed her of desire to keep herself looking her best. Either that, or the good doctor's income was not large enough to allow her fancy clothing and cosmetics. Emilie suspected the former, since she had already discovered that there were many native oils and remedies available.

Mrs. Madden's warm welcome could not be faulted, none the less, nor her curiosity denied. "We are pleased that you found time to join us," she said. "We had not heard of the shereef's marriage or that his bride was English. Have you known him long?"

Martha Drew cocked her grey head and her gaze was piercing. The teacup in her hand did not move.

Emilie deliberately smoothed the gossamer skirt of the caftan. "We've been acquainted sometime."

Denise Charing offered a tentative smile. Of the three, she seemed the least forbidding, though her Christian disapproval could not be completely hidden. "We're told your entire family came from London and lives in Tangier."

"Only last May . . ." Hortense Martingale said tonelessly. The inference that six months was scarcely enough time for any girl to know a man before marriage was clear.

"Yes. My father manages the Anglo-French Bank of Lyon." She was amused by their disapproval. How like a tea party in Belgravia among mother's friends! A tidbit of gossip to savour and dissect, a new presence to be examined from all facets, to be found wanting or not, and most of all to be approved or disapproved. Only these ladies had little choice. Regardless of their final personal deci-

336

ons, they were not in a position to make Emilie unwel-
ome. She smiled around the group winningly, and was
warded with a flicker of smile from the Swiss governess.

"I am only sorry that you will not take up permanent
sidence in Fez. We would enjoy having you among us.
here are so few Europeans, you would be a most wel-
ome addition," Mrs. Madden said.

"I am sure I shall be in the city often," Emilie an-
vered. "I'm told the palace is not far."

"An hour or more on horseback, not a trip to be un-
rtaken every day," Miss Charing said.

"Have you seen the palace? I admit my curiosity is
eat."

The five exchanged glances. It was Mrs. Madden who
nswered. "None of the women of our community have
ver been invited, though my husband has been. Not in-
de, of course, but close at hand when he travelled to
nd soldiers wounded in battle."

Emilie pursed her lips and set aside the half-empty cup.
Is there much fighting?" It seemed she heard of trouble
every turn. Taleb and Omar ben Hadj had been dis-
ussing an outbreak of violence . . .

"Much too much," Hortense Martingale said. "Brother
gainst brother, the ignorant against God . . ."

"There was talk of a revolt in Algiers." Emilie pursued
e matter. Taleb would tell her so little, and she was ea-
r to hear another viewpoint.

"The doctor has not yet returned, but Mr. Gregory
eard from the French Commandant that the number of
juries is high, though the invaders were successfully re-
lled and the revolt quelled in a short time."

"Algiers seems very far away," Emilie offered.

"Several hundred miles," Miss Drew said, "but Fez lies
the natural path between the mountain ranges, and it is
ere that the attackers raid most frequently. The tribes in
e hills to the east are never at peace. It is difficult to be-
ve that they are all of the same heritage and blood." It

337

was the first time she'd spoken except in murmured greeting, and Emilie was surprised by the soft, musical quali of her voice. She seemed well informed on military ma ters and geography. "It leaves one with a sense of inad quacy to know that our protection lies mainly in th hands of those who are blood brothers to our attackers."

"I don't understand . . ."

Miss Drew sat very straight like an instructress givin lessons. "The local army is comprised of Moors, with on a handful of French to train and lead them, and they a constantly called upon to fight their own countrymen. On wonders if they may not tire of it all and turn on the benefactors some day."

"You are giving a biased view, Martha," Mrs. Madde chided. "Emilie will have the wrong impression."

"That an uprising is possible at any moment? Can yo deny that we all pray each night that such is not in sto for the morrow?" Martha Drew would not relent.

"It was my understanding that the tribes surroundin Fez were at peace. Surely you have no fear from them Taleb—my husband speaks of the French in warme tones."

Claudia Madden quickly said, "Martha is speaking i general terms and makes no reference to the tribes you husband commands. The shereef is very highly regarde in Fez."

Miss Denison sniffed. "The shereef is not a Christia who can be expected to respect and follow the rules Go has set forth for the world. It is wicked to allow Mis Sloane to believe her life will not be altered drastically o that she is not in some danger."

There was an audible gasp from Denise Charing a such a bold statement, and Hilda Weiss paled and turne a nervous gaze to her employer.

"I value your friendship highly, Martha, but I must re mind you that Emilie is a guest in my home. I cannot per

it remarks that may upset her." Claudia shot the other a
warning glance that the matter was ended.

Emilie felt a tic of annoyance. What right had the
woman to assume that because Taleb was not of the same
faith that he was some kind of monster? He, too, believed
in God, and it would not surprise her if Taleb were more
devout in his faith than the preaching missionary.

"My husband is a gentle man," she said without smiling,
not caring if Martha Drew took offense. "He is faithful in
his religion which, though it differs from yours and mine,
is based on godly principles and behaviour. I know nothing of how he commands his people here, but I am sure it
is with a kind and loving hand. I assure you, I am quite
safe with him. He will not kill me in my sleep nor trade
me off like a head of cattle."

Mrs. Madden flushed and busied herself with the
teapot, refilling cups and passing the plate of honeycakes
once more. All eyes avoided Emilie and the rebuked Miss
Drew stared fixedly. The silence was mercifully broken by
the sound of running footsteps and the light, piping voices
of two little girls who swept into the room like a whirlwind. Miss Weiss was on her feet instantly, trying to capture the two before they could throw themselves at their
mother and upset the tea table.

"Here, little ones—" Hilda Weiss caught each child
with a practiced hand, hugging them to her, yet managing
to calm them without diminishing their exhuberance.
"Mama is pouring . . . there, little ladies now."

The two were blonde and blue-eyed, cherubic faced
and dressed in similar frilly organdy dresses of pale blue
tied with white sashes. They wore high buttoned boots of
white kidskin over knee-high white hose that were exposed as they went in turn to their mother to be kissed.
They were almost of a size, about six and eight, Emilie
guessed, pretty girls who resembled their mother in
fairness and bone structure.

Once greeted, they stood silent, looking at Emilie with

339

frank curiosity. The elder girl could not refrain from star
ing at Emilie's native garb, and her questioning glance a
Miss Weiss was bursting with curiosity.

"Madam Shereefa . . . may I present my charges
Miss Eileen and Miss Zelda . . ."

The children curtsied and Emilie smiled. "How do yo
do. I am delighted to meet you." Her eyes danced mis
chievously at the eager youngsters. "How pretty you bot
look in your blue dresses."

"Thank you . . ." Zelda, the younger took a step for
ward. Miss Weiss released her hand when Emilie beck
oned the child closer.

"Zelda is a very pretty name," Emilie said solemnly. "
hope that we will be friends."

"Will you really live in a palace, Madam Shereefa?"
Zelda queried.

Emilie ignored the governess' effort to quiet the child
"Yes, so I am told, though I have not yet seen it. But yo
must not call me Madam Shereefa. We are going to b
friends, and I want you to call me Miss Emilie."

"Are you a princess, Miss Emilie?"

"In a way, I suppose, though not a fairy princess o
anything so elegant. One day I shall invite you and you
sister—and your mama and Miss Weiss, of course, t
have tea with me at the palace. Would you like that?"

"Oh yes!" The child's eyes were round, as she turne
to see if such a magnificent promise were going to be de
nied by the adults who ruled her life. When her mothe
smiled, Zelda giggled and took Emilie's hand in her ow
chubby one. "A princess has invited me to tea!"

They all laughed, and the tension in the room vanished
The two girls were allowed to sit and nibble honeycake
as they answered Emilie's questions about their schoolin
and play. At each answer, Emilie showed solemn interes
and encouraged the girls to chat, much to their delight
When they had exhausted the topics of conversation Mis

340

Weiss skillfully herded the girls into farewells and from the room. They turned at the doorway and waved to their new-found friend, and Emilie smiled.

When they'd gone, she professed that she must be underway, too. Mrs. Madden looked disappointed but did not encourage her to tarry. The three missionaries rose, but only the hostess saw her guest to the door.

Claudia Madden took Emilie's hand as they stepped into the garden where a fountain gurgled near a row of cypresses. "You are always welcome at our house when you are in Fez. Please, call on me if I can be of assistance or you are in need of advice or help—" She regretted the word as soon as it was out and tried to soften its implication. "You may find it pleasant to have an English friend at times. The girls adore you and will be disappointed if they do not see you again soon."

"I shall keep my promise to have you visit. That is, if the palace is not too far for you to make the journey?"

"We would be delighted. When you've had time to settle. I wish you every happiness, Emilie. Please, do not let us lose touch."

Was it imagination or did Emilie detect concern in the other's voice and gaze? Like the missionaries, Mrs. Madden had reservations about Taleb. Emilie withdrew her hand as a servant brought *Bent Chitane* close to the gate.

"It has been a lovely afternoon. Mother will be delighted to hear that I have found such charming companions in Fez. I fear she worries about my well being and safety as much as your other guests, but it is because, like they, she does not know Taleb. Thank you again for having me."

"The pleasure was mine. Much happiness in your new life . . ." Her eyes had a faraway look for a moment before she smiled. "Enoch will be sorry to have missed you. Perhaps you will allow him the honor to call if his duties take him in the region of the palace?"

341

"I would be offended if he did not! Please extend m welcome to him. And now I must go."

She crossed the garden, pausing to smile before mount ing the mare and being led toward the gate.

CHAPTER NINETEEN

The evening spent with Taleb was delightful, with a leisurely dinner on a torch-lit terrace overlooking the gardens and vast span of black sky. The air cooled noticeably as soon as the sun fell beyond the hills, and Emilie wore a heavier caftan and robe Zohra set out for her. Hidden in the shadows of the garden, musicians played soft, stringed instruments in haunting tunes, and a parade of silent-footed servants served course after course of aromatic, spicy dishes.

Emilie and Taleb sat on a sea of cushions before the tiled patio where braziers warmed food and dishes. The quiet night gave the feeling of solitude, though they were in the heart of the city. Taleb was gentle and tender, with none of the harsh preoccupation that had marked his attitude earlier in the day. He questioned her about her visit to Gregory and Mrs. Madden, and listened as she detailed her impressions and disappointments. She mimicked the three missionaries so he laughed with her, and he smiled when she spoke endearingly of the two children. He was amazed at the tenderness in her voice, and he thought of the sons she would bear him.

That night he came to her chambers when the lanterns

343

had been turned low, and he embraced her in a wave of love-making that banished all doubts and fears that had been sown in Emilie's mind by the afternoon with the good ladies of Fez. She slept content and close beside her husband, one with him, and blessed by God and Allah.

He was gone when she woke in the morning, and she stirred restlessly running her hand over the pillow where his head had been. She wondered when he'd left, if he had stayed the night or slipped back to his own chambers? She imagined she could still feel his warmth on the satin sheets, and she hugged her arms across her naked breasts as she recalled the fervour of their lovemaking. Separate chambers were a nonsense that Taleb desired no more than she, she was sure. Perhaps it was a custom that he felt obliged to maintain befitting his rank but would use sparingly.

Slaves came to ready her for her bath. Since the sun was not yet high enough to warm the garden, she was led to an inside tiled bath where steaming jugs of water were brought to fill a deep tub under a slow, trickling fountain. She washed herself, though two girls stood ready to do her bidding, handing her soaps and oils, adjusting the temperature of the water to keep it just so. When Emilie emerged, they wrapped her in soft blankets to dry her, shod her feet with silken slippers, and escorted her back to the bedchamber where Zohra stood at the wardrobe waiting her mistress's selection of garments for the day.

Emilie had neglected to ask Taleb when they would leave, and when she tried to inquire of the girl, she was met with blank eyes. The girl did not understand. Sighing, Emilie walked to the table and lifted the silver bell. Its note was the clear tone of a bird at dawn. She had scarcely laid the bell back in its place when a small boned, well-endowed woman entered. She was beautiful with an oval face and flawless complexion the colour of wild honey, and large *kohl*-darkened eyes that were deep mirrors. Her hair was drawn back sleekly, held at the

pe of her neck by invisible pins; a narrow silver chain
ent around her crown, crossing her forehead where it
ngled a small, perfect ruby like a beauty mark.

"I am Hadra. There is something?" Her voice was like
e rustle of wind among soft leaves.

For some reason, Emilie felt awkward, as though the
oman had assumed command by her presence.
lutching the bath blanket, Emilie forced herself to meet
e woman's steady gaze.

"I wish to know what time we leave for Madawadi so I
n choose appropriate garb."

"The camel caravan has already departed, and the
hereef awaits your pleasure at breakfast. You will ride as
on as you have eaten."

Emilie frowned. "And the shereef, will he ride with
e?" Something in the woman's manner put her on the
efensive.

Hadra folded her hands prayer-like and bowed her
ad over them. "He has asked me to tell you that he is
stless with the dawn and with loneliness for you. The
orses are ready and you will ride together."

"Then I will choose a suitable *jellaba*—" She turned
ward the wardrobe. Hadra spoke a soft command, and
e slave extracted several garments from the rack for her
istress's inspection. By the time Emilie had selected one
 pale rose and magenta stripes, the other woman was
ne as soundlessly as she had appeared.

They reached the palace in just under an hour after
aving the walled city. Her first sight of it was breathtak-
g, and Emilie thought it could be better described as a
ty than a palace. It cascaded over a hillside and across a
nall valley, with natural fortifications of the hills in addi-
on to a high wall. There was a pass that afforded easy
ntry, and a line of sentries were in evidence all along a
rrowed ridge, men mounted and afoot, all with rifles.
hite robes fluttered in the wind as a silent signal was

passed to acknowledge the shereef's arrival. The pala
towered among the surrounding encampment. Its wal
bleached white by years of burning sun, the palace's re
tangular shape gave evidence that it was built around
huge court. Tops of cypress and fig trees relieved th
starkness, and numerous cases of green were scattere
here and there throughout the village.

A rider came toward them, reining in a dozen yar
distant. In spite of the flowing burnoose, Emilie reco;
nized Omar ben Hadj. Taleb rode out to meet him, ar
Emilie felt a flush of pride at the tall, straight figure h
husband presented on the magnificent stallion. He *looke*
like a leader!

The two men held a brief conference, then Tale
glanced back to command the rest of the party to follow
Emilie spurred the mare and caught up with the two ar
slowed her horse beside Taleb's. Though he smiled, h
did not interrupt his conversation in Arabic with Oma
Once again, Emilie had the feeling that she had trespasse
on territory where not even a wife had the right. It ar
noyed her, but there was nothing she could do, and sh
rode silently, pretending a total fascination with the sigh
around her as they approached the palace.

There were cook tents and sleeping quarters for so
diers at the perimeter of the settlement. Horses croppe
grass under desert palms; men sat on haunches near fir
drinking mugs of steaming tea; veiled women moved la
guidly, cooking over open fires, drawing water from well
Eyes turned to the party as it rode in, but faces were ex
pressionless. These were Taleb's people, and they ac
cepted his arrival as they did the dawning of each ne
day. The master came and went . . . and they waited t
serve. Emilie wondered if they had been told of her a
rival. It did not matter; she would be accepted as Taleb
wife and treated in the manner due the shereefa. Tale
was the law here, and there would be none of the siler

346

ndemnation she'd seen in the eyes of the English women
Fez.

They entered a walled enclosure that surrounded the
lace, and ben Hadj kicked his horse's flank and went on
ead as Taleb turned to Emilie.

"And so we are home, little shereefa. In a moment, you
l be at rest, our journey over."

"In the bosom of Allah," Emilie said with a mischie-
us smile.

Taleb laughed softly. "Yes, my dove, in the bosom of
lah. Come now, I long for the familiar comfort of my
me."

"It is so huge!"

He smiled. Even after seeing the palace of the Sultan,
e was child-like in her eagerness. It amused him, yet he
ew the depths to which her passion could be unfolded
well, and his loins stirred. She was child and woman,
d she was his. To him, the palace was without fascina-
n, an abode that served his needs, a center for his com-
nd, and a protection against his enemies. But he knew
would never lose the excitement that Emilie brought
n. Had he not already forgiven her boldness before his
d? Another woman would have been sent off like a
ck of sweet potatoes for such indiscretion. Emilie would
rn his ways in time, and her restless soul would find
ace and happiness. Yet he did not wish to rob her of
e spirit that made her so different, so appealing, the
rit that had attracted him from his first sight of her.
r heart and thoughts had been elsewhere, but her in-
lvement with Cartier was of no consequence—Taleb
ew he wanted her and he knew he would have her, not
an amusement for a few nights but forever. She be-
ged to him, and he would never let her go.

They walked the horses along a shaded path arched
th citrus and mimosa trees. The air cooled in the deep
adows, and the fragrance of flowers and blossoms
ared the dust of the desert from their nostrils. Gardens

347

were laid out among the trees, white paths crossing l
the brushstrokes of a calligrapher. Paper white narciss
wild anemones and lupins brightened the bank of a sm
stream that had been made to flow through the gard
from a fountain near the wall. The music of songbi
echoed the gurgling water.

Emilie looked this way and that, trying to see eve
thing at once, drinking in the wonder of her new hor
When they passed through another gate, the gardens w
lusher, the aromas more heady. And the palace loom
before them. Servants materialized to claim the hor:
and to help Emilie from her mount. Taleb led her throu
the thick carved oak doors that were drawn open by t
men. A prayerful murmur of greeting to the master w
up from his faithful servants as Taleb ushered her into
house.

Omar ben Hadj stood just inside, his face impassive
cept for the dark eyes which never left Emilie's face. I
hind him, half a dozen women were huddled in a strag;
line, pressing forward to glimpse the new mistress
things, their dark eyes guarded. One whispered sibilan
but was silenced by a glance from the elderly woman
the group.

Taleb had not mentioned other women, and Emi
looked at him questioningly.

"The women of my house," he said.

"The elderly one stepped forward with a bow t
seemed to warp her frail body. A red-palmed hand ca
from among the folds of the voluminous brown and g
embroidered caftan. Emilie thought she meant to sha
hands and put forth her own, but the old woman touch
two fingers to the tips of Emilie's, then brought them
her lips, murmuring an Arabic blessing of welcome.

"Zainab, the sister of my mother," Taleb said. Emi
smiled as the old woman stepped aside to allow a slo
eyed, honey-skinned girl to reach out a hand in the ki
ing gesture.

348

"Fatima, wife of Omar ben Hadj."

The others were introduced in turn, a sister of Omar, two cousins and an aunt, though Emilie was not sure she quite understood whose.

When the last had been introduced, Taleb said, "You will be shown your rooms and given the opportunity to refresh yourself. Though the other women live the the *iyal* I have ordered a private apartment for you." He gazed gently at her a moment, and she understood that she was being afforded a special privilege because she was different from the Moslem women. She was so thankful, she could have kissed him were they alone. There was so much to become accustomed to.

He said, "The *g'nafas* will tend your bath and wardrobe. I trust everything is in order. If you desire anything, make your wants known and they will be carried out."

"And you—?"

"I have been absent many suns and must see to my affairs. You shall never be far from my person and never part from my heart." Smiling, he turned and entered the doorway where Omar had already disappeared.

Emilie stood awkwardly, not sure what to do. The knot of women began to disperse, with only the elderly mother and Fatima remaining, still staring at Emilie. It was Fatima who spoke.

"It gives us pleasure to meet Taleb's *arusa*." Her voice was like a wind chime in a soft breeze, but her eyes were dark and distant. The fact that she spoke English took Emilie by surprise.

"Thank you," she murmured.

"I will show you the apartment Taleb has chosen . . . please, come."

The old mother stepped away to watch them walk slowly down the hall. Two slaves appeared from some recess and padded softly behind them.

349

"I am delighted to find other women," Emilie said. "I did not know—"

Fatima glanced sidelong. "It is custom for members of a family to live under the same roof."

Emilie did not say that she'd been unaware that Taleb and Omar were related. She'd been too conscious of Omar's hostility toward her, and she had the uneasy feeling that Fatima shared it. It distressed her that she would be judged before she had a chance to prove herself. They disliked her because she was a foreigner, because Taleb had chosen a wife not from his own people.

Emilie let herself be led through the palace, her annoyance vanishing as she was caught in the wonder of the vast patios and gardens, the balconies overlooking more gardens, magnificent rooms that rivaled those in the Sultan's palace. Every wall was tiled or painted in ornate scrollwork; archways were carved, pillars gleaming marble or intricate wood mosaics in a variety of colours. There were hidden courtyards and fountains everywhere that gave an air of eternal spring freshness. Man's will had banished the arid desert from this spot.

When they came to the quarters that were to be hers, Emilie could not stifle a gasp of astonishment. The room at Fez paled in comparison to the chamber she found herself in. The single room was the size of the entire Sloan residence on *el-Kebir* road! Draperies ruffled in the breeze and made the walls a shimmering mirage. There were a dozen doorways and windows leading to daylight beyond. No wall between had been left unadorned. Tapestries of gold thread and brilliant hues hung from ceiling to floor, which was itself covered with thick, soft carpets. The bed was screened by curtains and elegantly covered in brocade and satin. A wardrobe similar to the one in Fez occupied an entire wall, with more clothes than Emilie had ever seen in one place, even the finest shops in London! There were cushioned niches where she could lounge, tables on which tea could be served—and through a doorway

350

lendid bath as large as the outdoor pool in Fez. She
mply could not believe it, and stood gaping like a child
t alone in a sweetshop. She wandered about, touching a
tin pillow, feeling the texture of a wall hanging, examing the array of caftans, *jellabas*, tunics and shawls. She
uld dress like a queen, and she would never have to
n the same garment in a year's time! She was over-
helmed and dazzled, yet a tiny whisper of fear crept into
r mind. It was as though she were caught in a web of
ery and glamour that was unreal.

Fatima was watching her with something akin to
nusement in the dark eyes. Emilie forced herself to
ile.

"I shall be quite comfortable here. Are your own
oms near?"

"The *iyal* is at the long wing to the west."

Emilie accepted the curt answer and did not pursue the
atter. "I am surprised at your English. And delighted.
ere you educated abroad?"

The woman's eyes veiled as surely as if she had drawn a
tik over them. "The women of our country do not ven-
re beyond the walls of their houses. It is not the wish of
lah that a woman take to book learning or foreign
ays."

Chastened, Emilie felt her face warm. "But you have
arned English," she persisted.

Fatima was not ruffled. "My husband is chief *caid* to
s cousin's people. Like Taleb, he must deal with the En-
ish and French. His learning blesses me, and I please
m by acquiring knowledge so that I can speak with him
many tongues."

"I see." She still found it surprising, and she wished the
oman might have a friendlier attitude toward her. It
uld be pleasant to have someone . . ." And the ser-
nts, do any speak English?"

"None."

Emilie sighed but quickly covered it with a smile.

351

"Thank you, Fatima. I know we shall get on well, and am looking forward to our being friends."

Fatima inclined her head and pressed hands together a servant might. "You will want to rest." With that, s left, and Emilie was alone with the two slaves.

Emilie shrugged off the other woman's indifference. S was too excited to stay depressed, and she gave herself the luxury of her new life. The slaves were exper trained and anticipated her every wish, despite the la guage barrier. They indicated an archway and beckone and when Emilie followed, she saw an indoor bath wi sunken tub, high spouts for water and huge pitchers a jars of oils and perfumes. The room was tiled in colou soft and subtle as leaves along an English country lane October. The two girls stood waiting for Emilie to inc cate her preference. She pointed. She would bathe her the outdoor pool would be saved for another time. T two set about drawing the bath, perfuming it and readyi ointments and towels. Her dusty clothing was whisk away and she wrapped herself in the silken garment o girl brought. When the bath was pronounced ready aft much testing and pouring of water, Emilie let herself helped in and lay back on a slanted wall made for t purpose. How wonderful and luxurious! The wat swirled about her and she closed her eyes in relaxati and let her mind clear. She was home . . . how stran the word seemed applied to this magnificent palace. Sti she would soon be used to it, and with Taleb at her si nothing else mattered. In time, Fatima would overcon her reluctance to accept an outsider, and they would friends. The old woman had seemed pleasant enough, ar the others. She frowned, trying to recall names and p them to faces. Thank heaven Taleb had not sent her the *iyal* to live among them!

She was almost dozing when she became aware voices in the other room. She recognized one of th slaves', and the other was familiar as well. She frowne

352

and concentrated. The words were indistinguishable but she knew she was not mistaken. She had heard it before—Hadra! The English speaking servant who had been at her call only this morning in Fez. She had not ridden with them, yet she was here, and Taleb had clearly given Emilie to understand that none of the household staff moved from one residence to the other. And only minutes ago, Fatima had said there were no servants who spoke English!

Emilie leaned forward, glancing at the bit of the chamber visible beyond the doorway, but she could not see the two who were speaking. Then the room fell silent, and she busied herself with a sponge and bar of sweet-smelling soap, squeezing water over her shoulders and breasts, rubbing her flesh as though somehow it had managed to become unclean in a few hours time. Why did Hadra's presence disturb her? The servant had been polite and Emilie could find no fault with her behaviour . . . still, nagging worry ate at her.

One of the slaves appeared a moment later, her black face solemn as she knelt beside the tub. Emilie allowed her to wash her hair, rinse it and towel it dry before emerging from the tub and donning a thick soft robe. The girl fell to her knees again and dried Emilie's feet as she sat on a bench at the gold and blue tiled wall. She took each foot in her hands to rub it with oil and henna as she massaged muscles that had been confined to boots.

"Was that Hadra with you a moment ago?" Emilie asked knowing the foreign words would mean nothing but hoping for recognition of the name.

The slave started to rise. "Hadra . . ."

She thought Emilie was summoning the other. "No." Emilie lifted a foot and gestured the slave to resume rubbing. So it was Hadra, she had not been mistaken. She made a mental note to ask Taleb about the woman, then dismissed the matter from her head. She was eager to see the rest of the palace. the gardens and vast holdings that

353

were her husband's. And she was anxious to know what business matters were so pressing as to take Taleb away from her the instant of their arrival.

Would she ever learn to be patient about such things? Taleb's lifestyle was indeed different from any she'd ever known. How did the women fill their days? Fatima said they did not leave the house. Would she, too, be expected to laze and do nothing day after day?

She sighed and thought about the women she'd met in Fez. She saw little hope of relief from boredom with them, even if she went to the city often or had them here to visit. She giggled as she thought of Miss Drew's stern remarks about the Arab tribesmen. She'd made them sound like ungodly savages waiting to draw and quarter any Christian who ventured across their path. What would Martha Drew say if she could see the luxury that surrounded Emilie now, the comforts, the delicate red tint the henna had stained her feet? Taleb had told her henna was used to soften the skin and prevent blisters, but Miss Drew would deem it the handwork of the devil. The thought of the missionary's horrified face brought a fresh burst of giggling, and the girl looked up questioningly.

In the bedroom, Emilie paused at the wardrobe to frown over the selection; it seemed endless, and at last she decided on a silk and velvet caftan the colour of the desert sun. It enhanced the fairness of her skin and the darkness of her eyes, and she knew Taleb would notice.

She spent a few minutes examining the wardrobe and noted again that her clothing from Tangier was not among the others. The chemise she had worn during the journey from Tangier had vanished in Fez, and she had no idea where the others from her trunk might be stored. The girl seemed to understand; from a shelf she brought two white garments which she held out for Emilie's inspection. The top was a camisole of sorts, a high neck edged with delicate handmade lace, short, square loose sleeves, and the front opening fastened by gleaming gold

354

buttons strung together with a delicate gold chain. Emilie slipped into it and the slave's nimble fingers had it fastened over her breasts in seconds. She then shook out the lower portion of the undergarment, and Emilie was overcome with laughter. Drawers, if they could be dignified by such a name! Yards of material sewn into wide pantaloons, the waist huge enough to encompass Emilie several times around! They looked large enough to fit a horse rather than a woman, and Emilie could not stop laughing. The girl smiled and tugged at the ends of the drawstring to show how the garment could be made to fit. Still giggling, Emilie climbed into it and let the girl draw the linen strips snug. Seeing herself in the glass, Emilie thought how like a sack of patotoes she looked except for the pristine whiteness! But when the undergarments were covered by the caftan, the image that looked back at her was no longer ridiculous. It was quite stunning.

No matter what Fatima said, Emilie would not confine herself to her apartment, though she was wise enough not to repeat her mistake of searching out her husband while he was engaged in business. Instead, she wandered about familiarizing herself with the sitting rooms and vast halls that were probably used for large gatherings. Did Taleb hold court or entertain other tribal chieftains? Several times, she encountered servants on guard in corridors, and once she was sternly refused admission to a wing that jutted off at an angle from the rectangle and was lost among thick overhanging plants and trees. She was also refused admission to the chambers at a corner of the house not far from her own. Taleb's . . . with a connecting corridor as in Fez? She smiled and went on her way.

After numerous twistings and turnings, she came out upon a terraced balcony that overlooked a corner of the encampment surrounding the palace. It was the first glimpse she'd had since riding in, and she studied the forms and figures in the distance. Glancing skyward, she

355

realized that she was on the opposite side of the house from where they'd entered; the encampment seemed even more vast here. It stretched as far as the eye could see, lost at last among the shadows at the foot of the surrounding mountains. How many people did Taleb have? She'd imagined the tribe as rather small, perhaps a hundred or so, but she had seen thousands already, and there was no telling how many more were beyond the range of vision. There seemed to be an inordinate number of armed men considering the remoteness of the location. She scanned the distant mountains, which were steep and forbidding.

When she tired of the scene and solitude, Emilie returned to the hallway and started back toward her apartment. She was delighted to see Taleb coming toward her.

"There you are," he said. "I was told that you were wandering about like a lost gazelle." He embraced her gently and kept his arm at her waist as he walked with her. "Did you know that the word *gazelle* comes from an Arabic one that is translated as 'affectionate one'?"

She glanced to see if he was teasing and his smile was reassuring. "It is true," he said. "And so I think of you as my little gazelle, yes?" The pressure of his hand was as intimate as a kiss. "And now, come, I have a surprise for you."

"What is it?" She gazed at him with shining eyes.

"You will see. This way, through here."

They traversed an intersecting corridor and passed several rooms she had not seen. They were high-ceilinged, with pillars of gleaming marble and dozens of Persian and Oriental rugs covering vast expanses of tiled floors. Off another hall, he stopped to unlatch a carved oak door. Swinging it open, he drew her into a room which was bright with sunlight from windows and from a skylight-like dome that belled over a rounded niche. Carpets deadened the sound of their steps as Taleb led her into the wondrous place. The walls were panelled in wood,

356

and shelves had been built along three walls to hold hundreds of fine, leather-bound books. A library!

"My word! Taleb—wherever did they come from?!" She was so astonished she could only stare.

"I told you that you did not wed a barbarian. Here is evidence also that you have not married an unlearned man. I have collected the writings of many French, English and Spanish." He swept a hand to encompass the room. "I have read every volume," he said proudly.

"Good heavens, there is a lifetime of reading here." She drew a red-jacketed book from the nearest shelf. *Don Quixote*. Another, *Voltaire*. She moved along the wall, sampling the titles like new foods. *Dicken's Christmas Carol, Beowulf, The Iliad, A History of the French Revolution, The Life of Charlemange, Joan of Arc. . . .*

"I am impressed beyond words, Taleb. It is as wonderful a collection as I have ever seen."

"You have the freedom to choose what you will at any time. Until now, this room has been my private domain, but I welcome you into it."

"Thank you." She was moved by his sincerity and delighted by the knowledge that some of her time could be pleasantly passed in reading. His description of a "private domain" recalled the guarded passage, and she asked him about it now.

"Rooms in which I conduct business. You have no need to concern yourself with it. Is not the palace large enough to keep you occupied without that corner?" He was smiling and his words were gentle, and she forgot the matter instantly.

They remained in the library some time, with Taleb pulling a volume here and one there, asking her if she had read it, telling her his impressions, recommending some while bypassing others. The sun was almost directly over the skylight when they left to partake of the midday meal. Taleb, as always, left her alone for some minutes while he saw to his prayers and the house seemed to fall silent for several minutes. There was no cry of the *muezzin* here, and she was curious about how the Arab devotions were met. Enough time to concern herself with that later; she was sure Taleb would draw her into his life more and more as time went on, and what were puzzles now would become commonplace after a bit.

She did not remember to ask about Hadra until late at night when she lay in Taleb's arms. The curtains were drawn about the bed, but those at the windows billowed in the night wind like ghostly lovers reaching out in embrace. Their celebration of joy had been wondrous and complete, a fitting welcome to the palace of the shereef. Emilie lay nested against her husband's body, still aware of its power that brought her pleasure and fulfilment.

Her thoughts wandered over the day, the discovery and introduction to her new life, and the forgotten question was dredged from her mind.

"Is Hadra here?"

Taleb did not answer for a moment; it was as though he had withdrawn the harmony of their peaceful thoughts. Finally he said, "Yes."

Emilie felt disturbed. "You said the servants did not travel between the two palaces."

"Hadra is not a servant. She oversees many affairs of the palace that require a woman's hand."

"A housekeeper?"

Again he was silent momentarily. "That is an English title that cannot be translated to my language." He tightened his arm about her and stroked a bare breast as he murmured against her hair. "No need to trouble yourself with household matters. Leave them to Fatima and the others. You must only make your husband, the powerful shereef, happy."

His caress teased her flesh and she tried to turn to him, but he held her powerless while his hands and lips roused

358

her to burning passion once more. "You must only make me happy . . ." he murmured.

She whimpered softly as he took her again in a surge of need that drove all other thoughts from her mind.

Despite Taleb's assurances, she could not dismiss the beautiful servant from her mind. She never encountered Hadra about the halls of the palace, and when she asked the two slaves about her, they lowered their glances and shook their heads as though they did not understand. Curiosity impelled Emilie at last to take her questions to Fatima, and several mornings later she made her way to the _iyal._

The women's quarters occupied an entire wing of the palace and were as grandly furnished as Emilie's own. There was a large communal room where the women sat idling and talking; they seemed content with this and none had any kind of handwork or books to pass the time. Emilie recalled Fatima's remark about learning foreign ways. Off the central room were numerous smaller bed-chambers. Apparently each woman had her own, with slaves to tend her personal wishes and see to her comfort. Several black girls lounged on cushions near one of the cousins, and a fat woman with gold bracelets at her wrists, and heavy earrings jangling against her ebony neck, sat beside Zainab, talking as though the two had been friends a long time. When the old woman saw Emilie, she smiled and bobbed her head, motioning Emilie to join them. Fatima was not in sight, and Emilie crossed to sit beside Zainab. She had only spoken to the woman once, and it was apparent that she understood little English, but she talked now with profuse gestures and a rattle of words. From time to time, the fat woman nodded or added some comment.

When the old woman paused at last for breath, Emilie inquired if Fatima was about. Zainab blinked rapidly, then repeated the name.

359

"Fatima—" Her head bobbed and a leathery hand pointed in the direction of the garden.

Emilie rose and bowed to the two. It was a nuisance not understanding what people said, and she vowed she would learn enough of the strange language to get by in the household where everyone spoke it, save a few.

As she emerged from the *iyal* into the sunlit garden, she stood a moment looking about in search of Fatima. The garden was vast, several times the size of her own, with many small arbors under trellised vines or twining tree branches. There were pools and fountains, and the song of birds filled the air. She glimpsed two figures reclining on a soft mat under an arbor, a large bowl of fresh grapes between them. Fatima plucked a grape to pop in her mouth from time to time, but the other woman, whose back was to Emilie, chattered at a steady pace. Even without understanding words, there was no mistaking the anger in her voice, and her hands gestured impatiently or slapped at her fleshy things in bursts of anger.

It was not until Emilie was almost upon them that she recognized Hadra. Fatima looked up, a grape poised near her red lips, her eyes wide. The other woman's anger continued for a moment, then broke off as she, too, became aware they were no longer alone. She turned, and for a moment there was naked hatred in her eyes as she saw Emilie. She said something sharply in Arabic as she rose in a swirl of skirts and stalked down a path that would not bring her face to face with Emilie.

"I did not mean to interrupt," Emilie apologized without feeling as she stared after Hadra. Looking back to Fatima, she saw the other had resumed eating grapes and was watching with a curious gaze. Seeing Hadra had been unexpected, but had added to Emilie's curiosity. Though Fatima offered no invitation, Emilie sat beside her on the mat.

"It was Hadra I came to ask about."

Fatima looked impassive and said nothing.

"What is her position in the house? Taleb says she tends to some housekeeping chores or other, but I am not sure what she can be called upon for and what not."

Fatima concentrated on selecting a plump grape and chewed it carefully before answering. "Are your slaves unsatisfactory?"

"There are times when I would find it convenient to converse in English, and Hadra is the only servant who speaks it."

Fatima looked up with unreadable expression. "Hadra is not a servant."

Piqued, Emilie felt her annoyance flare. "Whatever. She *does* speak English. In Fez, Taleb told me to call upon her if I was in need of anything, but here I have no way to summon her."

"I see." Fatima's attention went back to the basket of grapes. "I will talk to her. Perhaps arrangements can be made." She said no more, and after a moment Emilie rose in a flurry of temper and departed. The woman was infuriating!

CHAPTER TWENTY

The days passed with the swiftness of the ever-blowing desert wind. Emilie soon discovered there was little to do, save roam the palace and grounds or spend hours in the *iyal* with the other women. She learned that Fatima had a son, a solemn lad of fourteen whom she saw only at a distance from time to time. As a male child, he did not live in the *iyal* with his mother but in rooms next to his father's apartment. There were two other children, girls, belonging to the cousins, but the toddlers scampered to hide at their mothers' skirts whenever Emilie was near, and she made no effort to become acquainted with them.

The chatter of the women was endless and incomprehensible, and Emilie found it wearying at best. She asked endless questions of Fatima about the house and encampment, and though Omar's wife was polite, it was impossible to feel any warmth toward her. Her disapproval of Emilie was all too obvious.

She did not see Hadra again, though once when she entered the *iyal* she was certain the woman hurried from the room and through the gardens. She did not speak about her again with Fatima, but two new slaves were sent to Emilie's apartment soon after the conversation in the garden; to Emilie's astonishment, the girls spoke and understood enough French so that conversation was possible. It infuriated her that neither Fatima nor Hadra had anticipated the possibility that Emilie's French was more proficient than her Arabic and sent the slaves sooner, but she said nothing.

The two were named Yakow and Toma, and Emilie immediately set about spending a bit of time each day adding to the girls' storehouse of knowledge. They conversed in French, and very patiently, Emilie began the task of teaching them English as well. They were bright and eager to please, and they learned quickly. At the same time, Emilie began to pick up a few words and expressions in Arabic as items were pointed out, discussed. She practiced alone in her bath or sitting on the terrace, and she decided she would hide her new skill from Taleb until she was proficient enough to surprise him.

It surprised Emilie how well the slaves were treated, far better than most servants in England. They seemed part of the family and had considerable freedom in action and speech. Fatima explained that a man of power like Taleb treated his people so they served willingly. To do otherwise was unthinkable, and he was rewarded by unswerving devotion.

The tribesmen and outdoor slaves were another matter. Emilie occasionally walked past the palace gardens and wall to stare at the encampment that surrounded it. On meeting Omar ben Hadj one morning, she requested his escort through the encampment so that she might see it firsthand. He ordered horses brought, and though he complied with her request, she knew it was reluctantly and only because she was Taleb's wife. His attitude toward her had not softened, though she did her best to be pleasant with him. His dislike seemed to grow out of their differences, which she sensed were unbridgable in his mind. She tried to win him over with smiles and pleasantries, but he was unreachable. He answered all her questions, explained what she wanted to know, but no more.

The encampment was vast. It lay around the palace for at least a mile in every direction. There were low, white-washed houses and tents set in rows and circles to mark off various groups. Omar told her that Taleb was shereef to a dozen tribes, many of which lived close at hand and a few that were nomadic and came to the palace only for special occasions or when they had need to consult the shereef. Omar's own people lived here, he said, pointing out a vast area where a mixture of houses and tents covered a sprawling hillside.

"I would like to see how your people live," she said.

His gaze skittered past her and off to the distance. "If it is your wish . . ." He nudged the horse between a row of tents until he came to one where the flap was tied back. He called out, and when a woman appeared in the doorway, he spoke to her in a guttural spate. Emilie caught a word and there, enough to know that the woman was being commanded to welcome the wife of the shereef.

They dismounted and she followed Omar into the tent. It was of good size, perhaps a hundred feet across. A reed partition divided it in two parts, one that seemed quarters for the four small children who stared at Emilie with huge round eyes and an elderly woman wrapped so heavily in her *haik* that only two sunken eyes showed. A grand-mother? The other half of the tent was the woman's domain. She, too, was shrouded in the sheetlike *haik* which she held close across her face. She had smooth skin and a huge purple star painted as beauty mark just above one black brow. Her hands and feet were painted with henna which was almost blood-red against the light colour of her garment. She made no attempt to follow Omar as he walked about the tent answering Emilie's questions.

The furnishings were sparse, several straw mats, a painted and arabesqued wooden chest for clothes, a small round mirror hung on a tent pole. There was a tripod built of cane and covered with a cloth; Omar explained this was to afford privacy for washing. There were also two large stones for grinding grain, the woman's daily chore in order to make *couscous* and pastries that were a staple of diet. Though the cooking was done outside, a reed table held jars, goatskin and plates for the family's use; a rusty tin lamp and a shining rifle were near the rear of the tent beside a weaver's loom. The rifle surprised Emilie, and when she asked Omar if all the people of the camp were always armed, he shrugged and told her that every man had need to hunt food.

Outside, they rode again, walking the horses along rows of tents where activity buzzed and people stared at the shereefa or women slipped quickly out of sight. They came to a walled section; when Omar would have turned to bypass it, Emilie insisted on seeing what was beyond.

Omar's face darkened but he acceded to her demand. They rode through the wide gate where two sentries stood with rifles in hand and came upon what appeared a drill field and several large storehouses, adobe that had not been whitewashed, with roofs of heavy tile and doors of thick oak. One door stood open as men moved and carried heavy cases from a tarpaulin-covered pile inside.

Omar said, "This is the center of our army. Our men practice riding and shooting." He pointed to a low embankment at the far end where targets against hillocks were shredded with bullet holes. The rear of the area was not walled but lay against the hillside, and a well beaten path showed where horsemen entered and left to the north.

Somehow Emilie had not expected such an organized military installation, but she hid her surprise. Taleb hinted of his power and importance, and she was only now beginning to realize the extent of it. She found a measure of comfort in knowing she was so well protected. As they rode past the storehouses, two men lifted another of the crates and lugged it toward the door. Emilie had a glimpse of the lettering on the sides of the box, too quick to distinguish words but not to determine that they were German.

She thought of the recent encounter with *Herr* Muller in Fez . . . he'd sold these guns to Taleb. She shivered despite the morning's blazing sun, and told Omar she wished to return to the palace.

After several weeks, Emilie tired of the routine of reading, wandering about the palace and grounds, or spending time with Fatima and the other women in the *iyal*. Fatima was no friendlier, and Emilie found it irritating to be tolerated in so casual a manner. To her dismay, she saw almost nothing of Taleb, who was fully occupied with the work of running his kingdom. They no longer dined together except on rare occasions, and she only glimpsed him in passing during the long days. She complained of it when he came to her chambers at night, and he told her that it was the way of his people, and he managed each time to kiss away her protests and fill her instead with rapture that made her forget. But no matter how closely entwined they were when she fell asleep, when she woke in the morning, she was alone in the huge, curtained bed. In the fourth week when Emilie pleaded the indisposition of her monthly time, Taleb did not come to her chambers at all. She was angry and lonely, and she snapped irritably at Yakow and Toma who tried to cheer her spirits. It seemed a turning point and her boredom grew to maddening proportions from then on. It was heightened by the fact that Taleb no longer returned to her chambers each night as he had from the beginning of their marriage. Now he visited only once or twice a week as it suited him.

January was gone and February well into its passing. Emilie pleaded with Taleb one night to take her to Fez so she might have a change of scene and some new faces to brighten her days.

"I cannot leave the palace, but if you wish, you may

go. I will send a message to *lella* Madden and *Si* Gregory that you will be in the city. Perhaps they can plan entertainment to lighten your heart."

"I do not want to go without you—"

"I cannot leave. You will stay at the house in Fez and have every comfort. If you wish, I will allow Yakow and Toma to accompany you, since you find them pleasant company and can converse with them."

How had he learned that? No matter. She was thankful that he did not suggest Fatima or any of the other women of the *iyal* accompany her. Though she was disappointed that he would not go, she began to plan eagerly for the trip. She would leave in two days and stay as long as she found the visit amusing. She began to list the many things she hoped to do. Could she shop, she asked Taleb?

"As much as you like. I will instruct the servants to guide you to whatever places you wish to see."

"You must guide me! If you cannot come, you must tell me about the city, what I should see, which places are most fascinating—"

He laughed at her breathless excitement and drew her to sit on a pillowed divan in a niche beside the cloistered walk surrounding a courtyard. The sun filtered through a lattice of vines and bougainvillea, and shadows played over Emilie's face and were reflected in the deep pools of her eyes. Taleb kissed her gently.

"I shall tell you all you wish to know. Already I grow lonely at the thought of your departure, and I will long for you each minute you are gone and hurry the hours until you return."

She nestled against his shoulder as he described the Sultan's palace, the *medrosas*, minarets, tombs, bazaars of Fez. He told her of the colourful *mellah* where the Jews lived and worked, the potters' quarters, and the *souk* of the *teinturiers*, where men dyed huge hanks of wool and hung them over the streets to dry. Her excitement began to grow, and she forgot the restless bordom as she began to plan for the trip.

They rode off early one morning before the sun climbed over the eastern mountains. Emilie was accompanied by Yakow and Toma, six armed guards and, to her surprise, several dozen soldiers who divided into four groups and rode a short distance from the party in each direction. Taleb had told her that she would travel under guard, but she had not expected one so extensive.

The messenger who carried word of Emilie's impending visit to the British Consul and to Mrs. Madden, brought back a penned note from the doctor's wife that she was eagerly looking forward to the pleasure of seeing the shereefa again and would be honoured by her presence at dinner. Douglas Gregory wrote a brief note that members of his staff would be at her disposal while she was in the city.

The journey seemed shorter than she remembered, or perhaps it was her anticipation and excitement that made it seem so. Emilie chattered with Yakow and Toma, and the two were almost as excited as Emilie herself. Yakow had been to Fez as a child, before she had been sold into the shereef's service, but for Toma it was a new experience. Her jet eyes gleamed and rolled when Emilie promised she would allow both girls to accompany her sightseeing or marketing. They would be a distinct advantage because of their knowledge of the language, but Emilie did not spoil their pleasure with a fact so mundane.

They arrived at the *bab Djedid* as the sun reached a halfway point in its climb from dawn. The bustle and activity after so many days of solitude in the palace was like a drug to Emilie, and not even the stench of waste and rotting flesh could dampen her spirits. She had eyes for everything, the crowded streets, slow-moving figures clad in white like a platoon of ghost walkers, merchants with laden camels and asses wending their way through the throng. Down side lanes, she saw tiny cubicles of shops with leather goods, copper and brass pans and pots spilling from ropes so they overflowed the street itself.

She was almost disappointed when the crowded native scene gave way to lush park areas near the river and the residential district where rich Moors and Europeans lived. The approach was different, but she thought she recognized the British consulate when she glanced along one lane.

At Taleb's house, she was helped from the horse and ushered inside by a dozen bowing servants. One woman spoke to Toma and Yakow, and Yakow related the message that the woman was in charge and it was her pleasure to do the shereef's bidding. Her name was Ilyan, Yakow said, and she had seen to it personally that the shereefa's apartment was readied.

Giggling and staring in awe, Yakow and Toma accompanied Emilie upstairs to the rooms she had previously occupied. The two slaves stared at everything, paused here and there to touch a wall hanging or a bit of sculptured plaster, as though comparing the house with the grandeur of the palace at Madawadi. They thought Emilie's rooms small, but they approved the baths and the gardens.

There was no unpacking, since Emilie had brought nothing save a few personal articles. An entire wardrobe awaited her here, and she had only to choose what she would wear. She decided on a light linen caftan of yellow and violet, and over it, a *ferragiat* of royal blue tied at the waist with a purple sash. She studied her image in the glass as Yakow brushed her hair, and she knew the brilliant colours highlighted her fairness. Her cheeks glowed with suntan, and her dark eyes stared back at her solemnly. She did not object when Yakow brought a small pot of *kohl* and touched it to her eyelids in the Arab fashion. The effect was dramatic, and Emilie smiled impishly.

369

Mrs. Madden and the good missionaries would be properly shocked!

They spent the rest of the morning exploring the city. Emilie covered her colourful garb with a stark white *jellaba* and carefully drew a veil across her face and hair so that she would not stand out as a foreigner. She wanted to experience the city firsthand, to fill her senses with its variety and colour. Despite her protests, the guards remained close at hand, thus robbing her of the opportunity to pass for an ordinary native, but nothing she said would dissuade them to alter one jot of Taleb's instructions. Yakow assured that she would be taken for the wife of a wealthy merchant or official.

They went along some of the narrow streets that led off from the Mansions Quarter like tendrils of hair blown in the wind. The three women stayed close together, flanked front and rear by the guards who kept the crowd from pressing too close. For all her concern, Emilie realized that her disguise was perfect, and that she was scarcely given a second glance by most. They went along lanes of beaten earth, winding among beshrouded merchants on fat mules, and hordes of men, women and children of every description. Afoot, Emilie was distinctly conscious that the horizon was never more than a few yards away, and she felt cut off from the world. Walls seemed to hug them, and when they chanced upon an occasional open doorway, it disclosed only the secrecy of an austere outer hall that gave no suggestion of what lay beyond. Here and there, a huddled figure sat in a doorway, head bowed as the world went about its business unnoticed. They descended a steep street, cobblestoned to prevent rutting by the rains and came upon a *souk* that was teeming with activity. Dozens of tiny stalls overflowed with all manner of wares, and Emilie was like a child at Christmas, staring and touching, whispering with Toma and Yakow about quality and cost. She bought a length of fine silk, a gleaming brass bell that rang with a note like a lark's song, pieces of pottery that caught her eye. Each time she expressed a desire to make a purchase, one of the guards came forward to haggle with the dealer before paying over coins to acquire the article, which was then handed to a towering negro who had been brought along to carry the shereefa's purchases.

Weary of the marketplace at last, Emilie informed the guards, through Toma, that she wished to see the section of the city along the river. After another perilous descent on a crowded street, they came upon a vast square closed on three sides by high battlemented walls with towers; the fourth side was bounded by the River of Pearls. In the square, military men, magistrates, officials and slaves were formed in lines, and beautifully decked horses pawed the ground impatiently. At Emilie's question, Yakow learned from one of the guards that the Sultan was in residence, his palace just beyond the rows of trees in the distance. His imperial guard, dressed in white, was drawn up in long lines; around the square thousands of foot soldiers in flaming red uniforms stood at attention under the broiling sun. Taleb's guide inquired if the shereefa wished to visit the palace and request an audience with the Sultan, and Emilie shook her head quickly. Without Taleb at her side, she would be distinctly ill at ease among people of high station. She was sure there were many rules of etiquette that must be observed in audience with the Sultan, and she did not wish to tackle that problem.

Emilie saw only a few white faces among the soldiery and recognized the uniforms as French. There were hardly enough to be called troops, only a handful of officers. The rest were Moors, boys for the most part.

They returned to the shereef's house by another route which gave Emilie a glimpse of the Sultan's palace and of several squat mosques, one large enough to accommodate thousands judging by its size. She was still gazing at it when she realized that the guards had changed direction abruptly and were reversing their direction. Emilie heard

Toma's soft indrawn breath as the girl averted her glance and bowed her head.

They were near a gate. There seemed to be a commotion of sorts, with a small band of soldiers and a crowd of angry, milling Arabs. A soldier on horseback slashed a whip angrily at men who would have pulled him from his mount, and when they had been driven back, he shouted a command. The crowd fell back and a wailing lament rose on the dusty air.

"Come away quickly," Yakow said to Emilie, grasping her sleeve to pull her. Emilie let herself be led, having no desire to become involved in whatever disturbance was taking place, but she could not resist glancing back. The air was charged with tension and anger, which she knew was directed at the soldiers. As she watched, there was another stir of activity at the gate and two heads appeared above the crowd. Another wail of agony rose in a crescendo, and a woman shrieked. Emilie jerked her arm from Yakow's grasp, and stared in horror as the heads continued to rise, red streaming like ribbons below.

They were suspended by the hair tied with rope . . . severed heads fresh with blood and the shock of death. One appeared to be that of a boy not more than fourteen, the other a man perhaps twice that age, both Moors. Nausea rose in Emilie's throat, and for a moment she felt faint. She gave a strangled cry and covered her face; the two slave girls shepharded her away, their arms protective as they stumbled along the crowded street.

She didn't know how she got back to the house or to her rooms, where Toma and Yakow bathed her face in cool cloths and coaxed her to drink steaming tea. Her stomach rebelled as the memory of the two grisly heads haunted her. She recalled Taleb's careless remark.

"We shall see many heads hanging over the gates of Fez . . ."

She had thought him joking! She shuddered and tears welled in her eyes as she pushed away the cup Toma was pressing to her lips. She cried out of horror and exhaustion. The day which had begun so enjoyably was soured. She wept until she had no more tears, then fell asleep until the sun was well into afternoon.

Toma and Yakow were seated close to the bed when she woke, their worried frowns vastly relieved when Emilie stretched and raked her fingers through her hair.

"You are well . . . ?"

"Yes, I am all right." Emilie blocked the image that would have returned to her numb brain. "What was the reason for such barbarism?" When she realized the girls did not understand, she said, "What did the two do? What crime drew them such a fate?"

"It is better to forget," Yakow said.

"I wish to know!" Emilie was drawn by a need to understand.

Toma looked solemn. "It is said they were prisoners brought back from a recent battle."

"But if they were prisoners they were no longer a danger—!"

"It is customary to present the heads of the enemy to the Sultan."

Emilie recoiled, as much from the placid telling as the information itself. It seemed impossible that people accepted such cruelty and barbarism. *Inch'allah*, Taleb had said. She shuddered again.

"Will you take tea now?"

"Yes." It was brought and she sipped slowly. The threatening sickness was replaced by cold numbness. She could not let herself dwell on the incident or it would spoil her entire visit.

There were notes from both Douglas Gregory and Mrs. Madden welcoming her and extending invitations. Mrs. Madden invited her to dine that night, saying the two girls were eager to see Emilie again and had been granted permission to stay up past their bedtime so they could do so. Dinner would be at nine if that was convenient.

Emilie took a moment to pen a quick acceptance which she sent off by messenger before she spent the rest of the afternoon in a leisurely bath in the huge outdoor pool. She dallied and splashed, enjoying the cool refreshment and banishing all ugly thoughts. When she tired of the water, she lay on a mat in the sun and let Toma cream her skin with a delicate almond scented lotion. And when the shadows began to lengthen, she returned to the bedchamber and spent another leisurely hour applying lotion to her face and letting Yakow brush her hair.

She had tea again and a plate of small cakes that rid her of the gnawing hunger pangs but would not spoil her appetite for dinner. She was amazed at her own strength in accepting what she had seen, though her mind still recoiled from such savagery by man against man. To continue a custom that dated from antiquity into the modern century showed an ignorance that appalled her. Was the Sultan an uneducated man? Perhaps the new leaders like Taleb would change matters someday.

She spent the hour until it was time to depart for the Madden house writing lengthy letters to her parents and sister. To her mother and father, she described the house in Fez and the palace at Madawadi, the people she'd met, and the invitations received. It was a cheerful letter, full of details but without emotion. The fact that she was separated by distance from the two who had given her life did nothing to bridge the gap that had always lay between them.

Her letter to Sara was another matter. She poured onto paper words that would have been spoken if her sister were close. She gave ecstatic descriptions of her joy with Taleb, the heady pleasure she found in his arms, the attention he lavished on her and the grand style in which they lived. She wrote of Fatima and the *iyal*, and of Omar ben Hadj who resented her but dared not speak against her. And she described in detail the three missionaries who so sternly disapproved her marriage, a story she

374

new would bring a smile to Sara's lips with its mimicry
nd humor. She begged Sara to come to visit soon. . . .

She stared at the page and wondered if her wistful plea
etrayed the loneliness she felt. She decided against redo-
ıg the page and scrawled her name, then sprinkled the
ık with sand to dry it *before* folding the paper and
ealing it in an envelope. She would take both letters to
Irs. Madden and ask her to relay them to the postmis-
ress. She felt guilty that she had not thought to write be-
ɔre this, but being at the palace was like being apart
:om the rest of the world and familiar customs.

CHAPTER TWENTY-ONE

She was received in the drawing room where she'd taken tea with Mrs. Madden on her earlier visit. The doctor was a short, rotund man, with wispy pale hair across a receding forehead. His skin was deeply tanned, with no tell-tale line to show where a hat was worn out of doors. He was dressed in a white seer-sucker suit that seemed slightly rumpled for all its cleanness and gave him the preoccupied air of a man who found work more important than personal pursuits. Like Pierre . . . She realized with a start that she had not thought in her letter to Sara to ask after Pierre!

"—sorry to have missed you on your earlier visit," Enoch Madden was saying. His voice was deep and loud, incongruous with his soft appearance. "Have you met the assistant Consul, John Link? No, of course not, you did tell me that, didn't you Claudia . . . ?"

A thin young man with a serious face and grey eyes behind owlish spectacles bowed to Emilie. "I am honoured Mrs. Mu'Min."

Emilie almost giggled at his formal manner and the title he had elected for her. Even after several weeks, the En glish of Fez had not come to comfortable terms with her marriage to Taleb.

"Mr. Gregory spoke of you," Emilie lied gallantly to put the young man at ease. He had obviously been invited as her dinner partner in a non-official capacity, and Emilie was touched by Claudia Madden's consideration.

John looked slightly flustered. "And he has spoken of you . . ." He slipped a hand inside his coat and withdrew an envelope. "Mr. Gregory has asked me to convey this to you. It came care of the Consulate about two weeks ago."

He handed her a letter and she immediately recognized the careful script. Sara! She was so eager to read the news, it was difficult not to tear open the letter at once and pore over the words. Instead, she tucked it in her reticule and at the same time, removed the two letters she had written.

"Thank you. May I impose on you to post these for me?"

"Of course . . ." The letters disappeared inside his coat.

"John has been with us since last fall," Claudia said, smiling and drawing Emilie to a sofa while her husband and John sat in two facing chairs. A servant offered round a tray of apertifs in thin-stemmed crystal glasses. "We discovered only after travelling halfway round the globe that we are both from Essex, our homes not thirty miles distant from each other, but we'd never met."

"You are from London, I am told," John said.

"Yes."

"Do you miss it?"

She hadn't given the matter thought, and she furrowed her brow. "Not really. I thought I would, but so much has happened in Morocco there's scarcely been time, I suppose. My life has changed so considerably that I have not given a thought to shops or theater or the dozens of things I believed I would miss."

377

Enoch Madden said, "Life in Morocco is a drastic enough change without marriage to a shereef." His wife looked scandalized, but the doctor paid no attention. "Do you find it to your liking, Emilie?"

Despite his directness, Emilie was not offended. She smiled to put Claudia and John at ease. "Yes, very much, though I admit I feel somewhat isolated at the palace. I could do with a bit more company. I find the women of the family somewhat sedate and settled in Moorish ways for my tastes. This has prompted my visit to Fez."

Madden nodded as if he expected just such an answer. His small blue eyes were steady under the colourless brows. "You've always a place to come to here, you know. Welcome anytime, anytime. Remember that."

Claudia blushed. "The shereef keeps a house in Fez, Enoch dear."

"I know that," he said impatiently, still looking at Emilie until she dropped her gaze under his scrutiny.

Claudia rushed on. "Hilda has allowed the girls to stay up. They have talked of nothing but your return. Would you like to see them, Emilie?"

"Of course!"

Claudia rang a silver bell on the table beside her, and a few moments later, Hilda Weiss entered with the two girls in tow. They were fairly dancing and the governess tugged to restrain them and make them walk properly as they had been instructed. They went immediately to Emilie who set aside her wine glass and welcomed them with a hug.

"How marvelous to see you again!"

"The princess came back!" Zelda said, giggling and clamping a hand over her mouth.

"And I have not forgotten my promise to have you visit my castle!" She looked to Claudia. "Will you come soon? Next week?"

Claudia looked to her husband questioningly.

378

He said, "Hmm, we'll see. I suppose if there's no more trouble out that way."

"Then it's settled," Emilie said, hugging the two to her again. "You shall come to the princess's castle and we shall have a wonderful time."

The girls squealed with delight and Miss Weiss shushed them softly. Emilie quickly included her in the invitation. "You must come too, Miss Weiss."

"All right, girls. Say goodnight to Miss Emilie and off with you," Claudia said. "It's considerably past your bedtime already."

"Goodnight, Miss Emilie," they chanted in unison.

"Goodnight, and I shall expect you next week. Your mama and I will arrange the details."

They giggled as they followed Miss Weiss from the room.

"I fear you may not know how demanding they can be," Claudia warned. "You must not allow them to impose."

Emilie tossed her blond curls impatiently. "I have more time than I know what to do with. I will adore having all of you." She looked to Dr. Madden. "You too if your schedule permits, doctor."

He shook his head. "Impossible, what with the damned Arab skirmishes we're hard pressed to keep up."

Again, Claudia looked stricken by her husband's lack of candour, and she smiled nervously. "Enoch's been very busy with plans for the new hospital."

"Tell me about it," Emilie said, thinking of Pierre and his work in Tangier. She wondered if by chance Dr. Madden knew him.

"Not much to tell. A hospital is a hospital, and God knows we need one here. Field surgery is scarcely more than butchery. The heat and flies make any pretense at cleanliness a farce." He shook his head and pushed back the wispy hair that fell across his forehead. "We need sur-

379

gery space and decent rooms where men can recuperate before going back to the barracks."

"I have seen the French hospital in Tangier," Emilie said.

Madden's brow creased as his brows rose. "That so? Fine place, excellent. Are you acquainted with Doctor du Bois and that young chap on the staff, Louvel?"

"Yes, both. My sister and I worked as volunteers at the hopital with Martine du Bois, and we knew Pierre—Dr. Louvel—quite well." How often her thoughts had strayed to Pierre in one day! As though her conscience were chiding her.

"Damned fine young surgeon and researcher. He's coming down to help us get things going."

"Pierre is coming to Fez?" She could not hide her delight.

"Yes, though we've no word when. I expect it's difficult for him to get away."

"I will be glad to send word when we hear of his coming," Claudia said, smiling at Emilie and trying to steer the conversation onto a subject that did not exclude her other guest. "John, perhaps the consul will enquire in its next despatch? I am told that there is a possibility that one of our countrymen may also journey with the next caravan."

"A botantist, I believe," John Link said. "Chap determined to catalogue every plant and flower of the desert."

"My word! That should keep him busy a lifetime!" Emilie said.

"Drivel, if you ask me."

"That's hardly fair, Enoch. To the botanist, his plants are every bit as worthy of devotion as your surgery is to you."

"Harummphh." It was obvious Enoch still considered the idea foolishness.

A servant appeared and Claudia set aside her wine

lass. "Shall we retire to the dining room?" She rose and
ffered her arm to her husband.

John Link peered from behind his round spectacles.
Miss Emilie . . ."

She slipped her arm through his and they followed their
ost. It amused Emilie that he called her, Miss Emilie, as
e children had. She supposed it was more comfortable
 his orderly English manners than anything else he had
ome up with.

The large, comfortable dining room faced onto an open
rrace from which the scent of jasmine drifted like a veil.
he room was well appointed; a Duncan Phyfe table and
airs, a huge sideboard that seemed too massive for its
indly legs, rich wall hangings and draperies. The table
as spread with a fine linen cloth and four places set,
aviland china with a delicate rose pattern, tall crystal
oblets, and heavy sterling tableware. Three servants cared covered dishes from some hidden area beyond an
ch, while two others stood close to the sideboard wait-
g to serve as soon as the guests were seated.

The food was a combination of native and English,
ith many courses and frequent hot-towel washings be-
veen them. Claudia Madden kept the talk on subjects
oper for the table, and anytime her husband seemed in
anger of straying to medical or military matters, she
eered the conversation back to safer channels. She was a
etermined hostess, and Emilie was surprised that Enoch,
 outspoken in manner, allowed himself to be dominated.
 was as though over the years of marriage, the couple
d worked out a division of command. The table was
laudia's undisputed domain.

The meal was enjoyable though somewhat heavy,
milie thought. No wonder the couple were overweight.
e smiled and chatted with her hosts and with John Link
ho semed to emerge from his shell under Emilie's coax-
g. She could not hear enough about England all at once,
d she found endless questions to ask.

After dinner, they retired to the drawing room again the men with cigars and brandy, Emilie and Claudia with small glasses of port. Enoch was back in power, and he began describing the latest military action in the hills only twelve miles distant from the city.

"We came off with four dead and a dozen wounded Damned shame the Arabs can't stay where they belong."

"Enoch, really. Please remember that Emilie is married to the shereef and guard your tongue." Claudia turned to Emilie with an apologetic smile. "He becomes so wrapped in the medical problems, he sometimes forgets that we are, after all, the intruders in the land."

"Do they consider us intruders?" Emilie said.

"Have you not been spat upon and cursed?" Enoch looked astonished. "I thought no one escaped their venom. 'Accursed Christians', that's what they call us."

"Why do you stay if you feel so strongly?"

The doctor cleared his throat and had the grace to look flustered.

"You see, he is bluster without fury," Claudia said "It's only that he is impatient with the lack of proper medical facilities and the conditions under which he must work. Isn't that so, Enoch?"

He mumbled and inhaled on the cigar.

"Do you find our people despised by the nation, John?" Emilie turned her gaze on the junior Consul.

He flushed. "I cannot deny what the doctor says is true, but in defense of the Arabs, I must say that many are most kind to us and work willingly side by side with us."

"The disturbance you spoke of," she asked the doctor "how did it happen?"

He exhaled a blue cloud of smoke. "Guns. Some had them and others wanted them. Guns are power, like horses, and a few dozen lives are worth the price. Turned into a bloody fullscale revolt and the army had to be called out. The big mistake is in allowing them to have

ns at all. If the French and English had taken a firm
nd on that from the beginning, there'd be a lot less
uble now."

"Impossible to control, of course," John murmured.

"Certainly—because they're armed to the teeth, every
st tribe. There are rumors that more guns are coming in
the time. For all we know, they may have caches of
em sitting in wait for the time when they'll decide to
mp the lot of us."

"Enoch!" Claudia was shocked.

He shrugged. "An exaggeration, perhaps, but more
ely close to the truth."

John Link swirled the liquour in the snifter. "I think we
st give credence to the basis for the rumours at least."
e glanced at Emilie with an apologetic smile. "The con-
late receives word on all that pertains to our people
re, and we do hear of these matters."

"What matters?" Emilie was curious and interested.
e felt as though she should defend Taleb, though he
d not been accused of anything thus far, but her con-
ence was burdened with the guilty knowledge of the
aling with *Herr* Muller and the bulging warehouse.

He glanced at his hostess and was silent, aware of her
sapproval of the subject. Enoch was not as cautious.

"A shipment of guns was recently brought to the in-
ior and sold off to some *caid* or other, and it's got the
litary damned worried."

Emilie felt a prickle of fear brush her neck. She forced
r voice steady. "How can you be sure?"

"The guns were smuggled into Rabat. A brisk trade in
em there, from all accounts. But before the authorities
uld close in on the people running them, they'd shipped
e lot out. They were traced as far as Beldeen. Imagine
e cheek of those beggars using our own railroad spurs
carry out their dirty business." Enoch finished his
andy and would have poured himself a second except

383

for Claudia's quick admonishing glance. He set the gla
aside and concentrated on the cigar.

Emilie was silent, her breath cold. Her mind tried
refute the picture being put together like a puzzle. The
could be a dozen explanations of the coincidence, si
would not believe the story without more concrete proo
Nor would she say anything that would sound like a b
trayal of her husband. Taleb had explained the need fo
guns and she could not dispute it—Madden had nothir
but surmise.

"The guns vanished after getting that far but you ca
bet they're hidden in the tents of one tribe or other."

"But this sort of thing happens all the time, you've sai
so yourself, Enoch. I do not understand why it is such
concern now," Claudia said.

John cleared his throat as though to warn the docto
he'd said too much, but Enoch was too engrossed in h
tale to heed. "Because there were machine guns amor
them. Do you have any idea what a machine gun can d
to a village or a regiment of soldiers on horseback?" H
shook his head and looked pained.

The room was silent for several moments, with the tw
women staring nervously. Emilie was frightened and an
gry, and she longed to escape the atmosphere of gloo
that had fallen over them.

"I think I should be getting back. It's been a long da
and I had a very early start this morning." She smiled
Claudia, who looked pale.

"Must you—?"

"Yes, but since I will be in Fez several days, perha
we can have tea together? Will you come tomorrow?" Sl
was talking too fast, saying the first words that came
mind.

"Of course . . ."

Enoch was on his feet as Emilie rose, John as wel
"Claudia will raise the devil with me for chasing you o
with my talk of guns and massacres."

"Not at all. It is the hour that takes me away, nothing else." She smiled to show she was not offended, but his critical blue eyes saw through her pretense. When he took her hand and bowed over it, his strong fingers were warm. Emilie declined John's offer to accompany her as far as the shereef's house; she had a dozen servants waiting, there was no need. She bade them goodnight and took her leave.

At home, she eagerly tore open Sara's letter and read it through three times. How like her sister to think to send a letter through the consulate, to await Emilie whenever it found her. She wrote of everyday things . . . their parents, father's business, her work at the hospital. She, too, mentioned that Pierre was planning a trip to Fez to cooperate in setting up a hospital there. There was no hint that Emilie's sudden marriage and departure had caused a ripple in the lives of those left behind in Tangier. Sara missed her, of course, and wrote that mama still cried in the privacy of her rooms but was stoic when father was about . . . she was recovering from the shock, Sara assured Emilie, and if Emilie was happy in her new life that was what mattered to any of them.

Enoch Madden's words caused her some restlessness after the dinner party, but by morning Emilie had pushed them from her thoughts firmly. Madden was gossiping, passing along bits and pieces that Emilie was now fabricating into a story of her own making. The guns smuggled from Rabat had nothing to do with Taleb—or if they did, his purpose was not the nefarious one the doctor implied. She would ask Taleb on her return, and the matter would be settled in her mind once and for all.

She spent the next days in a busy round of roaming the city, visiting with Claudia Madden. In a burst of impish generosity she invited the three missionaries to tea and was rewarded by Miss Drew's scandalized face when tea was served Moroccan style on a low table surrounded by cushions. The gray-haired woman looked like a fat bird perched on a branch that might collapse under her weight at any moment.

Before she left Fez, Emilie spent an afternoon at the Madden's and made final the plans for Claudia and the children to visit the following week. Despite the difference in their ages and interests, Emilie found herself looking forward to the visit. The children were enchanting and she knew their visit would be a delightful relief from the dull hours with nothing to do but sit about or pass time with Fatima or the others.

She posted another long letter to Sara, thanking her for the news and expressing delight to hear that Pierre was coming. She would make it a point to be in Fez so she could see him. If only Sara might come too! What a wonderful reunion they would have. She encouraged her sister to consider the idea.

Only after sending the letter off with one of the servants to deliver to Miss Charing, did Emilie realize that neither she nor Sara had mentioned Henri. He too was part of a past on which a door had been firmly closed.

The return to Madawadi lacked the spark of anticipation of the earlier journey. Emilie felt depressed though she concentrated on the pending visit of Claudia and the children. All the talk of battles and guns had unnerved her, and she wondered if Taleb would answer the dozens of questions that churned in her mind. She did not want to believe he had any connection with the trouble she'd heard about, yet she could not dispel the fear. What did she know of his affairs? Nothing. No more than he chose to tell her or what she could fathom from the veiled remarks made by others. He had not once taken her into his confidence, nor explained away her nagging doubt about minor matters. She knew nothing of his army except that it was well armed and very large.

She squinted at the soldiers flanking the caravan. Thirty? Forty men? Why did Taleb deem it necessary to protect her so carefully? She had not taken his remark seriously about there being some who would wish harm to the house of the shereef . . . perhaps she should have. Enoch Madden talked of a skirmish between tribesmen and the Sultan's forces. She shook the thought away like a bothersome gnat. Taleb was friend to the Sultan, another descendant of the prophet. Hadn't he stayed in the Sultan's palace in Tangier? Hadn't she been offered an audience with the Sultan by Taleb's guards?

She stared about the sunglazed landscape where patterns of heat danced on the sand. Omar ben Hadj had proclaimed the land for miles around as that of Taleb's people. From whom then did the danger come?

The palace appeared on the horizon like a shimmering mirage. How glad she would be to have the journey done and be in her own rooms again. She realized the trip had wearied her, not so much of body as of spirit. The news from home, the realization that she was cut off from what had always been part of her life. For the first time since Taleb's whirlwind proposal, the wedding and the glorious days of her honeymoon, she felt a strange loneliness that would not be dispelled. Even Taleb seemed remote, a stranger she barely knew, and no longer the eager lover who had thrilled her senses so totally that there was no room for doubts.

She sighed and studied a cloud of dust off to the right. All at once, the forward guards wheeled their horses and galloped off amid shouts and waving of guns. For a moment, Emilie was too startled to do more than sit tall and stare after the men who were heading directly toward the dust that was now discernable as a group of riders. The rear soldiers and palace guards spread around the women quickly, forming a tight circle as they spurred the horses to a brisk canter.

"What is it?" Emilie demanded, but her words were swallowed up in the buzz of dialogue exchanged between the men, who hurried her along.

"What is it?" she demanded of Toma and Yakow, who were staring at the men.

"We must hurry," Yakow said. "The soldiers say there is no time to waste."

"What is happening?"

"I do not know, but we must get to the safety of the palace as quickly as possible." The slave looked frightened, and when one of the guards yelled at her, she nodded quickly. "Come—" She kicked her own horse and one of the guards grabbed *Bent Chitane's* reins and would not release them, forcing the mare to keep up with his own. The furious pace did not slacken until they were within the walls of the encampment and escorted to the steps of the palace.

Word of the disturbance had preceded them; soldiers were mounting and riding out in a clatter of noise and dust. Women stared and children scurried inside or clung to their mother's skirts with wide eyes.

Shaking, Emilie dismounted and entered the palace, looking about immediately for Taleb. When she could not find him, her concern grew, and she sent Toma to ask Fatima his whereabouts. The slave came back saying Fatima had refused to speak with her or to admit her to the *iyal*. Furious, Emilie started to the women's quarters to confront Fatima, but stopped in the hallway as she saw a bustle of activity in the guarded corridor where Taleb kept rooms for his business affairs. Several robed figures were hurrying about, whispered consultations and much shaking of heads and gesturing. Something had happened!

She could only think of Taleb, and she changed course immediately to race toward the wing. One of the guards stepped to intercept her, but she pushed him aside and ran past before he could grab her, ignoring the cry that went up behind her. Two men had disappeared into a room where the door was ajar, and she pushed her way in.

Taleb was standing at the window; beside him, Omar

388

arguing angrily, the words caustic and threatening even though she did not understand them. The guard's cry caused both men to turn. Seeing Emilie, Taleb's face darkened with rage.

"What are you doing here?!"

"I—" All at once it seemed impossible to explain that she had been frightened about him, afraid something had happened and was being hidden from her. Her relief at seeing him safe was overwhelming, but she was caught in a storm of anger at being treated so harshly.

Taleb advanced on her. "These rooms are forbidden to the women. You were told so on your arrival here!"

She felt colour flood her face but she met his gaze defiantly. "I will not be spoken to in such a manner!"

"You will do as you are told!" He gestured to the guards, who came forward to grab her arms. "I will deal with you when time permits, now go to your apartment and remain there until I come." He waved a hand, and she was dragged off like a naughty child. Her anger erupted in a blaze, and she was speechless as Taleb turned his back and strode to the window to stare out once more. Beside her, Omar looked knowingly and the corners of his mouth raised in an ugly scowl before he turned back to Taleb and the argument that had been interrupted.

Furious, Emilie jerked her arms free of the restraining hands and walked along the corridor with head high. She glanced neither left nor right as she crossed to her apartment, but once inside, she flung herself on the bed and beat her fists against the pillows. How dare he treat her so?! She had never been so humiliated or angry! She turned, tearing at the bedclothes and pounding her fists until the rage exhausted her.

Toma and Yakow were staring from a corner, afraid to approach the mistress who had suddenly gone wild like an animal. When Emilie rose from the bed, they cowered out of her path.

"Oh, for heaven sake, I won't bite!" she snapped.

"Have you never seen a woman angry before!" She paced, thrashing at curtains, kicking aside a small table, and finally moving out to the balcony to stare at the gardens below. She could see nothing of the encampment from here, though she imagined she could hear horses and voices from somewhere beyond. There was an excitement in the air that made itself felt everywhere, and it portended trouble, she was sure.

She returned to the bedroom. "Yakow, go and talk to the women in the encampment. Find out what has happened and come back to tell me."

The girl shook her head. "It is not wise—"

"Do as I say or I shall have you flogged!"

Frightened, the girl slid from the room. Emilie was instantly sorry she had threatened violence, but it had accomplished its purpose. Yakow would learn what was going on and return with the information. Emilie sighed and pressed her fingers to her temples.

"Does the mistress of things wish a bath?" Toma's voice was placatingly full of fear.

"Not now. Set out clean clothes and I will change."

"What colour do you wish?"

"It doesn't matter—anything!" She could not control the outburst, and Toma looked wounded and slunk away to the wardrobe.

She was taking out her anger at Taleb on the slaves, Emilie knew. She tried to gain control, but new fury swept her each time she recalled Taleb's sharp tone and her embarrassment in front of Omar and the others.

It was an hour before Yakow returned. She'd had to talk to numerous people before she found out that Taleb's men had ridden out to attack a small band of soldiers who were patrolling a nearby valley.

"But why?" Emilie demanded.

"The Sultan's army rode against the shereef's men several days ago and took prisoners . . ." She looked away as though she could not finish.

390

"They took Taleb's men prisoners?" Emilie asked.

Yakow nodded, her eyes downcast. "The heads which were hung over the gates of Fez were those of one of the shereef's *caids* and the firstborn son of Omar ben Hadj . . ."

"My God . . . !" Emily fell back to the bed and sat staring at the girl. It couldn't be true. Her head reeled as the memory of the grisly sight erupted in her brain. Omar's son—

When at last she found her voice, she asked, "So Taleb ordered the attack?" Vengeance . . . the law he lived by . . .

Yakow was silent, her gaze resting on her mistress as though wishing she had not been the bearer of such tidings.

"Were the soldiers killed?" Emilie asked.

"Some. Others were taken prisoner."

"Brought here to the encampment?" She knew the answer before it was given.

"Yes."

"What will be done with them?"

Yakow looked away. "I do not know."

Emilie knew it was a lie, but she did not press the matter. Her own mind blanked at the thought of what retribution would be exacted for the death of a *caid* and Omar's son.

"You may both go. I wish to be alone."

They murmured protests, but Emilie shooed them from the chamber then walked out to the garden to sit beneath a fig tree and stare blankly. Part of her was numb, and part of her was tormented. She considered going to Fatima to console her, but she knew the guards at the door would follow Taleb's command to the letter. She would not be permitted to step outside the apartment until he gave the word.

She sighed. It was better that she talk with him first. She had to try to understand, to try to make him understand. She knew now why he'd been so upset at her bursting in as he talked with his leaders. She'd been a fool, and she would apologize. She acted without thinking, and she was sorry, though she still chafed at the thought of his cruel words and tone.

She lost track of time, and was startled when a soft voice called to her.

"Mistress . . ."

Toma peered from an archway. "I have brought food."

Emilie realized it was past noon, and she went in to find Toma had laid a tray. She had no appetite, but picked at the fruit and drank a cup of tea before pushing away the tray and returning to the garden. She was aware of Toma and Yakow rustling about the apartment, and when at last the sun grew unbearable, Emilie went in to disrobe and lay on the cool sheets of the bed and pretend sleep that would not come. Strangely, her thoughts went to Sara . . . and Pierre . . . and Henri. How uncomplicated life had been in Tangier, but she had not known it then. So many people had warned her of the difference in lifestyle and culture of the man she married, and now she could no longer ignore it. But what was she to do?

Her dinner was brought at dusk, and still Taleb had not come. Neither Yakow or Toma had any further news of what was happening, though the encampment seemed to have settled to an uneasy quiet. The house, too, was silent, and Emilie sat alone in the darkening room. Toma lit a lamp, but Emilie told her to let the others be. Somehow the dimness offered solace she could not find in her mind or heart.

Much later, the door opened and Taleb entered. Emilie looked up, but did not rise to meet him. The two slaves slipped out as though prewarned that their master wished to be alone with his wife. Taleb stood regarding her from the length of the room. She waited.

At last he said, "You were told not to enter the co

ridor where I meet with my chieftans. It was inexcusable, even for an English wife."

She did not flinch. "I have the decency to say I am sorry that I disturbed you. I acted foolishly, but out of concern for you. I saw the soldiers rush off and when no one would answer my questions, I was afraid something had happened to you."

The room was silent as he studied her with a dark gaze that did not soften. "Which of my servants would not answer your questions?"

She flushed. "I sent Toma to enquire of Fatima . . . I did not know of her bereavement and misunderstood her refusal—"

Taleb's breath was audible, almost a sigh.

"And now you know?"

She nodded. "I am sorry. How terrible for her, and for Omar. Oh, Taleb—I saw—the heads——" She buried her face in her hands and could not check the sudden flow of sobs and tears.

His heart wrenched in pity, and his anger relented. He crossed and knelt before where she sat and took her in his arms. There were no words he could offer to ease her shock and pain. He pressed her head to his shoulder and let the sobs wear themselves out. At last he lifted her chin and brushed away the silvery paths the tears had left.

"Do not think of it, my little one. It is impossible for the foreigner to comprehend the ways that have prevailed in my country for centuries. You must simply accept them because they are there."

"Such cruelty—a child—"

"He fought side by side with the bravest of my soldiers. His memory would be disgraced to hear himself called a child."

She gulped and bit her lip. Even in comfort, they did not speak the same language. "And what of the prisoners your men took today? Will they be tortured cruelly to pay for the crimes of others?"

393

The edge came back to his voice. "You are not to concern yourself with matters of the army nor my affairs."

"Taleb—please—"

"What would you have me do? Set them free so they can return to the Sultan with tales of my weakness? Do you imagine he will not send fresh troops against us in the hope of wiping us out before we can win a victory over him?"

She was confused by the talk of the Sultan's army fighting Taleb's. "It would have been merciful to kill them honorably in battle rather than bring them here for some horrible fate. Please—" she was begging again, tears overflowing. "I pray, do not make them suffer. I could not bear the thought of my husband demanding cruelty in exchange for cruelty—"

His arms withdrew and he rose to pace the room and stare out into the darkness. Emilie sensed her advantage and went to him, slipping her arms about him, and when he did not pull away, drawing her face close to his lips. "Please, this one thing I ask . . . for the sake of our love . . ." She stood on tiptoe and brushed her lips to his. For a moment he was unyielding, then he crushed her in his arms and let passion infuse the kiss. When they parted at last, she knew she had won. Then he took her to the bed and reclaimed her with fevered passion. They did not speak of the prisoners again.

CHAPTER TWENTY-TWO

In the morning when Emilie woke, Taleb was gone and she wandered restlessly about the apartment wondering what he had decided to do about the soldiers. She knew better than to seek him out, though her curiosity was boundless. Yakow and Toma related that there was no untoward activity about the palace; the women and slaves knew nothing, and the men were closeted in Taleb's private wing; whatever decisions were made took place there.

After breakfast, Emilie went to the *iyal* to see Fatima. She was admitted, but it was the old mother who met her and sat with her. The old woman's eyes were red with weeping, and when Emilie asked her, through Toma, where Fatima was, Zainab pointed toward the private apartments surrounding the common room and shook her head as she spoke softly.

"She says it is best to leave her daughter to her grief. The child's body is being brought from Fez today, and it will be entombed on the mountainside where the boy played as a lad."

"Please ask Zainab to convey my condolences to Fatima, tell her how sorry I am—" Emilie had no words.

Toma spoke again to the old woman. Zainab wailed, bobbing her head and staring trancelike with sorrowful eyes. Emilie left quietly and returned to her rooms.

Late in the afternoon, she was aware of a bustle of activity, though it was marked by a silence that was fearful. Peering into the hall, Emilie saw the women file from the *iyal*, each dressed in black, faces covered by veils. Even the slaves were garbed somberly, and two supported the figure of the old mother, and two others someone who could only be Fatima. The funeral was about to begin.

She had not been asked to attend, and she would not intrude, but neither could she ignore the sorrow that pervaded the house and all those in it. When the procession had gone by a rear door, Emilie slipped from her rooms and followed at a respectful distance, drawing a dark veil over her face so she would not be recognized. Her heart ached for the dead child and the mother's grief.

The entire encampment seemed involved; soldiers on horseback rode in solemn procession behind the mourning family; women and children from the tents joined the lengthening black line and wended a path past the military storehouses, through the fields and finally to the low lying hills at the edge of the mountains. The soft chanting became a trembling wail of grief that rose and fell in the afternoon heat, and it was measured by the beat of horses' hooves in the dust.

The boy's coffin was carried on the shoulders of four black slaves whose bodies were covered by mourning cloth. They walked in slow, even time so the wooden box seemed to float on a black cloud. The coffin was covered with elaborately embroidered silk, with bands of jewels adorning it and holding it in place. It was as though the child would pass to a greater reward with a rich offering to the powers beyond, and no restraint had been made on the elegance of the funeral cloths.

There were several tombs on the hillside, their domes almost hidden in the shadows of ancient fig trees. Emilie had never come this far before, and she stopped at the edge of the crowd that fell silent as a holy man began to recite the words that would commit the young soul to his maker. She understood not a word, but Emilie wept silent tears for a child she had not known. When the body was carried into the tomb and the wailing rose to a crescendo once more, she let herself be engulfed in the milling mourners who began the trek back toward the palace. Something of her seemed left behind in the tomb, something she had never known and now never would. A child that was not hers, and a harsh, hard lifestyle that she could never accept. Taleb . . . Taleb . . . her heart cried out in silent plea.

When she reached the gates of the military field, she was surprised that the moving crowd turned in instead of going past to their homes. She let herself be pressed along and stood against a wall, hemmed in by a knot of women with covered faces. Was there to be a military salute for the boy-soldier who had been taken in battle? A tribute to a fallen comrade?

A few minutes later, the crowd parted and Taleb and Omar strode through. Behind them, several soldiers, whom Emilie recognized from the conference she'd interrupted yesterday, followed. Behind them, the women of the family were led to a spot close to the storehouse. The doors of the building were open; several soldiers entered, reappearing a few moments later with five prisoners, hands bound, ropes about their necks tying them together like a chain of slaves.

Emilie's heart skipped erratically. Were the prisoners to face the bereaved family before being releasd? That was a cruelty more to Fatima and Omar than to the enemy. The five were led across the field and stood squinting in the sun as the ropes were untied from their necks and hands. They looked about warily, scanning the faces of the tribe that condemned them silently. One was a French officer, the others Moorish soldiers; all looked frightened.

One of the Moors whispered to the man beside him, bu the other shook his head and they fell silent again.

There was further activity near the storehouse a several men brought something out and placed it befor Omar and Taleb. Emilie could not see because of th throng, but she sensed the quick aura of terror that ros from the prisoners. Taleb raised his hand for silence, an Omar went to his knees, out of sight now, as Emilie won dered what was happening. Taleb called out a comman in a strident voice; Emilie recognized enough words t know he was telling the prisoners they were to go. Th five stood rooted, eyes on the kneeling Omar. Tale shouted again.

"Go, accursed ones, walk from thine accusers."

The five looked about in dazed fashion . . . at th crowd . . . at Omar. Their mouths opened as if to speak but they were pushed into motion by the soldiers. The shuffled, one shouted, then they ran, awkwardly, lookin back over their shoulders.

What was wrong with them? Emilie felt frustration a not knowing what was going on.

Then suddenly there was a sharp, horrid staccato o sound that she did not immediately recognize as machine gun. It rolled like drumfire, rending the after noon to fragments. The running men were hurled abou like dolls smeared red, cut to pieces by the continuin fire. They fell in all directions in a cloud of dust raised b the rain of bullets. The roar of the crowd, a cheer o triumph and vengeance, drowned out the sound of th hammering gun.

Stunned, Emilie could not move. The crowd shifted s she was able to see Omar kneeling behind the machin gun on a low tripod. His hand was still on the trigger, hi head bowed close to the hot metal as though it were prayer mat. Taleb's hand was on his shoulder.

She turned and fled through the gate and along th path to the palace. Everything swam a sick red, bloo red, before her eyes, and she threw herself into the apartment only moments before the terrible retching spewed uncontrollably. Alarmed, Yakow and Toma ran and helped her to the bed. They tried to question her but she babbled incoherently and writhed in agony. She squeezed her eyes tightly shut but nothing would block the horrible picture from her mind.

She was only dimly aware of the cold cloths put to her head, the gentle hands that cleaned her face and stripped off the fouled clothing. She shuddered, though she was burning, and turned her face away as some one tried to put a cup to her lips. She retched again and pushed it away, but the girl was insistent and finally managed to get some of the bitter liquid past her lips. Still sobbing, Emilie lay back and let a blessed fog envelop her and blot out memory.

Much later, she woke and the room was as grey as the fog from which she emerged. A lamp had been lighted, and in its mealy glow, she saw Yakow sitting on a cushion close to the bed, her dark eyes watchful. As soon as Emilie turned, she was at her side offering another cup to her dry lips. Emilie drank without resistence. What did it matter . . . what did anything matter . . . ?

She lay staring at the canopy about the bed. A shroud . . . a funeral cloth that had clouded her marriage to Taleb. How could he break his promise so monstrously? Only last night he had lain here with her, promising mercy to the prisoners as proof of his love for her. She closed her eyes and sighed. Lies, all lies. He'd quieted her so she would come to him and lie in his embrace, and she had been fool enough to believe.

Toma brought a cup of steaming tea and Emilie sat up to drink it. Her head hurt miserably, and she realized she had gone all day without food, but the very thought of it made her stomach queasy once more. When the servant spoke, she stared without answering, and when the tea was finished, she lay back again and closed her eyes. She did not sleep, but at last the two slaves withdrew.

She rose and drew on a silken robe and slippers, then sat on the terrace overlooking the garden. She could see a glimmer of light from the wing where the *iyal* was, and she wondered if Fatima slept.

Her thoughts would not stay on one path for more than a moment or two, and she let them wander where they would. Taleb's hand on his cousin's shoulder as Omar slew five men with a hail of bullets . . . heads hanging over the gates of Fez . . . Tangier—home, and Sara and mother and father. . . .

She heard the rustle of sound and turned, expecting to find Toma or Yakow again. To her surprise, it was Fatima. She stood under the light of the single lamp, staring about the room in search of Emilie. Emilie got to her feet. Fatima had removed the heavy mourning veil, but still wore the black, unadorned garments of her funeral attire. When she saw Emilie, her pale lips parted and the jet eyes caught Emilie's gaze and would not release it.

"I am sorry about your son," Emilie said weakly. What did one say to a mother who had lost her child?

The lamp hissed and the other woman continued to stare without speaking, until Emilie grew decidedly uncomfortable and turned away, moving to the cushions in an alcove and seating herself.

"Will you sit?"

Fatima advanced, her gaze unwavering. As she left the lamplight, her dark eyes seemed to retain its glow, pinpoints of flame from her soul.

"You have robbed my son's soul of eternal peace," she said in a voice so full of hate it was a physical thing. It stung Emilie like a blow across the face.

"I?" Was the woman mad?

"His death should have been avenged in the manner of our people—not as the stupid Nazarenes see fit!"

400

She *was* mad! Emilie rose to face her. "Five lives were given for your son's. Does that not satisfy you?"

"They died too quickly because you extracted a promise you had no right to ask."

Taleb's promise, so readily broken and thrown to the winds? It was ridiculous; Emilie gave a nervous, almost hysterical laugh. "Taleb kept no promise to me. Like you, he wanted blood to wipe away blood. Don't speak to me of guilt!"

Fatima reached to grab Emilie's robe, pulling her so close that their faces were only a breath apart. "The Sultan's soldiers were not merciful to my son! They made him beg on his knees before they sliced off his head, then hung it above the city for all to see and mock! His murderers should have suffered the most horrible tortures imaginable instead of the mercy of a quick death by a Christian gun." She pulled her hand away, almost pushing Emilie aside in disgust. "Omar would have seen to it, but Taleb spoke of the promise he made you, a promise not to make the prisoners suffer. No matter that my boy suffered. A promise to a Christian wife is more sacred." She spat and tossed her dark head. Her eyes were like glowing coals in the pit of her soul.

Emilie stared transfixed. The woman was saying Taleb *had* kept his promise. Her memory culled the words exchanged between Taleb and herself last night. "Do not make them suffer . . ." Her wording had allowed him to placate her and still have his warped justice! She felt sick with loathing and disgust.

Fatima smiled cruelly. "Come with me."

"No—" Emilie drew back, unwilling for the other to touch her again.

"I wish to show you something that I think will be understandable to your Christian mind, something you have asked about and no one has answered before. Come . . ." She was still smiling like a death mask, her face unnatural in the pale light.

401

Hypnotized, Emilie walked after her from the apartment. There was no one in the hall as Fatima led her toward the *iyal*. The large common room was empty, deep in shadows, with only two small lamps burning at each end. Fatima turned once to make sure Emilie was behind, then made her way across the room to a heavily draped doorway. On an earlier visit, Emilie had noted the private bedchambers opening off the common room; each woman seemed to have her own, but Emilie knew no more than that. Did Fatima have something in her chambers she wanted to show?

Silently, Fatima drew back the heavy curtains. The room beyond was dark except for moonlight that streamed through the arched windows. At a far doorway to a terrace, a curtain billowed and caught the light to make it shimmer across the bed. There were two figures sleeping, bodies entwined, their closeness obvious under the thin covering.

Emilie felt like a peeping tom, spying where she had no right. She tried to back away, but Fatima grasped her hand and drew her further into the room. Then they were over the bed, staring down at the sleeping figures. A woman, black hair loose about her perfectly oval face, the man's arm thrown in claim over her naked breasts. For a moment, she thought it was a trick of the light, then truth was a blinding flash. Taleb and Hadra!

The room was so still she could hear Fatima's breath, yet she could not take her eyes from the scene that was already etched in her mind for eternity. *Hadra is not a servant . . . Hadra sees to many things . . . Hadra serves me faithfully . . .*

Hadra's lashes fluttered, and for an instant her eyes opened lazily and she smiled. The lashes fluttered shut again and there was nothing but Fatima's raspy breath and the thundering blood in Emilie's temples. She turned and ran out, her slippered feet only a whisper of sound.

402

She fled the *iyal*, and Fatima's soft laughter followed her until she closed the door of her apartment behind her.

How could she have been such a fool?! A stupid, blind fool! She'd heard Arab words with English ears, and had not searched beyond the surface! *I have not chosen to take a wife . . . Would you be a concubine in my harem? . . . Housekeeper—a Christian word that cannot be translated into my language . . .* My God! How stupid she'd been! Hadra had been Taleb's woman all along! Before Emilie and even now!

She had no tears left and lay dry-eyed staring at the stars beyond the windows. Taleb had offered her marriage because he wanted her and there was no other way to get her. A marriage that was a farce. The nights of ecstasy, the love and longing she'd felt for him, a mockery. She was a cold, empty shell.

At dawn she watched the blood-red sun creep along the horizon and knew that she could not stay with Taleb another day. It was finished, and she had to go—back to Fez, then to Tangier. She would take nothing but the few things she could put into a saddle bag and carry with her. She wanted no reminders, no ties to her life here. It was finished.

The things were packed before Toma and Yakow came to ready her morning bath. Emilie answered their questions in a desultory manner, not wanting to alarm them into thinking she was ill but also unable to enter into any spirited conversation. They laid it to her depression after the funeral, but were pleased to see that she was up and about. They had been given strict orders to report her condition to Fatima and Zainab.

Toma brought a breakfast tray, and Emilie forced herself to chew and swallow, though each morsel threatened to choke off her breath. She would need strength for the ride; it would be midmorning before she could leave the palace. She always went riding about that time, and to set out earlier might raise questions. She was not sure how she would persuade the guards to accompany her to Fez, or to escape them if they would not, but she would find a way. She prayed that Taleb was too preoccupied with military matters to issue any special orders about her today. She was no longer a prisoner in her apartment, and she prayed fervently that she had regained her other freedoms as well. She longed to ask Toma if Taleb had been told of her tears and illness yesterday, but she did not dare.

She dressed in comfortable clothes but chose kid riding boots instead of slippers. When she made her way to the rear of the house, she glanced nervously toward the wing where Taleb and Omar had held their conference and planned their revenge. The corridor was silent, the guards watchful as she passed. All doors were closed, so if there were any talks taking place, they were well secreted.

At the rear garden where servants waited to fetch horses, the boy ran immediately toward the stables. Emilie paced under the gallery as she waited for the boy to return with *Bent Chitane*. It seemed an uncommonly long time for such a simple task.

"Where would you ride this morning, my dove?"

She whirled and found Taleb watching her, his face clouded with a scowl. He could not know—

She smiled nervously. "To the hills. I am restless and long for exercise."

He regarded her coldly. "And the garments packed in your *couffin*? Is it your intention to be gone so long that a change of garb is needed?"

Her pulse skipped erratically, the weight of the *couffin* a guilty burden in her hand. She tried to invent a plausible lie, but Taleb's gaze destroyed it before it reached her tongue. He knew what the bag contained, as surely as he knew every other move she made in his house. Many times he had reminded her that every servant and slave was faithful to him, that they did his bidding and none others. She'd allowed herself to be lulled to a sense of un-

404

real security because she was his wife. The slaves served her, but they belonged to Taleb.

She felt her cheeks pale at the realization that he meant to prevent her from leaving. For a moment, their eyes locked defiantly.

"You told me you would not kill those men," she said.

"I said I would not make them suffer. They died in an instant."

"They were massacred! I saw the blood and what was left of them!" Horror crept into her voice and she shuddered. "How can you speak so casually of death?" She turned from him and stared across the garden.

"You will not leave the palace."

She whirled. "You cannot keep me prisoner!"

He shrugged. "I have given orders."

"But why? I have done nothing—"

"I wish you to remain inside, in your apartment or with the other women. This is a day of much preparation and none of my men can be spared to ride about when they are needed elsewhere."

She stared at him. "Needed for what? You have thousands of men. If you would miss one, then I shall ride alone."

"You will remain in the house." He turned, the matter ended.

Furious, she raced after him and grabbed the sleeve of his robe. For a moment, she thought he would strike her so angry was his look, but then he smiled.

"Emilie, do not force me to exert my authority more strenuously. I have given orders that none of the women are to leave the house or grounds today. I expect them to be obeyed and if *you* are foolish enough to disobey, you will learn how unwise it is."

"Will you have me murdered as you did the Sultan's soldiers?" Her eyes were blazing and her voice shook.

He looked at her, the smile still on his lips but with eyes so cold she wondered if she had ever known him at all. He was like a stranger who was called upon to deal with a bothersome problem that was none of his concern. Deliberately, he released her fingers from his robe and dropped her hands. His own stayed between them like a wall.

"My people have lived by the law for many centuries. The law demands blood for blood, and it has been given."

"You are a barbarian!" The words fell between them like a whiplash.

"And you are a Christian." From his lips, the words were a stinging accusation.

Stunned, Emilie stepped back. In that moment, it was over . . . if it had ever been.

Taleb looked past her to where several soldiers could be seen beyond the gate. When he turned back, his expression was altered, though she could not say how. Perhaps it was she who was seeing him with new vision. Inside, she felt cold and angry.

"I would like to send a letter to my family. Can you spare someone to take it to Fez?"

"I have assured your father that you are well and happy. There is no need for a letter from you at this time."

"*You* have assured him—?"

"You forget, your father and I have business dealings. I would not like to see them jeopardized by incautious words from an angry woman."

Emilie frowned . . . the Pendash railroad . . . she thought again of *Herr* Muller and the guns. "You would use *my father* to supply you with guns as you have used *Herr* Muller?"

"Use? It is your father who profits from the company. He is a greedy man and cares nothing for my people or promises made them if his own purse can be lined."

"He would not sell guns . . ."

He shrugged. "There are many who will do that if the means to bring them to the interior is provided. *Herr*

406

Muller has held the balance of power too long. His greed has outgrown his wisdom. With your father's railroad, it will no longer be necessary for me to deal with him."

She shook her head. "The machine guns?" Her voice was a whisper.

He almost smiled. "A most effective weapon."

"Against whom will you use it?"

The smile vanished instantly. "I do not take women into my confidence on military matters." He started to turn.

Her words stopped him. "Not even Hadra?" He paused to look at her. She went on recklessly. "Fatima took me to the *iyal* last night, and I saw you with my own eyes! Do you think that I will stay with you knowing I am only *one* of your women?" Her eyes blazed.

"You are my wife."

"I shall divorce you the moment I can manage to do so!" Her hands were shaking and she blinked the tears that would betray her weakness.

In a mimosa tree near the gate, a nightingale mourned. Taleb regarded her with unreadable gaze. "I will never let you go, little shereefa." He turned and strode through the archway to vanish along the corridor. For a moment she was too stunned to move, then fury overwhelmed her once more and she raced toward the stables. At the gate, two soldiers with rifles drawn stepped to bar her path. When she tried to push past, she was seized and firmly escorted back to the house to be left sputtering helplessly. Trembling, she made her way back to the apartment.

Yakow and Toma were silent as she threw the *couffin* aside and removed the *jellaba* she had chosen for riding. The slaves had reported her actions so that Taleb had been alerted. She could not be angry with them, but she would be on guard from now on. She could trust no one in the palace, no one at all. And as sure as she was of this, she was also sure she could not stay. Her only hope

407

lay in seeming to accept her fate and waiting an oppor
tunity, or seeking some advantage she might pursue.

"I am unfamiliar with the ways of mourning," she sai
carefully to Toma, as they relaxed in the outdoor poo
splashing water and feeling the hot sun on their skir
"How long will Fatima stay secluded in her rooms?"

"Many days. She will come out only to mourn at th
tomb and pray for her firstborn as he passes through th
gate of eternal life."

Emilie tried to look appropriately sympathetic. "An
the others? Will they mourn at the tomb as well?"

"Yes."

"Whenever Fatima goes?"

Toma lifted a ladle and poured water over Emilie'
shoulders so it ran in cool trickles along her breasts. "Th
whole family goes once each day. A mother's heart take
her at any hour."

"And what of a father's heart? Does not Omar accom
pany his wife to the tomb?"

"He grieves and prays *Fajr* to *Acha,* but he must als
prepare to ride with the Shereef's army."

Emilie felt her throat constrict and controlled her voic
carefully. "Yes, I watched the preparations with Taleb. I
is a pity that Omar must leave his wife so soon."

"They have three days to comfort each other," Tom
said, "and they will be together in spirit, as they are wit
their son."

Emilie sighed to cover her excitement. Three days, :
would be three days until Taleb's men rode. Surely whe
he was gone, an opportunity would present itself for he
to slip away unnoticed!

Toma did not notice her mistress's preoccupatio
"And with Fez taken, there will be an end to separation
and loss." She smiled as Emilie glanced at her. "You wi
occupy the palace at Fez and every person will fall
your feet."

"The palace at Fez?" She could not help the surprised question.

Toma was excited and babbled on. "I pray that you will allow me to serve you then, shereefa."

"Of course, but tell me more. Taleb did not mention the palace."

"But when he captures the city, the Sultan will be banished and the shereef will rule!" Toma looked as though it were a most ordinary piece of news, to be taken for granted.

Emilie concentrated on the rippling water. "Of course," she murmured and let the matter rest. Her mind whirled and she felt dazed. Capture the city! Taleb was planning to attack Fez. His displeasure at the Sultan's dealing with the French was not a passive thing, to be accepted as the will of Allah. The Christians were to be challenged and beaten!

Enoch Madden had referred to a day when the Arabs would rise against the foreigners! It was Taleb who would lead that revolt!

She shivered and stepped from the pool. Her heart was like ice, and though Yakow rubbed her dry and wrapped her in a robe, the chill would not be driven away. She ordered tea and held the cup in her hands as she drank as though seeking its warmth. And as soon as she finished, she complained of weariness and took to her bed, letting Yakow draw the curtains and the drapes at the windows to shade the room in soothing gloom. The two slaves lay upon cushions, and Emilie closed her eyes to think.

An attack on Fez! That was why she was forbidden to leave the palace or grounds. Taleb feared she would ride to Fez, and he knew what danger lay there. She almost sat bolt upright as a new thought struck her. There was great danger to the Maddens and others! She had to warn them, give them time to flee. Three days hence—oh, God! It was the day Claudia and the children were to ride to Madawadi!

She put a hand to her eyes to stop the vision of thun
dering horsemen bearing down on the party of womer
and children with perhaps only a few servants in attend
ance! She could not permit it to happen, she could not!

She tossed and heard the slaves stir, so forced hersel
to lie quietly. She had to think. Her mind examined on
plan after another, discarding each futilely as she foun
its flaws and impossibilities. There was no way to send
message, no way to leave the palace! The smiling faces c
the Madden children, eager with expectation, haunte
her. Children, innocent children.

Her thoughts ceased the dizzying whirl. Children. Fa
tima's son's tragic death might give her the opportunit
she needed. If she could pretend to visit the child'
tomb—it was beyond the encampment, beyond the mili
tary tents and storehouses. It was a holy place, and surel
it would not be desecrated by the presence of soldiers.

She spent the afternoon in Taleb's library, since it wa
one place she could remain unseen yet watch the corrido
to the *iyal*. She saw Fatima three times, shrouded i
black, alone, walking slowly to the rear of the house t
make her way through the garden, past the encampmen
to the hillside. The third time, Emilie slipped quickly int
the hall and ran as far as the outer door so she could se
if Fatima was stopped by the guards. She was not. Sh
merely bowed her veiled head and passed unchallenged
The length of time she was gone varied, but it was neve
less than an hour all told.

As darkness fell, Fatima once more departed the *iyal* t
mourn at her son's tomb. She was met by Omar in th
corridor, and the two walked off. As soon as they wer
out of sight, Emilie who was dressed in the most sombe
of her tunics went to the *iyal*. As she expected, th
women were subdued, alone in their private chambers ir
stead of laughing and chattering as they usually did in th
common room. The entire *iyal* was in mourning, and th

en were occupied elsewhere with the shereef's business. A slave escorted her to the room of Hadra, who sat upon cushion, her nimble hands counting off the beads of a main as her lips moved silently. Even in black, she was rikingly beautiful, and Emilie's heart wrenched. Hadra oked up as Emilie entered, and there was no communiation between the worlds they represented.

"I wish to express my grief at Fatima's loss," Emilie aid. "I know she holds me to blame for my people's acons, but will you tell her I am sorry?"

Hadra's eyes slid past Emilie as though she were a puff f smoke that dissipated in a breeze. Her lips moved in ie silent prayer and her gaze returned to her beads.

Emilie retreated to the common room. Hadra's attitude id not disturb her in the least. She didn't care a fig for hat Hadra thought or did; let her believe she had triimphed, let her believe the shereefa groveled.

She glanced about quickly to be sure the slave was not a sight, then ran softly to Fatima's chamber. It took only ioments to find a black *haik* and wrap it about her body nder the caftan. She slipped from the *iyal* without seeing nyone. In her own rooms, she hid the black garment uner some cushions on the terrace where it would not be iscovered, then sat with a book until Toma and Yakow ame to prepare her for the night.

The next day seemed endless. Emilie read and watched ie *iyal* whenever she could. Several times she went onto balcony or terrace to see what bits of activity she could limpse in the encampment; it seemed Taleb's army numered into the thousands. There were horses and amels—and guns, though she could not see them. She hewed at her lip as she thought how her father had been uped in the matter of the railroad. Surely no mention ad been made of using it to bring guns into Fez. Her faier saw the lines as a step in the pattern of progress, and pportunity to transport supplies and products that would

411

ease the harsh life of the desert. Instead, Taleb was plan
ning an extension of his own power, steel locomotives o
death and destruction.

Was it too late for father to pull out, to stop th
scheme while disaster could still be averted? She praye
so. If only she could get word to him—perhaps the tele
graph at Fez! She swallowed hard. She was assuming he
own daring scheme would work, that she would get to Fe
to send the message.

As evening approached, she'd been over her plan s
many times it seemed part of her. She would not let he
mind dwell on the possibility of failure, for if that hap
pened, there was no future for her at all. Taleb woul
never forgive her.

She ordered her own dinner early, then waited until sh
saw the evening meal carried into the *iyal* before sendin
Toma and Yakow off to take their dinner in the servant
quarters. As soon as they were gone, she donned th
black *haik* and drew the veil to cover her face completel
as Fatima did. She slid along the corridor, heart poundin
and mouth dry. At the gate, she bowed her head an
walked slowly past the guards. She was so frightened sh
was sure they must hear her racing pulse, but there wa
no cry, no challenge. She stumbled once and smothered
quick cry as a figure materialized out of the darkness an
supported her quickly.

"Daughter of sorrow, let me help you." A soldie
steered her to the path she'd missed in the darkness.

She thanked him softly in Arabic, and he vanished i
the night as she walked on, shaken but reassured that he
disguise had not been penetrated. Fatima's shrouded fig
ure had become common these past days, and no on
found it exceptional now.

Past the military wall, she paused to catch her breath
In spite of the slow pace, she was panting with exciteme
and exaltation. She was away! Quickly she tore off th
veil and looked about. She could see several figures nea

412

he gates of the military enclosure, and people moved like
hadows in the encampment. She searched the darkness
or horses. There were several picketed near the gate, but
hey were too close to the soldiers. There had to be an-
ther! She moved silently along the wall, gazing in every
irection. Each horse she spied was well tended, tied close
) its owner's tent or in a compound where the soldiers'
hounts were kept.

Exasperated, she slipped off the black *haik* and tossed
. to the crevice of a tree branch where it would not be
ound readily. Her heart was thundering against her ribs
s she drew the dark veil about her golden hair, half cov-
ring her face. She made her way toward the encampment
/here dozens of fires were patches of light with women
uddled over them preparing night meals. Somewhere, the
otes of a lute rose in melancholy tune. A horse nickered
oftly and was answered restlessly by others.

There were several horses close to tents, but each was
ied securely. A man's wealth, his horse . . . She circled
he perimeter, still hoping she might find one carelessly
ended animal that could be spirited away. Then she saw
wo mules tethered to a low shrub. Neither was saddled,
ut one had a blanket tossed over its back and a rope hal-
er and bit. She looked about but no one was close. Taleb
ad told her mules were fast and dependable . . . the
aravan from Tangier used them to carry supplies and
vertake the riders who left camp earlier each day.

She slipped toward the animals. One brayed suddenly,
nd she almost fainted with the shock and fear. But still
o one came from the camp behind her. The people were
ccustomed to such outcries from beasts, and Emilie
lessed the primitive way of life. She slipped the rope
rom the bush and led the mule away from its companion,
"ho perked its ears and stared a moment, then went back
) cropping scrubby grass. The mule followed docilely as
he walked slowly from the camp into the darkness. There
"as no path but she could see the hulking mountains that

413

formed the natural fortress at the rear of Taleb's encamp
ment. She would have to make a wide circle to go aroun
the tents and get beyond the wall.

It seemed hours that she walked, not letting hersel
think beyond each step that took her further from th
palace. Each time a sound reached her, she turned froze
in fear, but there was no pursuit. Even if she were missed
it would be some time before anyone realized she'd lef
the palace. At long last she came to the hills and found
narrow path. Sobbing with relief and joy, she scramble
awkwardly onto the mule and kicked it into motion. Th
animal seemed reluctant to increase the leisurely pace, bu
she kicked its flanks until it set out at last at a brisk trot
Without a saddle, the ride was uncomfortable and hard
but Emilie would not give in to any thoughts of discom
fort. She wanted to get as far from the palace as possibl
in the shortest time. She had to reach Fez!

The loneliness of the desert was overpowering, with
miles of sand stretching to the black hills in the distanc
and the inky sky overhead blanketed with stars. Th
moon was not yet up, but the mule seemed to sense th
path, though Emilie could not make it out except at infre
quent intervals. It was well trodden, and the mule fol
lowed it because it offered the least resistance, an
perhaps because some instinct told the animal it had cov
ered the same ground many times before.

The silence was heavy, and from time to time Emili
glanced back to the fading lights of the encampment an
palace. It was like a toy village in the distance, unreal an
barely visible.

Occasionally she slowed the mule to a walk when
seemed unable to continue the fast pace, but her ow
fears closed about her too readily, and as soon as it wa
possible, she prodded the animal once more. What was a
hour's ride by daylight seemed like ten in the darknes
Few landmarks were recognizable, and several times sh

eared she had lost her way, but there was no choice but
o continue.

The moon scaled the peaks to her left, and she crested
. hill to be greeted by glimmering lights in the distance.
'ez! She recognized the slope leading down the side of
he bowl in which the city lay, and she could make out
he crenellated walls. Here and there she saw a torch,
ighted near a gate, and within the walls, numerous lan-
erns and torches along the streets or in houses. She could
ot control the tears, and she sat the mule as she wept
vith immense relief. She had made it! She would be safe
nside the wall, in the Madden's house or the Consulate in
. quarter hour's time!

She glanced back with a sigh, then started. A cloud of
lust rose pale on the horizon. She peered, praying it was
.n illusion of light and tired eyes, but it was not. Against
he silence of the night, she heard the roaring beat of
.orses' hooves thundering across the desert.

Frantic, she kicked the mule relentlessly until it gal-
oped down the precipitous hillside, slipping and skidding
.n the steep path, threatening to plunge her to the
ground. She slid about on the blanket and grabbed the
.nimal's short mane to keep herself upright. Her goal was
o close—how far behind were the riders? Distance was
leceptive and she could not be sure. Sobbing, she dared
.ot look back.

At last she reached the flat depression of the rim of the
.lain. She was almost to the wall—to the *Bab el Hadid!*
'he mule heaved and panted, protesting loudly, but
:milie slapped at it with hands and feet. She did not have
o look behind to hear the unearthly screams of the horse-
.en who crested the hill and were thundering down
oward her. She screamed and slid from the mule as it
eached the gate—but the gate was closed and barred for
he night! Frantically, she pounded and yelled, crying out
.n panic. Her head roared with the sounds of her pur-
.uers. How many? She could not tell, but they seemed a

415

screaming multitude as they dashed down the embankment.

"For God's sake! Have mercy! Open the gate!! I am English—help me! Help me!" She pounded and clawed at the wood as though to somehow open it by sheer force of her will. The horses clattered to the flat and were heading toward her at incredible speed. In moments it would be too late. She would be caught up and carried back to Madawadi, back to Taleb—

"For the love of God!!"

Suddenly the gate swung and she fell into the arms of two soldiers who pulled her inside as rifle shots whined in the night. Three other soldiers pushed the door shut and dropped a thick metal bar in place across them. Bullets splintered wood in rapid succession. Soldiers materialized from the gloom and climbed the parapets, returning the fire of the horsemen outside in a quick fusillade of shots.

Emilie lay sobbing, cradled in the arms of an astonished soldier who stared at her with wonder. She was shaking like a leaf in the wind, and quite suddenly she was aware of a terrible pain in her shoulder. When she reached to touch it, her hand came away wet with blood. Her head swam with dizziness, and she gulped air into her lungs.

"English . . . take me to the English . . ." And then she knew no more.

She woke with a throbbing head and her mouth brassy tasting with fear. The nightmare of the pursuit by Taleb's men and the narrow escape was still too real to be chased away by the quietness of the room in which she lay. She opened her eyes slowly and looked at the unfamiliar surroundings. A house . . . a curtained bed . . . and a soft pillow beneath her head.

The room was dark except for a lantern near the door with its wick turned low. She stirred, but lay still again as a fiery dart of pain shot through her shoulder—and she remembered the blood. She lifted a hand carefully and felt the bandage. A soft sound whispered close.

Claudia Madden smiled down at her. "Ah, you're awake. Enoch said it would not be long. How do you feel? Is there pain? He can give you something more for it."

Emilie's mind was pleasantly foggy and she tried to stir the muddy thoughts. "I am so relieved to see you—" There had been some dreadful terror, something more than the horsemen—she puckered her brow and tried to concentrate.

"You've had a bad shock and must lie still, Emilie. The wound in your shoulder is not serious but you have lost blood and must rest."

She bit her lip as the older woman pulled a chair close and sat to take her hand. "You are safe now."

"Yes . . . NO!" The fog cleared and ugly reality returned in full force. Emilie bolted up, ignoring the pain that almost made her swoon.

"Here—you mustn't! Enoch!" Claudia called out in alarm. She tried to ease Emilie back onto the pillow and comfort her with soft words. "You are safe. No one can reach you here—"

"You don't understand—Enoch, bring him, I must talk with him. It is not safe—I must tell him—"

The door opened and Enoch rushed in, snatching up his medical bag from a chair and opening it as he reached the bed. Emilie fell back to the pillows.

"No, please, I must talk first. The shereef's army is going to attack Fez!"

Enoch Madden stopped with a syringe in hand; his medical bag dropped to the foot of the bed. He stared at Emilie with a mixture of concern and genuine alarm.

"It's true—you must warn the military and the Sultan and all the foreigners! No one is safe unless the Sultan's army prepares for the attack at once!"

"But the Sultan's army rode out yesterday. His

Highness has returned to Casablanca—" Claudia's face was ashen.

The doctor sat beside Emilie, the injection forgotten. His round face looked like a solemn owl. "How do you know this?"

In halting words, Emilie told them of her return to Madawadi and the incident with the soldiers, the machine guns, and finally how she had learned from her slave that the attack was planned.

"You escaped to warn us?" Enoch regarded her with frank admiration. He knew that her ordeal could not have been easy, and if she had been caught—

"They will slaughter every foreigner they find," Emilie whispered. "The son of Taleb's chief *caid* was one of those slain by the Sultan." She turned stricken eyes to Claudia, and her voice was scarcely a whisper. "I saw the child's head over the gate—"

"There—do not think about it." Claudia's instinct to comfort overcame the horror of the news Emilie imparted.

"When is the attack to be?" Enoch was on his feet, pacing with hands clasped behind his back, stopping to peer at Emilie, then pace again.

Emilie tried to sort time into slots. Toma had said three days, but half of that was gone already. "Tomorrow, no, the next day."

"Unless he changes his plans now that he knows you have been able to warn us."

"My God!" How long would it take Taleb's men to return and report that Emilie had made good her escape? The shereef's army might be on its way this very moment!

Enoch came to the same conclusion and was at the door. "I will go to Mr. Gregory myself. There's not a moment to be lost. I'll send one of the servants round to alert the others and I'll have Dr. Louvel come here."

"Dr. Louvel? Pierre?"

"Yes, he arrived two days ago." Madden was gone, the

door left ajar in his wake so that the women heard the clatter of his boots on the stairs.

"Pierre is here—I cannot believe it."

Claudia was too frightened to occupy her thoughts with anything but her children. "I must pack and have Hilda ready the children. There is not a moment to be lost." She started from the room, pausing at the doorway. "Rest until the last possible moment. You will need every ounce of strength you can muster. It will be a hard ride this night." She hurried along the hall, calling for Hilda as she went.

CHAPTER TWENTY-THREE

Despite Claudia's admonition, Emilie could not rest. The effects of the sedative were wearing off, and she was eager to help in whatever way she could. She sat up, holding the brass bedstead. How long had she slept? How much time did they have?

She was no longer afraid as she had been within the walls of Taleb's domain, though the danger might be greater this moment than ever before. Taleb would not forgive lightly. *I will never let you go . . .* and she had defied him even in that. It was as though her past were unrolling before her with a new clarity; she could see the folly she had pursued, believing she could find love and happiness with a man she scarcely knew. She had let herself be swept off her feet by a romantic notion, Taleb's enticing words and his offer of marriage. Her own foolishness had left her ready for the drama and glamour of the dashing shereef.

She looked toward the door and though she could hear sounds of voices and footsteps, she could not see Claudia or the children. She got to her feet and would have fallen except for the tight grip on the bedpost. She was lightheaded—the sedative still hazed her brain. She closed her eyes until the reeling stopped.

"Emilie—?!"

She opened her eyes and saw Pierre hurrying toward her. The relief and joy at seeing him surfaced all at once and she stumbled toward him.

"Pierre! Pierre!" He caught her in outstretched arms.

"I could not believe what Enoch told me, but it *is* true. You are here!" He led her back to the bed and made her sit. "You're hurt."

"It's nothing," she protested and laughed with relief.

"Rest. We leave within the hour. There is much to be done."

"You are going too?"

He nodded. "Dr. Madden and the English Consul are rounding up everyone who would be in jeopardy. The caravan will be some miles along the road to Tangier before dawn. The shereef must come from the opposite direction."

"But what of the others, the people of Fez?"

He regarded her with compassionate eyes. "There are only a few companies of soldiers left, the others rode off with the Sultan. Mr. Gregory is telegraphing to Meknes to intercept the Sultan's party and have reinforcements sent back. God willing, they should arrive in time to prevent the fall of the city."

She sighed and closed her eyes momentarily, thinking of Taleb's army and the destruction it would cause.

"Are you all right?" Pierre asked gently.

His hand on her shoulder was warm and comforting, and she leaned against him. "It has been a nightmare."

"It is almost over. You must believe that and be strong awhile longer."

His words gave her strength. "I am glad you are here," she said honestly.

He smiled, kissed her forehead gently, then laid her

421

back onto the pillow. "Rest. Doctor's orders. As soon as the others are ready. I will return for you."

He left and she lay listening to the busy sounds of preparations. One of the children whimpered and was quickly soothed by a soft voice. Servants rushed up and down the stairs, and all at once there was a clatter of horses in the yard and Enoch Madden's voice rose in a shout.

Frightened, Emilie got up from the bed and stumbled to the door. Claudia was running downstairs, where Enoch Madden shouted. Emilie went into the hall and clung to the railing to look down. Near the head of the stairs, Hilda Weiss hugged the two girls close and stared at her employer with frightened eyes.

"What is it?" Claudia was asking as she raced to her husband's side. Pierre was already there, his mouth grim as he ran a hand through his sandy hair in an angry gesture.

"The guards along the wall have sighted riders—"

"Is it too late?!" Claudia turned to look at her children on the stair landing.

"How many?" Pierre asked.

"A formidable party," Madden said.

"There may still be time to escape by the northern gates—"

Madden shook his head. "They are surrounding the city. We must stand and fight."

"*Mon Dieu*! There are fewer than three hundred soldiers—"

Madden made a warning gesture that he was frightening the women. "The English Consulate offers the best protection. We must go there—quickly now. Hilda, bring the girls." He saw Emilie's pale face at the rail. "Help her—" Pierre was already racing up the steps to put an arm about Emilie and help her down the stairs.

The knowledge that Taleb's army was close at hand gave her a terrible shock, but Emilie felt power returning to her legs and clarity to her mind. "I am all right," she told Pierre as they reached the hall. "Here, let me take Zelda." She reached for the younger child who came to her eagerly, tears brimming in frightened blue eyes. Emilie petted her. "We must hurry, there is no time for tears," she told the child; the little girl nodded bravely.

"We can take nothing," Enoch said, shaking his head at the bundles the servants had collected under Claudia's direction.

"But my mother's silver—"

"Nothing!" her husband commanded. He already had the door open, and above the commotion in the streets, gunshots pierced the night.

"My God, it's begun!" Emilie uttered a quick prayer, then clutched Zelda's hand and followed the others from the house.

The streets were unnaturally quiet for several moments, then people woke from slumber. Servants yelled and dogs yapped and barked everywhere. In a very short while, an incredible pandemonium developed. Men scrambled over garden walls, shouting in the streets. Soldiers raced past on the way to their posts on the walls. The only hope was to repel the enemy before they breached the walls or smashed the gates to enter the city. Once inside, the remnant of army would never be able to withstand the frenzied attackers. An equal danger lay within the city itself; a great many Arabs would side with the shereef's forces against the accursed infidels, who were the target of the attack. Once Taleb learned the Sultan was not in residence and most of the troops were gone, he would take the city and dispose of the foreigners quickly. Except for Emilie.

They stumbled along the dark street. From time to time, Pierre offered a guiding hand to Emilie or the others in negotiating a turn, descending a steep grade. Zelda fell, crying out as she scraped a knee on rough stone. Emilie scooped her up and hugged her close, then carried her.

423

Her shoulder was aflame with pain but she clenched her teeth and shook her head when Pierre would have taken the little burden from her. Hilda Weiss shook and whimpered so that poor Eileen had little comfort, and Emilie told Pierre to take her. In spite of her husband's warnings, Claudia carried a small valise of clothing for the children, and in the other hand she had her husband's medical bag, somehow rescued from Emilie's room.

When they arrived at the Consulate, they were quickly ushered through the gates, past the stable and mill, into the house. The three missionaries were already there and a dozen other Europeans Emilie did not know. One spoke in French to Pierre, who nodded and herded the women to a rear office. The sounds of rapid-firing guns was a steady tempo now, and Emilie thought of the death and destruction Taleb's machine guns were capable of. Pierre and the doctor joined the men in the outer office. Emilie handed Zelda over to her mother who sat, palefaced, in a large, shabby Morris chair, then went to stand by the door. It was as though she played such an important role in what was happening that she could not abandon it now. Her flight from Taleb had precipitated the attack tonight, she was certain, and guilt was heavy on her. She'd meant to warn these people, to give them time to escape . . . but instead she'd brought Taleb's swift wrath upon them. And there was nothing she could do now to help . . .

The Frenchman who had spoken to Pierre was the French Consul, she discovered. It was he who now organized and ordered the men. Some would be left behind to protect the ladies in the event the walls were scaled. The others were to report to Major Biarnay at the garrison and fight alongside his men. Every gun was needed. The telegraph wires had been cut, and there would be no aid from Meknes. The two doctors would not fight but tend the fallen. That was an order from the Major himself. All medical supplies were being collected and an emergency hospital was to be set up in the deserted flour mill, within the walls of the British Consulate. It was windowless, so lights would not attract undue attention. The city was plunged into near darkness to avoid outlining the soldiers on the wall and give them better chance to fire upon the attackers before they were discovered. It was known that the shereef's army had machine guns; every extra precaution that could be taken would help.

Several women were weeping, but most were pale and quiet. Zelda and Eileen sat on their mother's lap, held close in her arms as she rocked them gently. Emilie smiled and crossed to kneel before them.

"You must be very brave and good. Very soon, we will ride to Tangier, and we will be safe."

"I shall not have tea at the Princess's palace," Zelda said, her lower lip trembling.

Emilie kissed her. "When we get to Tangier, we shall have tea in a very elegant house where the princess lived before she moved to the palace. And perhaps, if you are very brave, we may be able to visit the palace of the Sultan himself, where there is a zoological garden with all kinds of animals and birds."

Zelda's lips trembled in a smile. "Have you seen it?"

"Yes, and it is wonderful. Now close your eyes and try to sleep."

Emilie returned to the doorway. The men had dispersed, except for those assigned to guard the house. Pierre and the missionaries had collected blankets and bedding from the bedrooms and were staggering under the huge load. She ran to Pierre.

"Let me help—"

"Stay with the women."

"No, I cannot. I have caused this havoc and I must do what I can. I am able to bathe wounds and put on dressings—"

He looked at her a moment, then nodded. "Very well, come along."

425

They crossed the dark yard and entered the mill by a small door close to the rushing race. The sounds of gunfire seemed all around them, accelerated to a violent fusillade now and then, dying out to occasional sniper fire. Then it grew into a steady, deadly rattle as the attackers rode around the wall, screaming at the men inside as they fired off rifles and pistols as though ammunition were in limitless supply. To Emilie's mauled ears it sounded like ten thousand men and horses. From time to time the distant hammer of the quickfiring machine gun caused her to put both hands to her ears as she tried to close her mind to the bloody destruction she'd seen it accomplish.

Wounded were already being brought in. It was impossible for the soldiers of the city to ward off the attackers without exposing themselves, and many fell under Taleb's bullets. Others were wounded by rock chipped from the walls that cut like bits of shrapnel.

Martha Drew spread pallets and blankets as a bed, and the others lifted a young Arab soldier onto one. He had an ugly wound in his chest, his white tunic already crimson with blood. Martha cut the sodden cloth and sponged the wound. Emilie steeled herself against the sight of the blood and took up a basin to fill with fresh water. Pierre was tending a French officer whose leg bone was shattered through the flesh; the man's face was a mask of pain as Pierre gave him an injection, then set to work to pick out fragments of bone even before the medication had time to take effect. Emilie set down the basin, and was immediately called by Dr. Madden who required help to hold a man who was screaming and thrashing as the doctor tried to look at his bloodied belly.

The night became a horror of screams and pained silences. The mill filled quickly; the smell of blood hung in the air, and there were men laid everywhere. They ran out of blankets, and the wounded were placed wherever there was an inch of space. The man whom Martha had been tending when Emilie arrived was carried out, dead.

426

to make room for someone who could be helped. Emilie moved in a daze of numb horror. Several times, Dr. Madden or Pierre shook his head when one of the missionaries asked for sedatives for the most seriously wounded, and said the medicines must be conserved for those who could benefit from it.

Emilie's *haik* was bloodied beyond hope, and she discarded the filmy outer garment which hampered her movements. The screaming of guns became sporadic, but the pre-dawn sky was bright with the flames of fires set by torches tossed over the walls, or by spontaneous eruption as houses were hit and lamps spilled fuel.

All at once, as morning came, there was an unearthly silence. Those in the makeshift hospital looked up from their tasks to stare at each other. They'd been too busy to concern themselves with military questions, but now it was imperative to know what was happening. An Englishman with a bandaged arm in a sling, stumbled to his feet and through the doorway. It seemed a silent eternity that he was gone, unbroken except for the moans of the wounded or an occasional scream as pain penetrated drugged sleep.

Pierre walked to the door to stare out. Emilie wiped her hands on her tunic, now streaked with blood, and went to look at the pink sky beyond the Consulate wall. The smell of smoke was acrid, and the city seemed gray with ash. The orchard that separated the Consulate from the surrounding buildings spread blackened leafless branches in prayer to the sky. The two Indian Bride trees in the patio were unscathed but seemed to droop, weeping for the lost.

A soldier hurried from the gate, and Douglas Gregory appeared at the Consulate door. The soldier spoke to him quickly, then returned to the hospital.

"It is over. Their leader has fallen and the army has withdrawn."

427

Emilie's heart went cold and she gripped the frame of the heavy door. Taleb dead?!

The soldier continued excitedly. "They set up machine guns to draw attention to the west gate, while a party circled to the south and tried to breech the wall. Couple of our men saw them in time and gave them bloody hell. Dropped them like flies."

"The leader?" Emilie whispered.

The soldier nodded. "Why the devil he was with them, no one knows, but they got him right enough. The rest, what was left of them, lost heart. Picked up their shereef and carried him off while their gunners kept our men under fire."

Her hands were so tight the knuckles ached, and the pain finally brought back life. "The shereef is dead? How can you be sure it was him?"

"Couple of Moors swear to it. Saw him fall from the rope. The blackguards dropped back immediately and picked him up before they turned tail. And why else would they pull out, eh?"

Pierre came to her, alarmed by her pallor. He reached an arm about her. "Let me take you to the house."

"No, I want to stay here."

"You're exhausted—"

She looked at him with wide eyes. "He is dead . . . I cannot believe it . . ."

"Hush, do not think about it. The seige is over, and you must ready yourself to leave."

"Yes." The word was a painful wrench from the depths of her soul. She made no further protest as he led her to the Consulate and gave her over to Claudia and Hilda, who had already heard the news. The others in the Consulate were rejoicing and weeping with joy that the siege was over. If any knew of Emilie's personal tragedy, they gave no sign of it. It was agreed that the caravan, guarded by as many able-bodied men as could be spared, would set out immediately. It was imperative to get away before the shereef's army could be reorganized under another leader. It was also vital that the telegraph line be repaired so word could reach Meknes and Tangier and aid be sent. Finally, Douglas Gregory and Enoch Madden insisted on one other thing. Pierre Louvel would accompany the caravan to tend the wounded who were able to travel, and to take care of any accidents or illness along the way. The women and children were in poor condition for such an arduous trip, exhausted from the long night. They could not travel without medical attention close at hand. When Pierre protested, Dr. Madden reminded him that he was a visitor, while Madden himself was an official member of the English delegation in Fez. Besides, the three English missionary ladies refused to abandon their posts, and he felt it his duty to remain to watch over them. He sighed, committing his wife and children to Pierre's safekeeping. He also prepared a list of medical supplies that must be sent as soon as possible, and he urged Pierre to convince French officials in Tangier that not a moment was to be lost in hurrying troops to defend Fez. This would not be the end of it, he was sure. The death of the shereef was buying them only time, not peace. The matter had gone too far to be abandoned now, and the tribes of Madawadi still had the deadly machine guns.

The caravan departed by way of the *Bab Guissa*, the farthest gate from a direct line with Madawadi. It was reasonable that if the shereef's army returned, it would be from their own encampment, where they had undoubtedly taken their fallen leader to be entombed.

Emilie rode wrapped in her own thoughts. She was numb since hearing the news of Taleb's death, as if it were impossible to believe after the horror she'd endured. Still she felt pain and loss as memories of the physical love she had shared with her husband assailed her. Their bodies had met and communicated where their minds

429

could not. So different . . . their two cultures that were destined to remain centuries apart in manner and belief.

She thought again of the slaying of the five prisoners after the death of Taleb's *caid* and nephew. If such vengeance had been claimed for two lives, what would the chieftans demand for that of their leader? She shuddered to think of it. Her heart was heavy, yet there was a quiet joy in knowing she was going home. She had little chance to talk with Pierre, but she watched him as he rode in the lead of the caravan, sometimes calling a brief halt to check a bloody wound that he would not let go unattended until the noon or night encampment. He was especially solicitous of the two Madden girls, who were still slightly dazed by the unexplainable terror they'd endured during the attack on Fez. She wondered if Claudia would return to her husband's side when the troubles subsided. Would she again take two innocent children into such danger? The bond between husband and wife was strong, but even such allegiance had to end somewhere. Claudia's devotion to Enoch had been apparent in their tearful parting, and Emilie was sure they would not stay separated long. She only prayed that the girls would be sent to school elsewhere instead of being brought back to the desert.

She lost track of time as hour plodded after hour under the relentless sun. They followed the shortest route, through Petitjean, then north toward Larache. It was a slightly different course than Taleb's caravan had taken, but it was also more populated and followed the telegraph line all the way. The forward guards found the cut line some two miles beyond the city walls; it was repaired and the urgent messages sent. Troops could be sent by military railroad as far as Beldeen, then march into Fez; some would be there within days, others to come as quickly as they could be marshalled.

Throughout the journey, Emilie was keenly aware of Pierre's efficient and comforting manner. He was never too tired or busy to spend a moment with Eileen and Zelda, to bring a smile to their lips and chase the fear from their eyes. Midday camps were kept as brief as possible, giving the people time to eat and the animals a brief respite. There were an assortment of horses, camels and mules; the wounded were carried on makeshift stretchers between camels, a sort of canvas sling that some of the Moorish soldiers had improvised. On the third day out, one man died, though Pierre did all he could. The wound, a massive chest injury caused by machine gun strafing, could not be operated on in the crude hospital set up in the Consulate mill house, and Dr. Madden and Pierre had decided the man's chances were better if he could reach Tangier where surgery could be performed. But the wounds festered in the stinking heat, and the last of the antiseptics were used up. Men buried the body in a shallow sand-swept grave several yards from the camel track, marking the grave with a pile of stones, since the man was Moslem not Christian. This brief duty was carried out while the women were in the tents, but Emilie slipped outside to watch unobserved. She'd seen Pierre's despair when he realized there was no more he could do for the man, and she'd seen the anger and helplessness when he closed the soldier's eyelids in death.

As she watched the stark funeral, she thought of another she'd seen—Omar and Fatima's son entombed amid the grief of the entire tribe of Taleb's people. She wondered if this soldier's soul would pass as easily through the gate of eternal life with none to mourn.

Pierre walked off to sit beyond the perimeter of the campfire and stare into the darkness. She went to sit beside him on the sand still warm for the day's heat.

He looked about. "You should be sleeping. We've another two full days of travel."

She smiled. "I require less rest than most."

"Your shoulder—?"

She tilted her head indifferently. "It does not pain at

431

all." It was almost true; she barely noticed the dull throb. She was one of the lucky ones; her wound had been treated when there was still enough medical supplies to insure no infection, and it had been bandaged well. Sometimes her arm ached by day's end, but that too was passing. "I am sorry about him—" She looked off toward the new grave.

Pierre rubbed his eyes wearily. "There will be others, if not among those who travel with us, among those left behind. Without a hospital—"

"Dr. Madden told me of your willingness to help establish the hospital in Fez. What will happen now?"

"We will continue. My trip was a preliminary one to make plans and return to Tangier to raise the capital and backing we need to implement them."

"You will still build it?" She was surprised that he would go back.

"Yes. Now more than ever. It will be sorely needed in the years to come." He looked at her and smiled sadly. "The death of your husband will not end the wars, Emilie. He is but one leader, a powerful one, but there are others to fill his place and to cause more death and destruction. They will not take lightly the Sultan's agreement to a Protectorate under the French."

"Then why do the French pursue it? Why not leave the Arabs to their problems and lives. We cannot live like them, nor they like us." She thought of Taleb and her heart was heavy.

"You have discovered the truth . . ." It was neither a question nor an accusation. "If only the rest of the world might." He sighed. "But governments act out of need for power, not from the heart as you did. The Protectorate will come, I am sure of it. And my government and yours will reap their benefits, take what they want, and we will be left to salvage as much human life as we can from the carnage. The tribes will attack the city time and time again until there are no men left to die."

She bowed her head and felt sorrow well inside her. He was right. Omar, the others, would never relent until the foreigners were driven from their land . . . or until they had no army left to ride against the Sultan.

"Your family will be glad to have you back, Emilie." He said softly. "They have missed you. Sara has been worried and lonely since the day of your departure. She made me promise to look you up while I was in Fez."

"And would you have done that if fate had not brought me to you?"

"Yes."

She looked at him in the flickering light of the distant fire. His face was drawn and tired but his eyes were calm. She remembered how they'd ridden together, how they'd laughed and talked and made hours pass on light wings. How long ago it seemed. She leaned close and put her lips to his, and for a moment the months vanished in the tender kiss. Then she smiled and rose.

"Goodnight, Pierre." She lifted the ragged skirt of the caftan and made her way back to the tent.

At Larache, they were hailed by a band of French troops who had been sent out from Tangier to meet them. Medical supplies were delivered to Pierre, and another young doctor from the French hospital had come to help tend the wounded. Word of the siege of Fez had alarmed the entire European population of Tangier, and fresh troops had been despatched immediately, from Tangier as well as from Casablanca and Rabat. The Sultan had arrived in Casablanca after sending half his army to supplement the French troops moving to Fez.

Several litters had been brought, and the wounded were transferred from the slings to the more comfortable conveyances which were carried on the backs of pack mules. Pierre dispensed medications, including a mild draught of laudanum for Hilda Weiss, who had developed a fever and was near exhaustion.

433

They stayed the night at the house of a wealthy Mo[or] who was sympathetic to the French, having done busine[ss] with them in supplying horses and camels for the arm[y.] Renewed, they pushed on the next morning, determined [to] cover the last leg of the journey as quickly as possib[le.] The Larache merchant supplied each of the women wi[th] clean tunics and caftans from his wife's copious wardrob[e,] and each had enjoyed a bath that renewed body a[nd] spirit. For the first time since fleeing the palace [at] Madawadi, Emilie felt a lightening of her spirits. Th[e] nightmare was coming to an end.

The decision was made on the last day to continue ri[d]ing after dinner so that they would reach Tangier by ear[ly] morning. There seemed little to be gained by spending a[n] other night on the desert, and the comfortable rest [at] Larache had given them all a spurt of energy that wou[ld] not be dimmed. They halted only long enough for a qui[ck] meal and to water the animals, then went on. Darkne[ss] closed around them, and they were silent, each with h[er] own thoughts.

Emilie could scarcely believe by morning she would [be] in the arms of her family! She had to warn father abo[ut] Taleb's treachery in the matter of the railroad, and s[he] prayed he would listen. It was impossible that Taleb ha[d] acted alone. Who else among those father dealt with we[re] not to be trusted? *M'sieur* Augustin? The Ministers of F[i]nance or Foreign Affairs? Henri Cartier?

Henri. She sighed heavily. Pierre had not mention[ed] him. Perhaps he'd returned to France. She recalled ho[w] desperately she had wanted to go with him when he we[nt] before. She'd been so distraught at his refusal to take he[r] she had tried to kill both of them with the fire in the be[d] clothes. Now she tried to recall the hatred she'd felt f[or] Henri, but it would not come. No, she did not hate him; [it] was herself she'd been angry with and regarded an obje[ct] of loathing and disgust—so much so that she had escap[ed]

434

irst to Pierre, then with Taleb. *And all the time it was ierself she had been running from.*

A group of riders met them at dawn in the hills just outh of the city where the traveling camps were set up. Sent to welcome the weary travelers, the escort had been ilerted that they were nearing the city. One of the wound-d French soldiers cut into the telegraph line to send the :ommunication, knowing the relief the news would bring.

A single horseman rode out ahead of the others. For a noment, Emilie thought it was her father; all she could .ee in the gray haze before sunrise was a light business uit and panama hat. But as he neared, she recognized Ienri, and she felt a sudden surge of joy. He galloped the iorse across the distance and reined in at Pierre's side.

"*Mon ami*, you are safe? All—"

Pierre nodded, smiling and looking over his shoulder to where Emilie rode with the women banded together in a weary group. Henri kicked the horse and was at her side n a moment. His thin face looked pinched with worry, and his smile was joyful but hesitant.

"Emilie! Thank God you are all right!" His dark eyes earched her face. "You were wounded—?"

Her relief was so vast that she could only nod, then :hake her head to dispel his worry. When she found her voice, she said, "I am fine." It surprised her that her words came out a whisper. All at once her heart was hudding with more excitement than she'd known during he attack on Fez, more than she believed she would ever eel again. "I am all right now," she said again.

He drew a breath, then wheeled his horse so that he was beside her, lifting her from the saddle and sweeping her into his arms, so he could hold her close as he spoke oft words at her cheek.

"I shall never let you leave me again. What a fool I was! My own, my own precious Emilie!"

She thought her heart would leap from her breast. The

435

pain and anguish of the past days vanished in a moment, and she clung to him, heedless of the astonished faces of the women around them.

"I was stupid not to know my own heart when we were together," he whispered, "but as soon as we were apart, I became desolate. Life's joy vanished the day you wed the shereef." He drew back and looked at her.

There was no anguish in her answer. "The shereef is dead . . ."

He kissed her then, gently and lovingly, but with promise of passion to come when they were alone.

CHAPTER TWENTY-FOUR

The house at *el-Kebir* Road hummed with expectation. Charlotte fussed and worried that perhaps the stories of Emilie's injury had been modified to allay her fears. Wounded . . . in the midst of a terrible battle! Poor Emilie! How good it would be to have her home, away from that barbarian! Charlotte had known all along the marriage was wrong.

Roderick paced the library alone, his brow furrowed in deep concentration. He could still scarcely believe he had been so misguided in his trust. When Henri Cartier came to him five days ago and informed him of al Mu'min's attack on Fez, he'd been astonished and, at first, refused to believe the news. Mu'min's cooperation had been assured over and over by the Minister of Foreign Affairs. Plans for the Pendash Railroad had been ready, except for funds that Henri Cartier withheld. The Frenchman gave all manner of excuses for the delays, cautioning Roderick to move slowly and to wait until after Pierre's visit to Fez. He was adamant on that point: he would not sink one franc into the Company until Pierre's return and he had his friend's assurances that all was well. Thank God they'd waited! The news of the revolt of the Madawadi

tribes had shocked everyone in Tangier; when Roderic
sought out Ali ben Tashfeen, the minister of Foreign A
fairs would not see him. Repeatedly, a servant bowed an
regretted the Minister was engaged, the Minister was no
at home, the Minister was away on vital business. Rode
ick knew then that Tashfeen and Mu'min were conspi
ators against him. They'd used Roderick's eagerness a
they would his capital to endorse a railroad that woul
benefit them. Guns! Lord—and Emilie would have bee
caught in the middle of it! His own daughter!

Sara had been up since dawn, walking in the garde
and going often to the gate to see if there was any sign o
the travellers from Fez. She was torn between her desir
to see Emilie and going to the hospital where Pier
would be. The past months had been bittersweet. Sh
missed Emilie dreadfully, and worried about her mo
than she had ever admitted to her parents. She'd occupie
herself with work at the hospital—and with seeing Pierr
Her love for him had grown but she never spoke of it o
gave any sign. The forlorn look in Pierre's eyes o
Emilie's wedding day troubled her, and Sara knew that h
had been in love with her sister. The shock of Emilie
marriage to Taleb had hurt him badly, and it was
wound that was not easily healed. She felt pity for hir
and her own love was silent. When he announced h
plans to travel to Fez to visit Dr. Madden, Sara said far
well with a smile. But at night alone at her window, sh
stared toward the distant sky and wondered if the hope o
seeing Emilie was part of his decision to make the jou
ney. When the news of Taleb's death and Emilie's retur
came, Sara felt a moment of terrible anguish knowir
Pierre and Emilie were together.

The caravan arrived shortly after eight o'clock. Mo
hamet, who had ridden to the crest of the hill to watch
thundered into the courtyard, shouting as he slid from th
horse.

438

"*Señorita* come! Horses one mile—no more!"

Everyone ran out at once, babbling and crying. Jennie dabbed at her eyes with the corner of her apron to think her mistress was safely home again. Colleen kept a comforting arm around a pale trembling Charlotte, who kept saying, "My baby . . . my baby . . ."

It seemed an eternity before the straggly band rode into the yard. The wounded and sick had been taken directly to the hospital under the supervision of the French doctor who had joined them at Larache. Pierre rode with one of the small Madden girls in front of him in the saddle. Emilie had insisted that Claudia and the children accompany her home, since they had no other place to go. Hilda's fever had not abated, and she, too, had been sent directly to the hospital.

Confusion and excitement reigned as Emilie and the others were greeted and helped down. Sara hugged her sister, holding her at arm's length to look at her, then hugged her again. Charlotte's welcome was tearful and enthusiastic, and even Roderick took his daughter in his arms momentarily. Introductions were made, and everyone was ushered into the house. Asheema and servants brought hot tea, and no sooner had they finished the first cup, when breakfast was announced in the dining room.

"Is this where the princess lived?" Zelda Madden asked, looking about the elegant rooms.

Laughing, Emilie took her hand and promised to show her everything once they'd filled their rumbling bellies. Claudia looked so relieved to be there that Charlotte found strength in comforting her. Only Pierre made excuses and said he must leave for the hospital to talk with Doctor du Bois about the supplies that were to be sent to Fez. Emilie ran and put her arms about him to kiss him.

"Thank you, Pierre—" Their eyes met momentarily, and he smiled in unspoken understanding. Then turning, he slipped an arm through Henri's and walked to the dining room.

439

Sara stood with a heavy heart. "You must not work to day, Pierre. You are as exhausted as the rest."

He nodded. "Yes, it has been an arduous journey."

Sara did not look at him as she walked with him through the patio to where the horses had been left. "The plans for the hospital in Fez? Will they have to be aban doned now?" She knew how important the project was to him.

He sighed and shook his head. "Delayed until the present trouble subsides, but then it must be built with all possible speed. The situation there is critical. I have promised Dr. Madden to return as soon as I can."

"You are going to Fez?" She could not hide her sur prise.

"I will talk to Doctor du Bois today." He stopped beside his horse and looked at her, then reached to take her hand. "I know this is not the proper time or place," he said, glancing about at the barren yard where the horses waited to be taken to the stables. "Will you wait for me? I will not risk your life in that primitive place but neither can I bear the thought of being separated from you again."

"Emilie . . . ?" The whispered word escaped in sur prise.

He blinked. "She is safe now, and she will be the first to tell you that Fez is a harsh, cruel place for a woman. But I will only be gone some four to five months. We can be married as soon as I return—if you'll have me, that is." He sighed wearily. "I am not good at saying roman tic words. Perhaps first I should declare my love for you. I have loved you a long time, but I have only realized how much a part of my life you have become. Will you accept me?" His grey eyes were loving and pleading.

She threw herself into his arms. "Yes. I will marry you, Pierre. I will do so eagerly and with the greatest of joy!"

He stood holding her as though unable to believe his good fortune, then put his lips to hers. His kiss was gentle

440

ut it stirred her and made her senses reel. Pierre loved *her*, not Emilie! He returned the love she'd thought unanswered. Her heart sang and she met his kiss eagerly. When he drew away, they stood looking at each other for an interval of understanding and communication.

"I must go," he said.

"I will wait for you . . ."

Immediately after breakfast, the two children were put to bed; Claudia enjoyed the luxury of a bath before she, too, fell into a deep slumber.

Emilie walked to the garden with Henri to say goodbye, and they clung together in breathless ecstasy.

"How long must I wait before we can be married?" he whispered as he stroked her tousled hair.

"A decent interval, I suppose, but I do not want to wait—"

They kissed again and his arms were a comfort that she had longed for an eternity without knowing it.

"We will sail for Paris as soon as I can put my affairs in order here. We'll be married before we go." He smiled at her and put her fingers to his lips.

She thought of her father and the Pendash Company.

"What brings a frown to your beautiful face?" he whispered, kissing it away and rubbing her brow with cold fingertips.

"Taleb—" The name hurt her to speak. "Father's railroad was to be used to bring guns because he no longer wished to deal with a German merchant from Rabat."

"Hush, I know . . ."

"How—?"

"I look very carefully into any business venture which I am to be involved. I quickly learned the line at Beldeen was as close to Madawadi as the proposed Pendash line could come, and I wondered why the shereef and the Minister were so eager for it. It could only be that the shereef found it advantageous to control a railroad for his

441

own purposes. I suspected they were involved with illeg
gun traffic, but I had no proof. Then when you marri
him, I could not bring myself to hurt you in any way, lo
ing you the way I did."

She stared at him. He had loved her then? Her mi
whirled in confusion. He'd said nothing—Or was it th
she had not allowed him to speak?

He drew her close. "I tried to banish you from r
thoughts, but it was impossible. I would have left Tangi
long ago, except I hoped you might somehow be broug
back to me. And now you have." He kissed her linge
ingly and felt her lips tremble under his. "And now y
must rest. I cannot have you ill when there is so much
do. I want to spend every moment possible with you."

He walked her back to the door and saw her inside b
fore taking his leave. Emilie floated on a cloud throu
the hall and up to her rooms. She found Sara waiting f
her, her face wreathed in smiles.

"I am so glad to have you home safely!" Sara hugg
her again. "Rachma has drawn a bath. You look exhau
ed. It must have been a terrible ordeal."

Emilie sighed. "It seems long ago and far in the pa
So much has happened all at once—oh, Sara, I am hap
to be back. How foolish I was to not heed the warnin
you tried to give!" She burst into tears as Sara gather
her in her arms once more.

"It is finished. You must try to forget."

"Yes. And now I know what love really is . . ."

For a moment, Sara's heart caught. Did Emilie belie
that Pierre still loved her, that they would be togethe
But then Emilie was smiling through the tears and telli
her of Henri's proposal, and her own realization that
was *he* she loved all along.

"We will be wed as soon as possible, and we will live
France." Emilie sighed. "I cannot wait to esca
Morocco." She looked serious for a moment. "Do yc

think father will stay after all this? Perhaps you will go ome to England!"

Sara shook her head. "Not I. I am going to marry ierre as soon as he returns from his next journey to ez."

Astonished, Emilie gaped. "I did not know—"

"Nor I, until this very day. I am so happy!"

"Then I am happy for you!" They embraced again. To think that you will live in Tangier and I shall go. It ems ironic when I think back to our arrival and how re you were that we could not survive in this uncivilized nd."

"I can live anywhere as long as I have Pierre." Sara ushed at the admission.

"He is a wonderful person, and very fortunate to have ou."

Sara blushed again.

"And now," Emilie declared, "I must bathe and sleep fore I collapse where I stand!"

It was evening when she woke. Rachma told her the hers were in the drawing room, waiting her arrival be- re dinner was called. Emilie dressed, choosing from her ardrobe a gown of soft silk that she'd had made before aving London. She would give all the Moroccan style rments to Rachma to dispose of in some way. She never anted to see them again. She sat in front of the glass hile Rachma arranged her golden hair, in soft curls. It d grown these past months, and the face that stared ck at her from the mirror looked like the Emilie of old. nally, Rachma fastened about her throat the ruby and arl necklace that had been her father's Christmas gift. ith the dazzling array of jewels Taleb had given her, nilie had not realized she'd left the precious gift behind.

Rachma murmured approval, and Emilie rose with a st look in the glass, then turned toward the door. Before e could take a step, the curtains at the gallery arch were

thrust aside and she was face to face with a dark, scowing Taleb! One hand was upraised, the other held a kni
with its blade stained by a river of fresh blood th
dripped to the front of his white jellaba.

"Taleb!" What would have been a scream was
strangled cry of disbelief! Emilie felt faint, yet her hea
hammered as though it would burst. Behind Taleb, Om
slid past the curtains and into the room. Rachma made
dash for the door, her mouth opened to scream—b
Omar was upon her instantly, his knife slashing red acrc
her throat. She fell in a crumpled heap to the floor.

Taleb grabbed Emilie, his arm about her neck so s
could not cry out. "I took an oath that I would never
you go. Have you forgotten that the word of a shereef
not to be taken lightly?" He slipped the bloody knife in
his sash as he began to drag her toward the gallery.

She struggled and clawed at the steel band of his ar
gasping for breath and kicking wildly. But he lifted her
though she were an empty sack, and she was helpless
his grip. Panic was bitter on her tongue and her bra
would only repeat over and over that he was dead—
could not be here—he was dead!

His hand clamped over her mouth almost cutting
her breath as he swooped her into his arms and we
quickly and soundlessly across the gallery and down t
stairs. From the drawing room, Emilie could hear the sc
murmur of voices and the sweet lilting laughter of one
the Madden girls.

It was unreal, impossible—

They were across the patio and out through the re
archway toward the stables. By the light of the torch
Emilie saw the motionless bodies of three Rif guarc
their tunics darkly stained, their heads almost severe
She closed her eyes and fought the rising nausea.

There were half a dozen horses beyond the stable, a
Taleb hurried toward them. Four riders were mounte
and Omar snatched Emilie as Taleb swung into t

444

ddle, then reached out for her again. For an instant as
mar let go and Taleb took her, her mouth was free, and
e gulped air and screamed. Instantly Taleb silenced her
th his hand once more, but not before the cry had been
ard. Mohamet raced from the stable, pulling his rifle
om the strap at his shoulder. Omar leaped like a gazelle
d fell to the ground atop the lad before the gun could
fired. For a few moments, they thrashed and wrestled
the dust, then Omar's knife gleamed in the moonlight
d came down with a heavy thud as it sank into flesh.
ohamet lay still.

Without a word, Omar leaped to his horse. Taleb had
eady kicked the stallion into motion, a walk until they
re clear of the stables, then a thundering gallop as they
lowed the road toward the crest of the hill. Emilie
uld hear the other riders behind them, not caring about
ise now that they were clear of the house and beyond
e European sector. She was sitting in the saddle in front
Taleb, one of his arms tight about her shoulders so that
r face was pressed against his *jellaba*. She could smell
e sweat and dust in his robe, evidence that he'd ridden
rd. At his chest she felt the damp thickness of a ban-
ge—the wound which she had believed killed him!

Was there no end to the nightmare? It was beginning
over again . . . She tried to think but her brain reeled.
en, almost lost in the thundering hoofbeats of the
rses, she heard a rifle shot. Taleb heard it too and
ned to glance back but did not slacken the horse's
ce. It seemed only a moment until they reached the
est and were racing along the road that would take
m to the camel track heading south.

Clear of the city, Taleb released his grip on her so that
e could sit up. In the harsh moonlight, his face was
ney, his eyes glittering obsidian that never left her face.

"I took you with a veil of pride," he said, his voice car-
ng to her despite the noise. "Yet you saw fit to shame

me before my people and your own. May the sea be o
thee."

"Why do you want me back?" she demanded. "The
is nothing left of our love, and there never can be again."

"You belong to me. Allah has written it over us."

"I will never submit to you—!"

His gaze was piercing and cold, and he looked aw
dismissing her protests. She belonged to him and
would have her always.

Emilie's mouth was dry with dust and frustration, a
her breath was ragged in her throat. Her mind refused
consider her life if Taleb succeeded in taking her ba
to Madawadi! She began to beat at him again and try
struggle from his grip, but he held her fast. Her cries a
tears were carried away by the wind.

All at once there was a volley of shots behind the
and Emilie jerked up to look past Taleb's should
Riders! Racing over the crest of the hill—the staccа
notes of a bugle sounding charge. The uniforms of Frer
soldiers clear now in the moonlight!

She laughed and cried at the same time, throwing l
head back so that hair streamed past Taleb's shoulder.

"You shall not have me!" she yelled at him.

"They will not shoot and risk hitting you." His answ
ing laugh was ugly and he kicked the powerful stallion
a run. The others spread to let him pass between, th
lifted rifles and began answering the sporadic fire.

Taleb was right, the soldiers were firing over th
heads, but Omar and his companions were slowing in
der to take more accurate aim; at the same time, th
closed ranks behind their leader and his captive. Emi
knew that in minutes, the soldiers would have to fall ba
or be gunned down, since they dared not fire into the ti
group. Desperate, she glanced back, saw a soldier fall a
the rest spread out so they would present poorer targets.

Taleb glanced back from time to time; one of his n
was hit by a French bullet, and the man slumped forwa

446

the saddle but did not fall. Taleb cursed Satan and tightened his grasp on Emilie.

She could scarcely breathe, but her mind was clearer than it had been since the moment Taleb stepped into her bedroom. She knew what she must do. Her hand was already at the hilt of the knife in his belt, the knife that bore the blood of the Rif guards he'd slain to gain entry to the house. She held her breath, waiting until his attention was once more distracted by the commotion behind them, then pulled the knife free and plunged it into his side. His legs went numb and the horse slowed quickly without the pressure of his heels.

"Accursed Christian—" The oath faded as the pain spread.

Emilie grabbed for the reins and jerked the stallion's head about, so it veered sharply to the left. The other riders were intent on the battle and did not notice until it was too late. Emilie had full control of the horse now, and she was heading back toward the advancing cavalry. She circled widely so that they might see she was no longer in danger; as if in answer to her plea, rifle shots rang out in an angry volley. The Arabs returned fire, still racing straight ahead. It was Omar who noticed Taleb's horse leave the circle of protection, and he swung his own mount in chase. It took only a moment to realize that Taleb was wounded and Emilie controlled the horse. He raised the rifle.

Taleb summoned his strength to keep his seat as he grabbed Emilie's hands and forced them to jerk sharply so the bit cut into the stallion's mouth and it turned almost at a right angle.

In that instant, Omar's shot, which would have otherwise caught Emilie directly, struck Taleb and his life ebbed in a sudden rush. He slid from the saddle, dragging Emilie down with him, dead before he struck the ground.

She lay gasping under the weight of Taleb's arm across her breasts. The rifle fire was loud and rapid; a horse

447

screamed and fell heavily. Someone shouted, and mo
shots rang out as the horses' hoofbeats faded, the
stopped abruptly.

Someone was pulling Taleb from her, lifting her ar
brushing hair and dirt from her eyes.

"Emilie! *Mon Dieu*—! Pierre, come quickly, she
hurt!"

A horse, running steps.

Emilie opened her eyes and saw Henri's worried fa
over her. His relief was so enormous, she managed
smile as he hugged her close and covered her face wi
kisses.

"I am not hurt," she managed to say at last.

"You are covered with blood—"

She shook her head and caught her lip. Taleb's bloo
not hers.

Pierre knelt and struck a match to a lantern. In its ye
low light, he looked at her closely, moving limbs to t
sure they were not broken, feeling her head.

She sat up, insisting again that she was fine. Beside he
Taleb's body was sprawled in the dust, one arm ou
stretched as though to claim her in some final victory. A
a distance, the soldiers stood over the bodies of Omar ar
the others. She let Henri help her to her feet and lead h
away. It was over, this time for good.

She was perfectly capable of riding under her ow
power, but she made no objection when Henri took h
onto his horse and held her close during the ride back
the house. She smiled each time he bent to kiss her. Th
past was done, and this was a new beginning of true lo
and happiness. How long it had taken her to know h
own heart, but at last she had no doubts.